Global Predator

JACK MACLEAN

LEGEND PUBLISHING

2014

1

A convoy of three dented and mud-splattered SUVs roared up the forest track and jerked to a halt at a clearing overlooking the valley they had just left. A thickset, clumsy man in his late fifties climbed out of the middle vehicle breathing heavily. He peered through the thick pebble glasses perched on a large bulbous nose, scouring the track along which they had just traveled. He grunted in approval. No one was following. Meanwhile, the three vehicles edged forward until they were hidden from sight under a clump of pine trees. One of the drivers emerged with a pair of large army binoculars and handed them deferentially to the older man. He held them in front of his glasses before awkwardly removing them and then adjusted both lenses of the binoculars. First, he raised them to search the clear blue skies above and then lowered the binoculars to examine a village set in the valley below among a patchwork of irrigated fields. Families were out in the fields scything the autumn wheat harvest and bundling the stalks ready for threshing. Then he turned the binoculars to examine a large compound dominated by a domed white mosque. It lay a few miles to the west of the village and was surrounded by a high wall which formed a rough rectangle. At the corners were small guard platforms.

It was still mid-morning and a stiff breeze was pushing a bank of clouds from the west. The group of watchers waited in expectant silence. After twenty minutes, the wind brought the wailing sound of a call to prayers. Then almost a minute later, they heard a faint sound of a small motor engine and the watchers tilted their heads upwards, searching the sky for the source of the sound. There was nothing visible. Then, as the call to prayers ended, they saw streaks from two small silver missiles targeting the compound. Seconds later, the sound of two blasts echoed across the valley. The explosions created a cloud of dust and debris as the mud brick buildings shattered. The cloud swiftly rose into the air and then the debris fell as quickly. The mosque seemed to have survived intact. Then they could hear a new sound, a steady whop- whop from helicopters. A group of six Cobra attack helicopters appeared and within minutes they could hear the intermittent sound of machine-gun fire.

'Pakistani soldiers,' whispered one of the men watching.

The older man nodded.

'Allah has shown his mercy to you. Blessed is the name of the Prophet,' the younger man said sounded excited. 'They were coming for you but they failed again.'

Al-Zawahiri shook his head slowly. He did not share his followers' enthusiasm. Instead he felt a familiar intense anger began to burn inside. The Americans had somehow been tracking him and only a messenger carrying an urgent warning to flee had saved them. He had not known whether to trust the Pakistani or not. The Pakistanis had helped him escape their own attack but next time he might not escape in time. Another hour and the messenger would have arrived too late.

From the compound there was a hesitant and sporadic return of fire. Three of the helicopters lying low over the fields began strafing the walls of the compound. In the fields the farmers and their families stood and stared. A few figures began running back to their houses, while out of the compound, youths dressed in white robes and skull caps ran out and fled towards the village. In the seminary, another scattered group of men armed with a collection of guns and old rifles began firing wildly.

Within minutes, soldiers in dark olive and khaki combat gear were climbing down ladders dropped from the three helicopters as they hovered above the fields outside the seminary. Soon the troops began running towards the mosque. A pick-up truck and a minibus which tore out of the gates on to the road leading to the village were strafed by gunfire from other helicopters hovering just above the compound. Men piled out of the jeep moments before it exploded. The watchers could see more soldiers rappelling down from the helicopters into the compound. Three minutes later, the rhythmic bursts of gunfire suddenly stopped. The helicopter's wings stopped rotating. It seemed that resistance within the compound had ceased.

Al-Zawahiri slowly lifted the binoculars away from his eyes. Tears blinded his eyes and he let them trickle into his thick white beard. He murmured some instructions to the driver beside him. He went to the SUV hidden under the trees and returned carrying carpets which he laid down. The other members of the convoy joined the older man and the driver in kneeling down on the carpets prostrating themselves towards Mecca. The elderly Egyptian then sat up and began addressing the group. They listened in reverential silence awaiting his guidance. He spoke with a clearly and slowly. First he offered thanks for their deliverance and then he spoke of revenge.

'If we get martyrdom, so we achieve that we were looking for, for the flag of Jihad will never fall down until the Day of Judgment as we were informed by the prophet of Allah (peace and blessings be upon him). Oh brothers, if we die, we meet with our beloved ones, because the gardens of my Lord are prepared for us, and its birds flap their wings around us. So they await us in the eternal residence. Verily, Allah has chosen us for his call. Brothers, go ahead and don't look back, your path has been covered in blood. By the divine mercy of Allah, I call on the prophet thrice blessed be his name, to recognize the sacrifice of these martyrs. They are enjoying their reward in paradise but we here who have been saved must now prepare their revenge. By this hand, I swear that Satan's attack against a school, a place of holy learning will be avenged. These invaders will regret what they have done and will curse themselves for the use of these drones. We will turn them against our enemies and seem them weep over the destruction wrought on the children they claim to be protecting. Before the next Eid we will see them weep tears of blood at their folly. We will find a school and turn the sword of our enemies against their own bodies.' Then he stopped and raised his hand and brought it down in a savage chop.

2

In early autumn of 2011, Faiza Azhad was looking at a lined list of phone intercepts gathered by the National Security Agency's signals satellites when she noticed something odd. All the numbers blinking on the digital screen belonged to a mid-ranking al-Qaeda recruit, Salim Sinan, but the Jordanian native appeared to be using his phones from a location in North-West Pakistan called Bajaur. Salim was calling with a number of different sim cards to cover his tracks. She had been born in Afghanistan and had been recruited to deal with the vast volume of calls that was being gathered by speakers of Pashto, Dari and Urdu. She had no real business looking at these particular intercepts, but she was curious what Salim Sinan was doing in Bajaur, a region bordering Afghanistan, where the al-Qaeda Number One, Al Zawahiri, was believed to be living after the group fled Afghanistan because of the US invasion. It was not her job to monitor calls from Pakistan but anything to do with the

Egyptian was important. When she saw or heard his name, it caused a physical reaction of fear and revulsion inside her. She tried to pretend that he longer existed and every reminder felt like a physical stab of pain. When she forced herself to read on, her pulse would race suddenly and she felt the urge to run away. She had to use every ounce of mental will to override that initial response and force herself to concentrate because she knew that the only way she would ever conquer that fear was to destroy him.

The National Security Agency controlled the largest collection of eavesdropping tools ever assembled. It had billion-dollar satellites circling the globe and huge listening posts like moon craters, each with hundreds of satellite dishes which every hour pulled in millions of phone calls, e-mail messages and faxes. It accessed the countless phone call conversations made on fixed lines, and cell phones all over the world. To process this Nile-like flood of information, the NSA employed the largest collection of supercomputers on earth which sifted, filtered and searched for information by employing complex mathematical algorithms and pattern recognition techniques. Every day the NSA targeted around 7,000 people as part of its counter-terrorist brief. It recorded all their intercepted phone calls, but then someone had to listen to and sometimes translate whatever was captured. This information was then made available to other agencies, above all the CIA's Counter Terrorist Unit.

The linguists, intercept operators and analysts were grouped together into four giant operational centers across the United States. Faiza was sent to work at the Georgia center, a requisitioned former boarding school. The staff worked in dozens of old classrooms and many lived in the dormitories and ate their meals in the old dining-halls. The equipment, cables, computer screens had been shoehorned into the classrooms lining the corridors in a makeshift way. The windows were blackened out and the work went on round the clock in shifts, covering the different time zones around the world.

It was now past midnight and there were at least a dozen others sitting with Faiza in the dim room engrossed in their work. Like her, they were all intently listening and tapping away at their keyboards. Nobody spoke much; everyone communicated by sending messages through the internal network. She looked around at their earnest faces illuminated by the glow from their flat screens and took a sip of the coffee cooling in front of her.

No one was watching and she slipped on the headphones and began to click her way through the list of lined numbers. In the corner of the screen, a small box showed a map revealing the location of the calls from the satellite phone. The caller was near the village of Damadola and a small religious seminary.

The Jordanian had made five long distance calls, three to numbers inside Pakistan and two calls to the Gulf. They were all quite short in duration and she could glean nothing from them, but the last one was a lengthy conversation, lasting over ten minutes, to someone in Saudi Arabia. Salim Sinan sounded agitated and excited and he seemed to be raising his voice in order to make himself heard above the noise of a vehicle traveling over rough ground. He was not alone in the vehicle. She could hear other voices talking in the background. It sounded as if someone was giving instructions to the driver.

That person was speaking in Pashto, the common language spoken on both sides of the border, but he spoke it with difficulty as if he had learned it only later in life. He seemed to be shouting orders to the driver of the vehicle. The intercept had recorded just eight seconds of his speech, but it was enough for Faiza. She would recognize that voice anywhere. It was Ayman al-Zawahiri. She felt that stabbing internal pain again.

She played the passage back and forwards several times, and then isolated the track. She then searched for a digital voice imprint of al-Zawahiri's voice so she could compare the two recordings. He had rarely been caught using a cell phone, but he had made numerous propaganda broadcasts. The brief eight second burst was not enough to provide a good digital match but Faiza had seen and heard al-Zawahiri often enough to be sure. He was in Bajaur now, she thought, and they could get him if they acted quickly.

She was sure the Arabic-speaking linguists and analysts had missed it. Faiza felt momentarily blinded by the excitement of finding the quarry and then acted, writing out an urgent alert on the new Zircon instant messaging system. 'Al Zawahiri located in Darmadola traveling in vehicle with Salim Sina,' she typed and then attached the recording of his voice. She pressed send and waited.

Then she got up and left the room to find her supervisor in a room further down the corridor. By the time she reached Army warrant officer Sam Wilson, he had seen it. He was lounging on a black swivel chair staring at the stream of messages appearing and sucking the end of a pencil. He twisted his head round to look at her, opening his eyes wide to show surprise and then raised his two hands. She feared he might be angry, but he seemed pleased in a casual sort of way. With thinning mousy hair, pink cheeks and baby-blue eyes behind gold-wired glasses, he looked like a college boy to her. He was polite, well-meaning and, to her mind, too innocent for this kind of work.

She sensed he found her presence slightly alarming. For one thing, she was almost his height, with a long horsey nose and dark hair wrapped in a bright headscarf. Perhaps, though, it was not her appearance but her awkward blundering tongue.

'Please, what will happen now?' she asked.

'Well, I don't know for sure,' he said slowly. 'It's up to Langley now. We are just the messengers. They don't ever tell us what they do with the information.'

She nodded. She guessed that the information would be read by someone in the CIA headquarters who worked in the special taskforce dedicated to finding and killing Osama Bin Laden's second in command. She knew that the task force had already tried and failed to kill al-Zawahiri on many occasions.

'Maybe, they will send a Predator?' she pressed on. She imagined the messages bouncing between the satellites mobilizing the vast resources of the American military. Somewhere in Maryland or in the deserts of Nevada, a pilot would be steering an unmanned plane high above the mountains of Bajaur.

'Well, I can't be sure' Wilson started again, then noticed her irritation. 'Look, just because we know where he is doesn't mean anyone will do anything. They have to make sure no one else will get hurt. Maybe they have to consult other people like the Pakistanis. Who knows?'

'But they will do something?' she insisted.

Wilson sighed. 'We don't do ops here. We are not hunters but gatherers.'

She stared back at him, trying to control her growing anger at his indifference to the intense excitement that she was feeling.

'You had better go back and start listening. We need to know that he is still in the car,' he said, dismissing her and turning back to his screen

She turned round obediently, but then he said, trying to placate her, 'But hey, you did good. It's been duly noticed.'

She stood there stubbornly.

'But what made you check these intercepts? I didn't ask you to,' he asked, turning back to face her.

'I just want to see al-Zawahiri dead,' she said and walked out. Wilson stared at her retreating back and shook his head.

Over the next two days, Faiza noticed nothing more directly related to the Egyptian terrorist leader. But in the line of calls on her worksheet were some that made her wonder. They were all calls made from a location in the Nuristan Forest in Afghanistan, not far from the border with Bajaur in the North-West Frontier of Pakistan. They had been flashed up for her attention because one of the calls had been made to a listed phone number of an Islamic terrorist group operating in the Swat Valley, another part of Pakistan in the North-West Frontier. The one-minute call had been made to Maulana Sufi Mohammed, the elderly founder of the Movement for the Implementation of Mohammed's Law, an Islamic militant group that was fighting to wrest control of the hitherto peaceful valley. Faiza knew little about the Swat Valley or this particular group, but the software program was designed to analyze and identify any potential targets of interest by identifying chains of phone calls. She clicked on each of the ten intercepts lined and listened to each in turn. They were all by speakers using Pashto. She steadily and patiently typed out the dialog, forcing herself to carry out the task. Most of them seemed of little interest. The caller appeared to be a smuggler who moved back and forwards across the porous frontier collecting and delivering packages of what she guessed were heroin. Afghanistan was reputedly the largest producer and exporter of heroin and most of the harvest was taken over the passes into Pakistan, from where it was distributed around the world. Pashtuns usually brought the stuff on donkeys and the intercepted phone calls were mostly loosely coded talk about arrangements for these trips. The phone call to Maulana was also disappointing. The speaker, a young man in his late twenties, seemed poorly educated but devout and the phone call to the older man was mostly a tearful blessing calling on the Prophet to give thanks for his release and wishing him long life. There was nothing of interest there and she sent off the translations as soon as she had finished. There was five minutes left before she went off for a coffee break. She decided to search through all the phone intercepts from the same number and all those who had received his calls, looking for mentions of Darmadola. The software soon found three, all from one number. She called up the intercepts and listened to them. Someone with a British accent was talking in broken Pashto to the smuggler. He wanted him to arrange a safe passage across the mountains. He intended to travel to the Swat Valley. It was urgent, but the smuggler seemed reluctant. He said it would be difficult in the winter. The other man pleaded, saying it was a matter of revenge for an attack and would help Maulana's cause. The smuggler said he should wait until spring.

Faiza quickly searched for more calls made by the man with the British accent and traced all the numbers he had called over the past week. What sort of revenge could he be talking about? She started looking for any calls made to Maulana, or any of his associates in the Swat Valley. There were none made from this phone number, but she did trace calls to various NGOs operating in Mingora, the capital of the Swat Valley. In one day, the caller, who seemed to be called Ahmed, contacted the Save The Children Fund, Action Aid, the Anti-Poverty Welfare Organization, Caritas, and Children First. She listed to the intercepts. In each one, Ahmed asked questions, trying to find out if there were any Americans working in the Swat Valley. Many of the charity bases had closed down and the foreign aid workers had been withdrawn after a spate of violent attacks by the supporters of Maulana's Movement for the Implementation of Mohammed's Law. But it seemed there were no Americans left in the Swat Valley. It was odd, she thought. For moment, she toyed with the idea of asking Wilson to trace calls to all the foreign NGOs in the region. She knew what he would say. First it was against the rules, and secondly it was not her responsibility to investigate anything, her task was to monitor and transcribe. Perhaps, Faiza thought to herself, it was time she moved on and found another job.

3

It was Sunday morning and Sally Hodges had the day to herself. She switched on the radio just as the news was ending to hear Desert Island Discs on the BBC World Service. She had made herself in a large mug of strong sweet black tea in anticipation and settled down on an old armchair. She made a bet with herself that whoever was on would choose to play The Kinks and Vivaldi's Four Seasons. If she won, then she would open the last packet of chocolate digestives she had been saving up. Next week, she would be heading back to England and she could stock up again.

She liked the program because she was beginning to feel something of castaway herself although you couldn't describe the Swat Valley of Pakistan as exactly a desert island. The capital Mingora was chaotic, noisy and dirty and although it was easy enough to get lost in the mountains and pristine forests further up in the valley.

Sally was 28, a little on the plump side and wore her thick blonde hair tied at the back in a ponytail and had put on a thick chunky pullover because it was still cold even in the late November morning. The first luxury she would choose in London would be… she stopped to think. Maybe a brilliant hairstylist to dye her roots again, cut her hair and also do her nails. But that probably wasn't allowed under the rules. Actually, what she really craved was some company and some fun.

Most of the other foreigners who used to hang around Mingora had long gone. The backpackers who came to enjoy the crisp Alpine air and the stunning mountain scenery had been scared away by the fighting. Recently the gang of English teachers and gap year students had cleared off too and even the hard core of aid workers was dwindling rapidly. She felt pretty much on her own these days.

When she had arrived in the Swat Valley two years earlier to head up the local office of International Grassroots Literacy Foundation, she had been felt an immense relief to escape and be on her own. She could escape a rather dreadful relationship and all that dreary office politics. Here she was in charge, more or less. Actually, it was her local staff who were really in charge. They knew how to get things done and if they didn't, they turned to Aziza Yousafzai who was a local big shot linked to the Pakistan Coalition for Education. Ever since he had arrived Aziza had been her mentor.

Even so at first the sense of responsibility had been uplifting, even empowering. In fact, there wasn't that much too do at first. All the girl's schools had already been set up and were running smoothly. The locals didn't need to be taught about the value of educating girls. They had been doing it for hundreds of years, as they kept telling her. Nor did they need to know how to teach girls either. It wasn't like working in other parts of Pakistan where you had to fight total feudal patriarchal mega-ignorance and oppression. She suspected that's why they chose to send here rather than Baluchistan or somewhere.

Here in the Swat Valley all she had to was go around like a good fairy dispensing text books, computers and other learning aids and to make sure they stuck to the building plans. The Foundation was building a dozen new schools so there was a great deal of pernickety paperwork, collecting a jumble of funny-looking receipts and bills.

Sally sipped at her tea and listened as the Desert Island Discs guest, a rather smooth professor with a double barrel name who was an expert on Africa, started to select his first choice of music. He chose a pop song by a boy band just to show that he was not an old fogey. She fingered the packet of biscuits wondering whether to take her own bet seriously. Then after a conversation with the presenter in the studio about his travels in East Africa, he declared his second choice. It was Vivaldi, the Four Seasons. 'Yes, I knew it,' Sally said to herself out loud and then opened the packet and bit hard on the first biscuit.

She was enjoying the urgent silvery notes made by the strings in 'Winter' when she heard a banging at the door to the compound. She got up and went to the double fronted metal gate and then hesitated. 'Who is it?' she demanded.

'Aziza. Open the door. I have something to tell you.'

Sally recognized the voice immediately. She crossed the courtyard again and went into the office and picked up some keys and then fiddled with the large padlock. Normally, there was gate keeper cum guard who was in charge but this morning Sally was on her own. She opened the gate cautiously and poked her head out. Aziza was standing there alone but a few yards down the alleyway, her car and driver was waiting. The motor was still running and Aziza looked agitated.

'It's started again. They're burning the schools. They are attacking the teachers too. Those fools in Islamabad have let Sufi Mohammed out. That monster is back,' Aziza quickly, spitting out the facts. Sufi Mohammed, an elderly pious- looking man with a white beard, from prison, had founded the militant movement in the Swat Valley.

Aziza was older than Sally who thought her the most elegant and well-dressed woman she had ever met in Pakistan. She always exuded an air of inbred privilege and poise that came from her upbringing in one of the most famous families in the valley. Now she looked older and plainer but still very much in command.

'I came to warn you. Be very careful. Stay at home until the guard arrives,' she said. 'Now I must go.'

'Where are you going?'

'The Saidu Sharif College. They just called me. Someone has attacked it and its own fire.'

'But I was just there last week. I took 100 books there,' Sally said stupidly.

'I think this was only the first school they bombed this morning. I am going there now to look,' Aziza said.

'I want to go with you,' Sally said.

'No, it's not safe for you,' Aziza replied and gave her a hard look. Then she turned abruptly and walked to the car. As she got, she turned round again. 'Don't answer the door to anyone else.'

Sally nodded obediently and went back inside after locking the gate carefully again. Once inside her office, sat down in the sofa chair again. The radio was still playing and the guest on Desert Island Discs was making his final choice. She got up, turned it off and sat down again. She began listening to the sounds from the street half expecting to hear the sounds of gunfire. She couldn't hear anything. Then she thought, I can't just stay here and wait and worry, I am going out to take a look.

She got up and got dressed and then went outside into the courtyard. She opened the metal gate and looked outside into the alleyway. There was no one to be seen. She hesitated. Only last week, she had been at a school in Manglor village and had been touched by the way the young teacher there, a woman of her own age, had kept saying to her: 'We need you here, you must say,' she said. Then she had insisted on taking Sally to her home and cooking her a lavish meal that must have cost a week's wages. Ali, her driver, who had been invited along for the banquet had reassured her afterwards: 'People are just want to be sure you are happy here in our country. Not too lonely for home.' Everyone seemed more anxious than ever to welcome her and ask for her help in all kinds of ways. Sally felt a strong impulse to ignore Aziza's warning. She knew where the Saidu Sharif College for Girls was and Sally reckoned she could walk there in 20 minutes.

Sally went back into the compound and went to her room where she changed into a long black gown that reached to her feet. Over her head she put on a niqab that covered her blonde hair and hid her face except for the eyes. Then she walked out into the alley and headed towards the College. She kept her head down and avoided looking at anyone directly. As she reached the central market, called the Green Chowk, she noticed that the only other women were dressed the same way but were accompanied by a male relative. The shops selling music and videos had put up metal shutters. Sally kept her eyes to ground but an uncomfortable feeling that men were looking her did not leave her until she got close to the College where a small crowd had gathered and was too busy watching the scene to pay any attention to her.

4

In the courtyard of a half-finished building, some 20 miles north of Mingora in the Swat Valley, Maulana Fazlullah, rose to his feet. He looked down at the small circle of his men who were still keeling after they had finished their dawn prayers. It was damp and cold from an autumn mist and well before the sun would rise above the surrounding peaks and flood the valley with sunlight. There was enough of a dawn breeze to flutter the black flags stuck on the land cruisers and on the top of the unfinished concrete stairwell that would on day lead to the top floor of his headquarters.

Maulana Fazullah was tall and thick set with a large thick black beard. His hair and much of his face was hidden beneath a black headdress and from time to time he wiped his nose and then cleaned his hand against his clothes. Like everyone, apart from the old man who stood beside him, he was armed. His men had laid down an assortment of weapons next to them when they had prayed. They crouched under course woven woolen blankets, covering ragged looking trousers that stopped short of their ankles. Most of them were wearing sandals despite the cold.

Maulana had strapped on a gun in a leather holster around his waist and his hand strayed there. His men were not looking at him however but looking expectantly at the old man standing beside him. This was Sufi Mohammed, his father-in-law, a slighter figure wearing glasses above a white half beard that started at his chin.

'May Allah bless you. May God who created all mankind rain his blessings on you. For the order of Allah in the Holy Quran is very clear that Jihad is for the sake of Allah and to give with soul and money is a duty. Indeed the Jihad against the Zionist-crusader alliance is one of the main ways (after the grace of Allah) that we can destroy our enemies. O my Ummah grant us patience which suffices us to continue on the way of Jihad for seven years again, and seven, and seven again…Allah willing. Allah has chosen us for his call. Brothers, never glance back even if your path is strewn with blood.'

Maulana's fighters listened to him in grave silence. He had a calm air of authority and dignity and his voice started evenly and slowly. Then slowly it increased in intensity and volume as he spoke of his anger and indignation of his imprisonment.

'My brothers, we must clean these impious schools and fulfill our duty to return these people to Sharia law. As the Prophet laid down, men should not mix with women and the girls must be kept at home to obey their fathers and brothers and practise modesty,' he said.

'These schools are plot by the infidels which preach Christianity and sinfulness. They must be destroyed. Allah will show his mercy and compassion. I give thanks now in the name of the Prophet, blessed be his name,' he continued and then smiled. The men bowed their heads and repeated his words. 'Yesterday we won one victory. Today we will win another.'

Maulana had listened to his father in law with pride. His release had been a great victory that had boosted his own prestige and authority among the men after a series of deadly defeats at the hands of the army. Now they were ready to realize their dream and create a new caliphate in Pakistan. He motioned to the militants to get up and take their weapons. They rose to their feet and Maulana felt a thrill at seeing how readily they obeyed. He divided them into four groups. To each of them he distributed bottles filled with gasoline. Then they split up and got into four battered land cruisers. Maulana issued instructions to the occupants of each vehicle and then climbed into the front seat of the last vehicle.

Half an hour later Maulana and his fighters arrived in the village of Manglor, a small farming settlement off the main road which headed north from Mingora, the Swat Valley's biggest town. Only a few people are about. One or two boys were herding cattle to graze in the stubble fields around the scattered houses. Mangalor's primary school was quite large because it served four other villages. It was a small L-shaped building constructed of red brick topped by a flat concrete roof. There was small school yard graced by a couple of swings and a see-saw.

Maulana noticed with disgust that the entrance to the school had a large board with a faded photograph a class of girls modestly dressed with white head shawls sitting two to desk in rows behind a teacher. Above the picture were the words: 'Education for All – a promise to the new generation'. Above the metal entrance gate painted in blue was an arch with a demand in English: 'Support the Pakistan Coalition for Education'.

They had arrived before the school had opened its doors. Maulana, followed by his three fighters walked impatiently around the outside of the school to make sure that no one was in the building. He grabbed hold of the arm of one man, a fifty-year old man with a red hennaed beard. 'Grandfather, now you have your wish. It is your honor to destroy this place of pollution.' The older man, one of the poorest men in the district with eight children and had refused to pay for his daughters' education, and had been urging Maulana to destroy it for some months. He went back to the Toyota and lit the taper on each bottle of gasoline. Maulana took one and handed it over to the old man who took it, hurled it against the windows and shouted 'Alluh Akhbar'. The windows, papered by children's crayon drawings, shattered. The gasoline spread across the floor and Maulana watched the first blue flames take hold and begin to burn steadily. Then he slapped the old man on the back. The other three militants threw their bottles. Maulana watched the wooden chairs and benches catch fire and looked to see if the old man was watching too. Then the flames spread to the text books on the shelves at the back of the classrooms. The last to burn would be the blackboard. He had seen it before. Inside his heart, Maulana felt a glow of satisfaction begin to spread through him as the whole building began to take fire and the smoke rose back and thick. They had firebombed the biggest schools in Mingora and now his men would spread the laws of God to the rest of the Valley.

5

At his small desk, Stoner heard a babble of excited voices. He turned his head from his screen and turned to look through a frosted glass window. The bank's top executives were decanting out of the lift and walking up the big mahogany staircase to the meeting room next to the chairman's offices. At four in the afternoon, a December darkness folded around London. Every office block in Bishopsgate had turned its lights on. The main dealing room was two floors below and under the jolly Christmas tinsel and strings of cards, everyone was acting unusually animated as the markets closed and the weekend began.

Stoner opened his door a crack and recognized the lanky figure of the taciturn American, Felix Rosenbaum. Perhaps the moment had finally arrived. Rosenbaum had been commissioned to investigate the effectiveness of the bank's risk strategy management system. As chief auditor, Stoner should have been invited. That was odd – and why hold a meeting like this on a Friday afternoon?

Stoner hesitated. Then he grabbed his jacket off the back of his chair, adjusted the knot of his tie, and joined the crowd. Thankfully, there was no protocol in the seating and he selected a chair in the middle of a row but at the back. He squeezed between the rows, keeping a tight formal smile on his face, and avoided meeting anyone's eyes. He that all the members of the Asset & Liability Committee were there.

Last to come in was Brenda, the chief Risk and Compliance Officer, looking irritated but determined in a charcoal dark suit. She looked carefully at Rosenbaum, who stood sternly at the front, giving nothing away. If he had really found something, her career would be over. Then she caught sight of Stoner. He thought that a flicker of surprise crossed her pale features. He could feel a premonition, a knot of fear gathering in his stomach.

Mervyn, the chairman and the fourth generation of the Wilberwrights to run Grosvenor Bank, arrived finally to open the proceedings. 'No one will contradict me,' he said with a little self-deprecating 'Ahem' that brought respectful titters, 'when I say that this bank is proud of the fact that we have had one of our best results in the derivatives business. In fact, this year will be one of the most profitable in our bank's history.'

There was scattered applause. Mervyn was a bulky, florid man who relished boasting about the bank's history.

As he talked, a waitress came in wearing a little uniform and pouring coffee into tiny porcelain cups decorated with the bank's trade mark, a green griffin.

'Now, many in London feel that market ethics and codes of behavior have always been better than average. London has been at the forefront of most developments and will be for the future the prime source of best practice. Yet electronic trading is changing the world we live in and we have to change, too. Pride comes before a fall. And that is why I've asked the world's foremost expert on operational risk management information procedures to conduct a thorough review of the systems we have in place. Felix, I give you the floor.'

'Globally some two trillion pounds exchange hands every day. As these numbers have increased there has been a commensurate risk in the payment and settlement risk implicit within them,' he said. The rest of the audience shuffled in their seats, but Stoner listened carefully. 'Large operational risk-related financial services losses have averaged well in excess of ten billion pounds annually for the past twenty years. It could be ten times as much, if you include all the losses that no one really ever hears about because organizations don't want them out in the public eye,' he said.

'We all remember Nick Leeson who destroyed Barings with storied losses of 1.2 billion dollars. That was the defining moment for operational risk management. As Leeson showed us, settlements staff should never have the opportunity to undertake a deal or to write up a deal. But I am glad to say that we have at long last established a necessary segregation of back office duties and reporting lines.'

It is, of course, vital that there is no potential for collusion between a dealer and someone in the back office which could lead to trades being altered, payment instructions changed or revaluation rates being doctored.'

Stoner began to relax slightly as the American ploughed on.

'We have now an excellent operational risk management information system. All risks are being monitored daily by the Group's risk group, but we can still be at risk. Why? Unauthorized book entries.

'Colleagues,' Rosenbaum said, putting on a solemn expression like a newsreader announcing a plane crash, 'we are now at the precipice of a new risk management frontier.'

There was a round of polite applause, followed by some questions and answers before the meeting was over and everyone hurried out. Stoner walked out slowly, relieved that nothing more alarming had been announced. This had been more a prep talk than anything else.

At the bottom of the mahogany staircase, Mervyn's secretary, Janet, had been waiting for him. 'His Lordship needs a quick word in your shell-like,' she said with a bright smile. He followed her back up to the top management offices. Mervyn was standing in front of a small antique wooden desk, probably the only desk within a square mile without a computer terminal squatting on it. He gestured to Stoner to sit down on an antique green leather chair. Then he sat down himself and composed his heavy features into a thoughtful expression.

'Here at Grosvenor's we have always followed a certain philosophy. We trust our employees to take the initiative, to give them the freedom to work on our behalf, to find new ways of making money. We are, if you like, trusting. It's management by trust. It's about self-responsibility. Our tradition, if you like. In that ghastly American management- speak, we believe in empowering individuals. It's paying us handsome dividends this year, record profits.'

Mervyn is gabbling, thought Stoner. He's nervous.

'That Rosenbaum is a remarkable fellow, brilliant mind, got us a remarkable system in place. Best there is. But the question is – whatever the system, are we to be worried about the data? Or the, ahem, people, if you follow me? I mean to say, the data is only as reliable as the folks putting it in. Follow me? But we wouldn't want to make anyone nervous, start any rumors.'

Stoner guessed what he was driving at and nodded.

'You mean one of the traders has been inputting fake data?' he asked. As the senior auditor, it was Stoner's responsibility to reconcile all trades. When someone bought or sold a financial product, they booked the trade, making a profit or a loss. All open positions then had to be closed before the next and the trades matched.

'How much do we all really understand about all these derivatives anyway?' Mervyn said. He liked playing the role of the kindly and fussy schoolteacher dealing with a bright student.

'Well,' Stoner parried. 'You know what they say. They are like aspirins. If you have a headache, take one and they can make the pain go away. But take the whole bottle at once, you can kill yourself.'

Of course it may not be derivatives," Mervyn said.

'You mean it's not a trader inputting fake derivative trades?' Stoner said stolidly. 'Instead, you are worried about forex deals?'

Mervyn winced. 'The thing is, Rosenbaum's found a flaw in our system. It allows someone to set up a proprietary trading account, an account with a password that we can't open,' he said.

'You mean they have been using the bank's capital to trade on their own account?' Stoner asked.

'Yes, correct.' Mervvn took out the silk handkerchief from his breast pocket, refolded it neatly and put it back again.

'So how big's the hole?'

'That's just it. We don't know. It's been open for two years,' Mervyn said.

'Two years?' Stoner stared at him in open-mouthed astonishment.

'There's no evidence that we have lost any money. It's not like Credit Lyonnais, but somewhere in this building there's a rogue trader,' Mervyn said. 'If it's not derivatives – we can't find any records of that – it must be forex and we've no idea what our exposure could be. How can we? A profit could turn into a loss in the blink of an eye.'

'I see.' Stoner looked blank.

Mervyn locked his gaze into his eyes and the air of bumbling vagueness vanished. 'I want you to find him,' he ordered.

'I'll do my best, sir. But how?'

'I think you will find a way,' Mervyn said. Stoner nodded. Had he imagined that there was a slight and menacing emphasis on "you"?

They discussed the details of the work, and then Stoner left the meeting, went back to his office and closed the door. He shoved the three piles of print-outs piled on his desk on to the floor with a sweep of his arm. He sat down and for a long time he stared at the Christmas festivities he could see through the windows on the other side of the courtyard. He sighed and turned away. He pulled a cell phone out of his pocket, turned it on, staring at the small screen, and then put it back in his pocket. Stoner stood up, locked his computer, put on his coat and gloves. He went out of the room and carefully locked the door.

On the pavement outside the office he searched for a group of smokers braving the cold. He spoke to one of them briefly and then set off for the Pig & Whistle, a few minutes' walk away. Inside, it was heaving with dark suits, mostly traders all cheerfully shouting to make themselves heard above the din. Stoner elbowed his way through the crowd until he found Wilkins talking to a couple of mates from the quants department. The quants, who thought of themselves as a different tribe from anyone else in the City, set themselves apart by dressing like rich students. Wilkins was wearing a black t-shirt underneath a dark tailored jacket and his blond hair, parted in the middle, was long like a seventies pop star. The three of them were drinking expensive organic ale and entertaining two secretaries who were nursing glasses of white Chardonnay.

'You remember Sheryl, don't you?'

Stoner forced a grin, and she smiled back encouragingly. 'Sheryl, this is Stoner. Not that he is,' Wilkins said.

Stoner smiled humorlessly. 'But you are,' he said.

He knew Wilkins often took drugs and was probably going to spend the weekend high on them. Pointing it out was a way of cracking the whip, but Wilkins was enjoying himself too much to care.

Wilkins shook his head and then looked round the noisy bar. 'Don't you think it's too noisy here? Time we went home and curled up with a good book. What do you like to take to bed, Sheryl? A stiff hardback, I bet.'

She laughed. 'Very droll. Not.'

'My one tends to get a bit bent with use,' Wilkins said. 'Excuse me a moment,' Stoner interrupted and pushed his way to the toilets. He waited there until Wilkins joined him a few moments later. They stood next to each other.

'Jesus, Stoner, you've got so much money, you could lighten up a bit.'

'I don't need your help for that, thank you,' he retorted. 'Keep away from that woman. She's up to something.'

'What do you mean?'

'What do I mean? I mean we're in trouble.'

'Go on.'

'I've just been summoned to see Mervyn. They know.' 'What do they know?'

'About the account. Something.'

'Do they know how much money we've made?' 'No. At least, I don't know what exactly they know.' 'And what are you going to do?'

'He wants me to find out who has been operating it.' 'Well, just try and fail.'

'It's not that simple. There was a kind of threat. I've got to find someone.'

The door to the men's opened, letting in a blast of music.

Two other men came in, talking loudly.

'We shouldn't be meeting any more. It is too dangerous.' 'I rather think it's lucky we did,' Wilkins said and went to wash his hands.

6

The Predator swooped over a rugged and fissured landscape dotted with small scruffy settlements. It followed a river, a dark band in the grainy footage, as it wound through craggy hills past ribbons of farmland. A row of slender birch trees and fields of sugar cane and wheat came into view, then a small settlement, blocks of mud-brick housing with flat roofs.

The camera then tracked down the valley, following an unpaved road leading to a settlement dominated by the minarets of a large white-domed mosque. Each corner of the compound was marked by square watch towers. The camera focused on a number of bearded and turbaned men wrapped in sheepskin coats who manned machine-guns posts from the watchtowers.

A convoy of pick-up trucks and 4-wheel drive vehicles raced along a thin winding road throwing up a trail of dust. The black and white images were clear enough to be able to pick out the black turbans worn by all the men crouching in the back with Kalashnikovs. The convoy stopped and parked inside the compound of the mosque. The foreshortened figures got out and disappeared inside.

Seven thousand miles away the audience heard the voices of the pilot and console operator:

Pilot: 15,000 feet and descending. We are locking on to target.

Operator: Do you have any buildings in sight? Pilot: Sir, we have oversight. The target is in view.

Operator: There's a mosque. Do not target the mosque. Pilot: Roger that.

Operator: Target is the rectangular compound. Pilot: Can you see the vehicles?

Operator: Correct. You have line of fire. How many civilians can you identify?

Pilot: We can identify twenty people in the compound. Operator: Do we have authorization to fire, sir?

3rd voice: Mission is cleared. Repeat. Mission is cleared.

Fire at will.

Pilot: Thirty seconds.

Operator: There's more people moving around the compound.

Pilot: The guards can hear us, sir. They are opening fire. Operator: It's shot.

The Predator descended towards the compound. Figures started running out of the mosque towards the vehicles. The listeners could hear the voices of two men talking on the phone in Pashto, yelling at each other. The telephone conversation was abruptly cut short by an explosion. The video showed the cross-hairs of the camera narrowing in on the mosque, then a flash of white showing the heat from the explosion. Next, the video showed an explosion as the mud- walled compound blew apart under the impact of a single Hellfire missile. A gaseous ball of fire and then the debris collapsed in silence.

No one spoke in the briefing room. Then a confident figure in a double-breasted suit stood up and took charge. Floyd Blashford was in his early fifties, with swept-back blond hair and a florid complexion that matched his pink- striped shirt. His pugnacious style had earned him the nickname 'Brashford' and now he began aggressively to set out the arguments in favor of unmanned drones.

'As everyone here is aware, Ayman al-Zawahiri is our highest priority. Born in Cairo in 1951, he graduated as a medical doctor in 1974. He is the mastermind of 9/11 and every one of al-Qaeda's operations.' He paused to give everyone time to study the familiar face that appeared on the screen. It was a file photo of a scholarly-looking man who had a black beard flecked with white, a noticeable splotched birthmark on his wide forehead, thick heavy-framed glasses and a white turban.

Pakistani intelligence passed on a tip-off that al-Zawahiri would be visiting this madrassa near the village of Damadola in the Bajaur District to attend a feast celebrating the Muslim Eid holiday,' Blashford said. 'As you just saw, this time we failed to get him.'

He looked around the briefing room at the dozen men and women attempting to weigh their mood. Best to get the bad news out first, he thought. In fact, he had hesitated to show this clip because, impressive though it was in some respects, it would remind everyone of another frustrating failure. It was now his job to convince his audience, especially the four experienced politicians present, that Predator's effectiveness had improved and the new generation of drones would be even deadlier. He knew everyone wanted to see al-Zawahiri dead and claim credit for helping in his destruction, yet they still doubted that Global Predator could deliver.

Blashford had organized the meeting to convince a core group of legislators still reluctant to back an expanded program for a new version of the Predator. For years, Blashford had gone around telling anyone who would listen that the drones were the most effective weapon that the United Sates had to deal with the Islamic extremists operating in the Pakistan's bad-lands. He called the Predator a 'silver bullet' and boasted that it could finally kill off al- Qaeda.

He had invited four men to a briefing in one of the rooms in the basement of the Congress building. These were men whom he knew could sway opinion in the Senate Armed Services Committee, the Senate Intelligence Committee and the House National Security and Foreign Affairs sub-committee. The opinion he cared most about was that of Senator Bill Wright, a former criminal prosecutor, who had been the most persistent and respected voice questioning the legality and effectiveness of the drone program. If he could change his mind, then others would follow.

'As you know, this attack failed to kill al-Zawahiri,' Blashford continued. 'He was there all right. Pakistani intel-ligence confirmed they had given us accurate information. Al-Zawahiri had indeed been present in Damadola when the attack took place. He was arriving by jeep to attend an Eid celebration when we struck,' he said.

As he spoke, he was uncomfortably aware that Wright had a skeptical look on face. He was a slight man with untidy white hair and large bags under his eyes, but a sharp mind and a surprisingly strong and commanding stentorian voice that he had used to great effect in many courtrooms. As a former prosecutor, he had a well-honed technique of delivering an argument by speaking slowly and deliberately, with great force, a relentless and slow-moving bulldozer that could not be stopped. He knew that in principle Wright was in his corner. Wright liked the idea that more UAVs could cut defense costs. A single F-22 Raptor had a hefty price tag of 355 million dollars but a Predator cost a mere 4.5 million dollars. Blashford's real opponents were in the Air Force which feared that one day its pilots and indeed most of its expensive planes would go the way of cavalry squadrons.

Senator Wright raised his hand and spoke before Blashford could continue. 'Let me stop you there,' he said. 'This attack failed, and it failed in more ways than one. Pakistan's foreign ministry protested to the US ambassador over what it termed the 'loss of innocent civilian lives'. Pakistani News reported that most of the victims were women and children. So did the BBC. This is hurting us.'

Blashford was all too painfully reminded of how the news reports played out. They showed groups of wailing women dressed in black burqas digging through rubble while men struggled to remove bloodied corpses from beneath heaps of blackened bricks and timbers. One report claimed that eight members of a single family were killed in the attack. Another said that between seventy and eighty students died inside the compound.

'What rankles more is that it costs us hundreds of millions to run the Predator program and what does it cost them to send a suicide bomber? I'll tell you – a few hundred measly bucks,' Wright's bulldozer pushed on.

Not long after the Damadola attack, a suicide bomber had killed forty-two Pakistani soldiers in a revenge attack. One morning a man wrapped in a shawl ran on to the training ground where eighty recruits were assembled and said he had a vital message. When a platoon gathered round him, he blew himself up, leaving a huge crater and a mess of severed limbs.

'Not only that, no one over in Pakistan, and plenty of people here, don't think we have the right to fly around Pakistan blowing people up whenever we feel like it,' Wright said.

'Now if I remember rightly, we have tried and failed to kill al-Zawahiri at least four times. And it's not a shortage of clever technology but reliable intel that's the problem,' he continued remorselessly.

Blashford decided he had to jump in front of the bulldozer before it crushed everything. 'Sir, sir, – we all agree that we want al-Zawahiri dead, though? That the American people won't accept that we just give up while this man is at large plotting fresh attacks?'

Wright nodded. Reluctantly, he stopped talking. 'Please continue,' he conceded gruffly.

'As I was saying, I think we now know where he has found a new hiding place. It is here in Southern Waziristan. This is the fiefdom of the Mehsud tribe and the headquarters of the

Tehrik-i-Taliban Pakistan or TTP – that is to say, the Pakistan Taliban.' He paused to give his audience a moment to study the photo of another bearded and turbaned man.

'The TTP is led by Baitullah Mehsud, one of the most dangerous Taliban leaders. This man is believed, rightly in my view, to have masterminded the assassination of Benazir Bhutto. His tribesmen are now providing security for al- Qaeda and recruiting foot soldiers for many al-Qaeda operations. Thanks to the Predator's enhanced capabilities, we are now able to keep a 24/7 watch on his headquarters.'

He paused, again, to give everyone in the room time to look at more grainy video footage shot from a camera fitted into the nose cone of Predator. Taken from 15,000 feet up, it showed in clear detail a walled compound in a mud and brick settlement set in a wide, deep and treeless valley. On either side rose high snow-covered mountains. People could be seen walking up and down, working in the fields, or herding flocks of sheep.

'I think we are now one stop away from finding him. In fact, I can say with confidence we are getting closer to finding al-Zawahiri. You see, three weeks ago, one of his close lieutenants showed up, Abu Jihad al-Masri, an explosives expert who has trained many al-Qaeda recruits in major operations against our troops in Iraq.'

Blashford then played a clip taken at night with an infrared camera. The fuzzy images showed a small convoy of vehicles arriving at the settlement. It was possible to make out the individual vehicles and the number of people inside each of them, but not their faces.

'Here, he is arriving for a meeting with Mehsud. This time we were able to make a ninety per cent positive identification,' he said, 'and to take him out. This success has received almost no publicity. You are the first to see these images.'

He played another clip taken from Predator slowly descending on the convoy as it was approaching the outskirts of the settlement. In the background, a recording of several brief but agitated conversations played. Then one of the vehicles exploded in a burst of red heat.

'This time Mehsud escaped, but we got al-Masri,' Blashford said. 'When Mehsud heard the Predator descending, he panicked and called al-Masri, warning him to turn back. In his panic, he used his satellite phone. Al-Masri picked up the phone and answered so we locked on to it and could then track him. We also inserted a software package into his phone and activated the microphone. Even without his photograph, we could attack with a high degree of certainty because we had a voice recording of his speech. In seconds we could match the two.'

Bashford could sense that the audience was warming towards him. Now he had to close the sale

'What is more Mehsud is a hunted man and he knows it. He only travels at night; he never sleeps in the same bed twice. His men cannot train or gather in the open. They feel their safe houses are no longer safe, so at night they sleep under trees in the open. Mehsud cannot know for certain how we tracked him down. They suspect we have informers in their own camp or the general population.'

Bashford then paused for effect. 'In the past we launched strikes when there was a fifty per cent certainty. Now the current basic operational requirement is a ninety per cent certainty in order to avoid any civilian casualties. We can now do this.'

'And just what makes you so sure the next generation of UAVs will be any more effective than the ones we already have?' Senator Bill Wright said.

Blashford was ready for this. He got up and introduced a new speaker.

'That's a fair question which we can answer. I am now going to invite Lt. Colonel William Masterson from the Nellis Air Force Base in Nevada, home of the Predator, to introduce the new innovations,' Blashford said.

Masterson was a tall, slim man in his forties with a brisk air of technical competence. He was no showman like Blashford and got straight to the point.

'Let me introduce the MQ9-1B. We call it The Reaper,' he started and then began dryly describing the technicalities. At the same time he clicked through a series of photographs showing a sleek silvery aircraft with distinctive inverted v-tail wings. In the first one, it was shown standing next to the smaller Predator.

'This is the new MQ9-1B beside the MQ1. The new Predator is a real hunter-killer, equipped with four Hellfire missiles.

'We have a new Clandestine Tagging Tracking and Locating system. An individual can be invisibly tagged and tracked or located at great distance by unique identifiers. Once the suspect is identified, he can be tagged or painted by an infrared sensor which allows us to track his movements and contacts.

'Next, the new MQ9-1B is equipped with fine resolution Synthetic Aperture Radar. It can detect and locate up to six high value mobile targets at a time. The MQ9s even have voice recognition systems so we can be sure we have the right person.

'We also have a new Tactical Control System. What this means is that we can now maintain a twenty-four-hour vigilance over a suspect wherever he goes. At the right moment, say when the target is in the open or meeting with other Jihadist elements, the missiles can be launched with accuracy. If we do not wish to eliminate him – or her – then the technology allows us to tag other suspects with whom he is in contact.

'Lastly, the Predator's Hellfire missile can now lock on and then hit a target, even if the target is not in sight. It could be over the horizon and twenty miles away. The accuracy of the Predators has improved dramatically. There is now very little chance of a target escaping, or of inflicting an unacceptable number of civilian casualties,' Lt. Colonel Masterson finished. Blashford stepped forward again. 'Gentleman, this is the Reaper, the ultimate weapon that is going to change the history of intelligence warfare,' he said with a flourish.

Well, thank you, Colonel Masterson. Now I think we now know why they call these things drones. Of course, we can all congratulate the Air Force and the engineers at General Atomics on their technology,' he said. 'But I want to clarify a few things: do we really want these machines, ah drones, however advanced, to assassinate foreigners in foreign countries, or do we want them to help collect intelligence? Do we really want to kill al-Zawahiri or his associates, or do we want to capture them, and interrogate them so we can quickly destroy their networks?'

He looked round at the rest of the room. 'I think I already know the answers to these questions. Gentlemen, if you want my support I want to see fewer people killed and more captured, and above all, more leads: names and addresses, bank accounts, that sort of thing. Get their computers, phonebooks, that kind of evidence that would stand up in court. Don't just fly around blowing everything up – we already got enough damn rockets and bombs to do that.

'When are you people going to get hiring the sort of men, or women, who really understand this country? People who can speak the languages and understand the customs so we know what we are doing, ' Wright said. 'I think the lesson we have learned is that we cannot keep relying on Pakistan for help in dealing with our enemies and the Predator, or the Reaper – I mean, where do you get these names – is never going to provide the real time actionable intelligence we need.'

Blashford listened with growing irritation. Wright had to be stopped or he was going to smash his way through the whole morning's good work. Without reflecting, he threw himself again in front of the bulldozer.

'This machine is now close to tracking down al-Zawahiri and, with him, decapitating the whole al-Qaeda leadership.'

Wright looked angry, affronted at being interrupted, and then he forced his features into a more pleasant expression.

'Of course, if you were to destroy him, ah decapitate him, next week that would help,' he said with a hint of sarcasm. 'But as far as I am concerned, we don't need fancy robots but better human intel and better people to analyze it. This is not war but police work. Now, if you will excuse me, I have another meeting to attend.'

But if we did get his scalp, then we would have your support?' Blashford pressed him.

The meeting broke up soon after that. Senator was already standing up to leave, but he paused for a second to give a curt nod, and then stalked out of the room. The audience, too, began to make their excuses and drifted away, leaving Blashford alone in the room with Masterson.

Masterson looked at Blashford sympathetically. 'Did you, or did you not, just put your head in a noose by promising to deliver al-Zawahiri?'

'Maybe. Maybe not.'

'You know where he is then?'

'Not exactly,' he said. Masterson smiled slightly. 'But I think we know where he is going to be.'

'Where?'

'Ever heard of the Swat Valley?' Masterson shook his head.

'Well, maybe we need to start briefing your team right away,' Blashford said pleasantly.

7

Wilkins walked out of the pub into a thin drizzle of December rain and began to think hard. He was in the classic bind of the prisoner's dilemma, but it was not like studying abstract calculations of where betrayal or cooperation would lead. In real life, the mind is swept along by emotions, but he was not sure if he was feeling the emotions that he ought to be feeling, that he should be feeling. He descended the steps into the Bank tube station and got into a half-empty carriage. In his seat, he studied his illuminated reflection in the window opposite. The odd lighting turned his usual complexion from reddish to white and his mouth seemed drawn down at the corners. The blond hair, swept back and parted in the middle, seemed to be receding at his temple and he touched it for reassurance. Still plenty there. Not like Stoner with his shaven bald skull and those absurd thick black spectacles. But he would soon turn thirty and was no longer the golden boy student with open-ended prospects.

They had shrunk to just two. Which to choose, he wondered, as the train clattered along the rails. He had worked at the Grosvenor Bank for two years and was now richer than he had ever imagined, richer even than the flashy traders whose breezy confidence had awed him when he had started his first job feeling raw and unpolished. In the first week, he joined the smokers who gathered on the pavement just round the corner from the main entrance near Bishopsgate. It had even smelt of burning money. Stoner had been there.

'Meet Charlie Morden, the richest and most disgusting bastard in this building,' Stoner said, inclining his head at a tall elegant man chomping on a thick cigar. Wilkins noticed the dark suit of expensive wool and a gracious, charming manner. Charlie removed the cigar, blew out a cloud of blue fragrant smoke and then smiled back insouciantly.

'Just rolling the dice,' he said.

'Charlie cleaned up on 7/7 when the bombs went off on the buses and trains. We could hear the sirens but he went straight into action, speculating in insurance stocks, 'Stoner said. 'Thanks to him, it was the best trading day in the bank's history.'

'You make me sound like an unfeeling monster. As if I was blowing people up in the tube,' he said lightly.

'He made five million in nine minutes,' Stoner continued.

'Oh, well. It's just a bit of elementary psychology, knowing what the other guys are going to do before they do it,' Charlie had said with a little edge in his voice.

Then Charlie had asked Wilkins what he did, although he must have guessed just by looking at his clothes and seeing the roll-up in his hand. Wilkins had over-eagerly begun to tell him about the new trading program that he was working on with the other quants. Charlie had listened politely before cutting him off.

'No computer program will know how people, especially a crowd, will react, because people have emotions,' Charlie said. He remembered how Stoner had looked hard at him when Charlie said this, as if warning him to shut up. Of course, star traders don't like to hear that a piece of software can do their job better, so Wilkins had not responded. Yet Wilkins had proved him wrong and massively so. Then, as the little gathering broke up and returned to their offices, Charlie had fished out one of his long Cohibas, an Esplendido, and handed it him. Wilkins had been pleased by the generosity, ridiculously so, now that he thought back to a time when he was still learning that he was no longer a student.

Before joining the bank he had been up at Cambridge doing his doctoral research into quantum physics, or to be precise, quantum mathematics. Quants were just becoming sought after in the City. The branch of physics provides a mathematical description of the complex ways in which particles such as electrons behave, and it had become known that the science was surprisingly useful at predicting random movements in financial markets. The financial markets consist of individuals who react to what others are doing. So traders are very interested in understanding situations where there are only two choices, to buy or to sell. It is like dealing with electrons, they are either positive or negative. So you can marry quantum physics to game theory in order to search for patterns for probabilities and then perform a statistical arbitrage. That is why the so-called quant funds like to employ people with a background in quantum physics.

Stoner thought Wilkins could help him solve a problem. Traders who buy or sell stocks, or any other product, must play a version of a game called Prisoner's Dilemma, over and over again. The dilemma is simple enough and that is why it became one of the most studied games in game theory. Wilkins now went over it in his mind again. The basic idea is easy to grasp. It's all about guessing what would happen if one person and his partner in crime were arrested and charged with jointly carrying out armed robbery. The two partners are in prison and are being questioned, but separately. The police don't enough evidence for a conviction, so they visit each criminal with the same deal: if one testifies for the prosecution against the other and the other remains silent, the snitch goes free and the other gets the full fifteen-year sentence. However, the two prisoners know that if they both confess, each will get ten years in jail. If they both deny the crime then each will merely be charged with the lesser offense of gun possession, which carries a sentence of just three years in jail.

The best scenario is when one person confesses and his partner doesn't: the former will be rewarded for his betrayal by being released, while the other will get a sentence of fifteen years. The worst scenario, naturally, is if it is you who keeps quiet and your partner confesses. The optimal result for both is if both men keep quiet because that way each gets away with a lighter sentence. In the game, the key factor is that the two men have no way of communicating with each other. Each man is all alone. So each has to guess what his partner will do. If you could keep quiet, you run the risk that the other man could betray you.

The tricky thing is that you also know that your partner is bound to be making the same calculation. The most rational strategy for both is to confess, which is why in the language of game theory confessing is called the 'dominant strategy'. Yet when real people play the game in field experiments, the dominant strategy turns out to be 'defect', that is to grass.

Was that how Stoner would react? Wilkins' first thought was that it was unlikely, but then he asked himself how well he really knew Stoner. He knew little about Stoner's private life. They didn't share the same interests and he had given little thought to what motivated him. He was clever and secretive, he knew that, and had a passion for collecting antique Chinese porcelain. Stoner had once invited him to see his collection, but he had never bothered to do so. In fact, he had never been to his house.

Charlie Morden was right when he said that what always matters most is psychology because, as he had pointed out, people often act on irrational impulses. Wilkins knew, though, that Stoner was not an impulsive character, but a planner. Stoner was good at thinking far ahead and he had no qualms in deceiving the bank, so he was capable of anything. In theory it should be the case that half the time one player defects, and half the time the other player defects, but research showed that in fact about a quarter of the time the players choose to cooperate.

At the start of their collaboration, Stoner had asked Wilkins to create an algorithm to reveal what happens when the game theory is applied to scenarios in which the same calculation is made thousands of times in a day, and not by two individuals but by herds of traders in currencies, shares or bonds. The results then become very interesting and Wilkins suddenly became aware of an idea, unformed as yet, that was growing in the back of his mind.

When the train stopped at Belsize Park station, Wilkins got out, walked to the lift and once on street level, he walked to his basement flat, breathing in the refreshing night air. He enjoyed the ten-minute walk and at the door, he paused, wondering whether to walk some more on Hampstead Heath. He found it easier to think when he was walking. But the steady drizzle which had come on made him decide against it. Inside, he switched on a single light in the living- room. Then he poured himself a beer and took it to the sofa. He scrabbled around to find a remote control and switched on some guitar music, John Williams playing some classical Spanish pieces. He had bought himself the Hammacher Schlemmer, the most expensive Swedish stereo system one could find. Now the white speaker boxes with their triode tubes filled the bare whitewashed room with an intricate architecture of sounds. Wilkins reached under the sofa and felt around until he had located a small packet of weed kept in a small sealed plastic bag. He opened it and from the pack of roll-up papers deftly extracted a paper and began make himself a double joint. Then he lit it, inhaled deeply and exhaled even more slowly.

He felt calmer. The brief discussion with Stoner in the gents worried him, but perhaps there was less of a threat than he had feared. The fact that the management of the bank had entrusted Stoner with this delicate mission gave him every opportunity he could wish for to cover up their tracks. Perhaps, thought Wilkins as the drug began to wash through him, perhaps he wasn't actually dealing with a real life case of prisoner's dilemma after all. They had not been caught. They were not in jail, so there was nothing to confess.

But then the thought struck him that perhaps Stoner had not revealed everything he knew. Behind that those thick black glasses was a very astute and resourceful brain. Everything that Stoner did or said seemed intended to reinforce the impression that he was dull but straight, reliable and diligent but bereft of imagination. While Wilkins saw himself as a fox, a restless, busy, curious spirit, he saw Stoner as a tortoise; smaller, slower and plodding. He was never trapped by his emotions the way Wilkins sometimes was.

You couldn't ever imagine Stoner falling hopelessly in love with a girl, or getting obsessed by a piece of research, or playing a piece of music over and over again. The trouble with Stoner's personality was that his attitude to risk, in the first instance, was to avoid it. So Stoner might decide that in a vital sense being suspected of a crime was the same as being 'caught'. If he reacted that way, he would start plotting a way out and that could be dangerous for Wilkins. He might decide that the best means of protecting himself would be to betray Wilkins and therefore to 'defect', statistically the most popular option.

On the other hand, Wilkins did not have that option. He couldn't betray Stoner without endangering himself. The optimum option for both of them was to continue cooperating – and wasn't that why Stoner had told him what was going on? As he held on to that thought, he began to relax and let his mind drift. After fifteen minutes the dope was taking hold and he felt time slow down. It was a powerful pungent black resin called Afghan black that he had bought a few weeks ago for a ludicrous price. Smoking was something he always did when he needed to work on a difficult problem. His mind would work out the right solution by itself.

Normally on a Friday night, he would have been mixing some cocaine in an all-night bender with some of the traders or quants. The only thing he was not used to was being alone. He got up and selected a favorite guitar from the collection he had started building up. It was Stevie Ray's 1965 Fender Composite Stratocaster, a red and gold treasure that he had spent £350,000 on. He began to pick out the chords of Every Day I Have The Blues and half-hummed and half- crooned the lyrics to himself. After a while he felt drowsy enough and went to lie down on his bed.

The next morning, he woke up at ten to the sound of the sparrows and blackbirds chattering in the rear garden. He felt refreshed and his mind was clear. He dressed in a tracksuit and ran around Hampstead Heath, scaring the ducks around the dank lakes. Then he washed, changed and walked out to a coffee shop on the high street. It was a French chain and he ordered a large café au lait with croissants and some scrambled eggs. From the table at the entrance, he picked up a few of the Saturday papers. There was not much domestic news on the front pages in the run-up to Christmas. Some warnings of higher oil prices. The Daily Telegraph had a long feature on the search for al-Zawahiri. He glanced at it. Ten years after 9/11, and his escape from the caves at Tora Bora, the CIA still had no idea where he was. Reports said he might be in Iran, Yemen, Saudi Arabia, Afghanistan, but most experts interviewed said he was almost certainly hiding out in the North-West Frontier, the badlands between Pakistan and Afghanistan. He put the newspapers aside after his eggs arrived. When he finished, he felt his mind was made up. He would leave as quickly as he could.

There were two main factors, he reasoned to himself. He pulled out a pen and on the newspaper article drew some thick lines. On one side he began to list the pros of leaving and on the other, the cons. First point: he had already made enough money to last him a lifetime. Second, he didn't want to carry on working in the bank any longer: what for? Third, the risks that Stoner would betray him or sacrifice him would only increase with time. Stoner might come under more pressure to find a villain. The bank stood to lose a great deal of money if something went wrong. Even if it didn't, the two of them had been gambling with the bank's money. Sooner or later everyone gets caught and Stoner would have to cut a deal to save himself.

Fourthly, he hated Stoner and wanted to end the relationship. Once he had articulated the thought, the full truth of it hit him. The older man had a psychological hold over him and had manipulated him into working for the bank in the first place. If he had never met Stoner, it would never have occurred to him to leave research. Then he sat back and thought again. If he was going to leave, he had better do it sooner rather than later.

Stoner might start worrying about his loyalty. He could easily have him watched. In fact, if he was in Stoner's shoes, he would

already have done it. Wilkins looked around the half-empty res-
taurant to see if he was already under surveillance. He stared
out of the window and looked at the street and the people walking by. Even if Stoner hadn't done it yet, the very thought that
he might do it was disturbing enough. If that was the case, then
the sooner he disappeared, the better. The next question was,
where to go?

It needed to be a place from which he could not be extradit-
ed and somewhere he would not be found by anyone for at least
several years. He thought of Spain but dismissed it – too easy.
Then he thought of Brazil. Train robbers had hung out there for
years. Then there was Central America, places like Panama. All
these were too obviously places where criminals went to hide,
but not for long. It was sort of incriminating and obvious. Then
he looked down at his list again and began thinking hard. As
he looked at the paper, Wilkins saw he had been scribbling on
top of the feature about Afghanistan and Al Qaeda. If the most
wanted man in the world could hide himself there for years on
end without being detected, then he could disappear there as
well. It sounded the sort of dangerous and lawless place where
someone could lie low for a long time. No one would think
of looking for him there. Then Wilkins sat back and began to
think if he knew anyone who could help him in Pakistan. Then
he thought about Sally. He pictured those dimpled cheeks and
heard her low musical voice again. He had only seen her once
she had left for Pakistan. He wondered what she felt about him
now and whether she would see him again. There was one way
to find out. He would just call her London office and find out
when she was back for the holidays.

8

It was a lucky day after all. She had been going round the City pitching for money, feeling very upbeat, but as she was pushed along by the crowd funneling through the low-ceilinged tiled passage-way to the platform at Bank station, the optimism oozed away. Her face muscles felt tired from smiling and talking so much. The caffeine-fuelled buzz left her feeling jittery, as if she had been stretched out too thin. She had come away without winning a single firm pledge. Lots of happy talk about further discussions – our review panel will examine it at the next committee meeting – that sort of thing. Nobody else really cared to share her dream of turning around the lives of young women in the mountains of Pakistan. Why should these people care? she thought, standing on the platform in a crowd that smelt of damp woolen winter coats and hats. She squashed into the first train heading to the West End. The tannoy voice kept repeating, 'Stand clear of the doors. Mind the gap' but the doors didn't close. Inside it went as quiet as a funeral. 'If only there was a gap, I can't breathe,' she muttered to herself, but it was loud enough for her neighbors to hear. Then the train started with a big jerk and she staggered, crashing into the bodies behind her. A few heads turned to look at her and among them she recognized a familiar face.

'Bloody hell, Sally, it's you! What are you doing here? Shouldn't you be half-way up the Khyber, saving the world?' Wilkins said. 'Last I heard you were marooned in some god-forsaken village and were never coming back. And what a great loss, too.'

'Oh, and why would you say that?' she said coloring. 'As I recall you were only too glad to see the back of me?'

'Well, that was then,' Wilkins replied smoothly. 'Absence makes the heart grow fonder and all that. A lot has changed since you've been away.'

'Not you surely,' she replied.

'Outwardly no. I am still the devilishly handsome fellow you once knew. But inside,' and he paused and tapped his chest,' it's all changed. A different me.'

Sally laughed. He was looking particularly louche, in a blue suit with his blond hair pinned back in a sort of trendy quiff. They quickly agreed to get off at Tottenham Court and go for a drink.

'So what news on the Rialto? I never thought someone like you would ever settle down in a place like Grosvenor's. You know – "Helping the stinking rich since 1720"', she asked after they had taken their drinks to an empty table.

'As I was saying the power of luurv, not filthy lucre, is transforming,' he laughed. Then he eyed her speculatively.

'And are you still rescuing stray cats and saving the donkeys in Spain. How are el burros, by the way? '

She made a face and rolled her eyes.

'No seriously, I want to know more about what you are doing these days.'

'You do?' she said doubtfully. 'Gosh, I've been talking about it all day.'

She went into her spiel again. It had all started after the Pakistan earthquake in 2005 when a lot of aid workers had gone out to help. 'It was a sort of stampede really,' she explained. 'A big network sprang up and at first there were a lot of funds available. The great British public opened their wallets. Lots of public sympathy for the victims. There was a lot of building that had to be done. We had to get people out of their emergency tents and shelters. They needed hospitals and doctors, all that emergency stuff. There were all the children, some of them orphans that needed looking after. And that's when I got involved, but the money began to dry up a few years later.'

He nodded and cocked an eye.

'My outfit began to get really interested in the problem of helping the children long-term. We began to focus on the need to help the girls go to school. That's the key to everything – better health, better, education, higher living standards, more democracy, less violence, less oppression. You see, most of the girls in that part of Pakistan never get a chance to go school at all. It's partly because they are all so poor, but there's another reason.'

'And where exactly is this benighted region?' he broke in. 'Northern Pakistan. The North-West Frontier. The Swat

Valley, to be exact,' she said.

'The Swat Valley. Isn't there a poem that starts "Who or what is the Wali of Swat"?' he said.

'Yes, that's the place, but it's no joke. The Wali of Swat is long gone and now the Taliban are everywhere doing unspeakable things,' she said.

'The Taliban?' he said slowly. 'And is there a six-foot, six-inch man with a long beard who likes flying planes into tower blocks hanging around there?'

'Ha-ha. Of course, he is always mooching about wearing a big T-shirt which says 'COME AND GET ME,' she said.

'Actually, Osama Bin Laden was al-Qaeda, not Taliban, but there are a lot of al-Qaeda types there now who came over from Afghanistan after the American invasion. That's why it's become so dangerous. And that's why it is so important that we continue with our work. They are destroying the schools.'

'Go on,' he said. She was a little surprised that Wilkins was listening with interest.

'It all got worse after the Taliban's defeat in Afghanistan. All these mullahs and fighters crossed over the border and started setting up shop in Pakistan,' she explained. 'At first all the trouble used to be in Waziristan and the wild areas on the North-West Frontier that had never really been under the central government. It had always been pretty lawless there, even when the British were running the place. Tribal territories, they called it.

'Of course, they didn't like having foreigners there and they especially didn't like us educating the girls. So it's been getting pretty tricky.'

'I can imagine,' he said sympathetically.

'The government is supposed to provide the money for the schools, but a lot of it disappears – corruption, misman-agement. But most of all it is the prejudice against girls. They think there is no point educating girls. So many of them grow up without being able to read or write. Actually about seventy per cent and in some areas none of them get to read and write, that's why there is such poverty. They marry them off early and they start having twelve kids. So the poverty and ignorance gets locked in,' she said, in full flow now.

'I never realized,' he said. 'And what's the Swat Valley like? I mean, to go there?' he asked almost idly.

'It's a beautiful place, actually. They always call it the Switzerland of South Asia. It's got trout fishing, skiing, snow-capped mountains and lovely hotels.'

'I don't suppose there are any chalet girls, then?' He laughed, then got up to get another vodka tonic.

'Actually, all the women go around wrapped up in heads-carves. It was always a pretty conservative sort of place. But they do have these dancing girls,' she said after he had returned.

'Oh, yeah? So a bit like Thailand then?' he asked.

'It's very traditional dancing. Not the kind of thing that would suit you, you know,' she said, trying to match his tone. 'Now, you do me an injustice there. Plus I have always been very interested in the education of young women.

Passionately so. Always have been,' he said.

'Yeah, right,' she said. 'It is not like here in the UK. But most of the schools are in a terrible state. Sometimes there aren't enough desks and chairs. Some of the families don't even have enough to buy their children pens and notebooks. And even the teachers earn next to nothing,' she went on. No one had listened to her so attentively all day.

'We are a pretty small outfit, but you know, with just a bit of money, you can really change people's lives, even change a society. It's a lot better and cheaper than trying to bomb them into democracy. Once you educate people like that and open their eyes, then that's the end of all this religious extremism,' she finished.

'Sounds so simple.' Wilkins laughed at her. 'And so why are you here?'

Sally explained she had been doing the rounds trying to raise some more money and to tell existing sponsors why more help was needed right now.

'The people in Swat need to see that we support them.

This is the worst crisis they have ever had,' she said.

'So have you had any luck?' he asked and Sally put on a miserable and pouty face.

'Not much,' she said. 'And I thought at Christmas people would be more giving.'

'So how much do you need?' he asked. 'A million dollars.'

Sally said it straight out, expecting him to come back and say, 'Who would trust you with a million dollars?' But a thoughtful look came over his face and he went quiet for a bit.

'Half a million would do it, actually,' she said.

'So you say this place, Swat, is now off-limits?' he asked. 'Sort of. It's even hard now to get into the valley. They cut off the phones. The internet doesn't work anymore. The army has check points and there are all kinds of roadblocks. They are trying to flush them out.'

'No one can get in or out because of these mad mullahs? Nor airports, no trains, buses and everyone scared stiff?' he asked.

She hesitated. 'It's OK now. There was a sort of a truce but things are getting worse. They are robbing banks, too. That's how we lost a big chunk of our money last month.'

She paused and drank from her glass.

'Do you tell people about this? If you do, I am not surprised people are reluctant to give you any more dosh.'

She nodded somberly. 'Actually, we are almost the only NGO still working there right now. The others left,' she confessed. 'It's a bit desperate.'

Then he startled her.

'You should have come to me first. I know some very rich clients. For people like that, a million dollars is nothing, just small change, and they are always looking to do something noble. Besides, it's tax deductible anyway,' he said.

Sally looked skeptical. 'Who you know? You are just a computer geek, aren't you?'

'Ooh, I know people who know people. So I might just be in a position to help you. Wait here, let me make a few calls.' She watched him go outside the pub with his phone. He returned ten minutes later looking triumphant.

'Sally, old girl, I think your troubles might be over.' He beamed at her. Sally looked at him questioningly. Then he held up his hand.

'That's what old friends are for. There is someone who could help. Says, he wants to fund the schools. The only thing is, he wants to remain anonymous for the moment.'

'Well, that's no problem.'

'There is another thing. He asked me to go there first and check it out. Make sure you are not smuggling heroin or something.'

'OK, I suppose that's possible.' She looked uncomfortable. 'But is that really necessary?'

'But the only time I can get away is now, really, over the Christmas break,' he said hesitantly.

'Oh, I can't do that. I'm staying here, promised my folks.'

'Oh, well. Let's leave it for the moment,' he said carelessly. 'Let me get you a refill. I bet you can't get a bloody drink out there in Swatistan.'

Wilkins returned with two more glasses. He raised his eyebrows. 'Now, tell me what wicked things you have been up to out there. Is there some handsome shepherd boy you've been romancing?'

'One or two.' Sally laughed. Then, her thoughts returned to his suggestion. She pictured herself returning to the Swat Valley after Christmas and telling everyone she was leaving because there was no money left.

'Look, let me think about your idea. Maybe it is possible. I need to talk to the other people at the Foundation first. I can't just decide everything myself, you know,' she said.

'I think the donor could act quite quickly, but he's pretty insistent on keeping this quiet at this stage. You know, discreet.

Perhaps I could bring along a bit of cash now to tide you over,' he said helpfully.

'Really? Is that possible?' She was beginning to feel more and more tempted.

Wilkins shrugged his shoulders.

'You've got nothing to lose, have you?' he said.

9

Someone had put a barricade across the road heading north to Mingora, capital of the Swat Valley. It was just some logs and a rope stretched across the road. It was not enough to stop anyone determined. What had made the driver of Wilkins' car slow to a halt was the sight of three ragged-looking youths with straggling beards, each levelling an old rifle at them.

'What the hell's the hold up now? What do these stupid monkeys want?' Wilkins said aloud to himself. He was seated at the back of the big four-wheel drive which Sally had dispatched to pick him up from the airport in Islamabad. The driver, who had introduced himself as Ali, was a burly man with a big beaky nose above a moustache that stuck to his upper lip like a hairy caterpillar.

The three youths looked at Ali mistrustfully. He had wound down the car window, stuck his head out, and was now haranguing them in a fast and belligerent way. The boys didn't say much, just looked sullen, and kept repeating the same phrase.

Wilkins could tell from the scenery that they must be nearly there. On either side of the road stretched a wide valley bounded by high mountains of steely grey rock topped by bright glistening snow. They had been climbing steadily for an hour, following the banks of a wide river that ran somewhere out of sight behind the orchard trees and taller poplar trees. Up on the higher slopes, he could see dark pine forests. It was, as Sally had promised, pretty scenery.

He had read that the Swat Valley was famous in Pakistan for its skiing. It certainly wasn't ever going to be the next Gstaad, though, he thought, no gluhwein in the snow here. For one thing, he noticed a steady stream of trucks piled high with people and goods passing them in the opposite direction. Each truck was a work of art elaborately decorated with mirrors and sequins that belonged in a fairground. He had never seen anything as garish or elaborate, yet they were a sad sight. The people clinging on top of their chairs, tables, bedrolls and stoves looked miserable, even desperate. He wondered what they were fleeing, but put the troubling thought from his mind. He was feeling pleased with himself and wanted a drink to celebrate.

Wilkins had flown out of London without problems, passing through all the security checks. It was a good thing that money didn't show up on scanners, he reflected with satisfaction. But then, why should it? After all it was nothing but bundles of paper, right? Could be a novel or anything. He hadn't been so sure when he had been stuffing the notes in his trousers, in his shoes, in his back pack, even in the anorak by taking out as much of down filling as he possibly could. Now, if only he had taken more. There was no knowing when he'd next be able to make a withdrawal, maybe never. Around here, he was sure they weren't going to say 'That will do nicely, sir' when you flashed a bit of plastic at them. The beauty of cash was that you left no records. Still, it was a weird feeling, he thought, to be walking around literally feeling like a million bucks. In fact, there was enough dosh padded around his body to stop a bullet. The thought turned him cold. What if this was a hold up?

Wilkins took another look at the three youths, still listening to the driver, unconvinced and refusing to budge. He was trying to win their confidence by offering them some cigarettes, but they refused.

'They say they are waiting for someone called Zahid Hussein to come. Only he can let us go further,' Ali explained to him. 'This is not right.'

An hour earlier they had gone through a regular army checkpoint with barbed wire and machine-gun posts behind sandbags. The soldiers had been friendly enough, although they had checked through their baggage and supplies pretty thoroughly. Luckily, after a quick look at their passports, the boys in khaki had waved them through. What pleased Wilkins the most was that they didn't take a record of their passport numbers. They noted down the driver's ID and his car registration number, but that was all. It could not have been any better as far as Wilkins was concerned. There was now no record of him being in the Swat Valley. All that anybody could trace was his arrival in Pakistan on a BA flight. He hadn't checked into a hotel either, but had driven straight from the airport. So in a country this big, with over 170 million people, he would be hard to find.

He reckoned that all the authorities cared about were these British-born Pakistanis going to join the Taliban and all the other nutters. In a week or so, he thought, he could grow a nice beard and start dressing like a native with baggy trousers, one of those long shirts, and the brown woolen hats many of them wore. Rub in a bit of rancid sheep fat and no one would take a blind bit of notice of him.

Along the way Ali, who had once worked as a tourist guide, pointed out the sights with pride. The Swat Valley had once been the center of a great Buddhist civilization called Gandhara. According to legend, the Buddha himself had come here. The great ruler, King Asoka, was another visitor. Alexander the Great had come here. Winston Churchill, too. 'There are many temples, monasteries and carvings you can visit. I can take you. Swat had 500 tourist hotels, but now no one coming anymore,' he said. 'We have 400 Buddhist stupas in the valley. There is the Amluk Dara Stupa you can see, the Jahabad Seated Buddha, or the giant Buddha in Ghaligay.'

He rattled off the sites but Wilkins had listened with only half an ear. His thoughts were still in London. It was funny to think that beyond this valley, the markets were still churning. Prices going up and down. Currencies fluctuating. Indexes rising and falling. Profits made and lost. He looked at his watch. Back in Bishopsgate, the market would be closing with frantic sales calls and a lot of shouting and screaming. The only market trading going on here was in the bazaar haggling about the price for goats and donkeys. Nobody here cared about the Grosvenor Bank, let alone old Wilkie.

There were signs to Saidu Sharif and Sufaid Mahal, where, Ali told him, there was a white marble palace where the former Wali of Swat had lived. It was near to a golf course where visitors had once come to play. Soon they would pass by Churchill Picket, a hill near an old fort which had once guarded the capital of Swat where Ali said Winston Churchill had served during his time as a young soldier on the North-West Frontier.

'Fascinating,' Wilkins had said, feigning a minimal interest. He thought it would be another week before anyone would miss him or come looking for him. He'd told everyone he needed a week's sick leave for a minor operation and to make up for it had volunteered to come in all through the holiday season. 'It's just so that those who have the good fortune to have kids can take a break without worries,' he had said. Everyone was so pleased at this generosity, they didn't think twice about allowing him to take time off. Of course, sooner or later they would find out he had done a bunk. In the meantime, he thought he would have enough time to cover up his tracks.

'Hey Ali, do you think they'd mind if I went out for a piss? This could be a long wait,' Wilkins said. Without thinking, he opened the door and stepped out. One of the youths rushed over and started pushing Wilkins hard against the car door. Another one started shouting and fired some shots into the air. Wilkins, surprised, backed off and held his hands in the air.

A few minutes later, another group of men emerged out of the trees. Wilkins saw they all had guns and looked determined. A largish man with a big belly, streaks of white in his beard, and bloodshot eyes seemed to be in charge. He came up and looked over Wilkins carefully. Then he spoke to Ali, listening intently to what he said. After that he returned to Wilkins, looked at him, and smiled, revealing some uneven brown-stained teeth, and offered his hand.

'You are Sally's friend? Welcome, welcome, sahib,' he said. 'I am Hussein.'

Hussein explained that he had three daughters at one of Sally's schools and knew all about her work. Next he insisted they went back to his house for tea. They all got back into the car and drove into the trees until they reached a village, a group of two- or three-storey houses of wood and brick. They went into one of the larger houses and sat down on the carpet and talked. A young boy brought some tea. At first Hussein ignored Wilkins as he chatted to Ali, trading news.

'We call this gupchupping or gossiping, you know,' Hussein said. 'There are many bad things happening here in the Swat Valley. Do you come from Bunar?'

Wilkins shrugged his shoulders. 'I've never been here before. New to Pakistan,' he said.

'Last week, they blew up a police station in Bunar. A suicide bomber. Forty people dead,' he said.

'Who is they?' Wilkins said.

'The Pakistani Taliban,' he replied. 'Now you understand why we were stopping everyone on the road.'

'What about these people in the trucks? Your men were not stopping them.'

'They are refugees, running away from the fighting.' Hussein looked at Wilkins, studying him with open curiosity. 'The Swat Valley is now a very dangerous place. War is coming. 'People think the army is waiting and preparing for battle.

And the insurgents are arming themselves, too. They are getting help from the Afghan Taliban,' he said. 'There are several thousand of them here, many of them foreigners.'

Wilkins listened and nodded. Hussein watched him carefully.

'You are asking yourself, why is this fellow telling you all this?' he said. 'You are friend of Sally, no? You have come here to visit her?'

'Yes,' he said to both questions.

'It is not safe for Sally in Swat. You must tell her to go. The other teachers have left. All the foreigners are going. The Irish and Sri Lankan teachers at the Sangota Public School have gone,' he said.

'But surely no one cares about an English girl like her running schools? What harm do they do?' he said, forcing a laugh. 'Who could be frightened of old Sally?'

Hussein looked grave. 'My friend, you do not understand. The Taliban especially hate girls' schools. They are going to bomb and destroy them wherever they can. It may not be safe for Sally. If you are her friend, then you must help her,' he said.

Wilkins didn't like the way he looked at him after he said that. He was almost sizing him up and waiting for him to reveal his relationship with Sally.

'She has a mind of her own. She can be stubborn, but I will do what I can,' Wilkins promised.

Hussein nodded and then they finished the tea and left for Mingora.

'So Ali, how bad do you think it really is? That guy Hussein seemed worried about Sally's safety, said I should warn her to leave.'

Ali did not reply immediately and kept his eyes fixed on the road.

'Many people here very much appreciate what she is doing. Of course, they want to make sure she is safe. But do not worry, Swati people can protect her against all terrorists,' he said. 'It is right we do this.'

As they pulled into Mingora and drove along the streets, his first impressions of the place contradicted Hussein's dire warnings. The town lay at the foot of some modest hills and it had spread haphazardly up the surrounding slopes. The center of the town looked busy and even prosperous. People seemed to be going about their everyday lives in a peaceful way. The narrow streets were clogged by motor-cycle taxis, buses and trucks weaving around each other through noisy streets honking and tooting. The shops, usually four-storey houses made with concrete and breeze blocks with white tile balconies, were open. He noticed old men with long white beards squatted peacefully by the side of the road or sitting cross-legged on rope beds. In the bazaar, men sat on these beds eating from small tables. Wilkins turned to watch a man sitting on a mat holding a big knife between his toes with the blade up to slice off bits of raw meat for kebabs.

Most of the women were dressed from head to toe with these big shawls around them so he couldn't see their faces. Women's fashion, he thought, had got stuck somewhere in the seventh century, but at least they weren't all dressed in black. Some were wearing clothing dyed in bright crimsons and pinks.

'You see these men?' Ali said, turning his head and pointing out three men walking along the street. Wilkins looked at them. They were young men with longish hair and beards and were dressed like the rest in long shirts, baggy pants and running shoes.

'They are dangerous. See, their trousers do not reach their shoes. That is how you can tell,' he said.

'Tell what?' Wilkins asked.

'They are Taliban. They do that because they believe the Prophet said somewhere a man should keep his feet free,' he said. 'You must be careful.'

Soon after passing these men, he swung the vehicle down an alley, and then eased it round another sharp corner into a side street and then stopped before a metal gate with a small door in it. Ali honked and a guard came out and unbolted the gate, which swung open to reveal a small courtyard. It was an L-shaped building with three storeys and a small guard house at the other side of the courtyard. Sally came running out of the house, tripping down the steps, her face flushed and smiling.

'Welcome to my kingdom, fair prince,' she said brightly. 'Let me show you to your quarters.'

Wilkins gave her a quick awkward hug. He felt a stab of doubt, even guilt about what he was doing. He sensed that things between them would now be different from what they had been in London. They would have to be closer here, more trusting. It was going to be more awkward than he had imagined.

She showed him the office, a big room with two desks and chairs, files and printers on the ground floor. On the wall was a big map of the valley with pins stuck in it showing the location of the girls' school. On the other side of the courtyard there were a few smaller rooms, one of which was a cozy living-room with a nice fire going. Sleeping quarters were all upstairs and rather bare but livable. Out in the back was a kitchen where a couple of women were banging some pots together.

'Dinner will be served in an hour,' she said. 'We can talk then.'

After a wash and brush-up, and a change of clothing, Wilkins joined her in the kitchen where they ate a supper of tough mutton, flat bread and greasy rice. When the dishes were taken away, they moved to the living-room and picked at plates of nuts and dried fruits while sipping some sugary black tea. At first they chatted about his trip.

'Did you notice as you were coming here that there wasn't any music playing, not even in the bazaars?' she asked anxiously.

'No, I can't say I did,' he replied.

'Well, normally, you see, there's this tremendous din because everyone is playing their stereos at full blast. No one was selling any DVDs either. It wasn't like that before I left for London,' she said.

'Another thing, did you see all those families on the move with all their goods piled up? They are moving out because they think there is more trouble coming.'

'I did see that. We also met someone on the way, Hussein. He was worried about you, about your safety,' Wilkins said. 'Madam, Madam, it's not safe for white ladies here anymore!'

'That was very sweet of him,' she said. 'I wondered why you were late. I was worried.'

'But you are not really scared, are you?'

'No. People are frightened, but the militants don't usually target women, especially foreign women. It's a kind of taboo,' she said in her brisk practical way

'So it's jolly well "Carry On Up the Khyber", is it?' Wilkins joked.

'I don't want to alarm you just when you got here, but someone has been handing out leaflets around the town. They shoved this one in our letterbox,' she said, pulling out a crudely photocopied piece of paper from her pocket. She read aloud from it: 'Girls' education leads to obscenity and vulgarity in society. This is a conspiracy of the United States and other infidel nations to deviate our younger generation from the right path of Islam.'

'What does it mean?' Wilkins asked.

'It is by Mullah Fazlullah. He's the leader of the local Talban and he wants to close down all the girls' schools. We thought the army had chased him away, but he's back. He's the one who has been giving sermons warning people that playing music is un-Islamic. So is watching videos.'

'Is he targeting you?' Wilkins said. 'Maybe. It's hard to tell,' she said.

'What's this mullah like?' Wilkins said, grabbing a handful of almonds to chew on.

'He has a radio show on FM which he broadcasts every night around now actually,' Sally reached round and switched on a small old-fashioned radio, fiddling with the nobs for a while. They listened to a deep sonorous voice talking slowly and emphatically.

'He's announcing the names of female students who have stopped attending school and has promised them a high place in paradise,' she said. 'Now he is warning that they will destroy any schools where girls attend.'

She switched the radio off.

'This sounds bad, worse than I thought,' she said and fell silent.

Wilkins looked straight into her eyes and said firmly, 'If it's any help, I am willing to stay here and make damned sure that you get all the financial support you could possibly want. We won't let these buggers put the wind up us. A lot of people are counting on you.'

The last thing he wanted was for her to suddenly bolt, at least not until he found his feet. He was laying it on a bit thick, he knew, but she didn't seem to notice or mind his insincerity. She had given him back a plucky smile and then said in a tentative way, 'You know, I had second thoughts about inviting you to come, but now I feel, well, that it will all work out.'

10

Aziza had large green eyes, a prominent straight nose and a brilliant smile that displayed two rows of even white teeth. Wilkins judged her to be in her mid-thirties. She dressed with style and a striking sense of London fashion and he noticed that a pair of elegant pointed leather shoes peeked out from the bottom of her long dress. She was like no one else that Wilkins had met since he had arrived in the Swat Valley and her style and confidence unnerved him a little. Sally had brought him to meet her after she had taken him on a tour of the village schools the foundation was backing. When she welcomed him into her home, a large whitewashed villa that she shared with other members of her large family, he sensed it would hard to fool her with any fake enthusiasm for education. She looked at him directly and critically felt himself blushing as she seized him up.

'Ah, so you are Sally's friend from England,' she said inspecting him. 'I thought you would be older.'

Then she had invited the two of them into a reception room. There they sat down on some floral carpets with carpets and were soon nursing cups of green tea. Wilkins couldn't keep his eyes from her. Sally had told Wilkins that she ran half the private schools in the valley. She was a descendant of the Ahkund of Swat, who had united all the tribes in the Valley and created an independent princedom over a hundred years earlier which, until 1969, never paid any taxes to the Pakistan government. The Ahkund was regarded as a kind of Muslim holy man and was buried in Saidu Sharif. 'His tomb is a sort of religious shrine, something like the Canterbury Cathedral of the Swat Valley, so even the Taliban have to show her a lot of respect,' Sally explained. Her father had been a hereditary prince and she wielded a great deal of political influence and had strong connections with the politicians in Islamabad.

'So Mr. Wilkins, tell me about your impressions this morning,' she asked formally.

'Well, it was charming. First thing when we got there, this gaggle of little girls appeared out of nowhere all dressed in smart little blue smocks and white headscarves. When they saw Sally, they all started grinning and began chanting: 'Baa, baa, black sheep, have you any wool? Yes, sir, No, sir, Three bags full," he said. 'Then they collapsed into fits of giggles and rushed off. '

Then he laughed and was pleased to see Aziza smile too. 'The classrooms were very neat and tidy. In one of them, all the girls were chanting their times table. You know I think they are ahead of any girls in similar age in England.'

Out of the corner of his eye Wilkins could sense Sally looking at him speculatively. He guessed she was pleasantly surprised by his enthusiasm.

'Then I was quite moved when the teacher, a Miss Fatima, talked about how they were all determined to stand up to all these threats. She said: 'they keep saying that our schools are un-Islamic but Islam should be about truth and enlightenment and not about fear and terror.''

I will always remember when she then said: 'Teachers are a candle, showing us the only way out of poverty and darkness. We see the light through education. The real enemy is ignorance.'

Aziza nodded but said soberly: 'If there are no girls going to college, then there can be no female teachers. You can imagine what that will mean for the whole education system.'

Sally then added: 'People here don't like having their daughters taught by men and so, especially for secondary education, the lack of proper women teachers will be devastating.'

'I heard that the Taliban have already managed to stop women from working at health-centers and are disrupting a polio vaccination campaign,' Wilkins said.

'Yes, they telling the people that this a Western plot to make Muslims infertile and to prevent their numbers from increasing,' Aziza said. 'But these miscreants are losing public support in their campaign of murder and intimidation. The Taliban say that men have been given preference by God, but show me where it says in the Koran that you should not educate girls?'

'Yes, I don't know,' Wilkins said.

'My God, these people want to send us back to the Stone Age. But we are not going to become another Waziristan,' Aziza said, her eyes lighting up with indignation.

Sally interrupted to explain to Waziristan was where the Taliban headed after 2002 when they slipped into Pakistan after the Americans arrived in Afghanistan. A wild and remote place compared to the Swat Valley, it was under the control of a fearsome tribe called the Mehsuds.

Aziza continued: 'These kind of people have always been ignorant bandits who spent all their time killing each other or robbing other people. That is why they are in the pay of Al Qaeda. The Swat Valley had been a center of learning for thousands of years. We will never give in to these ignorant savages.'

'I heard what happened at the Shaidu Sharif College and some of the other schools, aren't you scared?' Wilkins asked. 'Can they get away with this?'

'Soon, the Islamabad government will send the army back here and destroy them for good. They are only a few hundred of these miscreants and a few thousand deluded ignorant followers, we are two million people here,' Aziza replied.

Anyone who thinks Muslim women are a subdued demure bunch, thought Wilkins, should meet her. When she fixed those striking green eyes on you, it was hard to say no to her.

'When Alexander the Great had marched through here on his way to India in the third century BC, Swat was already the center of a great civilization,' she went on working herself into a steely rage.

'Have you been to see the hundreds of historical sites, stupas and carvings we have here?' she asked Wilkins. He nodded meekly.

'Now the Taliban have gone around smashing them up and defacing these statues, just like they did in Afghanistan,' she said. 'People hate these people. They are destroying everything and are spreading ignorance,' Aziza said. 'They call themselves religious and pure, but they are nothing but common bandits trying to terrorize people.'

Wilkins tried to calm her down saying smoothly that he was sure he would be able to get them financial support, but she was now in no mood to listen.

'Mullah Fazlullah is just another bandit. He is not a holy man but stealing land and houses, forcing people to give two-thirds of their income to him,' she said.

'Listen to me, Sally,' she said taking her hand and then Wilkin's. 'You must not leave Pakistan now. You and your young friend here will see how we are going to fight fire with fire. If you show you are afraid, then the common people will be afraid, too, and people will run way or do what the fanatics want.'

'The key battleground is schooling for girls,' she emphasized. There were over 400 schools operating in the valley. 'Even though the militants are firebombing attendance has been going over the past ten years. Even poor farmers started sending their girls to school. They know we cannot keep half the population ignorant,'

'The girls are keener on studying than the boys because they knew that if they didn't resist they would spend the rest of their lives locked up at home,' Sally said.

Sally explained how unusual this was in Pakistan, where only a quarter of the girls ever went to school.

Wilkins nodded and smiled. 'That's why my donors have sent me here to see if we can help,' he said sincerely. 'Whatever happens, I am going to stay here until I am sure you get everything you need, I mean everything I can do for you. That is, I'll do my best to help you and Sally get the support of some donors. '

'You know, Mr. Wilkins,' Aziza said fixing her bright green eyes on him and holding his hand firmly, 'learning can take place without desks, without books, without classrooms, but it cannot take place without teachers.'

Then she let go of his hand and went out to organize some lunch. Sally and Wilkins sat in silence for a while. Then she said in her low musical voice. 'I want to thank you for this and for coming to help me. I didn't expect it.' Sally then turned looked up at him almost shyly as if he had become a different person that she didn't know.

Aziza returned and supervised two servants who spread out a meal, a mound of biryani studded with nuts and raisins and served with an orange drink called Thums Up. They chatted a little but mostly ate in silence.

Afterwards they had left Aziza's house, Sally went back to work. Ali and Wilkins went into the town to look around. Wilkins insisted on getting himself kitted out with some local clothes – a shalwar shirt and baggy trousers – because he wanted blend in more easily.

Wilkins wandered around the main marketplace, called the Green Chowk, inspecting the goods on offer and amused by the sight of the tins of Ovaltine and rice pudding stacked up in little pyramids. When they reached the middle of the square, they joined the back of a silent crowd of men and women. Wilkins thought they were just standing in a circle, gawping with idle curiosity at some accident. Perhaps someone had run over donkey or a dog.

At first they weren't close enough to see what was attracting everyone's attention, but then in the gaps that opened up between the bystanders, he glimpsed a body lying on the ground in a twisted unnatural heap. It was a woman and she was dressed in the sort of garish pink and lilac- colored dress that a local girl might wear to a party or a wedding. He pressed forward for a closer look. He couldn't see the face, but he saw next to a small pool of blood, a scattering of CDs, photos and pink rupee notes around the motionless body.

'What's happened? Has there been an accident? Who is she?' he said to Ali in a low tone.

No one responded. Perhaps, thought Wilkins, they wanted him to leave, or else they were so stricken by the horror of the scene that they couldn't move or speak. Then, it hit him that they weren't just dumbfounded, they were scared.

'Sahib, sahib you must go now,' Ali said. 'You must not be here. You can do nothing.'

Wilkins asked why nobody had called the police. 'Ali, where the hell are they?'

'Police no good. Police say in station, too scared to go out, like rabbits in a hole,' Ali said curtly.

He pulled Wilkins away and explained that the dead woman was called Begum and she was the most popular dancing girl and singer in the bazaar. She used to be invited to entertain men at parties or to sing at wedding parties.

'Taliban is warning her many times on radio to stop the dancing. If any girls found dancing they would kill them one by one, but she wouldn't listen,' Ali said. 'Taliban say dancing is like prostitution. Many girls run away to big cities, but not Begum."

When they stopped at a stall to buy some tea, Ali heard the full story. The previous evening some men had gone and knocked on her door. When she opened it, the men asked her to come to a dance party. She agreed and asked them to wait while she got changed. She came down and then these four men grabbed her and dragged her out of the house. She kept shouting for help, but no one dared open their door. When they got to the Green Square, they shot her and vanished.

Ali explained that two months back the Taliban had begun murdering anyone who refused to obey their orders. The executions took place at night when people stayed in their homes observing a curfew imposed by the Taliban. Then the bodies would turn up the square, or sometimes strung up on a tree. Most of them had been beheaded so, he explained, one wasn't always sure who they were or what they'd done.

Yet everybody knew who Begum was – she was a public figure, almost a celebrity. Her songs were popular and used to be sold everywhere. To murder an unnamed woman in cold blood was something else, Ali said. 'The Taliban want to tell everyone that they are back and in control,' he said. 'So they killed her and left her there for all to see.'

Wilkins thought he looked pretty shaken himself now. He kept taking his hand to the caterpillar moustache and pulling it nervously. They finished their tea in silence. Wilkins wondered whether he should tell Sally. She had been convinced that as a woman and a foreigner she would be safe. But no one was safe and the Taliban felt strong enough to do whatever they wanted.

'Ali, one thing I don't understand is why Begum didn't know these men were Taliban?' he asked.

Ali nodded somberly as if he, too, had considered this point.

'No one knows who exactly Taliban is and who is helping them. They have all kinds of supporters and informers. Sometimes, because people are scared, they obey anyone who says he is Taliban,' he said. 'This is not right.'

'You know Ali, I don't think we should tell Sally too much about this,' Wilkins said. Ali stroked his caterpillar moustache again thoughtfully. Wilkins guessed he was weighing up the prospect of being out of a job if Sally left.

'Let's just hope things get better before they get worse, eh?' he said and slapped him on his back. Ali looked uncomfortable.

'Sometimes the Taliban first give a warning,' he ventured awkwardly.

'Like what?' Wilkins said.

'One time I heard they throw a rose or something. Tied to it is message saying something like "Thinking about you, from the Swat Taliban,"' he said.

'Well, so far they haven't done anything like that to us, have they?' Wilkins said

Ali shook his head slowly.

11

As soon as Faiza entered the briefing room at the Creech Airbase, she knew it was going to be a challenge to assert herself. Lt. Colonel Masterson was going to start the briefing the team of pilots and console operators on the mission and then she would have a chance to speak. She studied the twenty men and women taking their seats in the small windowless room. Everyone else in the room was in uniform. Most of them looked very fresh- faced and untried. A few of them looked at her with curiosity but not much interest. They were too busy joking and horsing around.

In the meantime, Masterson had stepped forward on the podium and began the briefing:

'Good afternoon everyone, and congratulations, you have been chosen for a high priority mission. Within the next days, maybe hours, you – we – are going to get Ayman al- Zawahiri, the al-Qaeda number two,' he said and turned to look briefly at the screen behind him which displayed a photograph of the bearded Egyptian.

'We are now about to close the net on a man who has proved a deadly enemy of the United States. If we bring him to justice, everyone here will receive the gratitude of the American people and the world,' Masterson paused for the buzz of interest in the audience to die down.

The only problem would be Miller, Faiza thought. He was easily the oldest pilot in the audience. Faiza began to think how she would be able to use him. He had arrived early and taken a seat in the front and looked straight at her. He gave her a broad almost cheeky smile and she looked away quickly. Miller now seemed to think she was going drop into his arms at any moment. Tall and lanky, Miller had certain confident Texan charm and he seemed to like what he saw. She sensed he was often bored with his job and had decided that the most interesting part of the mission would be to nail this exotic woman. Faiza sat in the chair as stiffly as possible and tried to keep her gaze focused on the middle distance. She began thinking how she might turn his attention to her advantage. Perhaps he would be easy to distract and could perhaps even be manipulated into doing her bidding when the time came.

'Most of those selected for this mission will know what I am about to tell you, but for a few of you this will still be useful background. We are at a critical moment in the global war on terror, an important stage, too, in the development of the MQ1 and its successor, the MQ9. We want to show what this technology and the men and women behind it can do,' Masterson continued.

Faiza pulled back some stray hairs and tucked them inside her head scarf and then pondered how she would deal with

Masterson. Within a few hours the mission would begin and the hunt would start in earnest. She suspected that Masterson considered her ill-prepared for the role and would do his best to politely ignore her advice. He knew that Blashford had plucked her out of a low profile job at the NSA and enlisted her in the special team coordinating the hunt for Ayman al-Zawahiri. She was the only person on the nine-strong team without a career in intelligence work. She had no influence unless it was through Blashford. As a civilian attached to a military unit who was accountable to the CIA, she needed to get Masterson on her side.

They both wanted her to be on the spot at the Creech Airbase to be able to interpret events on the ground so she could guide the actions of the pilots and console operators as the operation developed. Above all Blashford had stressed to her that the priority was not just to find the Egyptian but to capture him and try to recover as much intelligence as possible. Killing him would be the last resort.

'We are now forcing many al-Qaeda and local Taliban leaders out of Northern and Southern Waziristan, Bajaur, Dir and Malakand,' he said. 'But they are now activelyAfter reviewing a history of the Taliban's movements along Pakistan's western borders, he turned the floor over to Faiza. 'To help us find them, Faiza Azhad has come from the CIA's counter terrorist center. She is now going to brief us on the latest intel. Faiza was born in Afghanistan, speaks fluent Pashto, Dari and Urdu and previously worked for the NSA. Over to you Faiza,' he concluded.

Faiza got up feeling nervous and thought her voice squeaked a little as she started talking. With great effort she forced herself to speak more slowly.

'Lt. Colonel Masterson gave us such a brilliant explanation of this region's tragic history. Full of learning and compassion,' she said and she turned gave him her sweetest smile. She had decided that it was best to flatter the older man.

'We at the CIA now believe that increased Predator surveillance has put such pressure on the al-Qaeda leadership and the Pakistan Taliban leadership that they have been actively searching for a new secure haven. This is the Swat Valley,' she said, pointing it out on the map.

She explained that how over the past three years; the Pakistan Taliban had tried to seize control over the Swat Valley through the efforts of Maulana Sufi Muhammed and his son-in-law, Mullah Fazlullah. Then she clicked on the PowerPoint to show photographs of both men. One was a grey-haired cleric in his seventies, the other a man in his early thirties who wore a black turban and had a beard covering half of his face.

'This time we don't want the Pakistan ISI to know about this mission – their ties with the Taliban have been too close in the past,' she said. 'For that reason, we cannot use the CIA Predators flown out of Pakistan.'

That prompted a flicker of interest in the audience.

'Any questions?' she asked and looked round at the sea of faces. Miller raised his hand.

'And why exactly does the CIA think al-Zawahiri is going to be in the Swat Valley?'

'We think that the Al Qaeda leadership believes that the Swat Valley is now secure from the Pakistan security forces. And because it is outside the North-West Frontier, they think it is safe from the Predators.'

'Is that what our Pakistani friends are telling us?'

'We now have reliable human intel that in the next few days al-Zawahiri will be in the Swat Valley as a guest of Mullah Fazlullah.'

'Why?'

'He and other high ranking leaders are attending a meeting, a Shura. We think Mullah Mohammed Omar, head of Afghan Taliban, his right-hand man Mullah Dadullah Akhund, and Baitullah Mehsud will all be there,' she said.

'So what exactly are we aiming to do? '

Masterson then stood up and interrupted the discussion. 'Our primary task is to locate al-Zawahiri, then it will be up to the CIA special fusion team to make the final decisions. They will be monitoring everything they do. The team leader in Langley is Blashford,' Masterson said. 'That's all for now.'

Then he called the team back. 'One more thing. We must keep this mission secret and confidential. Nothing we do must reveal our presence to anyone on the ground,' he warned.

Faiza felt relieved the briefing was over and pleased. The operating procedures were loose enough to allow many things to happen. As she left the room Miller walked with her. 'Nice job. Now we sure know what to do,' he said. Then, he put his hand on her arm briefly but she edged away. She curbed an impulse to say something cutting.

'I hope you are going to help me. I am very nervous now,' she said simply and turned up her face to look up at Miller appealingly.

12

Together Sally and Aziza had walked around the burnt out shell of the girl's college in Mingora with a builder to get an estimate of what the repairs would cost. Several builders had arrived and then gone promising to return with estimates. Many of the classrooms were intact and the damage was less than feared. The men stayed for twenty minutes and then left promising to provide quotes within a day or two. Both men seemed uncomfortable and anxiously to leave as soon as possible. Afterwards, the two women went to drink tea and sat upstairs in a tea house overlooking the Green Chowk. It was called the White Elephant and used to be a hang out when Mingora was on the backpacker's trail. The two women ordered hot chocolates and in the meantime looked at the activity in the marketplace beneath them in a shared silence. Sally knew that Aziza was thinking the same despondent thought. It was not right that all that money would have to go rebuilding something that should never have been destroyed.

'We can find the money,' Sally started to say in a soothing tone but Aziza cut in.

'But will these devils attack again. Who will be next? What will they do now?'

She looked on the verge of tears.

'I think Wilkins will be able to help. He's helping to raise some money for the Foundation from friends in London,' Sally said.

'Ah, yes, your mysterious friend. He's a nice boy. Good for you, I think,' Aziza said. 'But it is strange him coming here so suddenly.'

'Yes, I do wonder about it,' Sally said and looked down to stir her cup.

'Is he in love with you? Is that why he is here? ' Aziza asked. It was the first time she had talked to her about love.

Sally was silent for moment, thinking about her own feelings. She had begun to like the way the two of them were joining forces behind the same cause. It was sort of a more mature connection than anything they had before. In the past it had just been about having fun together. She felt though that he had never really tried to understand what drove her.

'It's true,' she said drawing in and letting out a deep breath. 'I am not quite sure why he is here. I didn't feel comfortable about it at first but when he offered to help raise so much money, I didn't want to say no. I didn't want to let my personal feelings get in the way.'

Aziza scrutinized her silently, waiting for her to continue.

'We did go out for a while but broke up two years ago.

He just didn't understand me. Thought I was just a bit of soppy blonde fluff.'

She suddenly felt the urge to tell Aziza more about her life. She explained how she had grown up in a small town in Surrey and her father had gone into the City to work for one of the big banks, while her mother had stayed at home looking after her and her two sisters.

'I was the middle one,' she said. 'The squeezed in the middle one.'

Later, her mother had started up her own home furnishing company specializing in design fabrics. They had all been happy until her younger sister had died in a road accident.

'A lorry going past their house had hit her as she was cycling. She was just six and I was eleven at the time. Then the terrible rows had started. It was the first time I ever heard either of my parents swear. My father blamed my mother for neglecting the kids and getting too involved in setting up her business.'

'What happened then?' Aziza said.

'The guilt tore them apart and divorced. It hurt me, as it was somehow my fault that my sister died. Now I can't stand anyone who hurts children. I am going to fight them.'

She stopped there feeling choked by her emotions. She wasn't sure of Aziza had any idea of what was talking about or could picture her life back home. Aziza had listened without comment.

'At least you are free to do what you want. To lead the life that you want. To love the man that you want. That is not given to everyone in this life,' Aziza said.

Sally stopped thinking about herself for the moment and wondered what Aziza was talking about. She had always seemed so self-assured and in command. Now Sally thought she was hinting at some kind of personal unhappiness. Perhaps there was some reason why she wasn't married at her age.

'Did you hear what happened to Begum? Aziza asked.

Sally shook her head.

'She was a dancer. They warned her and then they killed her. They found her body not far from here,' Aziza said. Sally opened her eyes in shock.

'When did it happen?' 'Yesterday.'

'It was not an accident like with your sister but murder.

Cold cruel murder,' Aziza said.

Sally couldn't find any words. She felt stupid for having talked so much about herself, and the next moment she felt scared, ignorant and defenseless.

'They want to make us so scared we submit to their will,' Aziza said with a cold faraway look in her eyes.

'Oh My God,' Sally said at last. 'Does everyone know?' Aziza nodded. 'We should go now. There is a lot to do.

We must not think about fear.'

They got and walked down the stairs into the market place. Ali was waiting for them in the car. Sally was relieved to see him. This was the last time she was going anywhere without some protection, she thought. Once in the car, she couldn't help start looking around to see if they were being followed.

'Let's take you back home,' she said to Aziza.

'No, I have one more person to see today,' Aziza said. 'Who's that?' Sally asked but Aziza didn't reply but closed the car door and smiled at Sally through the window. 'I'll see you tomorrow,' she said.

13

First there was a loud crackling noise when they switched on the big microphones at the mosque. Next the speakers came on and then a wailing and imploring call to prayer. Wilkins lay in bed listening to the call repeated from half-a-dozen other mosques. He already knew the routine. Next he would hear a tremendous hawking and spitting from nearby houses as if the inhabi- tants were all dying of throat cancer. Then they would all troop off for their prayers. There was no reason for him to get up early, so he lay there thinking what he would do with the day, maybe trip to see some of the sights or a bit of fishing.

Sally seemed pretty happy, he thought, after he had given her some cash to fix up the car and hire some more guards. After they had toured a few of the schools and inspected the damage done by the militants, he had also promised to pay for the repairs. 'Nothing money can't solve,' he kept saying in a cheery tone. Everyone seemed a bit happier.

In fact, he thought with satisfaction, Sally now thought of him as the savior of the mission and seemed mighty impressed by the heartfelt concern he was showing for the future of the girls' education. 'I just never thought of you as the caring sharing type,' she said in a sort of backhanded compliment. 'It just shows how wrong you can be about some people.'

He was feeling quite upbeat himself after the panicky anxiety of the first few days. None of the phone lines was working so there was no chance of any officials poking around asking nosy questions. Being more or less cut off now from the outside world made him feel oddly secure and he began enjoying the enforced idleness. Most of the time he could loaf around as he pleased. Funny how it is, he thought, propping up his head against the pillow and staring at the ceiling, but once you were away from the office, you just forgot about the markets. No figures dancing in blue and red on a Reuter's terminal – it was as if all that had just disappeared or, rather, it belonged on some other planet in a galaxy far away. Planet Money. Of course, he missed the thrill. In London it was always about the trade-off between fear and greed. Here it was just about fear.

In a few minutes, he thought he would get up and have some breakfast. The air in the Swat Valley had this well-scrubbed clean freshness which gave him a healthy appetite. Breakfast was usually hot tea, warm chapattis and jam. Today he would have another go at teaching the cook to make him some porridge. Sadly, there was no chance of getting any fried bacon here, but apart from that life was not so bad. All he had to do was lie low and hope the storm in London would blow over. Each day it troubled him less and less.

He knew on one level that Mervyn and everyone would be after his blood, but sooner or later they would forget about him. Besides, thought Wilkins, as he steeled himself to leave the warmth of his blankets, it was Mervyn's job to run the bank properly and supervise people like him. They only had themselves to blame. No proper risk management. Silly fools.

An hour later, he was ready to leave. He had changed into shalwar kameez over which he wore his padded blue anorak. On his head was a round brown woolly hat. Ali was waiting out-side washing down the jeep with a bucket and sponge. In the back, he could see some fishing rods and tackle.

'All set?' he said. 'Looks like a sunny day.'

Ali looked up at the blue sky and nodded. 'Sahib likes to catch trout? '

Wilkins decided he quite like being called sahib and grinned. 'We want them this big,' he said and held out his arms wide. On the way Ali entertained him with his stock of jokes about Pathans.

'Sahib, why did eighteen Pathans go to a movie?' Ali asked. 'Because below eighteen is not allowed!'

Wilkins laughed politely.

'Sahib, why can't Pathan dial 911?' Wilkins shook his head. 'They cannot find the eleven on the phone.'

'Sahib, Pathan is very religious. One day he lost his donkey, then Pathan got down to his knees and started thanking God. A passerby saw him and asked, 'Your donkey is missing; what are you thanking God for?' The Pathan replied, 'I am thanking Him for seeing to it that I wasn't riding the donkey at that time, otherwise I would have been missing.'

Wilkins laughed and was enjoying himself when he noticed they were reaching a small settlement by the Swat River. The Jeep was stuck in a small traffic jam of cars and vehicles. He could see they were heading to some sort of local festival. Further on he could see hundreds of people walking towards a green field.

'Hey, Ali why don't we go there and have a look at the festival?' he said.

'Sahib, this is bad place. This is Iman Dheri near Fazlullah's village,' he replied cautiously.

'Well, we better stay away. Can we turn back? Wilkins asked feeling nervous. The last thing he wanted was to get mixed up with the Islamic fanatics.

But there was no place to turn their vehicle around. The road ahead and behind was quickly becoming jammed by a motley collection of incoming Bedford trucks, pick-up trucks and old minibuses. They parked on a meadow by the river and found a space near the back among a few hundred families all sitting on carpets spread out on the grass. No one took much notice of Wilkins, although he was the only male there without a big beard. The families who had spread out round naan loaves, were pre-occupied with tending fires and stirring the food cooking in big black cauldrons.

It looked as if they were there for an open-air concert. Ali said it was a kind of local religious holiday and they had gathered here, excited by the chance to see Fazlullah deliver one of his sermons. After a while, a man riding a white horse arrived, followed by a group of a dozen men in black turbans on horseback or on foot, each with a gun slung over his shoulders.

'Good Heavens, it's Zorro himself," said Wilkins to Ali. A murmur of anticipation ran through the crowd as Fazlullah dismounted.

Wilkins noted the heavy-set man seemed to walk with a slight limp. A big black beard flowed down to his chest. Like all his followers, he wore a trademark black turban wrapped around his head but his woollen jacket and white trousers looked neater and more expensive than those of his followers. Many wore black masks with eye-holes and camouflaged combat vests and swaggered with Kalashnikovs or rocket launchers casually hanging from their shoulders.

'Shariah ya Shahdat!' he shouted several times into a microphone and the crowd applauded.

'He is shouting "Islamic laws or martyrdom,"' Ali said. 'That is his slogan.'

From time to time a new group of devotees arrived and came forward to embrace him like he was some kind of royalty. 'They are saying Amir Sahib – my commander, my master,' Ali said.

'So who is this guy? Why do they love him so much?' Wilkins asked, standing up to get a better look.

'Sit down, please sit down," implored Ali, pulling at his shirt. 'You have a camera. He never allows people to take a photograph of him. He believes it is against Islam to take photo-graphs or pictures.'

Wilkins sat down and put his camera away. Ali explained that this was near Fazlullah's birthplace and he was now building a new mosque and headquarters here. Fazlullah's father sent him to study with Sufi Mohammed and he then married his daughter. Actually Fazlullah's real name was Fazal Hayat and he had originally worked a ski-lift operator.

'When he was a child he had polio, but now he stops people getting polio drops,' Ali added with a sneer. 'Now he says anyone who dies of polio is a martyr.'

When Fazlullah started his sermon, Wilkins noticed he had a slight stammer, but his voice was deep and powerful.

'Now he is saying government cannot provide safety for everyone. That is why he must send his Shaheen Commando Force to fight crime. That it is his fighters who go to patrol villages and towns and punish killers, miscreants and car thieves. Now he says crime much less than before. Sharia law government better than real government,' Ali said. 'He is very much against democracy.'

The crowd listened with rapt attention, sometimes breaking out in laughter.

'The mullah makes fun of the police, saying they are too stupid and scared even to catch an old cow,' Ali said. He listened to some more of the speech.

'Now he says America is killing innocent women and children by raining down missiles from the sky. The Pakistan government is betraying their Moslem brothers by helping to overthrow the Islamic caliphate in Afghanistan. Every true Muslim in Pakistan has a duty to join the jihad against the crusaders invading Pakistan and Afghanistan.' Ali paused for breath.

Wilkins watched the crowd's response. They were getting really stirred up and chanting something.

'They are saying, "Give us the signal, Mullah, and then watch what we do!"' he explained with a note of disgust. 'These are just poor and ignorant farmers who think he can help them escape their poverty by stealing the land and money of the rich people, the landlords.'

'But you don't think he really is a new Robin Hood?' Wilkins asked him.

'Actually, Wilkins sahib, he asking money from these people to build new mosque to honor his brother who was killed by Americans in attack in Bajaur Agency. It is the duty of every good Moslem to give to charity. So people giving a lot of money, many lakh of rupees,' Ali said. Then he pointed towards an unfinished building which they could see beyond the trees. Wilkins looked at a grey concrete dome and the skeleton of some other half-finished buildings.

'I think it is madrassah where the Taliban are training suicide bombers to fight the government. He is asking people to pay taxes to him. If they cannot pay, they must give their children,' he said. 'That is not right.'

'The Taliban want to seize control over the whole of Pakistan and implement Sharia, the law of Allah. Then, they want to establish a great new caliphate covering the entire world,' Ali continued. Anyone who opposes Sharia is wajib- ul-qati – worthy of death,' he said. Fazlullah held up his hand for silence. His men hauled two prisoners in front of the crowd. They were boys with a fuzz of hair over their faces and their hands were bound with ropes. Wilkins thought they looked scared. They fell to their knees in front of him and began talking and holding up their hands in supplication. One of the bodyguards standing behind them was holding a stout stick, but Fazlullah wasn't ready to give them a lashing yet.

'They are boys who had been caught smoking hashish,' said Ali. 'Fazlullah says he is ready to show justice and mercy if people sincerely seek forgiveness from Allah.'

Then Fazlullah took a big knife out of his belt and cut their bonds, freeing them with a big smile. Each stumbled off, shouting 'Allah Akbar', and looking relieved. The crowd applauded and a few shouted 'Allah Akhbar' as well.

Fazlullah then looked stern again and held his hand up for silence for another lesson in public morals. His next prisoners were a couple of middle-aged men. Wilkins noticed that neither had the proper matted Taliban beards, nor did they look like the local farmers, but they seemed even more terrified than the boys. The prisoners were forced on to their knees as well and then, after their manacles were taken off, they were stretched out, face-down on to the dirt. Fazlullah then launched into another righteous speech, all the while holding aloft in one hand some hand-written letters.

Ali explained that these were complaints written by patients of the men, local doctors in Swat, who alleged that they were cheating their patents by over-charging them for medicines. In response, the Taliban had investigated them and decided to punish them as warning to all others.

Before either could raise a word in his defense, they were being held stretched out face-down and given a dozen lashes across their backs. One cried out for mercy, shouting the name of Allah. The crowd fell silent at this sight. Then the humiliated and bleeding men were hoisted back on their feet and given a kick to send them on their way. One of them stumbled a few steps and then collapsed, sobbing. The mullah lifted up both his arms and spread them out. He now had a fierce look in his eyes and he switched from the previous low growling voice to a higher and more hysterical rant, winding himself and his listeners to a pitch of furious indignation.

Two new prisoners were brought forward, a man and a woman, both with chains around their feet. The man had dried blood around cuts and bruises all over his face and neck. His hair and beard were matted with dirt and he had could barely stand on his own, as if he had been tied up for a long time. The woman was wrapped up from head to foot in a burkha, but out of the bottom he noticed a pair of fashionable pointed shoes. Wilkins thought he recognized them and felt a horrible fear grip his bowels. From behind the cloth hiding her face, a low sort of keening wailing sound emerged. A couple of men had shovels and were digging a hole in the ground as if they were going to bury her. Meanwhile, Fazlullah stood in front of the man, shouting and prodding at him with his knife like a man possessed, whipping himself into a fury.

Wilkins looked round at Ali to ask him what was going on and saw that Ali was looking ashen. 'Who is she? Isn't that Aziza?' he whispered. But Ali shook his head, and breathed one word softly, 'adulterer'. Then he held his finger to his lips. He looked around to see if anyone was paying attention to them, but they were all watching the scene before them.

'They will bury her and then stone her to death,' he said dully.

'Why, what can she have she done?' Wilkins said feeling cold with fear. He thought he knew who that was and felt an uncontrollable urge to get up and do something.

'The Taliban punish any women found outside their homes without an ID card and a male relative. So couples must carry a Nikah Nama or marriage certificate,' he replied. 'That's how they caught this couple.'

One of the masked men then handed Fazlullah a large curving blade, half-way between a sword and a knife. There was an audible intake of breath from those watching. Wilkins thought, they are going to chop his head off, right here on the spot. The prisoner made a big effort to summon all his dignity and to stand up straight. He spat noisily on to the ground.

Wilkins pulled Ali to his feet. A family near them suddenly noticed him and started shouting, and pointing at him, attracting the attention of the Fazlullah's men. Wilkins stood there uncertain whether to flee or stay. His heart began pounding. Without thinking clearly he grabbed Ali's arm and on an impulse he began walking towards Fazlullah. He had no idea what he was going to do but it was too late to turn back. His audacity took the mullah by surprise. Fazlullah was stopped in his tracks by the sight of the tall blonde stranger heading towards him.

'Salaam Aleikum, Salaam,' Wilkins said again and again when got close. Then he bowed deeply, reached inside his jacket and held up a big fistful of money. 'Zakat, Zakat,' he repeated.

'Ali, tell him I am a Moslem from England. I am here because I want to make a donation to his new mosque,' he said. 'Tell him I bring greetings from many believers who support his jihad. And who want to honor the sacred memory of his brother. '

The mullah looked with astonishment from Wilkins to Ali, who was translating his words. Then he looked down at the large pile of money that Wilkins had deposited at his feet. His eyes went back to Wilkins in disbelief. Wilkins babbled away for a good few minutes, throwing in as many phrases about Allah the merciful and his prophet Mohammed, blessed be his name, as came into his mind. Ali made some sort of sense of it all, but the mullah's eyes couldn't help but keep going back to the bundle of notes at his feet. Wilkins guessed that he had never seen that much money in his life. Then a breeze caught the notes and began to scatter them along the guards and the front row of spectators. It prompted a wild scramble as everyone rushed to collect them before they flew away.

'Tell him that a righteous man must show mercy and leave vengeance to Allah,' said Wilkins and gave a nod in the direction of the prisoners. Fazlullah stepped forward and embraced Wilkins, kissing him on both cheeks. No one else was watching; they were all scrambling after the bank notes. Fazlullah himself gave way to the temptation and bent down and hurriedly gathered up the cash, first examining the notes to see the currency, and then stuffing them into his shirt. Then he looked around at the pandemonium that had erupted. He could hardly now proceed with the execution and stoning. He barked out a few commands to his men and turned to Wilkins, making a gracious sweep of his arm which Wilkins took to be a gesture of invitation. 'Alah-u- Akbar,' he said gratefully and spoke a few more words. Ali said, 'Fazlullah Mullah say you are a good Moslem and he wants to invite you to eat with him.'

14

'I just don't get it,' Stoner said for the third time. 'How are on earth are you ever going find anyone in a country as big as Pakistan? I mean, there are, what 160 million people here? We only have days to find Wilkins. What can you possibly do? We don't even know that he is in this bloody country.'

After just a few hours in the country, Stoner was already finding its disorder and dirt quite intolerable. It was clear to him that getting the smallest thing done would be difficult and require protracted discussions. Nothing worked properly.

There was utter confusion even at the airport. Just hiring a cab was only accomplished after prolonged negotiations with numerous excitable touts. Even so, the cab driver demanded twice the agreed amount after he reached his destination. Of course, he refused to furnish Stoner with the receipt he demanded.

Mr. Khan regarded him from across the table with a troubled look in his eyes. He did not impress Stoner as possessing neither the needed sense of urgency nor any acumen.

Khan smoothed a large hand over his unshaven visage and sighed. 'Mr. Stoner, please, sir, you must trust me. We can find Mr. Wilkins, no trouble.'

In fact, nothing in Mr. Khan inspired the slightest confidence. He had failed to meet the flight on time, even though it arrived one hour and thirty-six minutes late. He wore an ill-tailored yellow shirt that barely constrained his large stomach and he had clearly struggled to fasten the collar around his neck. A garish purple silk tie issued by the Sindh Motor Industries Corporation hung around his neck. At least, thought Stoner, he wasn't wearing those pajamas.

outfits like most of the people, but instead a navy blue jacket and grey trousers.

'It is true this is a sticky wicket, sir. But do not worry, we are going into bat with full confidence. There are many ways to find a needle in a haystack, even one as big as Pakistan,' Khan said.

When Stoner had finally arrived at the Marriott International, they hadn't been able to find his reservation. A power cut had disabled the computers. Then he complained that they had put him in a suite when he had booked only a luxury standard room. Now they were sitting in the hotel coffee shop and all the waiters and waitresses were dressed in Bavarian costumes – all dirndls and lederhosen – because of a German food promotion week. Stoner had ordered fish and chips, Khan a beef roulade with sauerkraut and dumplings, most of which he had left uneaten.

On the table, a large foolscap file lay open with various photographs of Wilkins, copies of his passport and other assorted information drawn from his bank personnel files.

'So he is your friend?' Khan asked. 'Not exactly my friend; my colleague.'

'Ah.' he said. 'Then why did the bank send you to find him?'

'They thought I could persuade him to come back and face the music, you see.'

'Ah,' Khan said again and looked over Stoner in a way that suggested he wasn't very convinced.

'And he has run away with a lot of money? But he is not a crime suspect?'

'He was doing proprietary trading and lost a lot of money. Now the bank wants him to come back and recover this money.'

'A lot of money?'

'A substantial amount.' 'So he is not a thief?' 'Not exactly.'

'Ah. Not exactly.' Khan again rubbed his hand over his stubble and looked at Stoner.

'Do you know Burnleyside?'

'No,' Stoner said, but added that the flight had been crowded with the families of British-born Pakistanis going home.

'I went there. It is in Yorkshire. Yorkshire pudding and roast beef.'

'Aha.'

'You know a lot of Pakistani people living in England run away to Pakistan and then do not want to be found. Maybe they have not paid their taxes. Maybe they came here to join a madrassah and become a terrorist. Or maybe a daughter do not want to be married and want to escape their husband. Or husband run away from the family of his wife and relatives. I handle many such cases. These kind of people, they try to disappear in a big city like Karachi or Lahore. There are more than fourteen million people in Karachi. But many times such people are easy to find because they stay with the relatives. If we are having the names and addresses of their village or family, we can trace them. We can watch the relatives' house, where they go or whom they speak to. We are detectives, we know how to do this,' Khan explained.

'I see.'

'But you know, many times the police can do nothing because there is no extradition treaty with UK. That is why people come to me for help. They know the police cannot help unless this is political matter.'

'I see,' Stoner said with interest. It was clever of Wilkins to have gone to Pakistan.

'Mr. Stoner, is this a political matter?'

'No, good heavens, no. We don't want anyone to know about this. That's why we came to see you.'

Khan looked skeptically at Stoner.

'But I think this Mr. Wilkinson, he is an Englishman. He has never been to Pakistan, he knows no one here? Am I correct?'

'Yes, I think it is safe to assume that.'

'I think if he came to Pakistan, he would need a guide, someone to help him. Otherwise, what would he do after he got off the plane? We know he arrived three days ago. There is no evidence that he stayed in any big hotel or used his credit card.'

'He could just be using cash, changing money on the street.'

'Yes, yes, he could, but he would still be needing people to help him hide for some time.'

'But we don't have time. We need to find him very quickly.'
'Otherwise?'

'Otherwise, the bank's problems will become public.' 'Exactly. So Mr. Wilkinson's picture will be appearing in all the newspapers everywhere in the world.' 'That's exactly what we don't want to happen.'

'I know.' Mr Khan smiled at this and drank some of his tea. Then he lit a cigarette and stayed silent for a while as he puffed on it. Stoner looked around at the near-empty coffee shop and then up at the TV screen hanging from the wall above the tables. It was showing CNN's business news. Someone in Tokyo was explaining to the newscaster what the yen's sudden fall meant for Japanese exporters.

'We have to put ourselves in the minds of Mr. Wilkins.

He didn't have much time to prepare his escape? Correct?' 'Yes.'

'And he would want to go to a place where people would not be watching the news?'

'I suppose so.'

'And he is not afraid of danger.' 'Yes.'

'And he is not a Moslem.' 'No.'

Stoner looked up at the TV again. CNN was running the main news bulletin at the top of the hour. One story was about Pakistan, so they both watched it. A suicide bomber had killed dozens of people at an army barracks in the north- west of the country. A reporter was interviewing an eyewitness who de-scribed how someone dressed in a military uniform had driven up to the gate of the barracks. Then it showed a huge black column of smoke rising from a city. Khan followed his eyes and stared at the screen.

'It is in Quetta.' 'Terrible.'

The reporter explained that the authorities suspected that the Pakistan Taliban had organized the attack as a warning to the military not to push on with an offensive against the groups based in the lawless regions bordering Afghanistan.

'You know, Mr. Stoner, Quetta is now a safe haven for all militants. They are strictly enforcing Sharia law there. Women not allowed to go on streets alone. No watching TV or videos. The authorities do not dare do anything there now.'

'So what? You know, Mr Khan, I think it's time we called it a day. I am tired and we might do better in the morning when we are both fresh.'

'No, Mr Stoner. I am thinking we go to Quetta tomorrow morning. This where I would go if I were Mr. Wilkins. Quetta is a big town. I don't think he would want to go to a small place where people would be curious. And some foreigners are still living and working in Quetta, even though it is very dangerous. He could hide there a long time.'

'That sounds like a wild guess,' Stoner said, but he was intrigued. It had a certain plausibility about it.

'You know, al- Zawahiri, the al-Qaeda Number Two? People say he lived in Quetta safely for seven years, even though the whole world was looking for him. There is a twenty-five million dollar reward on his head. If Mr Wilkins is a clever man, he would hide there, I think.'

'But how?'

'I don't know exactly, but many criminals also living there. It's a center for heroin trade. The heroin comes from Afghanistan.'

'What if you are wrong and he is not there?'

'We cannot be looking everywhere. We must take a chance.'

'So it's just a hunch?'

'More than that. I am knowing people there. I will organize a car for eight tomorrow morning. Please be ready.'

Khan had made his mind up and Stoner was too tired to argue. At least it was a plan.

15

Ali drove the car with Wilkins beside him, his eyebrows knotted together above a face rigid in close concentration. He didn't saying anything and Wilkins thought he might be praying to himself.

Before he could defend himself further, the small convoy of vehicles came to a stop outside the gates to Fazlullah's headquarters. It was a large compound set in the fields and surrounded by a whitewashed wall that Wilkins thought must be over fifteen feet high. The massive wooden doors opened to reveal a collection of large buildings, some of them still under construction. They got out of the jeeps and waited for a while until Fazlullah's men went ahead to make the arrangements. Fazlullah himself had not yet arrived. He preferred to ride his white stallion with a couple of his bodyguards following him for protection.

Wilkins got out and stood looking about him with open curiosity while Ali stayed in the jeep. He could see a large white mosque. A scaffolding of poles covered red bricks and concrete and iron pillars. Next to it were some humbler buildings, which he guessed were classrooms or dormitories for the students. Immediately in front of him was a sort of parade ground and beyond it a three-storey building like an administrative block with a balcony running in front of each floor. The window frames were in a crudely done Arabesque style. It was the only building that showed any kind of decoration. The whole compound had a rather austere masculine, even military feel to it. Within a few minutes, he was conducted to another part of the compound to a more traditional style house made partly of wood. Through the twin door was a large hall covered by faded carpets. There were rolled-up mattresses around the sides. Upstairs, he guessed, there would be private sleeping rooms for Fazlullah's family. Out in the back was a kitchen.

He took off his shoes and then he was shown a space where he was politely invited to sit down on the carpet. Wilkins sat there cross-legged for a while wondering what was going to happen next. A young handsome boy with curly hair and long eyelashes came and brought him a small cup of sweetish green tea and smiled shyly at him. Somewhere a cassette box was playing loud music, a man singing hoarsely against a monotonous accompaniment of drums and a stringed instrument.

Over the next thirty minutes, a number of other men came into the hall and took their places on the carpet until there were about twenty of them sitting in a circle being served by young boys. Many brought their weapons, Kalashnikovs and grenade-launchers, with them and propped them up casually against the walls. Some had blue eyes, but rimmed with what looked like charcoal or mascara, making them look slightly fey. As it got dark, the youths brought in some oil lamps and in the fug of smoke and sweat, Wilkins began to relax. Nothing much was expected of him, at least until Fazlullah arrived and took his seat.

When Fazlullah arrived, he greeted everyone soberly and then sat down without ceremony. He clapped his hands once and one of the young boys came and served him tea and a towel. Wilkins stole a look at him and decided not to open the conversation. He couldn't make up his mind whether he was like a girl at a dance trying not to look at the boys or had joined Ali Baba and his forty thieves in their den. Soon a savory smell of lamb drifted into the room. Then a stream of young boys brought big plates heaped with greasy rice mixed with carrots, cloves and raisins. Next, came a stew in which Wilkins could see the glistening shapes of sheep kidneys. Finally, there were large plates piled with big chunks of roasted mutton. The men stuffed the rice quickly into their mouths using one hand. The meat was cut off the bone with long daggers and quickly and hungrily eaten. In no time at all, the food was all gone and the satisfied pack was wiping the grease from their beards. Fazlullah then belched and looked around the room at his companions with a benevolent paternal air, like a big bear looking at its cubs.

Many of the men began smoking and Wilkins joined them. So far he had been able to get away with smiling and repeating 'As-Salaam Alaaikum' whenever he felt it was appropriate. When they were all feeling cozy and sitting in a fug of smoke and unwashed bodies, Wilkins tried to work out who these men were and where they came from. He could hear a number of languages being spoken, none of which he understood. Then a small bird-like man with bright eyes came over and introduced himself as Malik. He was older than the others and spoke good, slightly formal idiosyncratic English and Wilkins was not surprised to learn that he was a former English teacher and he volunteered to interpret.

'Kind sir, are you enjoying your time in the Swat Valley?' he said as an opener.

'You are most welcome, sir,' Malik finished even before Wilkins had said anything. He didn't smile but looked at Wilkins and then he twisted his neck around, as if his collar was too tight, and blinked quickly.

'I have a brother in Bradford, Ibrahim,' he went on. 'Do you know him?'

'No,' Wilkins said, trying to express the maximum regret possible.

'Bradford is very nice place. Very nice to live there,' Malik said confidently. 'Yes, it is.'

'Yes, it is,' Wilkins agreed and was conscious of Fazlullah's eyes on him. He was sitting forward, pulling at his beard and staring at him with open curiosity. Wilkins pretended he did not find this disconcerting, but it was. Then the mullah interrupted his small talk with Malik and rumbled some words in Pashtun in his deep voice. Malik did his little neck twist again and explained.

'He said Daa Pukhtu dah. He is talking of the Pukhtu way,' Malik explained. 'It means that a Pashtun must be brave, truthful, straightforward and generous.'

The mullah continued speaking and Malik translated.

'He is saying you are an al-wahab. That is Arabic and means a generous giver. We are happy to receive this zakat from England. It is by fate that Allah the Almighty has brought you here.'

Wilkins hesitated and then, assuming this was an opening inviting him to explain himself and his presence in the Swat Valley, he gave the little speech that he had been rehearsing in his mind ever since he had sat down. He decided to keep it short and pious, explaining in a few simple unadorned sentences that he had been a rich but unreligious businessman until one day Allah had called him and he had come to the right faith. Then he looked Fazlullah directly in the eyes and explained that his fame had spread widely across England and in the mosques many people spoke of his deeds, his courage and his learning. His epic struggle to implement Sharia law and bring peace to this beautiful land was inspiring the faithful everywhere. Malik translated all this. Then Wilkins went into more detail, describing how he had traveled all the way from Londonistan to the Swat Valley just to bring them the generous donation and to support their cause.

Wilkins ended this speech by calling on blessings from the Prophet, then waited for the reaction. There was a hush as everyone waited to take their cue from Fazlullah's response. Wilkins knew it was a thin story and he suspected Malik thought so, too. Out of the corner of his eye, he saw him do that nervous neck twitch. Fazlullah grunted and made a comment to the others and everyone began talking animatedly amongst themselves.

'What are they arguing about?' he asked.

'Sir, they are talking about people around the world who are talking about the Swat Valley. They are very pleased that people know what is happening here. Some are saying that the American President is talking about Mullah Fazlullah in the White House,' he said. 'Now they are saying that the Zionist-crusaders cannot defeat their Jihad.'

None of them seemed to question his sudden conversion or thought it remarkable. It helped, thought Wilkins that everyone was familiar with the steady stream of British-born Pakistanis arriving to study at fundamentalist madrassahs in Pakistan and then joining the jihad.

Wilkins thought it better to try to steer the topic discussions away from himself and back to the jihad in Pakistan. He guessed that Fazlullah knew nothing and cared little about England, but would be only keen to talk about himself and the struggle in the Swat Valley.

'Please, Malik, tell Fazlullah, I would be honored if he would be my teacher,' Wilkins said and then made a show of taking out from his back pocket a notebook and then a pen which he held poised above a page. 'Ask him to explain the Pukhtu way.'

'Pa puktu ting pukhtun walaar da,' Fazlullah said with a condescending smile and happily launched into a lecture. He was not called the Radio Mullah DJ for nothing.

'This is the pashtunwali, the way of the Pashtun. He means that the Pashtun will always stick to be a Pashtun, no matter what,' Malik explained.

'It is our custom and our law, although some people don't understand that, even people in Islamabad who seek to impose their laws and courts on us. We have always followed our ways – even under the British or when Alexander the Great came here with his army many years ago.'

'Everyone knows the laws of the Pashtun, just as he knows how to eat,' Malik explained, adding that although nobody had ever written down the Pashto code, everyone knew it; or how else could they be a Pashtun?

'People in England had laws, courts and judges, just as the Pashtuns had theirs. They didn't try to tell us to do things the Pashtun way, so why should foreigners try to impose their way of doing things on the Pashtuns?'

In time, after hearing more than he ever wanted about the Pashtun, Wilkins steered the conversation round to the subject of adultery. He wanted to find out what would happen to the couple he had rescued. Malik posed the question to the room and it started another round of ani- mated discussion. In a quiet voice, he explained to Wilkins the concept of Toray Shaway. Tor means black in Pashto and death, Shaway, is the only punishment for adulterers.

'The risk is great and the price heavy for rare lips and beautiful eyes,' Fazlullah said. "It is Islamic law everywhere in Pakistan under the Hudood Law. Such people have dishonored their family and their village; they must be punished according to the Quran and according to the pushtunwali.'

Malik then whispered some further explanation to Wilkins. What happened was this: there had to be an investigation, then a jurga was held; if found guilty, then the man and the woman must face what was called had. The punishment according to Sharia law was stoning to death, or sometimes execution with a bullet. The criminals are buried up to their necks or tied to a tree and the villagers gather round and hurl stones and bricks.

'Even if they are not married?' Wilkins asked. 'What about that couple today? Were they married?'

Although he had not seen her face, Wilkins was now sure that the woman who was about to be killed for adultery was Aziza. He was also certain she was not married but she might be divorced or a widow. Then he wondered if he should press the issue right now and challenge Fazlullah's judgement.

Malik told him that the man was a widower and confirmed that the woman ran a school for girls.

'What will happen to them now?' he asked quietly. 'Will Fazlullah let them go?'

Malik said nothing, just looked at Fazlullah and gave his neck a nervous twist again.

'There is something you should know.' 'What is it?'

'Many people are discussing this case and asking whether Fazlullah has the right to do this. That is why he changed his mind,' Malik explained. 'He should now hold a shura Council to decide this.'

'I don't understand.'

'Sharia law requires the accuser to find four witnesses who have caught them in the, er, wrong behavior. This testimony is required by Islamic law.'

'So did you find four witnesses?' Wilkins asked.

'We know this woman. We are watching her and these schools,' he answered cautiously.

'What happens now?'

Malik looked away as if he was keeping something from Wilkins. After a pause, he leaned closer and said softly, 'He wants to show the people he can be merciful and perhaps he thought it is not always good for foreigners to see these things. '

'I mean the couple, what about them?' Wilkins asked again.

'Sir, you are now our Fazlullah's guest. My friend, please do not worry about such matters,' he said with a smile. 'We will do things according to our ways.'

16

Quetta's sandpaper desert and bare saw-toothed escarpments filled Stoner with foreboding. The drive from the airport revealed a deathly volcanic landscape of crags and winding canyons. The town, surrounded by sand brown peaks, was a cinder-block jumble of streets, white-washed mosques and low-walled houses of red brick scarred with graffiti. They drove past market stalls selling pomegranates and dates where dirty-looking men ate dishes of meat and beans steamed on open fires. It seemed dirty and chaotic, clogged by donkey carts. He saw beggars and sullen-faced men in baggy cotton pants with a coarse blanket thrown over their shoulders and brown woolen caps tilted over long dirty hair. In one area marked by wide roads, he caught a glimpse of colonial era compounds graced by neat lawns and whitewashed stone borders.

Stoner said nothing, but Khan kept talking. Quetta is the capital of Baluchistan, he explained, and most of the people are tribal people called Pashtuns but there were also many Hazars, Punjabis and Baluchis. He said you could tell them apart because they wore different ethnic clothing. Stoner nodded with little enthusiasm. They all looked the same to him.

Quetta was just sixty miles from the Afghan border, Khan said. When the mujahideen were fighting the Soviets, lots of Afghans had fled there. 'Many are still living there in refugee camps. That was why there are also many UN and other relief agencies here. That is why there are still many foreigners living here,' Khan said.

'You have heard of the Pakistan intelligence agency, the ISI?' Khan asked. Stoner shook his head. 'They trained the mujahideen here. So Quetta became the headquarters of the resistance against the Soviets. And now it is the base for resistance against the American occupation of Afghanistan,' Khan chortled, relishing the irony.

'When the al-Qaeda leaders escaped the American invasion, they came here to join their ISI friends. This is now their capital. They do what they want here,' he said. 'It is the Jihad Pentagon.

'Look, you can see shops selling Kalashnikovs and rifles.

They make them here.'

Stoner noticed posters of Osama bin Laden and other bearded clerics. He asked about the army presence. They had passed through a number of check points manned by anxious-looking Pakistani soldiers. To Stoner it seemed a city under tight martial law.

'I remember when Quetta was a beautiful tourist center,' Khan said, sounding wistful. 'People came here to picnic by the beautiful Hanna Lake or go trekking through the orchards of the Pishin Valley.'

From the taxi, he had pointed out the barber shops with signs telling customers they were no longer permitted to shave beards. Restaurants announced that they could not serve women because it would encourage 'immoral activities'.

'Quetta is worse than Bagdad now,' Khan concluded and warned Stoner to stay out of sight. 'These goons run everything and no one is safe. It is the Taliban, not the police, control the city. They warned the police not to leave their offices. A year ago the Taliban murdered two of the senior police officers here. They just drove past and sprayed their car with bullets. It is not the army but the Taliban who control the city and impose a curfew.

'The army is here, too, and they don't like the militants. There is a high command staff college here and last month the militants blew it up. A suicide bomb. Many died," Khan said. 'They thumb their noses at the army.'

They checked into a hotel called the Serena, a khaki-colored building which Khan said was the best in town. Stoner noticed how deserted it seemed, but he observed plenty of guards and people whom he assumed were plain-clothes agents in the lobby. The reception staff were helpful, even obsequious. At dinner, they were the only guests sitting in a cavernous dining-room. Khan ordered sajji, a local delicacy of barbequed and marinated lamb, which Stoner chewed through without comment.

'Please, Mr Stoner, try this green tea. It is very famous here. The people call it kawa,' Khan said after they had finished and had sat down in the bar of the hotel.

Stoner took a sip of the sweet and gingery tea. 'Very nice,' he said cautiously.

'You can have a drink if you like. For foreigners, it is permitted,' Khan said.

'Are you sure?'

'Oh, you British. So stiff upper lip.' Khan sounded exasperated and then settled back comfortably in a leather armchair. 'Where is your frontier spirit, Mr Stoner?'

Stoner tried to look amused at the gibe, but he was already beginning to tire of Khan. And somehow he felt that Wilkins would never have chosen to come to this bleached gray border town. Then Khan fixed him with a hard look.

'Tell me straight, how much is the bank willing to pay to find Mr. Wilkins?'

'It is very important that we find him and find him quickly. That is why we are paying you a very high bonus.'

'That is not what I meant.' Khan pulled out one of his Gold Flake cigarettes and lit it.

Stoner watched him and then said, 'OK, let's have a drink.'

Khan looked pleased. He went to the bar and came back with two large whiskies. He took a long sip with enthusiasm and then leaned forward so he was close to Stoner.

'In Quetta, there are many Taliban leaders living here openly. They even have hospitals here to look after the fighters when they are wounded in Afghanistan fighting the British or American soldiers. It is here that they organize many operations. Their people are coming and going from all over the frontier region bring them information and news for the fighting. So they know many things that are happening.'

Stoner was astounded. 'So you are suggesting that they would quickly find out if Wilkins was living here?'

'Yes, indeed. You must understand the border region is one thousand miles long and a hundred miles wide. Only they would be able to find out quickly if any new foreigners are coming anywhere in the north-west.'

'Well, why should they went help us – a British bank?' Khan took another pull of his drink.

'In Quetta, you can buy many things, anything. Here you can buy as many guns as you want. And it is nothing for these people to kill someone. We tell them some story and we offer them money, a reward.'

'My God!' Stoner recoiled with genuine horror. 'You are not suggesting that the Grosvenor Bank should hire al- Qaeda people to hunt down Wilkins? That's impossible. The board could ever approve such a thing.'

'The board? Mr. Stoner, please be realistic,'' Khan said. 'No. What I am proposing is this. We go to the Taliban and tell them that Mr. Wilkins is working for the Americans. That way they will quickly find him. The Taliban believe there are many people spying for the Americans. They will find this easy to believe.'

'OK,' Stoner said reluctantly.

'But we need to offer them good money or they will not bring him back alive.'

Stoner looked at him carefully. 'You think they might kill him?'

Khan nodded.

'And how much money would be enough?'

'That we will find out this evening. I am going to arrange a meeting with a very holy man called Noor Mohammed.' Khan stubbed out his cigarette and crushed the empty Gold Flake packet in his hand. He pulled out his cell phone and punched out a number.

17

It was easy enough to get to see Noor Muhammed but harder to get any sense out of him. He was an elderly man in white skull cap and white robes who lived in a kind of Islamic seminary. Stoner and Khan arrived after evening prayers and were ushered into a small side room on one side of a big courtyard in the center of a sprawling mosque.

Noor Muhammed sat cross-legged on a carpet patiently listening to Khan's explanation and fingering his beads. He took no notice of Stoner. After he had heard Khan out, he said nothing. Then he turned round and motioned to an attendant to come over. A young man popped out from an alcove and brought a tiny pitcher of tea and some white porcelain bowls. They sipped the tea in silence while Noor Muhammed turned the matter over in his mind. Then he asked for paper and slowly wrote out a letter. He folded the paper carefully and summoned his secretary, who bent over while Noor Muhammed whispered something in his ear. He then departed and they sat there again in silence, apart from Khan who fidgeted and scratched himself. Then Noor Muhammed spoke a few curt words to Khan and they were dismissed.

'So what was that all about?' Stoner asked once they were outside.

Khan held his finger to his lips. They got into one of the little yellow Morris taxis and headed back to the hotel.

'He says, he will help us, but there is a price.' 'OK, what is it?'

'This time he did not say. We must wait. First he will talk to the other mujahideen. Then we will have another meeting. This time in private.'

'Does he know how urgent it is?'

'Of course, but this is Pakistan. You must not be in a hurry. And these are dangerous men. Very dangerous men.'

They returned to the brown fortress-like hotel and sat in the splendid dining-room, once again the only guests. After they had finished eating, Stoner retired to his room. There was a television set but no signal. He wondered if this might be because some Taliban edict had outlawed watching TV and decided there was nothing for it but to go to sleep early. After midnight the phone at his bedside woke him. He answered it. 'Mr. Stoner? There is someone at reception for you.'

'Who is it?' he said. The man spoke good English and sounded polite and helpful. Stoner assumed it was the receptionist.

'Please come downstairs. You need to sign a form, for the police,' the man said.

Stoner got dressed and went down where he found a young man with a beard wearing a round white skull cap waiting. There was no one else present.

'This way,' he said, smiling pleasantly, before taking his arm and guiding him to the door. Outside strong arms immediately seized Stoner and bundled him into the back of car. A blindfold was put over his eyes and his hands were expertly tied. 'Sit down. Be quiet.' The man sounded firm but unthreatening. Stoner had no time to react before the car drove off. No one spoke for the next fifteen minutes. When the car came to halt, Stoner was pulled out, frog-marched through the chilly night air and guided down some steps. At the bottom, he heard a door being opened. He was pushed down on to the floor and left there for a moment. He could hear or rather sense there were other people present.

'Who are you? What do you want from me?' Stoner said, trying to sound more indignant than frightened.

That does not matter. We want to know who you are, Mr Robert Stoner,' a male voice answered. It was a different voice, an older man with a thicker Pakistani accent.

'I work for the Grosvenor Bank. You must have heard of us? We are the oldest, most respected bank in London. We are even mentioned in Pepys' Diary. And I am the senior auditor for the Grosvenor Bank.'

'I do not know this Peeps. You say it is a bank and you are an auditor. We want to know what are you doing here in Quetta?' The man's tone, though quiet, was mocking.

'I am looking for a colleague whom we believe is in Pakistan. A Mr Wilkins, who used to head our quants office.'

'Pants' office? I don't believe you. We believe you are working for the CIA. You are a spy, is that not so? Why would a bank in London send you to Quetta? We do not believe your story.'

Stoner deliberated what to say next. His story might sound slightly implausible, but there was no reason not to stick to the truth.

'It's like this. We are a bank, an old and respectable bank, and we believe Mr. Wilkins has stolen a lot of money from us and is in hiding here. I came here looking for him. My bank is prepared to offer a significant reward for any information leading to his discovery.'

'You have brought this money here with you?' Stoner hesitated.

'No, I don't have this money with me. It is too much money to carry around. It would be foolish to do so.'

'And Wilkins has this money with him? '

'No, I don't think so. He moved the money from his bank into another account.'

'And how much money are you willing to pay for this information, Mr Stoner?'

'A substantial amount.'

'Mr. Stoner, if you are not telling me truth, we could have you killed here and now. Are you CIA agent?'

The questioning continued for a while in the vein, but if they had any evidence Stoner was a secret agent, they didn't produce it. In the background, he could hear other voices talking, agitated and belligerent voices. If they really believed Stoner was CIA, and they were Taliban, then his position was hopeless. He could be here a long time, but Stoner assumed this was just be a shake-down.

Perhaps they were simply bandits after a ransom, something which Khan said happened a lot. In which case, this was simply a negotiation about money. The third possibility which Stoner considered the most plausible, was that his abductors were working for Noor Mohammed. So now they were simply trying to verify his story. That at least was helpful, although he couldn't be sure what exactly Khan had told them. But if this was all just about money, how much would they be satisfied with? After all, in a place where a prime form of transport was a donkey cart, a little cash must go a long way. So Stoner decided it was best to get the conversation back to money.

'You should be talking to Mr. Khan, who brought me here. He is a friend of Noor Mohammed whom we met today. If we were really CIA, why would we be doing that? But if you want to talk about money, we can talk about it now. But we can talk like civilized people. Please take off this blindfold. We can offer you a down payment now, a second payment on information leading us to the location of Mr Wilkins, and a third payment when we meet with him.'

'But if you have no money you can make a bank transfer, no?'

'Oh yes, of course.' Stoner tried not to sound too eager.

The last he heard was an urgent whispered discussion behind his back. Then a man came up behind him and struck him on the head. The pain exploded through his head and Stoner tumbled forward. When he had recovered, the room was empty. He was now alone, handcuffed and blindfolded.

The first thing he saw when they took off the blindfold was Khan's weary-looking and stubbled face peering down at him sympathetically.

'Mr Stoner, are you all right?'

Stoner noticed his eyes looked a little bloodshot and that he was still dressed in the blue blazer and with the same stained tie and ill-fitting collar.

'No. My head hurts and what about my hands?' Stoner held them up to show him. His head felt sore and he was sure there was a scab of dried blood on the crown.

'Mr Stoner, what were you thinking? I told you this was a dangerous city and you should stay in your room like I said.'

Khan tut-tutted some more as he untied his wrists. Stoner realized they were not alone. The room was lit by a single bulb dangling from the ceiling and he could half see a couple of men standing back in the shadows.

'Who are these men? What do they want? Why are you here? '

Stoner was relieved to see Khan, but he didn't reply. He helped him to his feet and they walked out the door and up some stairs. The two men followed them. Then they sat down again in a small room. On the wall was a lurid painting how one hand gripping a sword, and another with the Koran. It was early morning and through the shuttered windows Stoner could hear the honking from the motorized rickshaws and smell a whiff of fresh bread. They sat on the floor and the two men with rifles slung over their shoulders kept watch over them.

'You are a lucky man,' Khan said, sounding oddly pleased. 'They could be keeping you here a long time. Luckily I could find you, thanks to Noor Muhammed's generous assistance. And now I think we can do some business here. '

He opened a fresh packet of Gold Flake cigarettes, tapped one out and inhaled with pleasure. As he puffed away happily, Stoner thought he recognized that expression. He had seen it on traders after they thought they had snookered a good deal.

'So they've got me frightened, what happens next?' 'Don't worry. First we will eat something,' he said. 'Then we wait.'

After a breakfast of tea, chapattis and yoghurt, Stoner felt better, but still uneasy.

'So do they believe that I am telling the truth? Do they still think I am with the CIA?'

'No, they do not believe, but they do not disbelieve. They just wanted you to know that you are now in their power. And here in Quetta, they can do whatever they want.'

'OK. I believe them. I was scared.'

When I found you were missing, I was worried that you had been sold to another group. There are many warlords here. Goodness gracious, so many. Everyone has guns and little armies of their own. Any one of these could have kidnapped you and demanded a ransom. I could have searched for months to find you. Luckily this is not the case.'

'So what happens next?'

'Next we negotiate a price. Then you call your bank and ask your boss to make a charitable donation to a certain Islamic charity. That will be a down payment, so to speak, a deposit. After that they will start looking for Mr Wilkins.'

'So how much do they want?' 'Ten million dollars.'

'Christ!' Stoner said. 'That's a lot of money. Too much money, but I will try to get some-thing. You need to persuade them to be more reasonable.'

'We can try, but remember this, Mr Stoner, you are in a hurry. They are not.'

'Yes, even so, we can't just hand over the money like that. Besides, how do we do it? 'I know they are not going to take American Express, but do they have any banks here in Quetta?'

'Naturally,' Khan said. 'How do you think all these Saudi princes send all this money to fund the mujahedeen?'

'But can they find him quickly?'

'Of course. How many foreigners like yourself do you think there are in these parts? Look how quickly and easily they captured you. Everyone is looking out for American spies.'

'But how can we trust them?'

Khan chuckled at this. It was a foolish question. It didn't make any difference now whether he trusted them or not. He was their prisoner.

Another hour went by until finally a man came into the room with a cell phone and gestured over to Khan. They stood up talking to each other and the man gave Khan a piece of paper. Then Khan came over to Stoner and showed it to him and placed a phone in his hand.

'Please, now you dial your boss in London and ask him to transfer two million dollars to this bank account. The details are all here. Tell him, he must do it straight away,' Khan said. Stoner obeyed him.

The call went through to the switchboard in London just as the office was opening. Mervyn took the call and listened calmly to what he had to tell him. He didn't seem either too alarmed about Stoner's safety or question the amount of money involved, but instead focused on the practicalities of the deal.

'My dear Stoner, it is true that we are now very pressed for time and I am sympathetic to the problems you are facing. But remember: this is just a business deal. They have something we want, and we have something they want.'

'Yes, but with all due respect, Mervyn, your usual business-man isn't normally in the habit of cutting off your head if he feels like it.'

'In its time this bank has dealt with pirates, revolutionaries, kings and maharajahs for centuries. Why should these mullahs be any different, eh? Tell them about Pepys and that we were bankers to the Churchills, I find that usually helps.'

'But they want ten million dollars.'

'Offer them one million. Half now and half later. And I be-lieve it is customary that in such cases the kidnappers, or shall we say our new investigators, must first provide some proof of life or some guarantee that they can deliver what they say they can deliver.'

With that he rang off.

'Mr. Khan, he says you should tell them that Grosvenor Bank was banker to Winston Churchill and has been trusted by many great men. And that he will offer half a million now and half a million later if they find Wilkins. But he said they needed proof of life.'

Khan listened to this this with a half-smile on his face. He then went over and conferred with the other man for some time. The man went out and then came back after half- an-hour. There was another confab in the corner. The price came down to five million. Stoner went back to Mervyn. He raised the down payment to 750,000 US$ and offered a million if they delivered Wilkinson head and hands intact. After a few more phone calls they had a deal. Then he called Mervyn again and gave him the bank account number of the Al Rashid Trust in Quetta. Mervyn promised the money would be there within twelve hours. Khan looked pleased. He seemed very confident that they would soon have news of Wilkins.

18

Even before the muezzin's call to prayer Ali shook Wilkins awake. Well before dawn, they went straight to the mosque to perform the ritual washing, called wudu. After all the usual rinsing and spitting, Ali coached him on the correct way to pray before they entered the prayer hall. Start by raising both hands to the ears and face Mecca, he said. Then say 'Allah Akbar' and he showed him how to hold the left hand with the right hand on top and start bowing and kneeling with the words; 'Our lord, praise be for you only'.

Actually, Wilkins couldn't remember the words exactly and just mumbled something. The kneeling and prostrating towards Mecca didn't seem difficult, he thought, and since everyone was sticking himself bum-up and facing the same way, not much more was required than an earnest face.

Ali declared himself reasonably satisfied with his performance. 'You proper Pakistani man now, thumbs up,' he said, grinning inanely. It was kind of him to sound so reassuring, but there was no way Wilkins thought he could keep up the charade for long. It was one thing to pass unnoticed at such an ungodly hour while dressed in a flapping shalwar kameez and blanket, but another to keep this sort of thing up day after day. A good Moslem had to do this five times a day, but as Ali liked repeating, 'Allah wipes away your sins with five daily prayers.'

Ali pointed out that he didn't always have to keep going to the mosque. A devout Moslem could roll out his carpet and pray anywhere but that wasn't the point. It was essential everyone should see him demonstrating his piety. Ali was certain they were being watched and not just because the mullah would be careful about any foreigner in his little kingdom.

After they returned from the prayers, Wilkins went back to bed to catch up on some sleep. He wanted to stay out of sight as much as possible. He got up mid-morning and was sitting, propped up against a pillow and drinking tea when Sally burst in.

Sally was distraught. She had heard news of the fate of a friend of hers, Professor Muhammad of the Swat Government College. Fazlullah had sent his thugs round to the professor's home late one night and dragged both him and his eldest son away. They hadn't been seen since, but the militants were now searching for his youngest son.

Wilkins nodded somberly. He didn't know what to say. He put her off and said he would get dressed and come down. She agreed. As he got dressed, he tried to sort out his thoughts. The fear was spreading to people around them and it was getting harder to ignore what was going on around them. Fazlullah and his men were cranking up then tension in the Valley and they could be caught in the middle of civil war. He was no longer sure he could handle the pressure. He weighed up whether to tell her about Aziza but decided against it in case she panicked.

When he got down stairs, he found her waiting for him in the living room nursing a cup of tea. At first she was calm and explained that the Professor, a respected and educated dignitary had been doing his best to defy Fazlullah's efforts to close down all the schools. Matters came to head when the Professor had called on people to reject Fazlullah's decree ordering women working at the local government health centers to stop vaccinating children against polio.

Wilkins first reaction had been to shrug it off and say - 'Look, it's none of our business. Lie low a bit, blend in until all this blows over' - but stopped himself just in time. He didn't want to appear callous. Nor did he want to Sally to do anything foolish. In her hand, she held a crudely printed leaflet that she had picked up and showed it to him.

'Look at this,' Sally said. 'They are handing out these leaflets all over the place.

Wilkins looked at it carefully. There was a crudely printed photograph of Mohammed together with his two sons.

'They are demanding that they give themselves up and be tried at a Sharia court in Swat,' she said.

'It's not just Professor Mohammed who has been kidnapped. Aziza is missing, too. She's simply disappeared,' she said bitterly.

Wilkins looked at her in shock. Then she burst into tears, big tears that wobbled down her face. 'You've got to do something,' she mumbled.

He hesitated, then he put his arms around her and she leaned into him, heaving and gasping. 'I am sorry. I am just so scared now. Please, Wilkie, do something.'

What the hell do I do now? Wilkins had thought as he held her. It was the first time they had had this sort of physical contact and he felt a renewed tenderness for her. He began to kiss her and he felt her mouth reach up to his. Then he pushed her gently back. She looked up at him under tangled hair uncertainly.

'Sally, wait we need to think about things a minute,' he said. 'What can we realistically do?' He was on the point of telling her what he knew about Aziza, then he stopped himself. Per-haps it was time he did something otherwise the next step would be to start discussing plans to leave the Swat Valley.

'Wait, I have an idea,' he said slowly. 'We could try and get to some help from Frontier Constabulary. Ali talked about them the other day. They could give us some protection and help try to find whoever is missing. Or negotiate their release. I could go and see them with Ali and get some advice.'

Sally nodded and began to dry her face with her hand. 'At least it's a start,' he said. 'Wait here.'

He went out of the room and found Ali. They came back together and discussed it with Sally. The plan was to take the road towards Islamabad and head for the district headquarters of Alpuri where there was a large garrison. It might take an hour or two and they would be back by night fall. Ali seemed keen on the idea. He thought he could find someone there Wilkins could talk to.

'They will listen to a foreigner. They know they must protect them or it will look very bad for Pakistan,' he said. They could both see that Sally was not convinced any good would come of it but seemed relieved that something was being done. She made a visible effort to pull herself together. Once in the jeep and driving out of Mingora, Ali kept looking in the mirror and muttering to himself. There was plenty of traffic, lots of those gaudily-decorated trucks, battered old buses, motorcycle rickshaws and various old and new SUVs, all weaving in amongst donkey-carts and bicyclists. Ali seemed pretty sure they were being followed and he tried to drive faster, honking his horn and leaning out of the window to shout at people. Outside Mingora, the traffic thinned out and the pace picked up. Wilkins couldn't see anyone following them, but there was really no way of knowing. 'Why don't we stop somewhere and try and shake them off?' he suggested. Ali nodded his agreement and they turned off the highway at a place called Mamhderai. 'This is near my home village,' he explained. 'Someone here might help.'

They followed a bumpy road towards a group of houses and stopped outside one of the larger dwellings and went inside. Ali wanted him to meet the owner. For over an hour they sat in the house, sipping tea and smoking as Ali and the family discussed the situation in low voices. Eventually there were seven men in the room and several women listening in the doorway. Wilkins sat and waited. On a mantelpiece, Wilkins noticed a large framed funeral photograph of a middle-aged man in a western suit and tie. He learned this was Malak Bakht Baidar, the head of a prominent family and the deputy leader of the

Awami National Party. The Awami National Party had won the last round of elections and as result Baidar became the deputy mayor of the district. The previous year Fazlullah had sent a gang of eighty armed and masked men and kidnapped him from his house and then murdered him. Ali said that Baidar's family still had close contacts with the security forces and they should seek their advice.

They decided that if Ali was being tailed, it was safer if someone else went to speak to the police and ask them about Aziza and find out whether it was possible to negotiate terms for her release. A messenger could return in an hour or two and in the meantime they should stay put.

So they sat, waited and talked and talked. Wilkins began to get a clearer picture of the politics. It seemed that in 2002 immediately after the American invasion of Afghanistan the party of the Islamacists had won the local elections, but soon people began to tire of them. Five years later, the population turned out and voted for a non-religious Pashtun party, the Awami National Party. Fazlullah had done everything he could to stop people from voting. On several occasions suicide bombers had blown themselves up at polling stations, killing over forty people. He had sent gunmen who had murdered over fifty members of the Awami Party around the Swat Valley, sometimes by simply blowing up their houses.

Despite the terror tactics, the Awami National Party had won the elections. People rejected the coalition of religious parties. Yet the winners who had relied on the police and the military to protect them now found themselves exposed. The police had fled and even the Frontier Constabulary had not proved a match for the well-armed Taliban.   Finally, the regular army had come in and some sort of truce had been negotiated under which the army had released many of the leading terrorists, including Fazlullah's father-in-law.   The Taliban had then moved back from the hills and resumed their campaign of murder and intimidation. More and more people fled the valley, fearing for their safety and unable to carry out their business or to send their children to school. 'Taliban are taking power, they are going up in the world. They have guns, many weapons, they have got everything,' Ali said. 'So I think this makes some people want to join them.

'I can see in my village that they had painted signs on wall saying, 'do not smoke' and 'do not sell hashish'. It is frightening to see these things painted around your home. The militants entered people's homes and broke the television sets and beat the owners, using terrible force on them. Everyone is frightened now to say anything,' he said.

Wilkins was getting a better idea of who was supporting the militants. It was all the poor ne'er-do-wells who relished the opportunity to attack the wealthy educated classes and take over their houses and fields when they fled. So it was a sort of socialist revolution. Anyone who refused to flee would be kidnapped and held hostage until their family paid up hefty ransoms. And naturally these people, being mostly Pashtuns with their traditions of badal, there would be a lot of old scores being settled and new ones being created.

'If local leaders like my late uncle speak out against the Taliban, then they receive a pre-sent from Fazlullah – 1,000 rupees, black thread and a needle,' Ali said.

'What does that mean?'

'The money is for them to buy cloth to make a shroud and the needle and thread is for them to do the sewing,' Ali said. 'I think they are just using religion to grab power.'

'Aziza thought the Army was going to come back very soon and push them out again. Do you think that's possible?' 'Maybe,' he said. 'Maybe not. But maybe we need to help ourselves more. We need money to buy weapons and to fight.'

Ali gave him searching look. Then food arrived, plates of pilaf and lamb. They were nib-bling some nuts and dried fruit when the messenger returned from visiting the Frontier Constabulary headquarters. There was more earnest exchanges among the men in the room and many of them kept stealing searching glances at Wilkins.

'The police are saying they cannot do anything. Maybe Aziza has been captured by Fazllullah and he wants her family to pay him money and to leave the valley,' Ali said.

'The police also say that they have information. Some people have been asking for a tall westerner, an Englishman, who is living in the Swat Valley,' he said. 'Is that you?''

Wilkins smile froze on his face when he heard this. His first thought was to thank his lucky stars that Ali had brought him to this village and not straight to the police.

'No, do I look like a wanted man? I work for Sally's Foundation. We build schools for girls all over the world,' he replied as casually as possible. 'Do they have a photograph of the man?'

'No, they don't,' Ali said shaking his head. 'But they are warning everyone that it is dangerous for foreigners to be here now and maybe this man is a journalist. Remember what happened to Daniel Pearl. They will kill anyone they think is an American spy.'

'Well, so far we have been safe,' Wilkins said uncomfortably. He had felt that ever since he had showered Fazullah with all that cash, Ali had been looking at him in a different way.

They drove back to Mingora with Wilkins thinking hard. Had the bank contacted the Pakistan authorities? If so, the police might have received a routine request for information which was circulating around every police station. Yet it couldn't be very urgent, otherwise they would have had a photograph, he thought. And surely the police had other things on their plate now than to worry about a missing English banker.

At least, he had dodged one bullet, he thought, and they could reassure Sally with the news that the police were taking matters in hand and would try and get Aziza released. Ali kept breaking into his thoughts though to talk about his fellow villagers. They needed help to fight the militants and they needed it urgently.

In the evening, Ali and he went to prayers again and this time he felt even more uncomfortable, aware that people had noticed him and were staring and talking behind his back. It wouldn't do to be hunted both by the Taliban and the police. Maybe, he thought, it was time to get the Awami people to show a little more steel and take on the Taliban. That way they would all get so busy that they would forget about him and Sally. He began to wonder what they needed most, money or guns?

19

The ground control station was an oblong steel box, much like a shipping container with air-conditioning. Outside the early morning sun was rising into a crisp blue sky high above the desert. Captain Miller reluctantly opened the door into dark cramped space and was surprised to find Faiza already there. She was leaning forward in the console seat, absorbed in reading a report on the computer screen, frowning and biting her lower lip. She paid no attention to him as he edged behind her to speak to the pilot who sat in the other half of the cubicle monitoring images relayed from Pakistan.

Miller quickly scanned the panoply of screens. Overnight all four Predators assigned to the mission had reached the Swat Valley from Afghanistan, he noted with satisfaction. The map showed their positions, height and speed. Another monitor showed wind speeds, temperatures and air pressure. 'Be careful, Williams, the temperature is about to drop,' he remarked to the pilot and put a friendly hand on his shoulder. Flight Lieutenant Steve Williams took off his headphones, turned back and smiled. Miller had been one of his instructors when he had transferred to Creech six months ago after a tour flying F-16s in Iraq.

Miller dropped into the seat on Williams' right-hand side which was normally reserved for the console operator. Williams and Miller wore green flight suits as if they were in a real cockpit but there were none of the usual dials and meters found in a real aircraft. Instead, there were computer work stations and multiple screens displaying information and images. Williams was controlling all four Predators from a multi-aircraft control cockpit, making slight adjustments with a stick and throttle. It had the capacity to monitor and control up to a dozen aircraft. The flying was done through a keyboard and his skills only came into play during landing and take-off. Mostly, though, Williams just tapped on a keyboard. Once each of the Predators had taken off from Afghanistan twelve hours earlier, they traveled slowly and undetected across the Hindu Kush, too small to be spotted by the naked eye and almost invisible to radar. Once the pi-lot gave the Predators the GSP coordinates of the destination, the Trojan Spirit II system took charge and did most of the work of flying the UAVs. Via satellite links, it would monitor and execute the Predator's actions.

There was usually little for the pilot to do, but Miller was worried that when the sun set in Pakistan, the temperature would plunge rapidly. This could cause a layer of ice to thicken on the UAVs' huge wings. Williams tapped on to the screen and then pulled gently at the joystick.

'That should do it,' he said. Miller nodded and moved to the other side of the ground station to talk to Faiza. He wanted to be sure everything was ready when the other pilot and console operators arrived to start monitoring the multiple streams of video images.

'Anything the matter?' he said. She looked away from the computer reluctantly and adjusted her glasses.

'Could be,' she said. 'The body of a local tribesman called Mohammad Hussain has been found dumped in the mountains in the Datta Khel area of North Waziristan. He had multiple bullet wounds in the head. One of his hands was chopped off. He disappeared a week ago.'

'Was he one of ours?' Miller asked.

She nodded slowly. 'They found a note on Hussain's body which said he had been spying for the US.'

'Did you know him?' Miller asked.

'No. In fact he wasn't a real spy. But we made him look like he was,' she said.

'Why?' Miller, said, puzzled.

'Deception. The Taliban don't grasp the Predator's surveillance technology and we want to keep it that way. They think we are finding them thanks to some kind of mysterious electronic devices, homing devices, which they call 'chips' or pathrai, that's a Pashto word for a metal gadget. If they realized how easily we can now track them, they would take counter measures. So we have let them think it's the work of spies, and let them imagine they know how to defeat us,' she said.

'So some people get sacrificed,' he said with a little vinegar in his voice

'Look, almost every week the militants kidnap and kill tribes-men, accusing them of spying for the Pakistani government or for US forces. Very few have anything to do with us,' she said.

He shrugged but thought she was looking worried about something. 'Is there any more bad news out there?'

'Yes, someone in Quetta has warned Fazlullah he is un-der surveillance. I've just seen an intercept from my old of-fice at NSA. He has just ordered his men to start hunting for American spies.'

'Ah uh,' Miller said.

'They are looking for a British or American agent whom they now think is already in the Swat Valley,' she said. 'The fact is we don't have anyone like that there. It's too dangerous. They are looking in the wrong place.'

'But all we care are about is the shura, right? I mean, we are now monitoring all the passes from Dir and Malakand to track the targets as they enter Swat.'

'That is correct. Fazlullah is still busy organizing the grand Shura Council. He is expecting a dozen leaders to arrive for the largest gathering of al-Qaeda operatives for three years. Many are already on their way,' she said.

The door to the trailer opened and brought a waft of fresh-smelling coffee. The crew of three came in, the new pilot and two console operators, each carrying a paper cup of coffee, and laughing among themselves.

Faiza, irritated at their arrival, gave a barely polite greeting and resumed talking in a low voice.

'We do have a local agent. He's got a laser pointer and in-structions to paint Fazlullah,' she said.

Miller said this was good news which would improve the chances of success. In Iraq and Afghanistan a Special Forces unit would be infiltrated on the ground. They would take cover in a safe location and prepare to paint the target using laser pointers. These were small and portable and could look a bit like a handheld digital camera, although the device could be set up on a stand like a spyglass. The operator could hold it in the palm of his hand and only needed to be within 3,000 feet of the target. When the laser is kept pointed at the target, the laser radiation bounces off the target and is scattered in all directions. As soon as a missile or bomb is launched, or dropped somewhere near the target, it detects the reflected laser energy. As long as the missile is in the general area and the laser is kept aimed at the target, it will be guided accurately to the target. A smart weapon like the Predator's Hellfire missile would lock on and then hit a target, even if the target is not in sight. It could be over the horizon and twenty miles away and the missile could still hit within five meters of the target.

'Once Fazlullah has been painted, the Predator can lock on to his position at all times and we can destroy him and all the others at the shura,' Miller said.

'His instructions are to take action twelve hours before the shura opens. So it could be any time in the next thirty-six hours,' she said.

'OK, we will inform everyone here,' he said. 'But how is he going to contact you?'

'That's why I am worried. There's been no contact from him for six days,' she said. 'Can we assign one of the Predators to loiter over Fazlullah's headquarters? '

Miller nodded his agreement and went across to organize the two teams for the next four-hour shift. Williams and one of the console operators became responsible for flying three of the Predators which patrolled all the key egress points into the Valley. As night fell and the temperatures dropped on the other side of the world, their task became easier. The bodies of any travelers would instantly show up on the infrared.

On the side of the ground control station closer to the door, the new pilot and a console operator began to maneuver the UAV into position so it could loiter high above Mingora and Fazlullah's headquarters at Iman Dehri, about twenty miles to the north of the city. Faiza sat in a seat behind the console operator, a young black woman called Martha, and watched the screen. It took an hour for the slow moving drone reach Mingora and there it settled into an orbit above the town.

From high above, Faiza and Martha had a God's eye view of the city of about a million. Faiza could see a constant stream of traffic on the four roads which converged on the district capital. In the early evening, the city was busy but the stream of traffic leaving the city was tailing off. At first she wasn't sure what exactly she was looking for, but decided it was smarter to concentrate on any vehicles traveling between Fazlullah's headquarters and Mingora. Even though this narrowed the field, there was a stream of vehicles, including buses and trucks, traveling along the road. She discounted those and focused on those leaving the compound on motor-bikes or cars of some sort. Then she and Martha began to electronically tag and follow those that left the compound. The Predator had the ability to follow different targets simultaneously, even after dark. She could also plot the movement of any target against a map, making it possible to detect any patterns or unusual behavior. She was soon able to identify the Taliban headquarters in Mingora from the number of vehicles from Iman Dehri that arrived at a large walled house not far from the main market. She soon noticed that a high proportion of the vehicles were motor-bikes, usually with two men on, and began to suspect they were messengers. The Taliban, she guessed, were avoiding using phones as much as possible. Then she had an idea.

'Martha, keep an eye on these targets in Mingora for me,' she said. 'I am going to check something.'

She went on line to the CIA's Echelon database and began to hunt through all intercepts of phone calls from the Swat Valley. Echelon had been originally a Cold War project. All the listening stations run by the Americans and its allies pooled their intelligence on to one database. There was only one cell phone company operating in the Swat Valley and that made it particularly easy to intercept live phone calls. She stopped suddenly. The data log showed no intercepts and in fact no phone calls at all being made in the Swat Valley. The whole system had been down for twenty-four hours.

If the Taliban were communicating with each other, they must be using land lines or, worse, using Skype or Voice Over Internet Protocol (VoIP) phone services, all of which were harder to intercept. Unlike cell phones, it was impossible to identify the user's location. Even a cell phone could be adapted to use VoIP services. She realized with a shock that she didn't know if the switchboard in Mingora was being tapped. Pakistan intelligence would certainly be able to do that and in time such phone calls could be traced. She didn't think that the Predators now above Mingora could help much if Fazlullah and his men were no longer using their cell or satellite phones.

She turned her thoughts to the failure of the cell phone system in the Swat Valley. The coverage was operated by a Norwegian company, Telenor. She had to find out if the Taliban had deliberately blocked the phones or if it was caused by one of the frequent electricity black-outs. She fired off several e-mails to Langley, the NSA and one to Blashford.

'OK, Martha, what do we have?' Faiza said, switching her attention back to the visual surveillance. On a screen she could see the location of a dozen targets which the Predator had tagged but the infrared images confused her. In an urban environment there were too many sources of heat which showed up. The Predator's capabilities were better suited for tracking a moving vehicle in a desert than in a densely populated environment.

'Not much. I've been cross-checking the targets with locations. Several seem stationed outside residential houses,' Martha said. 'But once the targets mingle in a crowd or disappear in a building they are easily lost.'

The angle of the camera made it difficult to see revealing details of the building or of the two men. When the Predator was overhead, the figures were foreshortened, but if the plane moved further away, details of the objects were blocked by other buildings.

Miller came over and touched on the shoulder and she jumped.

'Sorry, but I thought you had better come over and see what what's happening,' he said. He seemed concerned. She crossed to the other booth in the ground control station. There was a live video feed showing three vehicles parked in a field not far from Fazlullah's headquarters. The infra-red camera was focused on the vehicles because the heat from the engines showed up sharper than the people. The fuzzy green images showed a group of men standing in a semi- circle.

'What is going on here? ' she asked.

'We were watching Fazlullah's madrassah when this group left the main building. One of the men is Fazlullah. We have a tag on him. I don't know about the other five,' he said. 'But it looks like they have a prisoner with them. They pulled him out of the car.'

She could see one of the figures had been pushed down on to his knees while the others stood around him. She struggled to recognize the faces, but there was something familiar about the prisoner. He or she was shorter and slighter than the others. The console operator began to adjust the images so they could see the scene from different angles.

'Who do you think they've got there?' Miller asked.

'It looks like an execution,' she said uncertainly. 'But why are they doing it out in the open?'

'I don't know. Is he one of theirs?' Miller said.

Faiza felt a stab of fear. 'Can we bring the Predator down lower?'

He looked at the altimeter. The Predator was at 30,000 feet. They could bring it down lower but the lower it flew, the louder the noise.

'We could, but they might hear it," he said. Faiza bit her lip and thought hard.

The drone responded well to the commands issued 5,000 miles away. There was a three-second delay as the data was transmitted to a satellite orbiting in space and then redirected back to the Predator. Then it took more seconds for the images from the Predator's nose cone to be bounced into space and back and fed into the terminals in the console room.

'How's the fuel?' Miller asked.

'Good for now. Copy that,' the pilot, Lt. Williams, said calmly.

'OK, we are set now,' said the console operator and gulped down some coffee from a paper cup.

'Targets identified. Watch the altitude there,' Miller said. Faiza stood behind him in the closed darkened space of the control station and he could sense her anxiety building.

'Captain Miller, can we take the Predator down right now? We need to get a closer look and ID this man,' she said, her voice tightening. 'I have to know if this is our agent or not.'

20

Stoner was startled when his cell phone rang. He had been left alone in a small room counting the hours by watching a pool of sunlight that moved around the corners of the room. He had listened to the calls for prayer and the men arriving and leaving for prayers. Sometimes, he heard students in a nearby courtyard discoursing loudly or reciting verses from the Koran in lowered voices, but mostly he sat and brooded.

'Hello Rob, this Jane. Please wait. I have Mervyn on the line.' The poised clipped voice from someone safe in their office in London irritated Stoner. With every slowly passing hour his fears had multiplied.

'Rob, hello, Mervyn here. Bad news, I am afraid,' Mervyn said. "The Al Rashid Trust is a blacklisted terrorist organization. We cannot transfer the money to their account in Quetta. It is against international law.'

Stoner's fears and doubts choked him and he didn't answer. All day he had asked himself whether he could really trust the bank to get him out of this. The way he saw it, he was hostage both to the terrorists and to the bank. Mervyn could now force him to confess to anything. He didn't trust Khan either. Khan had left him promising to return as soon as the money had arrived and the Taliban were satisfied. And the Taliban, would they trust Khan? He didn't share their faith in Sharia law and besides, he had worked for the government as a policeman.

'But you can't leave me here like this. They've got me here under lock and key,' Stoner said, trying to keep the panic out of his voice.

'That sounds bad. But we are doing our best,' Mervyn said.

Stoner thought hard. Mervyn sounded sympathetic and hadn't asked him anything further about Wilkie.

'What do you mean they are on a blacklist? Who are these people?'

'You ask them. You're the one who is there. But they are obviously linked to al-Qaeda or the Taliban, otherwise the Americans wouldn't have blacklisted them.' Mervyn sounded impatient and irritated.

'They could keep me hostage for weeks, even months. Time doesn't matter much to these people,' Stoner complained. Khan had told him that gangs in Quetta regularly kidnapped people. The victims vanished for months at a time and then turned up dead.

'We will find another way. Put me on to Khan.' 'He is not here. I don't know where he is.'

There was another long pause and Stoner could hear Mervyn consulting someone else

'We will call him and arrange the transfer through another bank account.'

'And in the meantime, what happens to me?'

'Sit tight. We want to get you out of there quickly.' He cut the connection.

Stoner leaned back and thought again. His suspicions cooled. It was true Mervyn would want to get him out if he believed he really could find Wilkins. The only way he could do that was if he believed that Stoner was guilty. Secondly, he would be sure that Stoner preferred to betray Wilkins, his accomplice, rather than cooperate with him and disappear in Pakistan. Stoner wondered what made Mervyn so confident about that.

He thought back to the meeting in Mervyn's London office when Mervyn had hinted Stoner was complicit in the fraud. When Stoner had protested that he barely knew Wilkins, who worked in a completely different department, Mervyn had said nothing. Then he had switched on a television screen and shown him a series of video clips from a CCTV camera. It must have been filmed by a security camera attached to a wall of the Grosvenor Bank building, because it was angled above the men in the shots. They showed Stoner and Wilkins meeting outside the office among a knot of smokers and talking. The time and date of each encounter were registered on the clips. It showed them meeting on twelve occasions over the past year.

'You see, I think you know each other quite well,' Mervyn had said.

Stoner was left to guess how much else Mervyn, or rather his investigators, had discovered – not everything, clearly. Yet it was a subtle and discreet tactic that had worked. Stoner had no choice but to go to Pakistan, but Mervyn had decided to leave it up to Stoner to find the solution to the bank's problems.

Just then Stoner heard the padlock on the door being opened. Khan entered the room smiling broadly. Three young-ish men dressed like Afghans with strong noses and beards, and wearing long brown shirts and round brown woolly hats followed him into the room.

'They have the money. Get up, you can go now," he said. Stoner got up slowly, looking at him with disbelief. 'How much did they get?'

'We should leave Quetta now,' Khan said, ignoring the question and looking at him with amusement. 'Unless you want to stay here longer.'

'God, no. But what happened? Can they help us find Wilkins?'

'Mr Stoner, we are in good hands. These men will help us. Imshallah. But we have no time to waste. Now it's our turn to go into bat,' he said.

He turned around and walked out. Stoner followed him obediently into the cool night air. Outside the seminary they climbed into a battered minibus. Khan sat in the front and Stoner was bundled into the back with the three men who said nothing. He didn't recognize any of them.

Soon they entered the lobby of the Serena Hotel and walked past the security guards. 'Your key, sir,' the receptionist said cheerfully and appeared not to notice the presence of the three mujahideen fighters.

'Mr Stoner, go to your room, relax, get changed and have a wash. I will send you some food to your room. Early tomorrow morning we will leave.'

'Where are we going? '

Khan hesitated and then said, 'Peshawar.' 'Where the hell is that?'

'Near the Khyber Pass. It is far. You will need some rest.' 'Why are we going there?'

'You will see tomorrow,' Khan said triumphantly.

'What about Noor Mohammed? Is he helping us?' Stoner asked.

'Mr. Stoner. You must trust me. You are free now,' Khan said.

Stoner shrugged and went up to his room. After a comforting bowl of hot tomato soup and a club sandwich, and fortified by a good cup of tea, he felt better. He tried calling Mervyn on his personal number, but when there was just a recorded message, he turned in. Khan had told them they were leaving at five in the morning.

21

Lt. Williams began gently pulling at the Game Boy-style joy stick so the plane banked and began to coast downwards. The camera remained fixed on the scene below and she struggled to tell what the greenly-lit spectral figures were doing. The images looked more like figures in a computer game without the sound effects. It was like watching actors in a movie with the sound turned off, she thought, making it all so unreal and unthreatening.

'When we get the plane lower, can we fly over at a horizontal angle so we can see the faces of the people?' she asked impatiently.

She was not even sure she could recognize Malik if she met him in the street. All she had was a file photo of him dressed in a suit and cleanshaven when he had visited relatives in Britain a year earlier. He would certainly have a beard now and be dressed Pakistani-style in shalwar kameez. All she knew was that he was slightly built and about five- feet six, making him shorter than Mullah Fazlullah and probably shorter than most of the fighters in his bodyguard.

Captain Miller checked the plane's location and the altimeter. 'Twenty thousand feet up, above the clouds and it's night and cold. But we could do it.'

Even more frustrating, thought Faiza, was the narrow view of the scene provided by the camera as it focused on the knot of figures. It was looking at life through a straw.

'Faiza, what are we going to do when if it turns out that they have got your agent?' Miller asked quietly. It was the right question, but she didn't know how to answer except with a question.

'Can we save him?' she asked.

'Not sure. We could try and do something. But if they know he is our guy, is he still any use to us?' Miller replied.

To take any aggressive action, she would have to follow a 17-step procedure and obtain approval from the Directorate of Intelligence and the military's Defense Intelligence Agency. For this mission, her immediate superiors were on the seventh floor at Langley, where Blashford was directing the special fusion cell hunting al Zawahiri. The cell's job was to pull together all the intelligence from satellites, signals, Predator feeds and so on. She knew they were watching the video stream in real time.

'I am going to call the fusion cell for help,' she said reluctantly. Fusion cells, staffed by up to a dozen analysts, had been initiated in Iraq in order to speed up the response time. It had taken six hours to get permission to fire a lethal missile, but even now in an emergency like this, it might take an hour to go up the chain of command.

'Descending at fifty miles per hour,' Williams said.

'Copy that. Stabilize the approach at five miles,' Miller said.

'Hello, Blashford there?' she said.

'Yes, Faiza, we are trying to confirm the phone network failure,' he said. She thought he sounded oddly neutral.

On the screen she could now clearly see a dozen figures milling around. Two men apparently wearing hoods over their heads were holding down a smaller man and forcing him to kneel on the ground. He was turning his head this way and that.

'No, look at the footage from MQ2,' she said, struggling to keep the panic out of her voice. There was a brief pause.

'Do you want us to go lower? We are dropping below 15,000 feet. They will be able to hear us but not see the UAV,' Miller said steadily. Unlike a manned civilian aircraft, the Predator carried no wing or tail lights. The dull metallic non-reflective paint of the fuselage would not show against the backdrop of a cloudy night sky. But its loud propeller driven engine would be audible and instantly recognizable.

'I see it now. Can you identify the man?' Blashford said.

She knew that if the Predator dropped below 10,000 feet, it would be able to clearly detect the heat signature of any human body more clearly than with the radiation which the infrared sensors picked up.

'I think it's Malik. It could be an execution,' she said over the phone.

It must be Malik. He was small for a Pashtun. The man on the ground had his mouth open as if he was screaming. How had they caught him? A group of other men stood to one side in a cluster, watching. The beam of headlights from one of the vehicles illuminated the scene.

'Copy that,' Blashford said.

'It's definitely an execution,' she said. She wanted to say, stop this, push the freeze button. Stop time. 'Bring it lower,' she said suddenly.

'We can go kinetic and start the kill chain process,' Miller said.

'Lock the infrared on one of the vehicles,' Miller ordered the console operator. 'The one with the engine running.'

'Copy that,' Martha said without turning her head. 'Target acquired. Missile locked on.'

'Do not fire, repeat, do not take action. We can't do anything, Faiza,' Blashford warned.

The Predator was now beaming back a series of purple and yellow blob-like images which were becoming clearer by the second. She thought she could see one man was lifting up a sword

'Faiza, we can take out the vehicles with a Hellfire missile. Any time,' Miller said quietly. The Predator could fire an infrared beam from the near the nose of the plane and the pulses would attract the laser seekers at the end of each Hellfire missile. Then the on-board computer would use the beam to calculate trajectory and distance.

'Bring the MQ2 up now. Whoever they are, we can't risk them seeing or hearing us,' Blashford said coldly.

Faiza struggled with her emotions. She knew he was right. It would be the first drone attack ever in the Swat Valley. And an attack made without notifying the Pakistanis. They couldn't take the risk of derailing the whole mission. Besides, she calculated, it might even work for the best if they executed Malik. If Fazlullah believed he had killed an American spy, a traitor, inside his camp then he would be confident it was safe to proceed with the shura.

'Listen to me. Attacking the shura must be our priority,' Blashford said. 'Besides, even if we fire, the missile might kill not only Fazlullah but Malik, too.'

'Captain, look at the altitude,' Williams interjected before she could respond. The images caught by zoom lens began to shake and blur slightly.

'Jesus, it's dropping fast! Bring it up now before the damn thing crashes!' Miller said.

There was an agonizing delay before they could tell if the Predator was responding to the commands. By looking at the altimeter, she could see that it was dropping like a stone.

'It's the wings. I think they must be covered with ice. When the UAV came down through the clouds, it must have picked up the ice,' Miller said.

'What about the de-ice controller?' Blashford said angrily. In the new models the edges of the wings were made of titanium and dotted with microscopic weeping holes that allowed ethylene glycol solution to seep out of internal reservoirs and break down any ice which formed on the wings.

'The V-tails are jammed frozen, sir. They are not responding.'

'Juice it up. Lift the cone,'

'Jesus, it's now at seven thousand feet. Do something!' Blashford shouted down the phone. He sounded panicky.

The figures on the ground couldn't see the plane but they could obviously hear the drone's engine. The Predator was heading straight to them. The knot of figures turned their heads to the sky, following the sound. It was a moonless, cloudy night and they wouldn't be able to see anything. Yet some of the men lifted up their guns and began shooting at the direction of the sound. Other figures on the ground began to run and scatter in all directions. Engines started and the vehicles began to move, dispersing in different directions at increasing speed.

'No, don't fire. Don't fire now!' she shouted. Just the presence of the Predator on the scene had caused panic. They hadn't killed Malik so far, she was sure, and it looked like they were fleeing in disarray.

'Copy that,' Miller said absentmindedly. He was now concentrating on saving the Preda-tor from its own destruction.

'Three thousand feet,' the pilot said tensely.

'Level the wings, man!' Miller barked. 'Do it now.'

There was an agonizing wait as they watched to see if the drone would respond. It did. The slender wings levelled out until it was flying parallel to the ground. It was still sinking slowly as the weight of the ice on the 66-foot wingspan dragged it down. If the Predator dipped its wings and caught a sudden eddy of air, the ice was heavy enough to destabilize the UAV. In an instant it could go into a terminal tail-spin, crash and burn. A crash would be as fatal to the mission as a misfired missile.

'C'mon, baby, get a lift,' Miller muttered.

The camera was still fixed on the execution scene. In the bubble under the cone, the lens could move in any direction, whatever the direction of the plane. The gymbal kept it steady, even though the Predator had by now passed over the heads of the surprised people at the execution ground. There was no way to look at the whole picture which a pilot flying a real plane could do just by twisting his head around the cockpit. She was busy trying to figure out what was happening on the ground when the console operator spoke up.

'Sir, we are heading towards a cliff,' he said. 'Look the map.'

He flashed up a screen showing a detailed geophysical map outlining the steep contours of the Swat Valley. The Predator's synthetic aperture radar provided another picture of the landscape on a second panel. The drone was heading north-east towards the steep side of the valley. Eastwards, the Swat Valley narrowed and the mountains rose to over 18,000 feet. In places the valley also narrowed as the river ran against the edge of the cliff. The Predator was now heading straight towards to a bluff that stood in the bend of the river. The UAV needed to rise up a thousand feet to get over the cliff and then head eastwards towards the neck of the valley. Otherwise there might not be enough time to ascend and clear the peaks rimming the valley. If it was to crest the cliff, the UAV would have to start a steep ascent quickly.

'Take her round south,' Miller said. Everyone watched anxiously to see if the UAV would respond. The pilot cautiously dipped the wings to begin the ascent. A stiff easterly caught the wings and it began to pitch. Of course, there was no camera to capture an image of the Predator's lonely struggle to stay airborne. She imagined the 950 horse- powered turbo engine laboring as the cold wind tugged underneath the struts in front of a dark dripping wall of rock.

'Stability augmentation system working,' Miller muttered. 'We just need to shake half a ton of ice off the damned robot.'

Astonishingly, the Predator's camera was still transmitting images from the execution ground scene. Some of the gunmen had been letting fly rounds as the Predator passed overhead. The thermography showed brilliant bursts of color from the guns and the deep red of the bullets flying past. Other men had run to take shelter in the bank of trees at the edge of the river. The faces of most of them were obscured by hoods and face masks, but as the group had turned up their faces to search for the drone passing overhead, she had been able to make a positive identi- fication of Fazlullah and several of his deputies. Then she noticed too that the Predator's infra-red signal was still locked on to the targeted vehicle which had started the engine. She had a hunch it was a Toyota Landcruiser for his personal use. It was certainly not big enough to be a pick-up truck. So now they could track it wherever it went.

What the live video feed couldn't show her clearly was what had happened to the prisoner. If he had been dispatched, then she doubted that a cold corpse would produce a thermal image. She had to decide quickly whether to track Fazlullah's getaway vehicle or keep looking for the prisoner. She reasoned coldly that if Malik was either dead or unable to use the laser pointer, then at least they had tagged Fazlullah's vehicle.

'Can we put a marker tag on that vehicle?' she said to the console operator. He nodded his head. It would only be useful as long as the Predator stayed in the air.

She hoped that the drone's malfunctioning had least distracted them long enough to give Malik a second chance. As soon as she could get away, she would review all the video transmissions from the last fifteen minutes and then decide what to do next. In the meantime, the struggle to save the Predator was not over.

Miller had taken over the controls of the drone and was trying to coax the Predator over the cliff. It was being buffeted by crosswinds but the plane had stopped sinking and was now slowly rising. He kept silent for a while, his eyes fixed in front of him on the two screens.

'Show me the ground,' he said tensely. The console operator swiveled the gymbal so the camera was now looking directly below the plane at the black ribbon that was the river.

If the UAV crashed, then the mission might have to be aborted. The militants would find the wreckage and announce a victory over the United States. The Islamabad government would be embarrassed and furious with the CIA. It might demand an end to all Predator flights over Pakistan.

She watched Miller push the throttle to the maximum and thought the Predator was gamely responding. Then it started to rain gently and she could see the drops falling into the river below. The rain would be warmer than the ice.

The Predator was now gaining in height, its wings close to the edge of the cliff. The camera showed the tree-lined cliff edge outlined against the sky. In another few minutes, the drone would be out of danger. Then a gust of wind made the plane lurch closer to the crags and there was another anxious delay as Miller adjusted the controls and waited to see if it responded.

'The damned thing is slower than a carthorse,' he said to himself. Its top speed was 100 mph and it was moving at just fifty miles per hour. At last the Predator crested the ridge and was in the clear. Miller could bank the plane gently round and, helped by updraft, turn it eastwards out of danger.

Everyone in the ground control station watched in stunned silence as the danger receded. Faiza felt relief, but no sense of triumph.

'Well done, Captain Miller,' Blashford said flatly. He did not need to say out loud what was obvious to everyone. The Predator's sudden appearance had probably jeopardized the entire mission. Fazlullah and the Taliban now knew they were being watched and monitored.

'I am going back look over the video feed,' Fazia announced. 'Let me know where that vehicle has gone.'

'Yes, ma'am,' said the console operator.

They were still talking as she closed the door, anxious to see if the recorded video images would provide a verdict on Malik's fate. Then she would call Washington.

22

Sally regarded Wilkins anxiously as he shoveled the first fork-ful of rice into his mouth. 'So what do you think?' she asked. 'Tasty?'

He looked doubtful. 'Hmm, a tad on the greasy side.'

'It's the plat du jour, served every day in these parts,' she said.

'And it goes under the name of?' he asked.

'Plov,' she declared. 'Or Pilau rice. Except it's got carrots in it, and its cooked in lamb fat.'

'You know they call these brown bits 'meat?' he said taking another mouthful and chewing slowly.

She laughed.

'You will get used to it. It tastes better with a pomegranate salad. Takes away the greasiness,' she said.

'I never thought I'd say this but I am beginning to miss your cooking,' he said. 'I think, I have been eating plov for days now.'

He gave the big 100 watt grin that she always fell for. Sally had been wondering where he had been and had been waiting for a chance to ask him about what he had been up to over the past few days.

'I heard Ali invited you round to his home,' she said. 'What do you make of him?'

'Well, Ali's been doing his tour guide stuff since you've been so busy these days. Introducing me to Islam and taking me to see people,' he said. 'I am thinking of growing a big brush on my upper lip too.'

'Oh, please,' Sally said. 'You really are going native in a big way.'

'Sir, that is not right,' he said imitating Ali.

She was actually quite impressed by the way he had settled in and was adapting. It actually made him much more likeable, less arrogant, more interested in what she was doing and who she was. And she liked having a man here on her own terms, she decided. Before it had always been about him. His music. His research. His friends.

'They really appreciate what you are doing here. So that's good news. Most people have made very welcome too,' he said. 'But they are all shit scared of Fazlullah and his merry men.'

'Why do you say that? What did they tell you?' she said. She noticed he hesitated at this and seemed to choose his words carefully. All the time she had been wondering how much longer he would stay. He didn't seem to show any inclination to leave. She didn't want to him to go now. It was reassuring to have him around and to feel he was getting more and more interested in what she was doing.

'Well, I heard a lot of stories about how he is threatening everyone again. Some are saying they can't put up with it anymore, and they don't trust the government to help them,' he said.

'You mean they want to fight back?' she said. He nodded.

'I don't think we should get involved, although it's hard not to want to,' she said. 'I went to a school in Mangalor today. The Taliban had burnt it down and warned everyone to say away from the schools. Everyone was scared. They were even scared to talk to me. They just wanted me leave. So I did.'

Every day, it is getting worse, she wanted to say but stopped herself. She didn't want to scare Wilkins off, or give him a reason to tell his rich donor to hold off. It's not fair, she thought, I feel so torn now. She wanted to confide in him her deepest fears but she held back again.

He nodded again. 'Why don't we have a drink and relax?'

She fished out the bottle of whiskey and went to get two mugs and boil some hot water. She came back from the kitchen with two glasses of steaming toddy mixed with a little honey and was pleased to find he had brought out a guitar and was strumming it.

'Look what I found,' he said. 'Ali got hold of it for me, actually.'

'Play it again Sam,' she said brightly.

'Okay, heard that joke before but it's still good,' he said and started strumming a familiar tune and singing. 'We don't need no educashin, We don't need no educashin, cos we're the Talee –ban.'

'Just another brick in the wall,' she sang.

When they stopped laughing, she gave him the hot toddy. They clinked mugs and drank it down.

'I am feeling better already,' she said and felt a rush of affection for him. She sort of hoped he would make a move on her but he didn't. Instead he started playing again, going through some of blues riffs. Then after playing his old favourite - Everyday I get the blues – he stopped.

'You know, there's something I should have told you,' he said suddenly. 'I actually ran into Fazlullah himself. He invited me to dinner, in fact.

'We went out fishing and ran across them. And there was no turning back. But the thing is I think it was a good thing. He's now bound by this pushtanwali thing. This local Pashtun code of hospitality so I am sort of his guest now and he can't harm us. Ali thinks it will protect us,' he said.

'I can't believe you did that,' she said slowly, feeling shocked.

'Well, I pretended I was a Moslem convert and had come to admire him,' he said.

'What was he like?' she asked.

'He's a pretty ugly monster,' he admitted slowly. 'The funny thing is, he seemed both stupid and clever at the same time. He thinks he knows more than he does so he is gullible.'

Sally struggled with her emotions for moment.

'Actually, I have a bit of confession myself,' she said. 'I think we are being watched. I've noticed some guys hanging around yesterday. I thought one of them had a camera or something. I didn't want to alarm you, earlier.'

'That makes sort of sense,' he said. 'I think he's now keeping an eye on me.'

She nodded, feeling relieved. Then she added. 'The other thing is that Aziza has gone missing. I don't know where she is. I haven't seen her since we met for lunch. I am worried about it. No one can tell me what's happened to her.'

She looked at him for further reassurance but he looked away.

'This place is really fucked up but, Sally, you can't help everyone here. They have to sort things out for themselves. It's not like looking after those stray cats and donkeys you used to rescue,' he said and picked up the guitar again.

'She is not a stray cat,' she said.

'Exactly, she is a brave woman with a lot of friends and influence around here. She must know what she is doing better than either of us,' Wilkins said.

This sounded reasonable too and Sally drank some more of the hot toddy and thought about it.

'Still, we should do something,' Sally insisted. 'You will help won't you?'

She looked up at him from under her blonde fringe giving him her most appealing look. She thought, he blushed a little. Then he laughed in a blustery uncomfortable sort of way saying; 'You know, I could never resist those blue eyes of yours.' Then he strummed some chords from Back Magic Woman and growled the chorus. 'You got your spell on me, baby, You got your spell on me baby,' he sang 'Trying to make a devil out of me.'

23

Khan sat in the front of the minibus next to the driver. Stoner was in the back, squashed between two of the men he had seen the evening before. They smelt of cardamom seeds and stale mutton fat. They had been woken before dawn and quickly checked out before climbing into a private minibus. The streets were still empty but the check points were manned by Pakistani sol- diers who emerged from behind the sandbagged guard post to carefully check their documents. In twenty minutes they were out on to a stretch of open road heading east where the sun was rising behind the pale lunar mountains.

The two lane blacktop ran by the side of a half-dried- out water gully with a trickle of brown water between a jumble of mud, sand and rocks. Square stones painted white marked the edge of the road. Flanking the other side of the road was a steep bank of rocks and trees. The bank on their side held a straggle of spindly winter trees sheltering some mudbrick houses. Stoner could see children herding flocks of sheep and goats. It looked a primitive place, inhabited by poor people. Goodbye and good riddance to Quetta, he thought. Khan had told him that the word originally meant fort and he wondered what anyone had ever thought worth guarding here.

The minibus drove round a blind bend and suddenly slowed. A casual and flimsy barricade made from rocks and logs blocked the way. Two men stood behind it holding out their arms and shouting. The driver braked, but did not quite stop. Everyone was watching the men in front when Stoner heard shots coming from the side. They punched into the thin metal doors. There was no hail of bullets sprayed by a machine gun, but deliberate shots. They killed the driver first and, as he slumped forwards, Khan grabbed the steering- wheel. But the bus lurched towards the gully on the left side, hit the big side stones and came to a halt.

The mujahedeen seated on Stoner's left had started to pull out a long-barreled hand gun from inside his coat when he was shot dead. The man on Stoner's right had begun to push his head down before the bus crashed to a halt. They both leaned down, pressed against the seat in front. Then the man lifted his head briefly to look around and was shot in the neck. He slumped across Stoner without a sound.

Khan was still alive when the ambushers reached the minibus. His head was cut from hitting the steering-wheel and Stoner could hear him groaning. Stoner heard the door being wrenched open. The ambushers dragged the body of the driver out of his seat on to the ground. They fired another shot into his body. Next they dragged Khan out of the bus and he stumbled and fell on to the road. One of the men forced him on to his knees and held a gun to his head. Khan held up his hands and started screaming and shouting.

So far no one paid any attention to Stoner, who was trapped in the back seat between the two dead men. He could see through the open door how a second gunman came from behind and kicked Khan in the back so he fell flat on his face. Stoner could hear him begging and pleading for his life. He figured the gunmen must have been hiding in the gully out of sight. When the minibus slowed, they had stood up and pumped shots into it.

'Kha-moosh!' Stoner heard the man holding the gun shout. Khan fell silent. The other gunman turned Khan over and started searching him, taking his wallet, cell phone, passport and papers. Around his waist they found a money belt and tore it off him. Then the man jabbed at Khan's head with the back of his rifle and Khan slumped to the ground.

Stoner thought for a second that he should try and escape. The gunmen were busy with Khan and his money belt. He tried to push one of the dead men off him and reached out a hand in an effort to slide open the door, but his limbs were trembling with shock and he could barely move. Then he heard the door being jerked open from outside. The dead men were pulled off and dumped on to the road. Stoner lifted his head and help up his hands. A short stocky man with cropped black hair and a bushy beard looked at him. He had a gun in one hand, and with the other he gestured, urging Stoner to come out. Stoner edged his way out and stood with his hands up.

'Eh up, Stoner, you look white. The man smiled pleasantly, showing strong white teeth. 'Like, you are not dead, are you?'

Then he turned round and shouted some orders to the other three men. They tied Khan's arms together, lifted him up and gagged him. He was now bleeding both from his mouth and the back of his head.

Next they lifted the body of the driver and shoved it back into the van. They put the two others in the back seat. Then they all heaved against the side of the minibus and pushed it into the gully. It tumbled and rolled half-way down into the gully and came to a halt. They tossed the rocks and logs that had formed the makeshift barricade into the gully as well.

'Some people are just careless drivers, aren't they?' he said. Then he turned his attention back to Stoner. 'I am Ahmed from Oldham. We are here to rescue you.'

Stoner stared back at him, speechless. Ahmed was short and stocky, about twenty-five, and dressed Pakistani-style with baggy trousers and rough woolen blankets thrown over his shirt.

'Don't worry, you are safe as houses,' he added and patted him on the shoulder. He watched the men finish their tasks. 'Now let's get going, like.'

He looked critically at Stoner, who was wearing a suit under an anorak and black city shoes.

'You need to get that blood off you. First you had better come along with us, quickly now. If you try to run, we will shoot you. Do you have anything in the van?'

Stoner nodded.

'Bloody 'ell,' Ahmed said and ordered one of the men to go down into the gully and to fetch the bags. He took a black attaché case and a suitcase from the back and held them up. Stoner nodded. When the man returned, they all started off down the road. Khan was dragged along with them.

Round the bend they reached a large gaudily- decorated truck. 'Get in the front,' Ahmed ordered. Stoner opened the passenger door and climbed into the cabin and Ahmed followed. One of the men got into the driver's seat and started the engine. The two others scrambled on to the back, taking Khan with them. The driver put the engine into gear, turned on a tape of loud music and lit up a foul-smelling cigarette. The truck rumbled noisily down the road. It was still empty, although the by now the sun had risen and Stoner could see smoke coming out of the houses in the villages near the road. He felt sure that no one had witnessed the ambush. It had taken no more than then fifteen minutes, maybe even less. Stoner felt he was in the hands of experienced men. Ahmed sat beside him cheerfully humming and watching the road. 'That was done very professionally,' Stoner said. 'Aye,' Ahmed said. 'And you're from Oldham,' Stoner tried again. 'Aye,' he replied.

'But who are you? What do you want with me?' Stoner said.

'We just saved your skin. You could sound a bit more grateful,' Ahmed said sharply. After a pause, he said, 'Your friend Khan sold you out to the United Balochistan Liberation Front. You were about to be taken to a farmhouse and kept hostage. Probably for a very long time.'

'What?' Stoner said. 'Who on earth are the United Balochistan Liberation Front?'

'That bugger Khan sold you out to them. He double-crossed us and sold you to the highest bidder. Then he kept the money your bank had sent.'

'And you are?"

'Taliban,' he said proudly.

What are you going to do with him?' Stoner asked but he did not answer the question. Instead he started talking about the United Balochi Liberation Front. Ahmed said it was one of dozen armed groups fighting for an independent homeland. The groups had mounted hundreds of terrorist attacks and the Army had arrested thousands of these rebels. Ahmed said that while Khan was waiting to hear back from Noor Mohammed, he had contacted one of the Balochi po- litical parties, the Baluchistan National Party, and proposed a deal: he would hand Stoner over to them, then the Balochis would keep him hostage until the government returned some of the hundreds of people who were being held by the Army. When the deal was successfully negotiated, then Khan would get another cash pay-off.

Khan had given the Grosvenor Bank details of an account which he knew would be rejected. That enabled him to per-suade Mervyn to pay the $500,000 deposit directly into his hands. So Khan could double his money. 'He's a clever bugger, that Khan. But he just got too greedy for his own good,' Ahmed concluded. 'Allah will punish him.'

Stoner thought that Khan's punishment would not just be left to Allah. 'And what now? You have our money,' he said.

'We are going to take you on a nice little trip. We think that your friend Wilkins is hiding out in the Swat valley. People there have seen a foreign man in Mingora who might be your friend,' Ahmed said.

'You think you know where he is? Good grief, but what if you are wrong?' Stoner asked. 'Khan said we should go to Peshawar.'

'He was lying,' Ahmed said. 'But think about it. The North-West Frontier is bigger than the whole of Britain Do you think it is easy to find a man hiding in these mountains? Even a foreigner? And to identify him with any accuracy? '

'Can't you just bring him to me? I could wait in Islamabad,' Stoner said.

'No, it's complicated,' Ahmed said tersely. 'It's not safe for you there anymore. We need to take you into the valley so you can identify Wilkins. And getting there is not that easy. There are army checkpoints. We need to find a special way.'

24

Ali had been right when he said the new imam who took over the Friday prayers spelt trouble. Wilkins hadn't wanted to attend, but Ali insisted that it was essential. 'It is the duty of every good Moslem to attend. He must smell sweet to attend the jumma prayers at noon, prayers are the key to paradise,' he insisted. Wilkins pulled a face. He was finding it trying to keep up the pretense of being a devout convert.

'I think it's more important to keep out of sight. There could be someone there who recognizes me,' he argued.

Ali looked offended even angry. 'Don't be a fool. Maybe they are watching you anyway,' he said. Wilkins thought he was right. Anyone in the household could have seen him drinking, for instance and reported him. So on Friday morning, Wilkins took a bath, put on his long shirt and baggy pants, and applied some kind of cloying perfume.

Inside the mosque, Wilkins estimated there must have been a couple of hundred men there, many more than during the week. This time, he thought, he attracted a number of curious looks. He followed Ali's actions, performing the bowing and prostrating, in a Simple Simon sort of way and hoped he would pass muster. The imam first led the congregation in prayer and then Wilkins watched him stand up in the pulpit and talk. He had a glassy stare, a white beard and a turban and he put Wilkins in mind of an owlish magician. The imam seemed to mention America a lot and each time raised and chopped down his right hand as if he was going to crush it. Wilkins also thought that he brought up the name Harry Potter.

After the sermon was over, the men poured out into the courtyard and hung around for a while chatting. 'Who is this Happy Potter?' Ali asked. "Do you know him?'

The imam had warned everybody not to read his books. According to the imam, it was all about a Zionist plot to corrupt the youth and get them to worship Satan, the devil. Ali explained that the prayers he had been mumbling always included a plea to seek Allah's help from Satan who is everywhere accompanied by a pack of smaller devils called jinns. Moslems must constantly be on guard against them.

'Is that all he talked about?' said Wilkins, trying to keep the amusement out of his voice.

'No, he talked about American spies. He says they are here.' Ali tugged at his moustache.

'So that's why people were looking at me,' Wilkins said. 'I told you I shouldn't have come.'

'He talked in a very angry way about America, the great Satan, and the Crusader West. He praised the mujahedeen for heroically defeating the mighty Satan's efforts to conquer Iraq and Afghanistan. Before you never heard such talk in a mosque in Mingora. He belongs to the Deobandi sect. They are very strict. So people are asking themselves why he has come here to say such things,' he said.

Wilkins looked around quickly and noticed that a lot of the men stood in knots talking earnestly.

'The imam said the Americans have many spies here in Mingora and they will catch them and kill them,' he said. 'That is why many people are very scared. They can call anyone a spy, and kill him just like that.'

It now began to dawn on Wilkins what this meant and he felt a prickling of fear.

Then Ali lowered his voice further. 'There is a rumor that that an American spy plane had been seen, but the mujahedeen shot it down. That is why they are now hunting for spies.'

Wilkins had assumed the imam was just putting the frighteners on everyone: oppose the Taliban and risk getting shot out of hand as a spy. Within a few hours, he realized how mistaken he was. After leaving the mosque, they went to the Green Square. It was deserted and there were banners up warning women to stay away, another indication that the Taliban had taken control of the city.

Some of the narrow streets were still bustling with business and they mingled with a large crowd who were waiting expectantly, held back by five hooded men holding semi-automatics and phones pinned to the top of their waistcoats.

The crowd fell silent when another group of black turbaned men wielding wooden sticks pushed their way forward, dragging with them three prisoners with their hands and ankles in chains. They were brought into the middle of the circle and the first prisoner, a man in his mid-twenties, was thrust forward.

One of the masked gunmen asked some questions in a soft voice. Then he lifted a revolver and shot him point blank. The prisoner staggered back and fell to the ground. Then the gunman casually stepped forward and fired three more bullets into his body and head. Nobody moved or said anything. Then another gunman took out a piece of paper and pinned it to the man's shirt. The dead man had been a burglar, Ali whispered, and he had been executed in accor- dance to Sharia law. They finished off the second man in a similar fashion.

Wilkins thought he recognized the last man. It was Malik, the interpreter at Fazlullah's dinner. He had already had the stuffing beaten out of him. Behind the dried blood on the cuts and bruises around his swollen face, he wore a sullen, apathetic expression. This time the chief gunman gave a bit of a longer speech. Malik didn't say anything and kept his eyes straight ahead with an unfocussed look. Then he was shot in the head and slumped to the ground. Another note of paper was pinned to his waistcoat. It condemned him as an American spy. Then the hooded enforcers shooed everyone away and the crowd dispersed mutely. The bodies, each lying in its own pool of blood, were left for any latecomers to see.

So much for the Switzerland of the East, Wilkins thought. Now they were killing people in broad daylight and this time he didn't need Ali to tell him what this meant. They did not speak to each other as they made their way back..

If even Fazlullah's cronies weren't safe, who was? Wilkins thought. He wondered if Ali would stick by them. Sally had come to depend on him and so had he.

It turned out that Ali had other ideas. In the evening he insisted on taking Wilkins back to his relatives' village. 'There was something important they want to discuss with you,' he said.

Wilkins agreed and as the sun was disappearing over the mountains they left the town by a long roundabout route. Ali said little by way of explanation, concentrating on looking constantly at the mirror. This time he didn't tell his usual jokes.

The atmosphere was tense, too, in Ali's village. After the usual show of hospitality, Wilkins found himself seated amongst a group of a dozen men in a small room lit by lanterns. As the best English speaker, Ali did a lot of the talking. He delivered a bit of a preamble by saying that Englishmen had been very good to the Swatis and how there had been peace and happiness when the Brits had run India. The valley had been left in peace and prosperity. He even brought up Winston Churchill and told Wilkins how he had come to Swat Valley as a young man and how everyone remembered what a brave and noble fellow he was. There was much nodding of grey beards.

Ali was laying it on pretty thick, thought Wilkins, and waited for the pitch.

Next, he praised Wilkins as another Winston Churchill who had already shown himself to be a great friend and benefactor of the Swati people. Ali had told everyone how he risked his own life to help people in trouble. It was remarkable, he said, that even though he was a Christian, he had managed to befriend Fazlullah and to gain his trust. And how he was proving to be a good Moslem who showed respect for their traditions and religion.

'The way you are talking, I can hardly recognize myself,' Wilkins said modestly. If only they knew what he had really done, he thought privately. It was a great pitch, but he still had no inkling of what on earth they wanted from him.

Ali didn't cut to the chase immediately. Instead, he summoned a young woman from the kitchen. She was all in black with a black headdress tight around her pale face and her eyes looked bruised and swollen by weeping. She described how a week earlier she saw fifteen to twenty armed men come to her village. They stormed her house and were carrying weapons, including rifles and grenade launchers. All of them had their faces covered. When she saw them coming, she ran and took shelter in a cattlepen. From there she witnessed the gunmen shoot her mother, her sister and her brother-in-law.

'I want to see these killers brought to justice,' she said. She didn't look directly at Wilkins but down on the floor, but Wilkins was aware that everyone else's eyes were on him. Then Ali took up the baton.

'The only thing we want is peace. We ask that the Taliban, the government and security forces stop killing us in the name of religion or restoring the government. Let our children go to schools and let us live how we like,' he said, putting his hand to his heart. 'Soon there will be nothing here but shops selling coffins.'

Of course, there was no way to resist this, thought Wilkins, not with everyone looking at him expectantly as if he was about to turn the water into wine. He nodded weakly and volunteered in a voice which sounded a bit feeble even to his own ears, 'What can I do to help?'

Ali smoothed the caterpillar moustache on his upper lip and leant towards him. 'You must ask the British government to help us. Tell them what is happening here. Tell them to send soldiers who can restore the peace here. Ask them to go the United Nations and appeal for help. We are dying here.'

Wilkins was moved and then relieved. He explained as gently as he could how they should really get help from their own government first and that the British government wasn't very likely to send troops to Pakistan unless Islamabad asked them first.

They chewed this over a bit and a debate broke out which became quite heated. He had the feeling that they had discussed this many times before and everyone was just rehearsing well-known arguments. Of course, it was unlikely that the Pakistan government would do anything more than they had before. Islamabad had sat on its hands while the Taliban were murdering all the elected members of the Awami Party and had then made a bungled attempt to tackle the jihadists with military force.

'No one else will help us. We must fight ourselves,' Ali said to him quietly as the discussion raged on.

'We need to get arms and fight them. There are enough of us and we can raise a lashkar.'

By this he meant that they had to raise a militia of their own. He threw this into the debate and then there was a lot more shouting and gesticulating.

'No one here is a coward,' he said. 'But they are afraid. Two years ago the Gujar community formed a lashkar and the Taliban attacked them, destroyed their houses and cut off their heads in public. They attacked a tribal council and took over sixty hostage. This time we be wiser.'

'How?' Wilkins said.

'We need to get better weapons, more guns, but we are poor farmers here,' Ali replied.

'And what sort of weapons do you need?' Wilkins said. Ali smiled at this as if Wilkins had just fallen into a trap. 'You can help us buy guns?' he asked.

Wilkins turned this over in his mind. 'How many men can you raise?' he asked.

'Maybe three thousand,' Ali said. 'More men than Fazlullah has.'

Wilkins pointedly looked around at the men in his room and his skepticism must have registered on his face.

'I know you have money. You are a rich banker,' Ali let slip in a quiet, off-hand way. Wilkins hadn't expected this.

'Nonsense,' he laughed. 'Of course, if my mates are in trouble, I am going to do what I can. But how much are we talking about here?'

'You helped Fazlullah. I saw you give him a lot of money. You are a generous man, so you must help us,' he said.

'If you help us, we can protect you. And Sally,' Ali said and smiled.

'Where are you going to buy these weapons, anyway?'

'In the Peshawar bazaar, you can buy whatever you need. They make Kalashnikovs there. You can find things stolen from the

Americans, too: grenade launchers, small mortars, detonators and machine guns, everything. A Kalashnikov is a hundred American dollars. Grenade launcher fifty dollars. A mortar twenty. Whatever the Pakistani army uses ends up in the market,' Ali said.

'Most of it comes from China and is dirt cheap. Then there is the stuff that the Americans give to equip the Afghan army to fight the Taliban. A lot of it is stolen from the supply convoys that truck the goods from Pakistan ports up through the Khyber Pass to Kabul. Even in the bazaar in Mingora you can buy any amount of ready-to-eat US army rations,' Ali said.

'Yes, I've noticed that,' Wilkins said. He still couldn't picture himself as a sort of Lawrence of Arabia, but then he thought, how much of a stretch is it to go from being a renegade banker to an arms dealer?

'You know, I am no Rambo,' he said with a modest laugh. 'But I believe in a good cause, though. I think I could help you with some cash, a small loan.'

He did a quiet piece of arithmetic in his head. To arm 3,000 men at say $50 a head would cost no more than $150,000. Even so, Wilkins did not think that they had the organization and training to take on the Taliban who had been through training camps run by Osama bin Laden in Afghanistan. Still, he thought, it was their fight and while they were all busy blowing each other up he might be safe. At the end of the day, he had bought some protection from Fazlullah and some extra protection from the other side would do no harm.

'Mr. Wilkins,' said Ali triumphantly, flashing his white teeth under that ridiculous moustache. 'I knew you were a good man.'

25

Alive satellite uplink allowed them to see and speak with the fusion team assembled in a grey meeting room at Langley. Blashford's anger showed in his beefy florid face. Faiza sat in the conference room at Creech, isolated and determined. She felt certain Blashford wanted her out and sensed that everyone around her thought so too, but in the last hour she had come up with fresh ideas. As she waited for a chance to speak, she mentally rehearsed what she was going to say, practicing it in her mind.

Blashford, she knew operated according to his own code, something he called in private the Snowflake principle of business. It was his own universal theory about how to make life work. It didn't matter whether you applied it to picking investment stocks or to intelligence work. He had once explained it to her where the name came from. As a young man, he had worked in Saigon during the Vietnam War where in a bar he ran into a very pretty girl. She was a hooker and her nickname was Snowflake. She puzzled him. The hookers would hang around drinking and gossiping, chatting up customers and asking high prices. What he couldn't understand was why they waited until two in the morning and then drop their prices and then go with whoever was still around. Then one day Snowflake explained to him what was going on. The girls knew that every so often, one of them would hook a really rich guy who was so rich or drunk or crazy about a girl, he would pay ten or twenty times the usual market price. Or best of all, he would marry them so they wouldn't have to work again. And it was landing one of those customers which made the whole business worthwhile. That was why they waited so long each night.

Later on, when Blashford went to work on Wall Street as an investment broker, he discovered to his surprise that the Snowflake principle applied there, too. He found that most deals rarely do better than break even, but once in a while there was one deal that came along and really turned golden. Now and again, he bought a stock that unexpectedly shot up ten times, and that was the one which made the whole business profitable. It was the juice-maker.

When she joined the intelligence service, Blashford had explained that it applied to intelligence work. 'Many people make the mistake of thinking that success comes from slow and patient field work with incremental gains in a war of attrition. This is wrong,' he said. 'You spend a long time waiting around and doing stuff which doesn't really make much difference, but now and again there comes along an opportunity that could turn things around.'

She knew that Blashford believed that the killing of al-Zawahiri at the shura was one of those opportunities. It was her opportunity, too; all she had to do was put the raw intelligence into the right light and she could carry Blashford, because deep down he badly wanted to hear good news. In the meantime, he made no pretense of hiding his frustration, pacing up and down, shouting and glaring at the camera.

'What the fuck is going on? You can't operate this toy plane. And then the fucking Taliban pick up our man and blow his brains out? What the fuck is going on? I want some fucking answers,' he stormed.

Masterson had tried to take responsibility for the errors made by the Creech team and had blamed the mishap on poor meteorological data inputs. Masterson had calmly pointed out that it was an older model which lacked the de- icing technology and that it was Blashford who had picked that particular drone because there was no other available. 'Jeez, how smart do you have to be to spot a fucking rain cloud?' Blashford replied dismissively. By this time, everyone had reviewed the video footage of the previous twenty-four hours and seen Malik being executed in the Chowk Square in Mingora. Yet Blashford insisted on showing it again.

Masterson had tried to shield her from as much of the blame as possible, but there was no doubt some of it fell on her shoulders. The fusion team who had intercepted phone calls and footage from three different Predator shifts had been able to piece together and construct a sequence of events. As part of the security preparations for the shura, the Taliban had searched everyone's personal belongings and had found something suspicious hidden in Malik's room at the madrassah. They weren't sure what it was, but the discovery had led to his interrogation. When the Predator suddenly appeared over their heads, they were trying to frighten him into making a confession. The Predator's appearance had scared them, but had closed the case against Malik. She should never have allowed it to be heard. Blashford was now certain that the Taliban believed that they had been infiltrated and, since they thought they were under such tight surveillance, it was inconceivable that Fazlullah would consider the Swat Valley secure enough to host the shura.

'Six weeks of planning down the toilet. This mission is blown now,' he concluded glumly. 'We are totally screwed. And at the worst possible moment for the Predator program.'

Everybody understood what he meant. The Joint Chiefs of Staff had approved the Defense Advanced Research Projects Agency's new budget to expand the fleet and build the new generation of Predators dubbed the Reaper. A sub-committee of the House Defense Appropriations Committee had heard strong doubts expressed about the Predator's usefulness. Some experts stressed the shortage of qualified and experienced pilots and emphasized the difficulty the existing pilots had in maintaining their concentration over long boring shifts. Yesterday's events could be used as an example of this. No wonder he now sounded bitter and disappointed. 'We've got ourselves a magic carpet, but we just don't know how to fly it,' he liked to say, but that wasn't all that was on his mind.

Other critics emphasized the gravest defect of the Predator: the challenge of collating and interpreting the sheer volume of data it gathered. Every Predator could theoretically produce a Nile-like flow of 16,000 hours of video and audio recordings in a month. With four Predators operating on this mission that was 64,000 hours or over 2,000 hours of footage a day. No one could filter that much information fast enough to respond to events in real time. Plus in the Swat Valley, the enemy was communicating in more than a dozen languages and dialects: Uzbek, Tajik, Arabic, Urdu and Pashtu, plus local languages like Khostani for which there just weren't any trained interpreters at all. It was why Blashford had brought Faiza out of the NSA and sent her to Creech so that there was someone on the spot with a feel for the local culture and languages.

Another obstacle to the acceptance of both the Predator and the Reaper was that their use could be challenged on legal grounds. A drone was a lethal weapon for assassinating foreign nationals on foreign soil without anyone going there and getting their hands dirty. Killing a terrorist in a military operation in Afghanistan might sound unobjectionable, but executing a suspect living in Pakistan on executive orders was different. Just because it was done by a machine oper- ated remotely didn't change the legal objections. Illegal or not, the CIA and the military had introduced a set of safeguards and procedures. All the right boxes had to be ticked before they were authorized to fire the Hellfire missiles and make a kill.

As an Afghan-born American, Faiza couldn't see that it mattered. Revenge was revenge and every Afghan and Pashtun understood the principles of badal. Yet for the Americans, these laws and procedures meant so much more. It was something she would never fully understand about America, but she had thought of a way of getting round that. One analyst at Langley argued that the intelligence all pointed to a cancellation of the shura, followed by another declaring that to continue would risk forcing al-Zawahiri into deep hiding, making it next to impossible to find another opportunity to catch him for at least six months. As they were speaking, Faiza thought this was her moment to jump in. She raised her hand to get Blashford's attention and he nodded coldly in her direction.

She stood, smoothed some hair which strayed from her shawl, and then opened her mouth. 'I think we can still destroy al-Zawahiri. The shura has not been cancelled,' she declared boldly. Then she rushed on without waiting for a reaction. First, she pointed out that none of the intercepts mentioned the shura. Next, it had been too late for Fazlullah to send messages to all the participants. As he would not have dared use any electronic means to contact senior al- Qaeda leaders, he would have sent handwritten notes by individual messengers traveling by foot or donkey. Third, she said it was odd that the phone system had been reactivated in the Swat Valley after the Predator had been spotted. 'Why are now they now allowing us to listen in to their conversations?' she asked and before anyone could respond she continued, 'Now look at this.'

She showed footage taken over one of the passes into the Swat Valley during the previous night. The Predators had picked up infrared footage of several convoys, each with a dozen men, heading towards Swat along a long-distance smugglers' trail. Each convoy was made up of a dozen men. She insisted that these were important Taliban leaders traveling to attend the shura in the Swat Valley.

'And how do you know that?' Blashford challenged her. 'To avoid detection they were not using motorized vehicles. None of them is using mobile or satellite phones. If they were smugglers, we would have at least a signal from their cell phones,' she said. 'But we haven't got even one.'

She explained that most Afghans didn't realize that even when the phone was not in use it gave off a signal which revealed the owner's precise location. But the Taliban would know that. On the screen, she could see Blashford listening with a frown on his face.

'Shit, that's just an assumption,' he said. 'How the hell do we know who these guys really are?'

She sensed Miller and the others present in Creech turned to look at her to see how she would respond. She took a deep breath and ploughed on.

'We have to put ourselves in Fazlullah's shoes for a moment. He wants to demonstrate his cleverness to the other leaders at the shura. This is his chance to shine by pulling off a dramatic publicity coup,' she said. 'I think he is planning to use the Predator and the shura for his own purposes. Here's how.'

She showed a piece of grainy footage taken over Mingora. There was a close-up of two men watching a house. One of them held what looked like a camera with a long lens hidden in a bag.

'These are Fazlullah's men. It looks like they have a camera and that this is just a simple stake-out. Then I checked the coordinates and discovered who is living in this compound. It belongs to the International Grassroots Literacy Foundation, a British charity which funds the edu- cation for girls in Pakistan.

A number of foreign aid workers live and work there. But what are these men really doing there?'

Now she had everyone's attention, she pushed on.

'What if this is Malik's laser pointer? Maybe the Taliban are trying to manipulate us by pointing it at a location which they hope we will destroy? They activate the laser pointer, the Predator locks on and blows up an international charity helping schoolgirls, killing a bunch of do-gooding foreigners. What could be more damaging for the Americans? And for the Predator program?'

This made everyone sit up.

'You are saying that Fazlullah is planning to switch on the laser pointer so the Predator will hit the charity's headquarters?' Blashford interrupted.

'Exactly,' she said. 'He wants to turn the tables on us.' 'You really think he's that fucking smart?'

'We assume that men like Fazlullah understand nothing of modern technology or science. It is true that he never went beyond tenth grade at school. After that he attended a religious seminary, memorizing the Koran and interpretations of Sharia law. But that doesn't mean we should underestimate his cunning.'

'So he would use the shura as bait to entrap us?' Blashford said, warming to the idea.

'The Predator is proving our most effective weapon against the al-Qaeda leadership. In the last six months we have targeted and killed nine senior commanders. If Fazlullah could turn that weapon against us and discredit it, it would be a huge reversal for us,' Faiza said coolly. 'And a great boost to the Jihad cause.

Just think how people in Pakistan and in the US would react if we killed foreign aid workers by mistake.'

Blashford turned the notion around in his mind. Everyone else in Virginia kept quiet, waiting for him to speak first. She could see he was undecided. She herself wasn't so sure that they had captured Malik's laser pointer or knew how to use it. There was no proof they had found it, but she was certain they were planning something.

'There's one another thing. Maybe this has been planned by al-Zawahiri. Back when I was still working for NSA, I picked up something. It was just after Darmadola. Someone was caught talking about revenge. And there were phone calls made to the Swat Valley and inquiries about NGOs.'

'This is their Snowflake moment,' she added quietly.

'Say you are right, but could this really work?' he said uncertainly.

In the Creech Airbase meeting room, Masterson took up the challenge.

'It is possible. They couldn't trigger a Hellfire missile launch just by turning on the pointer. On the other hand, if we launched an attack, especially a multiple strike attack, the Hellfire missiles would certainly home in on any target designated by the laser pointer,' he said.

'You mean the computer wouldn't be able to differentiate between the different signals?' Blashford asked.

'Yes, and we wouldn't have enough time to stop the missile once it homed in on a target painted by the laser, even assuming we realized what was happening,' Masterson said.

'So if we ordered a strike against Fazlullah and the other leaders at the shura, then the Hellfire missiles might blow up the Grassroots Literacy Foundation,' Blashford interjected.

'But if we do know what their plan is, we can take precautionary countermeasures even when we do strike at the shura,' Faiza said quickly. 'We still have an infrared location fix on Fazlullah's jeep, don't we? We are still tracking him, aren't we?'

Masterson nodded his head in agreement.

'So all we need to do now is to ascertain the location of the shura meeting. Then wait and watch,' she said. 'We need to concentrate all our efforts on this task alone.'

'If what you say is true, then he is going to have to let us know where the shura will take place,' Blashford said slowly. He sounded relieved and he looked around the room for any dissenting voices. There were none.

'Yes, I think that's why the cell phone network is operating again,' she said.

'OK. It's a chance. Let's give it a try. Let's see what we can get in the next twelve hours,' he said. 'Back to work everyone.'

26

After leaving behind the fields and orchards, a shale path tracked the side of a fast-flowing river. Beneath the grey buttresses of rocks, they followed the path that climbed through black fir woods. It was almost dark but the donkeys knew the way and trotted forward. Apart from the occasional slap of a rein against the flank of a donkey or the jingle of a bit, they traveled in silence. Ahmed said little except to issue the occasional order. The others in the party kept their silence, too. After an hour, Ahmed slowed his donkey and waited until Stoner drew alongside.

'Islam is about mercy and justice,' Ahmed observed stiffly. 'It was unfortunate about Khan back there, but remember, he would have killed you.'

Stoner, who had been unable to focus his mind on anything around him since watching Ahmed execute Khan, did not respond.

Stoner remembered hearing Ahmed talking on the phone in an animated loud voice while they were in the truck and nodding his head in agreement. Then, before they reached the airport, Ahmed ordered the driver to stop the truck and walked round to the back. In the wing mirror, Stoner saw Khan, rumpled and disheveled, but still wearing his blue blazer and tie, being pushed and dragged into a copse of spindly trees. The sun had come up, but had not yet dried away the early morning mist. The group of three men, the gunman at the back was the third, came to a stop with Khan falling to his knees. The younger man stood frowning as he listened to Khan's pleading. Stoner saw him trying to pull out his wallet from his pocket to show Ahmed something. Ahmed snatched the wallet from out of his hand and quickly rifled through it. The gunman looked on from the side, holding his Kalashnikov on his hip, ready to fire, as Ahmed read something. Then Stoner watched with a stunned and horrified as Ahmed toss the wallet on the ground and spoke a command. The gunman fired two shots which echoed dully from the hills and Khan fell down dead. Ahmed had then walked back and climbed into the cabin of the truck and sat beside Stoner.

'Traitor,' he had said. Then he nodded to the driver to start the engine.

After that Stoner and Ahmed had barely exchanged a word. Stoner felt alone and tired. A dazed exhausted lethargy settled over him. He obeyed Ahmed's commands mutely and passively. He followed Ahmed through the airport security procedures and on to the plane for Islamabad without making any effort to escape. Ahmed's command reached his brain as if from a vast distance. At the airport they were met by a battered SUV and driver. They traveled into the coun- try-side. It was late afternoon when the jeep turned off the road and bounced down a dirt track until it reached a group of flat-roofed houses surrounded by bare brown fields edged by stone walls. In the dwindling light, Stoner could half see, half sense the high mountains around. The wind carried the scent of pines and flowers. In a village house, they were served a plate of cold lamb and greasy rice. Stoner ate little but drank some of the hot tea. Afterwards they went out- side and found a party of a dozen or so men waiting for them. There were no introductions and the men, wrapped against the cold with hoods and blankets, spoke quietly amongst themselves. Stoner noticed that some of the men carried guns. Then they all got on to the donkeys and set out without ceremony. The animals were so small his legs dangled almost to the ground. His luggage was lashed to another animal. They set off in line with Stoner and Ahmed at the end.

'What was he trying to tell you? 'Stoner asked. Ahmed considered this for a while.

'Eh, so you want to, like, talk now,' Ahmed said, looking at him closely. He had caught the emotionless tone of Stoner's voice.

'He said he worked for the ISI, the Pakistani intelligence service,' he said.

'So why did you kill him?' Stoner said.

'Sometimes the ISI helps us. But like we can't, like, let them know everything we do,' he said. 'Anyway, I didn't believe him. People will say anything to save their skin.'

Stoner thought about this for a while. He tried to work out what it meant for him, but his mind felt fogged. At the end he had rather liked Khan and his cricketing nonsense. He felt dimly that Khan, whatever game he was playing, was less dangerous than Ahmed and his friends. If they had no compunction in murdering Khan, then they would kill him, too, when they had what they wanted from him.

'Ahmed, where are we? And where are we going?' Stoner asked.

'The Swat Valley. To find your friend, Wilkins,' Ahmed replied.

'And what then? '

'Then you pay us the money,' 'And we are free to go?'

Ahmed stopped his donkey for a moment, and shook his head. 'You are not listening to what I said. The Prophet, blessed be his name, said, 'Truth takes you towards virtue and virtue takes you towards heaven.''

'And what about this Pakistani intelligence organization?

Won't they come looking for him?' Stoner asked.

'Khan was a scumbag. He was working on his own trying to sell you,' Ahmed said.

Stoner tried to think through the consequences, trying to battle his way through the fog in his mind. Nobody, including the bank, now knew where he was or what he was doing.

'But surely the authorities will try to find me after they find his body?' he persisted.

'You don't know owt, Stoner,' Ahmed said, and kicked his donkey so it cantered forward.

By this time, the trail had passed beyond the trees and, exposed among the rocks, Stoner felt a keen wind cutting through his thin city clothing. He was still dressed in a suit and anorak. At midnight they stopped for a break. The men lit a small fire, brewed some hot tea, and handed out some flat bread to chew with it. Stoner watched Ahmed pull a small portable radio out of his pocket and tune into the BBC. An announcer's faint but steady voice delivered in a sing-song chant the results of the Premier League.

'Man City 'ave been trashed by the Gunners again,' he said. 'Who do you support?'

'Oh, I don't know, Liverpool,' Stoner said dully.

Ahmed was keen to chat about soccer and volunteered the fact that the Premier League was also very popular among the other militants. 'The brothers like kicking a ball around whenever they have the chance,' he said. 'I used to play quite a bit myself as a lad.

'My dad came from the Punjab to work in a textile factory before I was born. When I finished school there were no jobs, so I went to college in Huddersfield to study accountancy, but I was bored like. No good at it. And I was sick of being called a Paki. One day a friend brought me to hear this lecture and see a film about the murder of Moslems in Palestine, Iraq and Afghanistan,' Ahmed said. 'I began to understand more about Islam and to realize how it would end all the injustices in the world.

'Then I heard you could study Islam properly in Karachi, so I went. That's how I went back to Pakistan,' he said.

Stoner listened without much interest, but he recalled there had been race riots in Oldham some years before.

'Only the best students in the seminary were selected to get military training. I was one of them. By then I had already decided to sacrifice my life to the Jihad. So I went to one of the camps in Waziristan.'

'Waziristan?' repeated Stoner puzzled. 'That's up north near Afghanistan,' he said.

The others had finished their break and were mounting their donkeys again. Ahmed was still chatting as they set off. The path then rose steeply out of the gorge and began to wind ever higher, hairpin bend by hairpin bend, taking them out beyond the tree line. Now they were higher, the moon and stars shed a pale light on the snow-capped peaks around them.

'The Americans watch all these trade routes, that's why we have to travel by night. They've got drones and satellites so we have to be careful,' he volunteered.

'So they could be watching us now?' Stoner asked. 'Could be, but what would they see? Just some donkeys going along a trail in the mountains. We could be anything – shepherds, farmers, smugglers, traders,' he said.

Ahmed explained that they were following an old smugglers' trial. Soon they would reach the top and then go down on the other side to the Swat Valley.

'The Pashtuns have used this route for hundreds, maybe thousands of years,' he said. When Swat had been an independent kingdom, smugglers used it to transport tea and to avoid import duties.

'Fascinating. So you have done this before?' Stoner asked.

'Loads,' he said with pride. 'Let me tell you a few stories. One time I went this way to Afghanistan and the Americans caught us.'

At the top of the pass, he said there was another trail which skirted the head of the Swat Valley and then headed north towards the Afghan border. There was no real border between the two countries, certainly none that the Pashtuns recognized. In the old days British officers came into these mountains to hunt ibex, wild sheep or leopards, but they never controlled these regions or maintained real border posts. After the Soviet invasion, its troops had never managed to control the long mountainous border. There had been patrols and mines planted, but never enough to stop local families and their herds from moving freely backwards and forwards across a line on the map. The Pakistan Army had never patrolled these packhorse trails either. After the Soviet invasion, the mujahedeen had used the trade routes to smuggle men and weapons across the border. Now they moved not just supplies but opium, which was grown in the fields of southern Afghanistan.

'We were traveling like this transporting stuff from Helmand, about twenty of us, when we were spotted,' he said.

'You mean opium?' Stoner interrupted.

'Yeah, but if it wasn't for the opium these people would have nothing,' he said.

'Anyway, we were trekking through the high mountains when we heard this noise. It was like an old lawnmower engine. Man, we were scared,' Ahmed said.

'Why?' Stoner asked.

'It was a drone. An American spy plane. We thought we was done for,' Ahmed said. 'Before, you would feel safe as soon as you crossed into Pakistan. This time it followed us all day. They can watch you for hours. Like a CCTV camera in the sky.'

'You mean, they can track you wherever you go?' Stoner said.

'Of course. Everyone was freaking out, like. Some of us wanted to shoot it down, but the others said, no, we couldn't hit it anyway, we should just pretend we were local shepherds going into the mountains. In the summer months, you see, the shepherds take their animals to graze in the high pastures.'

'But can these drones fire weapons? 'Stoner asked. 'Sometimes,' Ahmed said cautiously. 'We just rounded up some sheep and cows and covered our faces. Then it left us. But that's why we travel at night now and avoid the roads and towns.'

'I see, that easy,' Stoner said.

'Think of all the billions the Americans waste on this technology. It is their religion,' Ahmed said. 'But look how little it costs us to defeat them. Just a penny shawl is enough to hide from their spying electronic eyes. And a single bullet can destroy a traitor. It costs them millions of dollars to fire one rocket, but it costs us a few hundred dollars to recruit and equip a human bomb, a martyr. No matter how much money they spend, we will always win because we have faith.'

After that speech, Ahmed fell silent. They rode until they reached the top of the pass. A stiff wind was blowing a fine drizzle. A group of horses and donkeys huddled near a wall sheltering from the wind revealed the presence of another party of travelers. There was a windowless shelter made from drywall stones and some of the men had unslung their rifles. Stoner heard the faint click of safety catches. The men in Ahmed's group were consulting in whispers. Then there was a great shout of greeting and a lot of cries of Salaam Aleikum.

Stoner got off wearily. He stood and looked up at the sky for some time. 'Don't worry, nothing there,' said Ahmed. 'You are safe.' Stoner made a wry smile, and then Ahmed gave him a shove towards the entrance of the shelter. He could smell dried dung burning in a fire. Inside he saw some heavily armed and bearded mujahedeen squatting inside. They turned curious gazes at Stoner. In the farthest corner Stoner noticed an older man with a beard and glasses who was be-ing treated with great respect. He quickly wrapped a shawl over his face when he no-ticed Stoner. It unnerved him. There was something else going on and he wondered what these men were doing here.

27

Wilkins walked along the main street at Darra Adam Khel, a flourish small town half an hour's drive north of Peshawar, and thought he had never imagined anything like it existed. At first sight it looked like any other small market town in Pakistan. The grubby shops had the same cheerful friendly owners offering their wares and shouting 'Come look, my friend.' Yet they sold nothing but weapons. He was even more astonished to find how many of them were made here. Off the main street, he toured a series of small workshops which he could see workmen hunched over workbenches drilling, hammering and soldering pieces of metal tubes. Some were working electrical lathes. They turned out every kind of gun and ordnance favoured by the Pashtun.

'What do you need my friend? Russian Kalashnikov, Chinese Kalashnikov, American Muzzelite? Here look at this RPG! Very good. It can stop a tank. You want pistol, we have

Glock, Sig Sauer pistols. Mausers? Or machine guns?' a man in a dirty white skull cap put down his pocket calculator and began picking up each of the guns in turn and showing them to him and Ali.

Wilkins smiled pleasantly and looked at Ali who kept them moving from shop to shop with the air of a man looking for a bargain.

'Let's go see the American market first,' he suggested. Ali had wanted to go to Darra Adam Khel ever since they had first hatched the plan to raise a Lashkar. It was the main arms bazaar for the North West frontier and its existence was an open secret. Wilkins had heard that the government was trying to keep foreigners away from it and had been reluctant to go. He was worried that anywhere along the way they could be stopped and searched by the military or by Fazlullah's men. And then he had trouble making up a convincing story about a fishing trip to tell Sally and to explain their absence. Yet in the end his curiosity had been so great that he had decided to go.

Now he walked around wearing a turban and scarf that covered most of his face with some sun glasses that hide his eyes. Soon he found himself having fun. At the so-called American market which was full of stuff pilfered from American convoys to Afghanistan, he looked at the wide selection of Dell and HP computers, sniper rifles, boots, combat jackets, Kevlar armor, landmines, night vision goggles, mortar shells - in fact everything one could possibly need to equip their little army. The prospecting of taking on the militants seemed at once a real possibility.

'It's all so cheap too,' he kept marveling to Ali. 'Look at this a 9mm gun is just 50$. An assault rifle is just one hundred.'

'First we try them out. Then we talk prices,' Ali said pragmatically.

His mood lifted even further when Ali suggested they should try out some of the weapons. They followed one of the salesmen up some stairs to the flat roof of his shop. He took some machine guns and a selection of assault rifles to shoot. He gave one of the guns to Ali and painted at the hills. Ali cautiously pulled the trigger and the recoil took him by surprise. The next gun he let fly a burst and then laughed out loud. Wilkins took hold of the next gun, aimed through the sights and top of the hills and pulled. He loved the sound of the rounds going off and the shell cases hitting the floor. 'Damn, that's fun,' Wilkins said grinning. He tried a couple of revolvers and liked that even more.

Then they followed the salesman back down stairs. He pulled up some comfortable wicker chairs so they could sit outside in the sunshine. A boy brought them tea and biscuits. I am beginning to like this more and more Wilkins thought to himself. He thought he could grow into this new persona of local warlord. If they could see me now, he thought. He struck a pose - adjusted his shades, lit a cigarette, slid back in his chair – then surveyed the street with an air of bored malevolence. No one paid him any particular attention.

Inside canvass bag at his feet, he had bricks of dollar notes, some 30,000 in cash. Despite the fact that everyone in sight was probably armed or could be, he felt safe. Ali had a school notebook in which they had written a list of what they need. Ali had consulted with his relations and friends and agreed on the shopping list. Ali took out the notebook and ran his finger down the list stopping now and again. The owner of the shop then came out and the two of them talked quietly while Ali penciled in figures next to each item on the list. The merchant, a heavy unsmiling man called Noor Mohammed, used his calculator from time to time. After half an hour, the two seemed to have reached an agreement and shook hands. Then they went back into the shop and Ali asked him to show the money to Noor Mohammed. Wilkins opened the bag so that he could see the cash and then closed it. Next they all went down the street and then turned left into a back street and walked on until they came to small brick warehouse. Mohammed opened the locks with a series of bulky keys. Inside, they could see a whole armory neatly piled up.

Ali called their truck by phone and they waited until it arrived. The driver, Amir, a scruffy small man with a stubble spotty face, backed the gaily decorated old truck into the alley and lowered the tailgate. Soon they were watching the weapons being loaded into the back of the truck. Ali ticked munitions and gear as it was loaded. Wilkins felt pleased. The quicker they were out of there, the better, he thought. Some items were out of stock and Noor Mohammed sent off some runners to collect them from another store. By five o'clock the truck was full and they had enough to equip a small army. He handed over the money and there was another wait while he counted it, occasionally checking to see if the bills were not counterfeit.

Then the heavily loaded truck rolled out of the town heading towards Peshawar and Wilkins felt his mood began to lift. Ali too was as euphoric as a schoolboy who had just robbed a sweet shop. 'Now we are going to fight!' Ali told Wilkins and hugged him as he had already won the war. 'Don't look so worried, my friend. Be happy.'

Soon the front cabin began to get warm and they were talking and laughing. Amir keeping one hand on the wheel, used the other to pull out a large plastic bag of weed and then dexterously rolled a joint. After they passed Peshawar, the road took them over a pass and down the other side along a series of tight bends. The more the truck swayed and rattled as it swerved round the hair pin bends. At first Wilkins wanted to stop him. Didn't he realize that if they crashed they could be blown to smithereens? He looked questioning at Ali, who shrugged with blithe insouciance. 'All drivers here smoke,' he said. 'They spent too long on the road.' Then after taking a few drags of the shared joint, he began to feel a little high. It was warm in the cabin and a flood of warm feeling of brotherly fatalism coursed through him. What the hell, he thought to himself.

At every chance, Amir honked his horn enthusiastically at the passing vehicles. Sometimes he slowed down to shout greetings at passing trucks when he recognized a fellow driver. Amir grinned at Wilkins too. Snapping his fingers in front of Wilkin's face, he went 'boom, boom.'

'What a blast,' Wilkins giggled.

'Yes, it is explosive,' Ali concurred in a serious tone, then burst into laughter at his wit.

'I just hope he won't drive me round the bend,' Wilkins added. Ali thought this very funny too. Amir didn't understand much English but it didn't seem to matter. He also seemed to find everything Wilkins said deeply amusing.

'I do recommend the cash and carry shopping in Pakistan. The service is impeccable. The staff helpful. And the home delivery service is unique,' Wilkins said.

'Yes, customer satisfaction is always guaranteed at Pakistan's number one arms bazaar. A customer with a gun is always being right,' Ali riposted.

Wilkins was laughing hard. The more he thought about things, the merrier he felt. Piled in the back was a ton of munitions and guns which they had bought in Peshawar. The crates and boxes crashed loudly against the metal sides at each corner. Wilkins was in the seat next to the passenger door and when he glanced out he could see down the steep mountain side to the river bed below. He saw the rusting remains of wrecked vehicles.

'She'll be coming round the mountain, when she comes,' he sang,

'She will be coming round the mountain, driving a wagon full of AK 47s, six bazookas, and a bag of grenades.'

Ali joined in the chorus and had thrown his arm over Wilkins' shoulder as they swayed backwards and forwards.

28

Sally looked round at Stoner with surprise. She was yawning over a mid-morning coffee and a desk scattered with papers when he knocked at the door of her office and stood there watching.

'Can I help you?' she said. 'I am Sally Jones.'

'Rob Stoner. Actually, I was looking for my old mate, Wilkins. I was told he might be here,' he said casually.

'Oh, who told you that?' she bristled and then smiled. 'Sorry, bit grumpy today. Got to do these wretched accounts.'

She waved dismissively at the piles of receipts and chits heaped around her opened lap-top.

'Have to do them every bloody month. What a pain.

Anyway, he's not here.'

A headscarf hid most of her blonde hair and framed a pretty but drawn face. She wore a sexless woolen jumper and blue cotton trousers. Stoner looked at the wall behind her with photos of school buildings and classes of girls and boys dressed neatly in uniforms.

He nodded at them. 'Are these your schools?'

'Yes, this is the Swat Valley branch of the International Grassroots Literacy Foundation. We help finance schools, especially for girls,' she said, pleased to talk about her work.

'Fascinating,' he said.

'It's not going so well. The Taliban are closing the girls' schools down. Quite a lot of violence and intimidation,' she said.

'I never realized. It looks so peaceful,' he said.

'Well, it's not. It's getting hard to keep them open because the Taliban want to shut them down.' She picked up a wad of receipts and put it down again.

'The Taliban? Really? So they don't like what you are doing?' Stoner asked.

'They've blown up some of the schools but for some reason they've left us alone, for the moment.' She looked at him with open curiosity. 'Not many foreigners come to the Swat any more. It is nice to see a fresh face but you are a bit of a surprise.'

'I am in banking, actually. I used to work with Wilkins. I heard he was down here and thought I'd drop by and catch up.'

'Really? Does he know you were coming? He never mentioned it.'

'Not exactly.' Stoner forced a laugh. 'It will be a bit of a surprise, I suppose. I would have called, but the phones aren't working very well.'

She gave him a hard look. Stoner grasped that she didn't believe his story.

'So what exactly is Wilkie doing here? I mean, he is not here for the skiing, I take it? Or for the beer. Nightlife a bit quiet here, I reckon,' Stoner inquired.

'Well, he has been helping us here with our work,' she said picking her words carefully.

'Oh I see, you two are…?'

'Oh, no, crikey. It's not like that. He has been helping us, er, raise money from donors, benefactors, that sort of thing. We needed to do a new fundraising round. So he volunteered to come out here and look around. Said he knew a lot of rich people.'

'Indeed, he does,' Stoner said and smiled. In the strained silence that followed Stoner realized it wasn't only his story that rang false. Sally herself had her own misgivings about Wilkins. He wondered what sort of story he had cooked up to explain his sudden appearance in the Swat.

'So what exactly made Wilkie suddenly pop out here?' he asked in turn.

She explained about Wilkie and how she had bumped into him on the tube one evening. And how he had decided to offer to help out with raising money. Then, fixing him with troubled blue eyes, she asked, 'I think you had better tell me the truth. Are you with the government? Is Wilkie in some sort of a mess?'

For a moment Stoner toyed with the idea of deceiving her with a cock and bull story about government intelligence agents. Then he thought better of it. He wasn't good at improvising stories. It was safer to stick to the truth. He needed to get her on his side or she might alert Wilkie before he had a chance to confront him. He guessed, too, that if he stayed with her long enough, Wilkins would turn up sooner or later.

'The truth is he is in spot of trouble,' he started, 'but not the kind you think.'

He smiled pleasantly at her. She stared back without comment.

'It's more of a sort of misunderstanding,' he said. 'Go on,' she said.

'He is a very clever boy and the bank urgently needs his help to sort out some technical problems. I, or rather we, need to persuade him to come back and help us out.'

'Is this all about money?' she said abruptly.

Stoner sat back and drank some of the coffee. It tasted of sweetened condensed milk.

'Have you ever heard of something called the Alpha Generation Execution Platform?' he asked. Then without waiting for a reply, he continued. 'Wilkie invented a special algorithm which we used to make money on the foreign exchange markets.

'The forex market is the largest market in the world. Trillions of dollars change hands all the time. The money market is the largest in history. The trading goes on round the clock and every hour people all over the world are buying and selling billions of dollars' worth of currencies,' he said.

'When I first met Wilkie a few hedge funds had already started using quantitative analysts, or quants, to design programs that would hunt out bargains among the prices quoted for shares and other securities. The quants use Algorithms for data mining. They could conduct a fast search through a mass of financial data to find the optimum price for stocks and shares,' he said.

'I never did understand why someone like Wilkie suddenly went into banking. It was most unlikely. When we were going out, he was just into physics research, and singing in his rock band,' Sally said.

'Well, it was my fault really. When I met him he was doing his Ph.D. in quantum physics. The Center for Quantum Physics in Cambridge hosted a reception after Glover's famous lecture on fast factoring algorithms. I went along hoping to find someone who really understood quantum physics,' Stoner said.

'You see, what the hedge funds were trying to do was not unlike the way physicists studying particle physics use computers to search through a mass of random data, so they set out to recruit physicists from universities,' Stoner said.

'We had a glass of Madeira. As I recall, he wore a ponytail then and a scruffy beard which emphasized his precocious youth. He wore a T-Shirt printed with the grungy faces of a rock band called The Big Bang. Or was it just Big Bang?'

'Yes, I remember he always had a glam rock purple velvet jacket,' Sally said with a laugh.

'By the way, are you expecting him back any time soon?' Stoner asked.

'I am not sure,' she said carefully, 'but go on.'

'His natural gifts lay in mathematics, not music, but he was bored by his research. As we talked about Glover's lecture, it became clear that he was the right person. He immediately grasped the practical implications of Glover's Algorithm. It dramatically enhanced the computational power of any working quantum computer, making it easy to find the proverbial needle in a haystack,' he said.

'Not everyone is drawn to high risk activities but intuition told me that Wilkie had one of those personalities which craves the rush of doing something dangerous and unpredictable. The life of a research scientist was not for him,' Stoner said. 'He was totally uninterested in financial markets or indeed anything to do with money. So I realized it would be hard to corrupt him with offers of generous remuneration packages.'

'So what did you do?' she asked.

'The only way to get him hooked was to introduce him to the drug. Successful traders are given to impulsivity and sensation seeking. All I had to do was to find a way of introducing him to the thrill of dealing.'

'Impulsivity? What's that?' she said.

'One day he came down to London. He was in his customary ragged T-shirt. We had a splendid lunch at Wilmot's – I had to lend him a jacket and tie – and over devilled oysters and grilled Dover Sole I outlined the challenge.

'The task was to create an algorithm to use in foreign exchange trading. No one had yet applied this technology to the global foreign exchange market. It is, as I explained, incredibly liquid, but every millisecond counts when making trades. Yet the sheer speed of the single dealer platform which Wilkie eventually agreed to devise allowed us to seek out hidden liquidity,' he said. 'We called it an Alpha Generation Execution Platform.

'Wilkie relished the technical challenge and on the white linen serviette, he immediately began scribbling down the clever equations he would use. I think it was the notion of do-ing something covert and undercover that held out the greatest attraction. He was entranced by the idea of doing something so subversive and clever in the staid and dull world of banking.

"That's wicked, really wicked," he told me with a grin. 'The first time we tried the Alpha program, trading on the yen/ euro pairing, with 10,000 pounds of my own money we cleared 200,000 pounds in just one night. Wilkie was delighted at his own cleverness. "Ye gods, I've invented a machine that makes money out of thin air!" I remember him saying. "It's spinning straw into gold." Then I knew I had him hooked.'

'So you were like Rumpelstiltskin in the story?' she said. 'Yes, I suppose so. From that moment on the trading mania set in. The last doubts vanished. The next day, he bought himself a Hugo Boss pin-striped suit, a set of button-down blue shirts and twenty fat silk ties. We soon wangled him an entry level job and I made sure that he was rapidly promoted to a senior position,' Stoner said.

'And that's when he dumped his girlfriend and abandoned his old friends,' Sally broke in.

'You see, traders are like gamblers. They get addicted to the adrenaline-stirring risk-taking of wagering vast amounts of money. He wanted to take ever bigger risks and began to leverage up our trades to a reckless level, ultimately endanger-ing everything. No computer, however clever the program, can successfully remove all risk from market transactions. Markets' movements are at the end of the day random movements. Only God is infallible and unfailing.'

Sally nodded.

'So there you have it, Sally,' he said. 'The trouble is, Wilkie went a bit over the top. He built up massive positions on exchange traded positions. Now he needs to come back and unwind them before the whole thing ends in tears. For everyone.'

'Oh, I see,' she said, looking rather relieved. 'I thought he had broken the law or absconded with some money.'

'Goodness, no. No one thinks of it in that way. Just a case of irrational exuberance,' Stoner said sweetly. 'He got in way over his head. Then he just panicked and took off. And Mervyn – he's the head of the bank - asked me to come here and persuade him to come back. As I recruited him, he thought it was best that I did it,' Stoner said, watching her closely. He let her take it all in.

'Are you sure that you can persuade him to go back with you?' She still hesitated.

'I need to explain to him why it's in his best interests. He can't remain a fugitive, you know,' Stoner said. He smiled reassuringly.

'Well, this does explain why all of a sudden he found my project so interesting,' she said at length. Stoner thought she looked a little disappointed. 'I suppose it won't do any harm for you two to meet. Why don't you come back for dinner?'

'It's probably best if you don't tell him much. I don't want him to panic or anything,' he said.

'OK', she nodded.

Stoner hadn't expected to track down Wilkins so easily or quickly. After descending the pass, they had arrived at one of the walled compounds outside the town. There Stoner had rested and slept for a while. After eating some food, Ahmed had taken him here straight away and then left him outside the entrance. Somehow his friends had known exactly where Wilkins was staying. Out on the streets of Mingora, he began thinking what he would say to Wilkins. He knew Wilkins cared nothing for the future of the bank and its employees, which he continued to hold in contempt. 'Bankers and wankers,' he called them. Unfortunately, he suspected Stoner of having betrayed him. Why should he believe anything he said now? As he walked through the shabby town past the half-destroyed buildings and shouting stallholders, he pondered all the possible lines of approach. Then Ahmed appeared in front of him. 'You found your man?' he asked. Stoner nodded dumbly. 'Business settled? Time to pay up then.'

Of course, the Taliban now wanted their reward. As they walked on, they discussed the arrangements and then Stoner had an idea: perhaps there was a second way of resolving every-thing.

29

As the early dawn lit up the peaks around Swat Valley, the Predator circled above tirelessly transmitting a stream of images to Creech Airbase via a satellite circling the earth. Faiza clicked on the keyboard so she was now looking at the grainy white and black pictures of Min- gora. The top down view showed a jumble of aerials, tin and flat concrete roofs and the muezzin towers with their loudspeakers. The call to prayer had already been made and she could see men walking to the mosques around town. A few cars were in the street and the markets had yet to open. The operator toggled the camera for her so they could now see directly over the charity's offices compound. The jeep was still parked in the center. There were few signs of life, just smoke drifting from the chimney.

She sighed with frustration. She needed some caffeine, a cup of hot cardamom-flavored coffee with a roll and then a quick walk in the desert air would clear her head. Instead, she had a battle on her hands to convince the team to concentrate its resources on the shura. There were only two Predators now available instead of four. One had to been taken out of service after it nearly crashed. Another had returned for refueling, and Blashford had insisted that the remaining two be diverted to keep watch over Fazlullah's madrassah. She had pleaded with him for more time to keep up the surveillance of the charity headquarters but he had listened to her with increasingly obvious impatience.

'We have been given a new priority,' he said. 'The NSA has intel which suggests that al-Qaeda is preparing to use a white foreigner in a major suicide operation aboard a plane over the United States.

'Intercepts of cell phone conversations refer to an Englishman who has joined Fazlullah bringing a large amount of money,' he said. 'In fact, there may not be just one, but several new recruits. And there is this footage.'

At the planning conference a buzz of surprise had gone through the room as they watched a clip of a blond-headed man with a fuzzy beard greeting Fazlullah reverentially. The camera caught them in crowd which had gathered in a field by the Swat River. The man was surrounded by a group of militants, but he could be seen handing a package over the mullah.

'Has anyone ever heard of any white Taliban in the Swat?' he had asked. Faiza had shaken her head. She knew that there was Predator footage of westerners being trained in Taliban camps. It was always assumed they were being prepared to undertake suicide missions in the belief that they could enter the United States without arousing suspicion.

'What about the shura?' Faiza had asked. 'We are tracking the arrival of the delegates. We are narrowing down the list of potential meeting places. I think it's going to be at a village in the Madyan Valley...'

'Good work,' Blashford had told her. 'Keep me informed. The two may be connected. But for now we concentrate all efforts on identifying the white Taliban and this means watching the madrassah.'

She was surprised by the sudden change in plan and had pleaded for more time.

'There is nothing I can do. We think they could be planning to use him in a terrorist attack in the United States,' he had insisted. 'It takes precedence.'

She had arrived at the seven o'clock meeting in high spirits. She had fresh Predator footage to show which backed her theory that the shura was still on. One clip showed a party of mounted Taliban emerging on to a pass from the neighboring Dir Valley. There were clips of two other groups trekking into the Swat Valley along two different passes.

'These must be the Taliban leaders on their way to the shura. It looks like they are converging from different directions,' she had declared.

The nighttime photography was too indistinct to reveal anything conclusive about the identities of the men. All the figures were heavily wrapped up, usually in dark clothing.

'Sure, they are. Do we know where they are heading?' Blashford had asked skeptically.

'We must have more time to wait and watch,' she had said. 'We cannot afford to lose them now. Once they are out of the mountains, they could disappear in a town full of people and buildings, or go underground where we couldn't trace them.'

Blashford had put on his glasses and looked down at his report before looking up again.

'Just get me something on this blond guy, will ya?' he said and had then closed the meeting.

Now she sat at the console's desk looking at the images of Mingora and thinking hard. At eight o'clock in Mingora, she saw a western woman come out and start loading the car with the help of a driver. After a while Wilkins came to talk to her.

'They look pretty relaxed, don't they? It looks like she is preparing for a trip,' Miller said. 'I think we can strike them off the list of suspects.'

'Maybe,' Faiza said.

'Look we are wasting our time here. We should be looking elsewhere,' Miller said. 'Who knows why they were staking out this house? We don't even know that they really have a laser pointer, do we?'

She nodded slowly. 'I still think they are something to do with this shura. There is some connection. They were watching this house. We know that,' Faiza said, avoiding his eyes and staring at the screen. But she felt more and more uncertain. She knew the militants' reign of terror in the valley had frightened most of the foreign aid workers away, but so far they had left this small operation alone. It was plucky of them to stay on.

At around eight am Pakistan time they watched Sally and a driver load up a jeep. She noticed they were carrying boxes of what looked like computers.

'Well, these people don't seem very nervous. It looks like a routine trip. They aren't taking any precautions,' Miller noted.

They watched the guard open the gate to the compound and then saw a tall western man come out into the compound to see them off. He waved them goodbye and went back into the house.

'We are wasting our time and the Predator's valuable time. The action must be somewhere else,' Miller said impatiently.

'No, wait a minute,' she said. 'Isn't that the white Taliban? Freeze that image.'

She studied the frame for a minute. 'Yes, I think that's him,' she said. 'But who the hell is he? And what is he doing there?'

Faiza went to sit in the console's empty chair on the other side of the ground control station. She logged on to Echelon and began to trawl through all the cell phone intercepts over the previous six hours. She was still sure that there was connection between the Taliban and the International Grassroots Literacy Foundation. What she really needed to do was to find the cell phone numbers of the staff from the charity so she could track them wherever they went. It might even be possible to download software into the phones which would turn them into listen- ing devices. If the microphones in the phones were activated, she could listen to whatever was said. She fired off a request to Langley.

Next she decided to play back and listen to the recordings of the phone intercepts from numbers linked to Fazlullah. She found there were two hours of recorded phone calls. First she put them all on one single file and then used the voice recognition program which allowed her to search for certain key words. She knew from experience that the militants preferred to speak in an elusive coded manner.

First she tried 'shura' and then 'meeting'. She found ten conversations which used both. She selected these and began to listen to them with excitement. Fortunately, the word 'shura' was used in a number of languages. It was evidence that suggested the shura was imminent but none of the recordings revealed where it was taking place. Then she tried 'al-Zawahiri' and 'Baitul-lah'. She was not surprised that both names came up negative. None of the militants would risk using the correct name or place. They would be too afraid now of being eavesdropped, but they might reveal some clues. For one thing, she would be able to tell something from the tone of the voices, the urgency with which matters were discussed. She felt a certain excitement that she was now on the right track at last and her tiredness vanished. There was nothing for it; she would have to sit down and listen through all the tapes.

She decided to call Blashford and ask for fresh instructions. It was now more important than ever to keep watch on the charity's headquarters and the madrassah. He was excited to hear that the white Taliban had been found. The top priority now was to track him and establish his identity.

'Fantastic job, Faiza. It's all about predictive analysis,' he congratulated her. 'Let's get this fucker. Whatever else happens, keep an eye on him.'

The ground control station now had a full complement of two pilots and two console operators. One team kept watch on Mingora, waiting for the white Taliban to emerge and the other hovered over the madrassah.

Faiza turned to watch the activity at the madrassah. Around nine, there was suddenly a lot of fresh activity. During the night the Predator had been able to fly lower because the crew was sure that the militants couldn't spot it so easily, but as the sun rose it had moved higher. It changed the angles, making it harder to identify each of the actors on the ground. She counted the arrival of four, no five vehicles, two minibuses and three motorcycles. Small groups of armed men were milling around the courtyard inside the compound.

'Can we get closer and see their faces?' she asked the sensor operator. The top down view made it hard to study their faces, but the images became sharper. She saw men with black turbans and shawls which hid their faces, although a few wore white skull caps and the round brown felt Tajik hats.

'It certainly looks like they are getting ready for something,' Miller said. 'It is odd, though; they normally prepare for these sort of things at night.'

'Maybe something urgent has come up,' she said.

'Can you use the facial recognition and identify any of them?' he asked.

'No use, they have all covered their faces,' she said, but she noticed some of them were speaking into the cell phones they had clipped to their vests.

She went back to the console in the other room and began to hunt for the calls that she hoped the Predator was picking up. The surveillance software allowed her to eavesdrop as the signals switched from one cell phone transmission tower to another. There was a great deal of chatter. The militants were clearly intent on some sort of action which had a high priority. One speaker listed the weapons that were needed – automatic rifles, mortars, explosives, grenade launchers – as well as supplies of picks and shovels, cement and wood. She overheard a lengthy debate about the possibility of getting more RPG-7s, a favorite anti-tank weapon, and RPK machine guns.

'What have you got?' Miller asked.

'It sounds like they are preparing a mission, maybe a suicide attack,' she said. 'But I can't tell when and how.'

She listened again for a while. Several of the militants talked about a school and discussed how it could be defended against a possible attack. However, she was unsure what they meant by 'school'. It could be anything, a religious school or a secular school, or simply the name of a building. Then she tried a word search through the recent recordings. She tried 'mission' first in Pashto and then in two other languages. It came up fifteen times. Next she tried 'martyrdom'. That scored seventeen hits. So they were planning something that was certain and probably a suicide mission, but when and where?

And if it was a suicide mission, why would they need to defend themselves? One man had talked about the 'wolves', another mentioned 'hawks' and a third had discussed rumors of resistance by a new lashkar. But who was organizing such a militia in the Swat Valley? She knew that there were a number of possibilities and in the past the Taliban had easily outgunned the local militia. It would be different if the Pakistani military had decided to arm one of the local militia groups. She decided she had better get some help on researching this and was about to call Langley when Miller came back.

'A group of Fazlullah's men is just leaving the compound on a truck,' he said.

They both turned to look at the screen, which showed the truck with half-a-dozen militants perched on top moving through the open countryside, kicking up a trail of dust.

'They are heading north, towards the Madyan Valley, away from Swat,' she said. 'That must indicate they are not going to attack the military or the police.'

'And it doesn't look much like a suicide mission either,' he said. 'They don't seem to care whether they are seen or not.'

Faiza wasn't sure this was so significant.

'It does look like they mean business, though,' she said. 'We have to tag and track them.'

The console operator tapped on to the key board and boxed the truck. Soon they saw that other vehicles were following them. She watched the convoy for ten minutes, trying to figure out what was going on. Perhaps it was connected to the shura in some way. If that was the case, she was determined that to ensure that one of the Predators should be reassigned to follow the vehicles.

She called Blashford again and told him what was going on. He listened carefully. 'We will find out about the lashkar,' he promised. 'But you can't have one of the Predators. Not now.'

'But why?' she said, taken aback.

'Look at what else is happening,' he said.

She looked at the images being relayed back. She watched with surprise as a large western man got out of a car at the entrance to Fazlullah's compound. He could be seen speaking to one of the guards and then waiting.

'It's him, the White Taliban,' Blashford said. She could hear the excitement in his voice.

Fazia watched the scene for a moment, thinking hard. She knew she had to find the means to persuade Blashford to allocate one of the Predators to follow the militants. Or find another one. There was something about this story of the white Taliban that didn't make sense to her. If he had been recruited to a special mission, why would this man turn up unannounced and unexpectedly in a taxi?

30

There were black and white Islamic flags flapping in the breeze above the village mosque but Sally had not noticed them. She had been enjoying the sights and smells of a beautiful morning as they drove from Mingora to Karram, one of the prettiest villages north of Mingora. Through the windows, she sniffed the smell of cows, sheep and horses mixed with freshly cut hay carried by the brisk north wind. The village was a group of mud-and-stone homes sheltered by willow trees and apple orchards. The village lay below dark clusters of virgin pine forest that crowded up the lower slopes of a range of grey rock peaks. She was thinking that she had once taken a fine trail that followed a noisy stream up to the summer pastures and would like to get there again in summer, perhaps with Wilkins. They would take a picnic and collect some flowers. No we won't, she thought stopping herself. He's only here to get out of some trouble in London.

She had been brooding about this all morning. The thought still hurt.

Karram had one of the best junior schools in Swat because its leading families had eagerly seized the opportunity to finance the building of a new school. Aziza had persuaded the village chief to provide the labor and land and Sally's foundation had stepped in to provide the finance. A condition was that the new school would provide enough places for the girls to stay in education long enough to pass the exams and go into higher education. Like everywhere in Pakistan, infant mortality rates were exceptionally high. Most women still gave birth at home.

In their enthusiasm the villagers had put up a rather grand school building next to the village mosque. They had felled trees themselves, hauled logs down the mountain and weathered the timber. So instead of the usual jerry-built cinder block and concrete structure, the school was a solid handsome building. It had several floors, a strong roof and a large meeting hall which served the whole village as a community center.

Sally had found an architect in Islamabad who had delivered the plans for free. You couldn't mistake it for anything but a school. It even had real plumbing with proper toilets and showers for both boys and girls. Some of the kids lived there for part of the year when their families moved up into the high mountains during the summer months to graze their flocks. The children could stay behind and, by staying in dormitories, they could continue their schooling. So it even had a kitchen attached where school lunches and dinners could be cooked.

Everyone else in the valley was envious of Karram. The villagers had built a high wall around it so the children could play inside in safety and it was right next to a mosque with the usual domed roof and minaret. All these things must have attracted the militants' attention. Outside the bigger towns, there was nowhere else as well equipped in the Swat Valley.

Sally had been anticipating a warm giggly welcome with all the girls in their long blue dresses and white shawls coming out to greet her. Many of them knew her by name as she had been there so often. In the back of the jeep, Sally had brought a stack of Oxford English-language text books, but she knew they wouldn't care about that. What they wanted were the eight Toshiba computers, each with a 1.6 gigawatt memory and 500 RAM, eight flat screens, six HP black and white laser printers (second hand), ink cartridges, ten boxes of white A4 paper, eight headphones and all the necessary cables and a bunch of pirated software programs on disks. It was all she could lay her hands on.

For months the teachers had been begging her to install some computers and to bring the village into the digital age. The older kids wanted to go online and connect with the rest of the world. Just how they were going to make that happen, she wasn't sure. They planned to power them up by hooking up some old car batteries. They could access the web later when the telephone lines were restored, although Sally assumed that sooner or later someone would figure out how to get online with a cell phone connection. Still they would be able to start by getting used to working with computers and writing on a keyboard.

It was funny, even here in rural Swat, where Alexander the Great's soldiers had marched,   everyone seemed desperately keen to keep up with the times and be as modern as possible. It was the girls rather than the boys who agitated for the computers. In fact, they were the most disciplined and conscientious kids she had ever seen in her life. It was their only ticket out of the isolated existence of their mothers who spent all their lives shut up in their homes. Even though they could read and write, which was more than could be said for most rural women in Pakistan, they still lived cut off from the world beyond their village. So attendance was high: nothing dented their enthusiasm, not even the threats by the Taliban. They just didn't want to grow up like their mothers. I mean, who does? Sally thought. And because everyone in the village had chipped in to help build the school, there was a real solidarity here. No one here wanted to side with the Taliban if they could possibly help it.

That was why it didn't really click when Sally saw the flags with black Arabic script fluttering over the village. The militants must have descended on to the village late in mid-morning, not long before she had arrived. There was usually just an old watchman on guard and most of the men would have been out in the fields or away on business. They would have met with little resistance and must have quickly herded the frightened girls and teachers into the classrooms.

Sally had first noticed a truck parked in the lane outside the mosque, but had thought nothing of it. If only she had reacted quicker, she thought, they might have got away and raised the alarm. The militants hadn't been expecting them either. When she glanced up at the roof of the mosque, she saw two men in black turbans. One of them was looking in another direction and engrossed in talking into a phone pinned on to his khaki jacket. The other was holding on to his weapon but when he spotted the jeep, he looked uncertain what to do and began slowly raising the weapon to chest height. At that moment Sally's driver saw them, too, and started saying something, but Sally wasn't sure what because she started yelling: 'Zahid, turn round! Now, turn round! Get out of here!'

Zahid put the Toyota Landcruiser in reverse, twisting his head around to steer the jeep through the village. Sally kept her eyes fixed to the front, staring at the man on the roof as he lifted his grenade launcher to his shoulder. She started in disbelief as he hesitantly began to take aim and prepared to fire. The jeep careened wildly from side to side and Sally was thrown to one side. A grenade exploded into a mud-brick wall, showering the car with bits of mud. She started screaming as Zahid swiftly turned the car around so that some of the other houses were now between them and the mosque.

The car bounced down the dirt road as it accelerated. Sally looked at the wing mirror but there was no one in view. When they were 500 yards further down the road, she looked round again to see one of the pick-up trucks in pursuit. 'They are coming,' she shouted. Sally's jeep was faster but some of the fighters who were holding on to the bucking truck began firing with bursts of wild gunfire.

Zahid had his eyes fixed on the road ahead and held on to the steering wheel with both hands, his mouth shut in grim determination as he tried to control the bucking vehicle. At the back the supplies bounced around, shielding them from the gunfire. The gunmen could not steady their aim, but Sally could hear steady bursts of fire behind her. She felt a growing sense of elation. The road took them into a grove of trees which momentarily shielded them from their pursuers. Sally thought that if they could get on to the main road and amongst the traffic, then they would be safe. No one would dare shoot at random with so many other people around.

Then, as the Toyota Land Cruiser came out of the trees, Sally saw a herd of cows led by a young boy ambling across the road. Zahid braked suddenly to avoid hitting them. Sally threw her hands in front to stop herself hitting the dashboard. She heard a sickening thud and then saw Zahid's head against the steering wheel. He was motionless. He had not been wearing a seat belt and his head had struck the hard plastic of the wheel stunning himself. She felt dazed and in shock. She raised her hand to her forehead and felt something wet. She was bleeding. The cows ambled past unconcerned. She pushed at Zahid and he groaned but did not move. She considered pushing him out of the way so she could take over the driving. She could hear the militants' truck getting closer. Then she turned her head round and saw their truck come careening out of the trees and round the bend. It stopped behind them. Three black turbaned men jumped down and approached the jeep slowly. Sally froze in fear unable to force herself to move. They wrenched the door open and pulled Zahid out. He slumped on the ground and one of the men clubbed him on the head with the butt of his assault rifle. Another opened the rear door and began riffling through the boxes of supplies.

The third man looked at Sally through the window and shouted something at her. Sally felt she should not move or do anything to alarm them. He stared uncertainly at her and then began talking to the others. After a brief discussion, they hauled Zahid into the back seat and two men climbed in and sat on either side of him. A third man got into the driving seat and started the engine. They drove back to the school in silence. Sally noticed all the men wore black turbans and long beards. Their faces were hidden behind woolen balaclavas with eyeholes cut out of them. Sally thought it was a good sign that they had not been planning to abduct her but then she began to think hard about their presence in the village. Why were they occupying Karram? What were they planning? When they reached the school, they stopped the jeep and motioned her out. She obeyed and opened the door slowly and started to say something and then thought better of it. Within seconds, they had shoved her into a classroom and bolted the door behind her.

31

Can they hear us?' Shaleema whispered. Her head was hidden in the scarf and she had her arms around one of the younger girls who was crying in deep shuddering breaths. Sally knew Shaleema well. The studious and plump sixteen-year-old with glasses was the star of Karram village's school who had just won a scholarship to study medicine at the Swat Government College and said she wanted to specialize in maternal health care. When she finished, Shaleema said she would return and become the first female doctor to serve the village families.

Sally shook her head slowly and creased her face into a grimace. A crack of light entered through a gap in the crudely made door and glinted off Shaleema's glasses when she lifted her head. Outside the door several men were talking urgently in low voices. Inside about twenty girls crouched huddled together on the beaten earth floor under the teacher's blackboard, clutching each other and whimpering. Sally struggled to keep her own panic in check and to control her thoughts. She steadied herself by taking deep breaths in and out.

Shaleema was now staring at her, waiting for her to take the lead. "These are bad men,' she whispered.

'Sssh, don't worry, they will not hurt us,' Sally said. 'Keep quiet.'

'Sally, I very afraid, very scared. These are Fazlullah's men. They don't like girls' school,' Shaleema said.

'Look I am not scared,' Sally said, keeping her voice steady. She looked directly at the earnest round face with its glasses.

'They hurt you?' 'No, of course not.'

'Yes, you bleeding,' Shaleema said. Sally put her hand up to her brow and found the cut.

'I bumped my head in the car,' she said. 'Nothing to worry about.'

As they talked in low voices, Sally saw the other girls had stopped crying and were beginning to listen to them.

'What happened?' she asked.

'We were studying, before lunch, when these men came in with guns. They shouted at us. They took away the teachers and put us here,' Shaleema said. 'Sally, what do they want?'

'I don't know,' she said. 'Maybe they just want to close the school.'

'Sally, they could just bomb it then, like the other schools.'

The trouble was that Shaleema was too smart to be fobbed off with easy answers. It was true, what she said. If these were Fazlullah's men, then that was their usual practice. Firebombing a school was usually enough to frighten anyone. These men seemed to be following a differ- ent sort of plan.

'Shaleema, where are the other girls?' Sally asked. She reckoned there were about thirty girls here, so there must be another forty somewhere else.

'I think they are in the other classroom,' she said. 'And the boys?

'They told them to go home,' Shaleema said.

'I think your father and the other men will find the imam and they will bring the police,' Sally said. 'Then they will let us go.'

That didn't seem to make much sense even to her, but Shaleema said nothing and seemed to be thinking. They must be hostages, Sally thought. They were being held here for a purpose, but what was it? Even if the news got out, the village men would not dare come out and challenge Fazlullah's men. No one would doubt that Fazlullah was ruthless enough to kill some of their daughters if it served his purpose. What about her? Sally asked herself what he would do to her. She guessed that he would not want to harm a foreign woman. She had arrived here by accident, so her capture wasn't part of any plan. So much was clear. Yet she was now a hostage like all the others.

'If they are keeping us here, they must be having reasons,' Shaleema persisted with obstinate logic.

'Yes, I suppose so,' Sally said after a pause. The trouble was she couldn't think what these reasons could be. Was it money? Karram was a relatively prosperous village. Perhaps some of the men who were working in the Gulf or in Europe could be forced to hand over their savings. Or did they want to blackmail the government as part of some negotiations that she wasn't aware of? Seizing a whole school would certainly send a powerful message. She began to won- der how long they would be prepared to keep them as hostages. They would need to sleep there, and be given food and water.

Sally got up and quickly walked to the door. It had no lock and she stepped out, surprising two men squatting outside and smoking. 'I want to speak to Fazlullah. Now,' she said with all the resolution she could muster. She spoke first in English and then in Pashto. Both men had covered faces so she could only see their eyes. They both stared back blankly. She took another step forward, determined to show confidence. 'We need food and water for the girls. You have no right to keep us here like this. Who is in charge here?'

The taller of the two men stood up, blocking her way, and shook his head slowly. He was wearing loose black trousers and a ragged khaki vest with pockets stuffed with hand grenades and clips of spare bullets. On his bare feet he wore cheap plas- tic sandals. Then he spoke in a surprisingly soft voice to the other man. Sally couldn't recognize the language. It was neither English nor Pashto or any of the other languages spoken in the valley. Perhaps they were Fazlullah's Uzbeks, she thought. The other man laughed. He stood up, too, and nodded. Then he opened the door and indicated with his head that she should go back inside. Sally hesitated. Then she shook her head and folded her arms. The other man laughed, too. He put down his gun, made a shushing sound and gestured with his hands as if he was herding goats into a fold.

The classroom door opened into a small sheltered courtyard which served as the play-ground. In the center a large tree with benches around the trunk provided shade. It was the classroom nearest to the entrance gate, two metal doors which opened into the street. The compound had three other classrooms and the washrooms and dormitories were in the rear. Opposite was another wall with a small door which led into the compound of the mosque. Above the wall Sally could see the dome of the mosque and looked up at the small minaret tower. There were two men up there keeping watch, holding up binoculars and staring into the distance, scouring the skies.

'Look up there,' she shouted and pointed. The two men turned round immediately. Sally took off, running hard for the door. She reached it and pushed it open before they could follow. In the street, she stopped, looked right and then left. There was no one in sight. In one direction, she could saw the road which went out of the village into the trees. In, the other she spotted the jeep, still parked behind the truck. Her heart gave a leap. It was still there and she could make it. She sprinted for the jeep and reached in less than a minute. She darted round to the driver's door and was relived to find it was unlocked. Sally felt a breathless hope. No one was going to stop her now. She wrenched open the door, praying that the keys would still be in the ignition lock. Behind her she sensed the two men chasing her were just behind. She dived across the driver's seat and stretched across to find her bag still lying between the seats. One of the men reached to grab her right leg. She kicked out at him. He stepped back, surprised. It gave her enough time to slither into the driver's seat and put her hand on the ignition key. She managed to start the engine. The engine began to fire. This time the man grabbed her shoulder violently with one arm and with the other, slammed his fist into her face. She twisted her face away so he struck her head and at the same time reached for the stick shift, and the jeep jolted forward. This time the man used all his strength and dragged her out of the jeep as she held on to the steering wheel. She fell awkwardly on to the ground as the jeep slid forward.

'Let me go!' she screamed. She continued screaming and felt oblivious to the pain just a kind of hysteria. He struggled with her, grabbing her arms and then slapping her hard in the face. The shock stunned her and stopped moving for a second. This gave the other man the opportunity to grab her legs but by this time she didn't care. She had done what she had hoped to do and she went limp. She knew that the men believed she was trying to escape. Together, the two men picked her up and carried her back through the door into the courtyard. Then they pushed open the door to the classroom and tossed her in like a sack of potatoes.

She lay in a sobbing heap for a moment. None of the girls moved for a while. Then Shaleema came over to her and wiped her face clear of the hair and tears. 'Why did you do this?' she said.

Sally lay for a while, breathing heavily, until she recovered. Then she raised herself and took out of her shirt a small cell phone that she had concealed and held it up. 'For this,' she said triumphantly.

32

From the moment that Stoner had walked in the door, Wilkins had started thinking about escape. Of all the thirty-six strategies, he had read somewhere, running away was the best. Stoner he could have dealt with alone, but he had walked in with a couple of armed men in tow. Stoner didn't introduce them, but then he didn't need to; they had the long hair and beards of militants. They simply leaned their weapons against the wall and squatted on the ground, smoking and looking at the two men.

'Well, if it isn't Dr Livingstone, I presume,' Wilkins said. Out of his white pasty face, Stoner's small eyes looked at him coldly for a moment. Then he smiled. 'No, that's my line, isn't it? I think you will find that my role has been that of Mr Stanley. And besides, we have already been formally introduced.'

It was typical of him to sound cleverer and better informed than anyone else. 'You must know that the Grosvenor Bank is very concerned about you and your unexplained absence.

Mervyn asked me especially to come and find you. This was not an easy matter.'

'Come off it, Stoner, cut the crap. Tell me what you want.' Wilkins looked him straight in the face. 'Does Mervyn know what you are really up to?'

Stoner said nothing, but raised his eyebrows.

'I thought so. He still thinks you are the good guy. Have you told him how you recruited me?'

'Mervyn and all the rest were too stick in the mud to grasp the brilliant opportunities. No one running that wretched bank had the faintest idea about the potential of sophisticated computerized trading,' Stoner said evasively. 'Every trader knows that big money is made when new products start up and only a few firms are getting in on the action. This is when risk management controls are slow to catch up. We had to move quickly.'

'So he doesn't know yet,' Wilkins said. 'Does he realize that it was you who was mismarking the overnight forex trades?'

'He knows it was you who ran away. He knows you blew a huge hole in the bank's capital, but he doesn't know how exactly. And he knows we have to find a lot of money quickly, very quickly or the Landesbank deal is off.'

'You mean that the bank goes under." 'Precisely.'

'And so? It looks like I am well out of it.'

'Not so fast. You misunderstand one thing. Mervyn thinks very highly of you. Your trading skills, that is, not your morals, of course. Actually, he thinks you are a bit of a financial genius, even if you have trouble hiding yourself. The absurd notion that you have a Midas touch is an idea that I have actively encouraged. He wants you to come back, reinvest the money that you have stolen and cover up the hole in the capital reserves.' Stoner stopped there.

'And all would be forgiven?'

'The alternative is that you go to jail for a very long time. Or worse,' he said and then looked at the two men who were watching them curiosity.

'You are bluffing. Why on earth do you think that I would fall this crock of shit?' Wilkins said. 'You and the Grosvenor Bank can go to hell. I am staying here.'

Stoner sighed heavily. 'You can unlock the money and use the program to make up for the losses, and you can be back here in a month or so – if, of course, you really do like it here so much,' he persisted. 'Which I for one very much doubt.' He looked around the compound with a sneer.

'You blackmailed me into working for the bank once, but you won't do it a second time," Wilkins said as obstreperously as he could. He thought that the more he was hard to get the better.

'A few weeks after I met you, the college received an anonymous tip-off that some research students were indulging in dealing and consuming Class A drugs,' he said. 'My rooms were searched and, surprise, surprise, they found some smack. Funny, that. The affair was hushed up, of course. The college was averse to bringing in the police, so there were no prosecutions, but I had to find a new career.'

Wilkins was still taken aback by the fact that Stoner had found him so quickly. How had he done that? As he fenced with Stoner, one part of his mind focused on answering the question. He could see that Stoner had a drained, exhausted look. There were dark patches under his eyes and two days of stubble on his face. His clothes, khaki safari pants, had the sort of wrinkles you only get from sleeping in them. Somebody must have helped him to get into the Swat Valley and he certainly had not arrived here in an air-conditioned jeep. If someone was helping him, they must be exacting a price. Stoner must be being squeezed by both sides.

'Whichever way you look at it, you have a great deal of money which does not legally belong to you. You cannot realistically expect to retain such a large amount, can you?' Stoner said levelly.

'You forget I invented the algorithm. I was the one who applied quantitative analysis,' he said.

'You would still be a feckless student playing in a rock band, if it wasn't for me,' Stoner countered swiftly.

'So you are saying the money is yours?' Wilkins said. It was easy enough to needle Stoner but somehow he had to negotiate a deal with him.

'Wilkins, we are offering you a way out here. It's a risk, I see that, but we thought someone like you would not be frightened of a gamble,' Stoner said reasonably.

'OK,' Wilkins said, 'you'd better come inside.' They went into the sitting-room of the charity headquarters and took seats on the tatty sofas facing each other. The two Pashtuns stayed outside. Sally had not returned yet and they could talk in private before the evening meal was served. Wilkins decided his best option was slowly to give in to Stoner's arguments. He made it clear that he wasn't going to give Stoner the password to the accounts in London, but instead concentrated on negotiating the terms for his return to the bank. Stoner was prepared to offer certain guarantees for his safety and security once in London. Yet the reality was that he was already Stoner's prisoner, whether he was here or in London. The chances of escape were better here, though.

When Sally didn't return, they ate a meal of mutton and noodles at the kitchen table. Wilkins told Stoner about his experiences in the Swat Valley, the trout fishing, the efforts made to help with the girls' schools, and his encounter with Fazlullah. He explained how he had been forced to pretend to be a Muslim convert and that he was now required to behave like one, which meant attending regular prayers. Stoner listened in silence.

Wilkins also tried to draw out Stoner on the identity and loyalties of his bodyguards, but Stoner was evasive. He said they were there for his protection in view of the general lack of law and order in Pakistan. Wilkins told him about the violence in the Swat and the murders he had witnessed, so when he said that next morning he would have to return to the mosque.

'If I don't go it will be suspicious. They would come after me, I might not be able to leave,' he explained. 'Fazullah's men have check posts along the main roads.'

Stoner looked unconvinced.

'The mosque is close by. You could send one of the guards with me,' Wilkins proposed. 'We'd be back before you were awake.'

Stoner reluctantly nodded his head. He looked too tired to argue. Wilkins thought that he convinced he had won and that Wilkins was now prepared to cooperate with him, one way or another.

Before they retired to bed, Wilkins overheard heard him speaking on the phone and talking to London telling someone, he presumed it was Mervyn, that he had found Wilkins and that they were now making plans to return to London. Wilkins started making his own plans. He lay wide awake for a long time.

33

Just as the prayers were ending, Wilkins stood up and dodged round the front row of worshippers just as they were rising to their feet. Wilkins looked straight ahead and was sure his guard was still prostrate. Step one, he thought. Step two, don't look back and keep moving confidently. All night he had been rehearsing in mind what he would do, going through the sequence of events in his mind. He had broken in down into steps There would be only seconds to get out before the guard realized what he was up to. His first worry had been to get to the mosque early enough to grab a spot directly opposite the small door which opened behind the imam's pulpit but not too early that he would attract any unwelcome attention. As he stood up to move, he felt so nervous that he jerked upright and stood there for second. Then he lowered his head and in six strides reached the door, stretched out his arm and grasped a small knob. He had no idea if it would be locked but it opened easily. Step three done. He had a loud red and white checkered head scarf around his neck and he wrapped this now around his head. Once through the door, he passed two offices was then reached a small yard through an open doorway. He forced himself not to run.

Across the yard there was a back gate which opened into a busy street which would take him straight to the Green Chowk. He sensed behind him that the guard was following. He knew the back gate was open. He pushed through and turned right along the wall that ran around the mosque. Wilkins was now momentarily out of sight. Step four accomplished. He whipped off his red and white shawl and pulled another one out of his jacket. It's a drab dark brown shawl. He wrapped round his head so it covered most of his face and stuffed the other inside the front of his jacket.

In front of him, he saw that the stallholders were busy setting out their wares, but there were plenty of people about. He moved quickly into the street which was filling up with motorcycle rickshaw taxis and farmers pushing carts of vegetables to the market place. Step five, he noted. He was sure that anyone looking for him in the street would be searching for the red and white checkered head dress because that would be all that was visible about the trestle tables and awnings of the market vendors. In a few minutes of fast walking he had reached the bus station where there were more people milling about. Then Wilkins began breathe easier. He squeezed through an alley between two houses and hid himself in the ruined walls of the burnt out police station. Then he stood still for a minute holding his breath and straining to hear any sounds of pursuit. Step

5. Then he changed out of baggy shalwar kameez and buried the trousers and shirt under a pile of rubble. He was now dressed in a western shirt and jeans under his thick winter jacket. He kept on the shawl and put on some sunglasses and headed off in a new direction to find a taxi rank.

I've done it, he thought to himself. A clean pair of heels. Now the guard will be looking for a man in a chequered scarf wearing a white shalwar kameez. Once the guard had lost track of him, his only option would be to head back to the charity offices and summon help. The seventh step would now to get in a taxi. Mingora wasn't a big city, but big enough to get lost in. All Wilkins now had to do was to get into one of the beaten-up taxis or a motorized rickshaw and he was free.

It can't be that easy, Wilkins thought as he headed off in the direction of the taxi pick up spot. He walked more slowly confident no one was paying him any particular attention. At the far end of the market place, he found the usual group of men standing around their taxis. He picked one which had a roof and plastic flaps which would make it hard for anyone to see who was inside. Without looking the driver in the face, he gave the name of Fazlullah's village at Imam Delhi. The driver, pleased to get a long distance fare, nodded his head and Wilkins squeezed into his seat. It wasn't the fastest mode of transport, he thought but it was probably the most inconspicuous.

The noisy two-stroke engine took them through the town and they were soon out of Mingora and heading north. After ninety minutes, the motorcycle stopped at a turning which led off the main road to Fazlullah's headquarters. Wilkins got out and paid the driver and then stood there uncertainly.

A dirt road shaded by poplar trees led past the fields to the white walls of the compound. It had the forbidding look of a prison with high walls and several watchtowers. Now that he was here, the idea of putting himself in the hands of a murderous fanatic like Fazlullah no longer seemed so appealing, but he could think of no better idea. He couldn't just take off into the mountains and try to disappear.

As he walked down the road, he knew he was being watched. At the entrance two guards patted him down and motioned for him to wait. Inside, he stared at the main building, a half-finished long white concrete building with arches. Normally the space in front of the building should have been packed with loads of students, militants and visitors milling around. He wondered why it looked so quiet and whether Fazlullah was still there. After a while, one of the guards brought a cup of black tea, but he rejected it impatiently, asking again for Fazlullah and then for Malik. No one seemed to speak English and Wilkins felt worried. The euphoria of the escape had gone.

At length a tall bearded man in a white shalwar kameez, a white skull cap and sneakers came out and looked at him curiously. He stood up to look him in the eye. He was nearly as tall as Wilkins. 'What is your business here? What do you want?' he said, unsmiling. He didn't offer his hand or introduce himself. Wilkins explained that he was a Muslim convert from England, a friend of Fazlullah who had given him zakat and needed to see him on an urgent matter.

'Fazlullah is very busy now,' the man said curtly. 'What about Malik?'

'He is dead,' the man said flatly.

'I have very important news for Fazlullah. He needs to know this,' Wilkins persisted, giving him a big confident smile. 'He is in danger from American spies.'

The man eyed him coldly for moment. Then he turned away. 'Wait here,' he commanded. He walked across the square and disappeared into the white building. After half an hour he came back and motioned Wilkins to follow him. They walked into the building and then down some steps to the basement. Fazlullah was there and he greeted Wilkins without a smile. This time he was wearing a camouflage jacket and looking deadly serious. Wilkins pretended not to notice and strode forward with a generous smile and said Salaam Aleikkum. Fazlullah didn't respond, but motioned him to sit on some cushions on the ground. A small handsome youth came in, bringing cups of sweetened tea.

'You may talk now,' the other man said. Wilkins felt his confidence ebbing away and a sense of fear. He started talking quickly and nervously, explaining that Fazlullah was in danger from a spy who had arrived in the valley several days ago. He told them he was working for the CIA and must be arrested. Then he launched into a description of Stoner, describing his features. Fazlullah pricked his ears at the mention of CIA and listened intently to the translation without moving. When Wilkins had finished, he spoke in his low rumbling voice. The two men ignored him and carried on their conversation in low intense tones.

'What do you know about CIA drones?' the interpreter said, looking at him closely and judging his reaction. Wilkins was caught off-balance.

'Nothing,' he said.

'Then how do you know this man, Stoner, is a spy?'

Wilkins couldn't see the connection. He wasn't even sure he knew what a drone was and whether he should admit this. The man stared at him hard and then said something to Fazlullah who just grunted. Wilkins felt uneasy.

'Fazlullah thinks it is you who are a spy,' he said. He stood up and clapped his hands. Three men came into the room. Two of them pulled Wilkins to his feet and grabbed his arms. He felt so surprised and scared that he barely reacted. A third took out a blindfold and covered his eyes. Then he was marched out of the room and pushed down the corridor. He heard a padlock opening before being shoved into a room and left alone. His hands had been tied and he staggered against rough concrete walls. He walked around the small space and then sat down on the floor.

It had all happened so quickly that he'd had no time to respond. Wilkins realized that he was now a prisoner and no one knew where he was. They could do anything they wanted to him, even kill him. At least, he thought, he was out of Stoner's hands. Yet he felt very alone for the first time since he had arrived in Mingora. Then he began to think that perhaps there was a way to turn this to his advantage. Surely there was but what was it? It would be very convenient if the world believed that he was dead, a victim of the Taliban's brutality. There had to be way out of this, if only he could figure what they had been saying about these drones and why that was so important to them. That must be the key, he thought, to getting their attention back.

If they really thought he was an American spy, then they would have to interrogate him. They wouldn't just leave him here to rot. And surely they wouldn't just let Stoner run around Mingora as he pleased? All he needed to do was somehow give them something that would bolster his credentials, but what would that be? If he didn't he could rot here for weeks. No one even knew where he was.

34

Stoner had been slow off the mark when he woke up. He had needed a long sleep. The thick woolen blankets smelling of old mutton fat had made him warm and drowsy, reluctant to get up. He knew there was a long drive to Islamabad ahead but this nightmare was ending. By the end of the day he could be sipping a flute of champagne in first class, the FT on his lap, back in the familiar civilized world. He had walked downstairs and gone into the kitchen and made himself some instant coffee, helping himself to the kettle which was boiling on the stove. There was no one else around, so he imagined it was still early. Looking through the kitchen window at the back of the building, he could see over the rooftops, the sunlight spreading across the snow on the lofty peaks. He had felt sort of warm himself; it was the glow of self-congratulation and contentment.

It took a while for him to realize that he was all alone. The complex of office, kitchen and living quarter were so quiet he could hear a fax machine printing out sheets of paper. The office had an answerphone, too, and he could hear the beeps and recordings going on. Hullo, he thought, someone sounds desperate. They keep ringing back and leaving more messages. It sounded like Sally's voice. So he got up and went outside into the courtyard to see if anyone else was about. It was empty.

He ran back into the living quarters and saw that Wilkins's stuff was still there scattered on the floor and on the bed, a great confusion of shirts, pants, vests, a few paperbacks, a notebook and all sorts of other rubbish. His bag was still there, too, but there was no sign of him. Stoner felt a knot of fear like a contraction start in his stomach. He began to search through the bag for Wilkins' passport and wallet. Neither was there, but everything else was.

Then he heard sounds in the courtyard and ran down the stairs to see one of Ahmed's gunmen slouching back through the gate. He had a scowl on his face. Seeing Stoner, he turned away, looking frightened and angry. The other man came in and they both ignored Stoner and embarked on a loud shouting match in Pashto. When they had exhausted themselves in the argument, they hoisted their guns, slung them over their shoulders and stalked out.

Stoner shouted at them in English, 'Where is he? Where's Wilkins?' They looked back at him blankly and walked on. At Stoner's request, Ahmed had given them instructions. They had to intimidate Wilkins and make sure he went back with Stoner. All they had to do was to keep an eye on him until he got into the jeep that would take them to Islamabad. Stoner didn't even know their names. They must have lost Wilkins somehow and were now clearing off.

At that moment, Stoner's sense of unease turned to fear. He knew this had gone monstrously wrong and he had to fix it quickly. He had to move fast or Wilkins might disappear for good. He went through the options: he could wait for Sally to get back, or at least wait for her staff to turn up for work. That was the sensible thing to do. Yet he felt it was odd that no one was here now. Or should he go out and try to find Wilkins himself?

Stoner stood there, hesitating. He knew he couldn't find his way around Mingora by himself. The best option was to find Ahmed. He had the men and the contacts who could track Wilkins down once more.

Stoner pulled on some pants and ran out into the street. He thought he could retrace his steps. He had left Ahmed at the headquarters of the militants. There couldn't be more than one or two in town, so he should be able to find someone who could speak English and show him the way. Without further thought, Stoner left the compound, turned left down a narrow street and headed towards the center of town. Now he cursed himself for being panicked into rushing. He wished he had stopped for one moment, and at least scribbled a note to say where he was going.

He had walked on impatiently, pushing past the other pedestrians, consumed by a growing anger at Wilkins' betrayal. The attack took him unawares. His assailants seem to come out of the blue. The first thing he felt was a man aggressively grabbing his left arm and then a thud against his back and a sharp pain across the back of his legs. He looked round in surprise but before he could take anything in, he fell to the ground on his knees. Several more violent blows on his back knocked the wind out of him as he struggled to get back up. One of the assailants wrenched his arms behind him and he cried out in pain. Stoner struggled to raise his head and made an effort to shout at the passersby for help, then he was hit again, this time a blow against the side of his head. He was aware the street was crowded with people but no one seemed to be paying any attention. At the same time, he became aware of a loud and insistent honking from a car that was edging its way closer through the street. Then he saw a Landcruiser that drew up beside them. Before he could offer any resistance, the men bundled him into the back seat. One got in next to him and the other climbed in on the other side.

'I've been kidnapped,' he thought despairingly. Before he could open his mouth, he felt a hood being thrust over his head. One of the men shoved his head down, keeping a strong grip on the back of neck. No one said a word and the jeep started jerking forward. By now, Stoner had met enough Taliban to know who these men were. Next he heard some wailing Pakistani music being played and the vehicle gradually gathering speed. Stoner could feel the fear rising in him and he began breathing faster and faster, struggling to catch his breath. He fought hard to control his body and struggled with the panicky feeling that he was suffocating, that he just couldn't get enough air inside him. Everything he done since coming to Pakistan had been wrong, he thought. There was no one here he could trust and the thought made him feel that he was drowning underneath a wave and whatever he did he could never make it the surface.

The journey wasn't long and it was still mid-morning when they shoved him out of the car and dragged him stumbling and staggering into a building. Two other men seemed to be waiting for him inside and felt himself being held on both sides. Stoner sensed their impatience. They kept his head in the hood, re-tied his hands more firmly behind his back and then thrust him down onto his knees.

'What is your name?' he heard a voice ask.

'Stoner,' he replied. 'Please, take off this hood and tell me what you want from me.'

'You are American spy, a CIA man,' the voice stated coldly. 'What are you doing here?'

Stoner shook his head.

'I can't help you. You have made a mistake,' he said trying to remain calm and to sound reasonable and cooperative.

'Where have you hidden the laser pointer? We know you brought it with you. Give to us. When is the Predator coming?'

'What the hell is a predator?' he said. 'What laser pointer? What is this about?'

In the brief silence that followed, Stoner wondered what they would want. A laser pointer was something you used in a Power Point presentation. What did these psychos want with such a thing? It was almost laughable. Imagine Osama bin Laden in his cave doing a point and talk slide show. Key points; torture, murder, bombs, and jihad, plus the consolidation of budgets

The man repeated the same questions three times with mounting irritation. Then Stoner heard another voice speaking. This man started shouting in Pashto. Then he heard the first man speak in English. He kept his voice steady and neutral. 'If you do not cooperate now, we will kill you,' he said. 'You must believe this. Tell the truth and you will live.'

Then the beating began. After each question and answer, he was struck by a stick or a truncheon just above the elbow or on the leg just behind the knee. After some time, he didn't know how long, the questioning stopped. He heard the interrogator with the deep voice leave the room. 'He is very angry,' the translator said. 'You must talk or he will simply kill you.'

Stoner groaned. When the beating stopped, he felt a fierce tingling pain spreading through his limbs. He could barely move but he summoned his last strength and made another plea. 'I keep telling you again and again. I am not American. I am not CIA. I am English, I work at the Grosvenor Bank in London and I came here to find someone. Look at my passport. Call the bank. If you want money, they will help you.'

At one level, Stoner assumed that even the most stupid interrogator would realize that they had the wrong man. If the threat of immediate execution didn't elicit the response they expected, he thought they would have to reconsider.

The other man now sounded almost sympathetic. 'It is no good saying these things. This is not about money,' he said. Then he lifted the hood over Stoner's head enough to bring a glass to his lips. Stoner drank from it and felt relieved. He felt a glimmer of hope that at last he was understood and believed. A sense of gratitude towards this stranger welled up inside him. The man was tall and thin but with large dark liquid eyes but he didn't seem cruel or stupid. 'Tell me how money you want. The Grosvenor Bank is rich, they can pay you million, two million, three million dollars. I can help you arrange this,' he pleaded.

'You do not understand, it is not because of ransom. We are Jihadis fighting against the American dogs for Islam. We do not fear death and we not care for money. That man is Fazlullah. He controls the Swat Valley. He has killed many enemies before. He can kill you whoever you are, wherever he chooses,' the man said with soft concern.

One of the men brought out a large meat cleaver and placed it in front of him so he could see it.

'This is what they would use for the execution, if you do not cooperate now,' the man said. Stoner looked at it. Its edge was dark with encrusted blood.

'We cut off the heads of infidels and spies, that is the Islamic way,' he said patiently.

The soft earnest voice reminded Stoner of a teacher patiently censoring a difficult student but he realized, too, that whoever he was, he wasn't a student or a teacher but a fanatic. It was the voice of someone who was impervious to reason.

35

Stoner felt someone else was in the room. He had thought he had heard the door open and then the click of the light switch. He tried lifting his hands to his eyes and scrabbled at the blindfold. He could lift his hands up and down the pipe and duck his head forward but not far enough to reach his hands. As Stoner sat chained to the pipe, he heard that voice again. 'Get up,' it commanded. Stoner did as he was told. The man came over, unlocked the chains, freed his hands and helped him on to his feet. 'You come with me,' he said and held his arm as he steered him out. They walked up some stairs and then came out of the building and into the open.

Stoner's hands were pulled behind his back and tied tightly with string. Then the man took off his hood. The sun was high in the sky now and bright. Stoner looked around him and saw a group standing at the other end of the open ground. There were about five of them and two were prisoners, a man and woman.

Stoner could see they were locals from their dress. It was the woman who caught his attention. She was dressed in a black shapeless dress and shawl with her head and face covered, but she stood erect and defiant without moving. The man was bare-headed, with cropped grey hair and a handsome clean-shaven face and he had tears on his cheeks.

The interpreter, who was standing behind him, spoke: 'This is for you. If you do not talk now, Fazlullah will execute this man and then this woman. They are adulterers. They have broken the law and are already condemned.'

Stoner looked at them without speaking. They were about twenty yards away. He could see the executioner holding the cleaver loosely in his hand, awaiting a command.

'If you do not start speaking now, they will meet their deserved punishment.'

Stoner dropped slowly on to his knees wincing with pain. He held out his hands in supplication. 'I beg you, you must believe me. I have no information or knowledge whatsoever about drones or the CIA. Even if you kill them, I will not be able to help you.'

The interpreter spoke first in Pashto and then switched to English. 'We do not believe you.'

The condemned couple did not look at Stoner, but turned their heads upwards to look above Stoner to a man standing on the balcony. Stoner twisted head round and looked up and saw a big bearded man standing there, surrounded by a group of other gunmen. He realized this was Fazlullah and saw him nod his head and growl 'Allah Akbar'.

Across the courtyard, two of the militants grabbed the man and forced him on to his knees, while a third stood to one side and lifted the cleaver. In an instant, he brought the cleaver down on the man's neck, severing the head. The body fell to one side.

The woman screamed. Stoner noted with revulsion that the whole thing was being filmed by a man with a small camera who had hovered around the execution group and then stood over the corpse taking close-ups of the head and the pools of blood.

Stoner felt sick and dizzy. A bout of nausea came over him and he began to retch dryly. In his shock he could barely hear what the interpreter was saying to him. He was lifted to his feet and shaken by the man. He was speaking to him in that earnest patient way, talking about Islam and Islamic justice, but the voice reached him from far away. Fear paralyzed Stoner and he could not respond or take in what the man was saying to him in his ear. Within a few minutes, he knew that they were going to kill him, too. He was helpless to stop it.

The thought came to him with a sudden clarity. What if he was the person they believed him to be, a CIA operative, and what if he told them what he wanted, would they let him live? No, not a chance. Stoner began to shake his head from side to side, anything to drown out the urgent whispering from the man behind him. He kept shaking his head, beginning to cry hysterically. There was no way out of this. He had been just a few hours away from finishing the job and clearing out of Pakistan; now he would die in this nameless place.

The man shook him by the shoulders. Then he started slapping Stoner's face on either side. 'Listen, sir! You must stop this. Give up this pretending. You are fooling no one,' he said.

Stoner stopped crying. Then his despair swung suddenly to anger and he struggled with his tied hands and tried to hit him, screaming with rage. Unable to free his arms or hands, Stoner tried to butt him with his head. The man stepped back, surprised by the aggression.

Before Stoner's anger burnt out, Fazlullah came up to him and began to strike him with a stick. Stoner fell to the ground and lay there in a fetal position until the beating stopped. He could hear Fazlullah and the other men deliberating. They ignored him for a moment.

Stoner slowly lifted himself and got up. He was shaky, but OK now. His composure returned to him and he began to breathe in and out slowly and to think rationally again. Maybe being ignorant had its advantages. Until he gave them what they wanted, they wouldn't kill him, would they? His only hope was to keep stringing them along and just to bluff his way out of this. What the hell did they know about drones and that stuff anyway? He would just have to wing it.

As Stoner was thinking these thoughts and getting a grip on himself, he heard a kerfuffle behind him. He turned round and saw another man being dragged up the steps and frog-marched to the killing ground. He had a hood over his head and was dressed as a Pakistani in a shalwar kameez. But the big physique and the gait struck Stoner as familiar.

The prisoner walked and was half pushed across the square by two guards. When they reached the execution spot, they tied his hands firmly at his back and then took off the hood. It was Wilkins.

His hair and beard were matted and disheveled, but it was him. He stood straight as a pillar, with the corners of his mouth turned down in a half bitter smile and looked straight at Stoner. He stared back stunned.

'If you do not speak now, we will kill your friend,' the interpreter said.

36

The Predator was orbiting six thousand feet over the Karram village in the Swat Valley unseen and unheard. Over seven thousand miles away, Faiza sat in the darkened control room concentrating hard on the images displayed on half-a-dozen LED screens. At mid-day in Nevada the desert sun hit directly on the GCS's trailer, heating the metal roof. The air-conditioning unit kept it cool and above its low efficient hum Faiza could hear one team, two intelligence coordinators and a pilot, calmly talking amongst themselves. Another sporadic conversation took place in the adjoining room between another pilot and two senior coordinators.

She could hear Miller talking to someone about his weekend trips to the desert. He was talking about copperheads, a kind of snake. 'They are unique. They wait patiently at night in ambush for their prey, but they can't see or hear them. They just sense when the mouse or rat is nearby because they sense its body heat.'

She tried to shut their voices out her mind and focus on her own thoughts. Something was wrong out there and it was up to her to see it. Then she listened, intrigued by the story.

'A copperhead has this heat-sensing nerve between its eyes and its nose. It's like they can detect infrared radiation. They sense the warmer body nearby and then they pounce,' he was saying.

She overheard someone expressing disbelief.

'It is true. A scientist did an experiment. He filled one balloon with cold water and another with hot water. Then he put the snake down and turned off the lights. The snake attacked the warm balloon and sank its fangs into it, bursting the balloon,' Miller said.

If a snake could do it, then so could the Predator, Faiza thought. Four hours earlier three Predators had taken off from bases Jalalabad and Shamshi in Pakistan. Each of the Predators was loaded with two Hellfire missiles but Captain Miller told her that two missiles would be enough. They planned to strike at four am so there were three hours left.

Faiza could hear the members of the two teams chatting calmly amongst themselves. She could see why they felt there was nothing to worry about. There was nothing moving in the school compound, the mosque or the village streets. At one in the morning the whole village had settled down to sleep. The Predators' cameras swept the whole area around the village and the roads leading to it.

It was a clear night with a bright moon. The greyscale images showed up the shadow cast by the minaret tower on the square roofs of the schoolrooms next door. She could see their flags flapping in the breeze. There were a dozen vehicles parked on the road outside, but their engines were cold. If they had been running, the heat would have shown them up on the screen as a brighter white shape. The infrared was good enough for her to identify the position of the guards on the minaret, another group inside the school gates and a third group guarding the entrance to the village. If any of them had used their guns recently, then it did not show up on the infrared.

Each group of men had been tagged, so even if they moved, the Predators could simply track and destroy them at the press of a button. The vehicles had been tagged, too. The Predators had tracked Fazlullah's Toyota Landcruiser from the headquarters to the village. A dozen other vehicles had arrived after him.

As long as the bodies targeted were the right ones, the missile guidance system left almost no room for human error. The 45 kg Hellfire missiles were accurate to within a meter. One could destroy a single classroom and leave the others standing. The village itself would be left completely unharmed, provided that the team had correctly identified the right people.

That was the question. She stared again at screens and the indistinct images of the buildings. Who exactly was in the school? Was she really sure al-Zawahiri was there?

They had relied on deductive analysis rather than positive identification. After night had fallen, the Predators had shown parties of men and animals moving along mountain tracks from two directions. She had no doubt that a gathering of some sort was taking place in the village. After she came on duty she had read the summary report of the operation. It had said that the villagers had been ordered to stay in their homes. Around the village she could now clearly identify both the distinct shapes of sheep and cattle and the Taliban guards. All of them produced a core thermal image, a reddish brown and yellow glow.

Yet none of the Predators could provide a definitive visual identification of any of the men they sought. Once the men had entered the buildings, the thermal imaging was useless because the walls blocked the emission of heat. Even with the best image enhancement, the intelligence team had not been able to identify any of the men as they entered the village either by vehicle or on foot. They had never been able to paint al-Zawahiri with a laser designator.

She hated the man with his pious white beard and earnest glasses and she could not stop herself going back to the memory of her father and his savage death in Kandahar nine years earlier. She could still see her father's body swinging from a tree near the center of Kandahar after the Taliban had seized power in 1999. She relished the thought of him getting up and winding his turban, preparing to go to his morning prayers and unaware that the short stubby missiles would soon drop from the Predator and fly as a fast as a bullet until they struck him at the center of the crosshairs. She saw in her mind the cloud of black and white dust convulsing in the air. She would have preferred that his death would take place in a more public and humiliating manner, with the man pleading for his life. It was a pity that he would never know that she had been responsible for his death, but it was still revenge. She would be proud that she had managed to play a role in his death.

For a moment, though, she wondered if her thirst for revenge was blinding her judgment. She wanted to be certain, to make this count, in case she never got a chance like this again. Before returning to duty, she had lain awake in a small sterile room, tossing and turning. Her excited mind had refused to stop working. Several times she got up to adjust the blinds and shut out the strong Mojave Desert light. Why, she wondered, had the Air Force at Creech been assigned to take out al-Zawahiri at the shura? Why were they not using the drones operated by the CIA from the Langley Airbase?

She reached an obvious conclusion: if the mission failed, the Air Force could be blamed and the CIA would minimize its responsibility. And why had Blashford designated her as the intelligence coordinator here at Creech? She was one of the first non-US born citizens recruited by the CIA in the war of terror. Of course, they needed her because she spoke Arabic and Pashtun, especially the Kandahar dialect. But maybe that, too, was a way of reassigning blame in the event of a disaster.

In the propaganda war, successful suicide missions in Pakistan counted for little in comparison with a strike in the United States, preferably against a prominent target. That was why Blashford had become so convinced that he would use a white convert to Islam. An individual with no record in terrorism could slip unnoticed into the United States because they would be on no one's watch list. When he saw the Predator's footage of a white man going into the Fazlullah's headquarters, he was sure that he had been enlisted for a major mission so important that al-Zawahiri had arrived in person to oversee the planning. Then there were transcripts of intercepted phone calls which had been analyzed at the National Geospatial Intelligence Agency, all of which supported the theory that the shura was taking place. Phone intercepts had clearly referred to a shura taking place in the Swat Valley.

For Blashford, it was a perfect example of the Snowflake Principle. It didn't matter how many small screw-ups there might be along the way, as long as you hooked the big one. He knew that if the Americans deployed the Predators in the Swat Valley, they risked raising such an outcry in Pakistan that it might bring an end to the use of drones in the North- West frontier. But if they got al-Zawahiri, the real mastermind be-hind 9/11, they could deal with that.

But who was that white guy? And why was he walking around in broad daylight? His head and face and been largely obscured, but he was unmistakably a westerner. She could even tell that from the way that he walked. They still hadn't been able to clarify his identity but she thought there was something fa-miliar about him. She felt sure he had appeared in some earlier footage, but where she couldn't recall. She had viewed so many hours of real time video transmissions, sometimes it showed what you were looking for, but often it showed something im-portant but you didn't realize it at the time. There were three shifts of analysts working on the opera-tion and 250 pilots on hand and a squadron of drones was circling the skies above the Swat Valley. With military drones and CIA drones taking off from fields in Pakistan and Afghanistan, it needed thousands of analysts to digest all this information. None could keep track of it all, let alone make sense of it.

Then she considered the role of Pakistan intelligence. Blashford had been wise to keep the ISI out of this operation. Some suspected that the ISI had tipped off al- Zawahiri about previous attempts on his life. She reasoned that the ISI couldn't be entirely ignorant of what was going in the Swat Valley. Too many senior Taliban figures were involved for that to be possible.

Faiza then considered the whole story from the perspective of the Taliban. It was always going to be risky for them to hold such a meeting. They knew the Predators were monitoring them all the time and they seemed to be aware of some, if not all its capabilities. But they seemed to assume that without humintel, the Predators were essentially blind. That at least was the conclusion al-Zawahiri might have drawn from incidents such as the failed attack at Dar- madola, so they concentrated on killing spies and, after eliminating Malik, they had removed the chief threat. And they may have banked on the fact that there had never been a drone attack in the Swat Valley in the past. If Blashford's theory about the White Taliban was right, then maybe al- Zawahiri was also ready to throw caution to the wind, gripped perhaps by the ambition to commit another high profile attack on the United States. Perhaps he, too, was possessed by his own version of the Snowflake Principle.

There were two things that troubled her about this scenario. One was Malik's execution. She thought they had not fully understood how he had been discovered and was puzzled by how little concern Blashford had shown after the execution.

Without Malik, they had no way of being certain what exactly the shura was about, or who was present, or when to strike.

The other was al-Qaeda's decision to attend a shura in Karram Village. It was her fault that Blashford had become convinced that the shura was not being held at Fazlullah's madrassah but in this obscure village. On her own initiative, she had persuaded Miller to fly the MQ2002 from Afghanistan. It was the drone which had nearly tumbled out of the sky and it was the only one available. They had been able to track the convoy of militants until it reached Karram, but the delay had meant that they had lost a vital two hours. She had not seen what the militants had done after they entered the village. Yet the Predator had provided enough footage to show that they were involved in a major operation. Blashford had been off duty at the time, but later had been furious with her when he found out.

Then, after he had watched the footage showing how the militants had taken over the village with growing excitement, he had told her, 'You did good' It was the scenes of the two groups of travelers reaching Karram that had finally convinced him to start planning the operation which was about to start. They had tracked Fazlullah's jeep to the village. The decision to destroy the mosque and the school had been taken while she was asleep. Blashford had ordered her to get some rest at the end of the morning briefing, reminding her that she had been up all night and was exhausted.

After a quick breakfast in the canteen, she had arrived on duty tired, anxious, but determined. She had learned that the mission had been approved, based on a series of phone intercepts. She hadn't listened to any of them, but she had seen the intelligence summary. There had been a burst of phone calls late in the evening, all explicitly talking about a shura, the arrival of important guests and their accommodation. In one call, they had even recorded Fazlullah talking on his cell phone announcing the arrival of al-Zawahiri. She guessed that had clinched it for Blashford.

As she turned over the evidence, she tried to find flaws in the analysis. For one thing, there had been the executions at the madrassah that the Predator had recorded. How did they fit in with the story?

She looked up at the clock. There was still ninety minutes to go. Then she turned on a digital map of the area and studied it. She noted that the village stood at a key crossroads. It was connected to the main highway by just one good road. At its back were forest and high mountains and the village was a staging post for several trading trails that led out of the Valley. It was convenient for men to arrive unnoticed and to flee in a hurry. The intelligence team had concluded that the al-Qaeda leaders would be in the group of men sleeping either in the minaret or in the attached madrassah. It was more likely that they would be sleeping in the seminary. They had decided to launch the attack at dawn just as the men woke for morning prayers. Faiza looked again at three classrooms and could see that in each there were what looked to be large groups of people sleeping on the ground.

Yet she was sure that the village had no strong connections with Fazlullah's insurgents or his clan. Surely he had much more secure hideouts in the caves in the mountains, she thought. Could there be something else about it that had attracted Fazlullah? She looked again at the images on the screen, taking her eye from the school and mosque to study more closely the other houses in the village and the orchards and field around them. It all looked much like any village in the Valley, perhaps a little more prosperous than the average. Some of the houses were large and well- built and the villagers had obviously had some money to build a new school. Then she stopped at that thought. It was a large new school with a high wall around it, made of red bricks instead of the usual mud walls with good facilities, large enough to accommodate important guests.

Then it struck her in a rush of intuition. This was a new girls' school, one of those built by the International Grassroots Literacy Foundation. Fazlullah's men had been watching the Foundation's headquarters, hadn't they? And Fazlullah would never have chosen to host al-Zawahiri in a girls' school built by foreigners to promote female education and emancipation. Fazlullah was notorious for burning these schools down. The villagers must have built the school in defiance of Fazlullah's brutality.

A horrible churning excitement began to well up inside her and her hands began to sweat. Those weren't Taliban inside the school, but schoolgirls. The guards were there to keep the girls inside. The Predator was armed and primed to massacre a girls' school full of girls. She reached for the phone and began calling Langley. The strike had to be called off immediately.

37

It took Sally less than two minutes to realize that the cell phone would not work without a ladder. It was absurd. The twenty-first century technology of microchips and satellites was of no use to her unless she could somehow climb on to the roof and get a signal.

Once back in the classroom, she had pressed the button on her Samsung phone and it had come to life with the jingly welcome tone. Its small screen cast a faint glow in the semi-darkness of the classroom. Sally cupped it in her hand and saw that the battery was half charged. Her relief turned to disappointment when she looked at the small triangle in the corner. There was no reception. She knew there was only one company, Norway's Telenor, that had coverage in the Swat Valley, but its signal was so weak that outside Mingora there was no reception indoors. Sally sat back against the wall fighting back a wave of despair as the girls looked at her expectantly.

'No signal, Missy?' Shaleema asked. Sally shook her head, but she tried to make several calls just to be sure.

'You must go outside,' Shaleema said. 'Then you can be calling anywhere.'

Sally smiled bleakly. As the afternoon turned to evening, she kept running through a number of schemes, none of which seemed realistic, even with a strong dose of optimism. She had been lucky once, she couldn't expect to outwit them again. Or could she? All she had to do was get out and climb on to the flat roof and make a few calls. She could even call London, or Ali, or any number of people who could rouse help. At best, she could just send out some text messages.

In a traditional Swati house, it would have been no trouble to climb up from the inside of the room. There was always a wooden ladder to the third floor. The farmers stored hay under the wooden roof and sometimes it had a little window, or they had a flat roof with a little balcony running round it behind which she could duck down. But the school was a brand new rectangular building made of concrete with walls thick enough to keep out the signal.

If she could climb out of one of the windows, then she could somehow heave herself up on to the roof. She got up and looked at the windows, but they had iron bars and wooden shutters firmly locked on the outside. She tested them all, but they did not budge. Given enough time, she could force them open and squeeze through the bars, but she couldn't make the slightest noise without alerting the guards outside the door.

Shaleema and the others watched her. 'We need to wait, Missy, until we can go outside,' she suggested. Sally wondered how much time they had to wait. The guards had brought them some water and tea. Sooner or later they had to go out to the bathrooms or the kitchens at the back. She was pretty sure the windows in the toilets were not barred. They were the usual squat toilets and she could picture herself climbing out of the small square window and then pulling herself on to the roof. She was sure they could do something and began to feel apprehensive.

She remembered the watchers in the minaret tower. They would spot her. So the best chance would be to wait until it was dark. During the long afternoon, she sat and watched as the girls got up, knocked on the door and demanded to go to the toilet. The guards consented and accompanied them back and forth. The men were brusque but polite although showing signs of increasing irritation.

Then it was time. Sally got up and went to the door with the next girl. Shaleema saw this and got up with her. Her plump round face framed by the shawl looked earnest and but determined. Sally felt a warm comradely affection for her and nodded at her and smiled. 'I will do it now,' she said to the girl.

Together they filed out through the doorway after it opened and the guard motioned them forward with the end of his Kalashnikov. He scowled at Sally, but said nothing. They walked across the courtyard to the row of outhouses. It was now turning to dusk and in the evening air she could smell the blossom from the peach orchards and twitter of evening bird-song. 'Hope, and pray,' she said to herself.

As she walked past the two other classrooms, she noticed the location of the other guards. There seemed to be more of them now. Shaleema tried to speak to their guard and carried on talking, even after he ignored her.

Once inside the toilets, Sally went straight to one of the cubicles and opened the door. 'Oh no,' she thought. There was a window of sorts, but it was just a slit where a couple of bricks had been left out. It was too narrow to squeeze through. She took out the phone and stuck it outside. A faint flicker of coverage showed, but nothing worth taking any risks for. 'I can't get signal here. I have to get on the roof,' she whispered to the girl.

After a few minutes, the two of them came out together. This time Shaleema boldly stood still and started shrieking and screeching at the other guards until they looked embarrassed. Sally felt scared. What was she doing? She could see that she was accusing them of something and the big ragged-looking men seemed intimidated, even bewildered behind their beards and turbans. She was pointing at one of them with her finger and then at the toilets as her voice reached a crescendo of indignation. One of them got up angrily and went towards her, but the others held him back. Soon they were standing in a semicircle around her, all arguing and gesticulating with passion.

Sally, who had shrunk back against the door to the toilets, edged her way round the group and headed towards the kitchen. She thought Shaleema was overplaying her hand but took courage from her example. She took a deep breath and started moving slowly. It was a separate building with the large hearth and a brick stove over which hung a blackened kettle. Dried cattle dung and bundles of small branches and twigs were piled nearby. It was used to provide the children with lunch and other meals for the children who lived as boarders if their parents were away in the summer months herding livestock in the high pastures.

At the back, she could dimly see some tables and benches where the children could sit and eat. She was surprised to see that no one was in the kitchen preparing any food. It was dusk and she would have expected to see someone cooking rice or noodles in a large pot over the fire. Everyone, including the Taliban, would want to eat, she thought, but no one was there. Several bare bulbs dangled from the ceiling, but no one had switched the lights on.

Sally edged her way into the kitchen so she was now standing unnoticed in the shadows. Any one of the Taliban who stood just ten yards away could have turned his head and seen her. Sally pretended to take an interest in cooking, picking up a heavy iron ladle that lay nearby and sidled further into the dim interior. She guessed there must a door leading to a backyard where they would throw the cinders and other rubbish. A few more feet and she reckoned she would be invisible to the Taliban.

Then the shouting stopped. She saw one of the Taliban had seized Shaleema's arm and was lifting his other arm to strike her in the face. Sally froze for a second, fighting the urge to go back and intervene, then turned on her heels and threaded her way between the tables and benches and found a door. It was really just a woolen blanket hung over a gap in the wall. She ducked out and found herself in the open. She looked around and saw the mountains and the darkening sky. It stank of rubbish and shit, but Sally felt a rush of hope. Bless that girl, she thought.

She looked up at the roof, measuring the distance. Too high to reach. She looked around for a ladder or something to climb. No dustbins here. She edged round the back of the school and stumbled into a ditch that ran along the wall. From here she could reach up and grasp the bars of one of the windows. She wondered if she strong enough to pull herself up. She put both hands on the bars and put her feet against the brick wall. It was not so hard and she hauled herself up until her feet were on the window sill and she was holding onto the bars. Then she was standing on a window ledge.

The big challenge was getting from there onto the flat concrete roof above her. Holding on to a bar with one hand and with the other she stretched up but could not get finger tips onto the flat concrete roof. Damn, she thought. I can't do it. I am too short. She leaned back and looked up at the ledge above. She reckoned she was a foot short of what she needed to be. Even then it would be hard to pull herself up. She put her hand up and tried to feel along the bricks for anything she could grip. There was nothing. She was conscious that there was little time to waste. Yet she was so close. I have to try, she thought. Let's see what I remember from those old gym classes. She put one foot against the side of the window recess and the other against the other side. Then she leant back holding onto the bars. She could support her weight. Then she gradually edged one foot up and then the other, until she could get higher. It was awkward but the window was wide enough. She went up as far as she could and then she jammed one foot into the gap between two bars. It's now or never, she thought. One big heave and then she would take a leap of faith and try to grab the top. Is she failed she would have to drop to the ground again.

Here we go she thought. One deep breathe. She put her weight on her left foot and launched herself up and threw her right hand up. Her foot slipped but she managed to get hold of the edge for long enough to let go with the other hand. She now had two hands on the roof and pulled herself up. It took all her strength but she jammed her second foot against the bars and left herself up.

Done it, she congratulated herself as she scrambled across the top. She realized that she might be silhouetted against the sky and dropped down until she was lying flat. From below she could hear Shaleema still screaming and shouting. Not far away she could hear the village dogs barking. When one started, the others joined in. Then the barking died away for a few moments before starting again. She twisted her neck up to look at the minaret tower and froze. The Taliban guards were there and they could easily spot her if they turned in her direction. Instead, all three of them were staring up at the sky looking for something.

For a moment, Sally thought she detected a faint hum like a lawnmower engine, but she ignored it. There was nothing in the sky. She pulled out the cell phone from her pocket and switched on. The light came on and she cupped her hands around it to shield the glow from the small screen. Then she looked at the icon in the top left hand corner. There was enough of a signal showing to try a call.

She first sent text messages that she had prepared, hoping to avoid speaking, then waited for confirmation that the messages had been sent. 'Message not delivered,' the screen said each time. Then Sally watched in horror as the phone's screen flickered just seconds before a call came through. The phone vibrated and emitted a ring tone. Ali the driver had chosen it, a top selling but irritating Pakistani pop song called 'Dil Dil Pakistan'.

Sally was too startled to respond quickly and the first few bars rang out before she could stop it. Fumbling with the buttons, she pressed the receive button with its green phone icon and whispered 'Hello.'

'Hello Foolishness, Mother Hen here,' Jennifer's brassy confident voice boomed all the way from London. 'Why haven't you called in? I got worried.'

'Shut up, for God's sake shut up,' Sally whispered. 'Why? Are you in trouble?' Jennifer asked briskly.

'No, I mean yes. I am being held hostage by the Taliban,' Sally said. 'Call my office in Mingora. Tell them I am in the girls' school in Karram Village. Do it now, Remember, Karram Village.' Then she hung off, cutting dead Jennifer in mid-flow.

It couldn't have lasted more than forty-five seconds but Jennifer had been loud enough to have woken up a sleeping Buddha. It was the ring tone with its irritatingly familiar 'Dil Dil Pakistan' which might have really given the game away. She lay still and listened.

In the courtyard the quarrel between Shaleema and the Taliban was still going on, although the girl was now getting the worst of it. She could hear the dogs' chorus still ricocheting around the village and a particularly hysterical dog was barking somewhere close. Perhaps she was safe and no one had noticed. Now she had to get back.

Sally inched along the roof until she reached the edge. Then she swung over and dropped over and fell to the ground. She found her shoes and crept back into the kitchen and through to the shadows. Her clothes and shoes were muddy but in the gathering darkness she hoped no one would notice.

By this time the row was over. One of the Taliban, a stern man with a strong hooked nose and brown woolen flat cap, had arrived to impose his authority. He pulled Shaleema to her feet and then shoved her towards the classroom so she stumbled and half fell. Then he turned to look at Sally, staring at her intently.

Sally took in his gaze for a second, feeling an acute intelligence in his greenish eyes. She lowered her eyes to the ground submissively, but she could feel him examining her from top to bottom. She felt he must have noticed the tell- tale muddy stains on her baggy cotton pants and sneakers. For a moment, she feared that he might order her to be searched and discover the phone.

After a long minute, he seemed to make up his mind and calmly issued orders to the other men. They obeyed without protest. She was accompanied to the classroom and walked across the yard meekly. As she did, he could feel his eyes on her back and before she walked into the door, she heard him whistling the catchy chorus to 'Dil Dil Pakistan'.

Inside the classroom, she slumped into her customary spot under the blackboard and let the fear drain out of her. The girls let her be, but whispered excitedly amongst themselves as they heard Shaleema tell her story. Sally listened numbly. Although she had got away with it and there was now hope of a rescue, she felt no relief. Why had the Taliban leader deliberately let her know that he knew what she had done? It made no sense to her. Among the cluster of girls, there was a brief burst of laughter and giggles. Shaleema came over and sat beside her. 'So how did you do it?' Sally asked, taking her hand in hers.

'I told them they were dirty dogs spying on girls in the toilet,' she said. 'For a religious man, that made them feel very shameful.'

'You are very clever," Sally said and put an arm around her shoulders and gave them a squeeze. 'And a very brave girl.

'You know, it worked like a charm,' she continued. 'I got on to the roof and the phone worked. I spoke to the office in London and she is going to get help.'

'Your boss?' Shaleema said, sounding disappointed. 'Yes, and she's going to call everyone she can. You'll see,' Sally said confidently, but she, too, felt a twinge of doubt. It might have been better to have dealt directly with the UN or the Pakistani authorities, or best of all with someone in Mingora. Yet in the end she had no choice, it would have been too dangerous to make another call.

Sally reassured herself that if Jennifer sprang into action, she would not be shy of brow-beating any number of foreign office officials in London, but she wondered who else she might contact. She reckoned that it would be close to mid- day in London so if Jennifer had any sense she would be trying to reach people in Mingora. Many people might be wondering what had happened to her and the parents of the girls in the school would not be sitting on their hands either. She was not sure what anyone would do, even if the rescuers arrived at the village.

She still could not understand what the Taliban were up to. Maybe, she thought, they actually wanted people to know what was going on. That meant they wanted to put forward some demands. Wasn't that what hostage takers did in a siege? Perhaps they wanted to force the government to release Fazlullah's father from jail or something like that. Sally puzzled over it until an hour had passed. By then it was past nine. They had already been held captive for nine straight hours.

The door opened without warning and three of the guards entered the room carrying a bucket of rice and lamb and another full of water. The girls fell on it hungrily. Sally joined them, sitting on the floor with a spoon and bowl of food. Then she raised her head up and saw the stern man with the hooked nose standing in the doorway looking down at them. She looked back at him, but he said nothing and gave no sign of recognition.

With a shock, she realized something was different about him. He was now fully armed with a gun slung over his shoulder and a military vest loaded with hand grenades and bulging ammunition pockets. His face was different, too, paler somehow.

Then she realized that he had shaved his beard off. She looked at the other men and they had done the same. This was what the Taliban did when they expected to die. She had seen it before. They were preparing to fight, not to negotiate. And if the Taliban didn't expect to survive this, what were their own chances? Then he was gone, taking the other men with him.

Another thought hit her and she was gripped by a sudden panic. Suicide bombers shaved their beards in preparation for entering paradise. This might be their last meal. Shaleema and the other girls had been so hungry, falling upon the food, they hadn't noticed anything. Sally stopped to listen. Outside she could hear more vehicles arriving and leaving with the dogs barking furiously. She got up and went to the door and pushed as hard as she could. It was now locked and barricaded. Then she pressed her head against the door to listen. There seemed to be no one outside. Sally started hammering at the door and shouting 'help, help' as loudly as she could.

38

Wilkins turned his back on Fazlullah, holding his breath, and walked shakily to the Land-cruiser. He could still feel the brush of Fazlullah's beard on his cheeks after he had embraced him in an extravagant display of pashtunwali. As he climbed into the back seat, he sensed that Fazlullah was staring at his back pondering whether he had made a mistake.

It was only after the car had pulled out of the compound, bumped down the dirt road and hit the smooth tarmac road towards Mingora that he breathed out. It was more like a stifled sob and he covered his face so the men with him would not see the tears which he could feel welling up behind his eyes. He was still in Fazlullah's power. Fazlullah had assigned three men to go with him to Mingora but Wilkins felt confident he could deal with them later. He hunched himself in his padded anorak and he could feel the weight of the money inside it when he leaned back against the seat. All he had to do now was go back to the charity headquarters and find Stoner's stuff and give it to them and then he was free. Free to get the hell out and to disappear for good.

Wilkins stared unseeingly at the road ahead, savoring the small beating knot of hope that had now formed inside him. The moment he had met Stoner's eyes across the courtyard, he guessed Stoner would cave in. His cold white podgy face had a beaten look with streaks of sweat running down it, but Wilkins had given him a wink and flicker of a smile and his pale blue eyes had opened wider. One of Fazlullah's thugs was holding Wilkins down and the other had lifted a great meat cleaver aloft in his hand, but Wilkins felt that Stoner was more scared then he was. The fucker knows that if I die, he'll never get the money. Then he banished the thought.

Stoner would tell Fazlullah anything and the crazy bastard would believe it because he wanted to believe it and Wilkins had filled his head with a load of nonsense about the Great Satan and Stoner's CIA mission. It hadn't stopped Fazlullah's men from beating the crap out of him, but Wilkins stuck to his story and kept reminding him of melmastya and the pashtunwali code of hospitality.

Fazlullah had taken him to his home and had fed him and taken him under his protection, so he was entitled to ask for panah. So Fazlullah would look a fool now if he had been taken in by his show of being Moslem convert. He had accepted a charity donation from him in front of the whole world, so Wilkins reckoned that Fazlullah was now in his debt.

In truth, that wouldn't mean anything to a man like Fazlullah with his utter conviction of his own infallible sense of righteousness, but it meant that he couldn't be treated like a total stranger. Pashtun obligations meant something, especially towards a fellow believer. Of course, they may have had their doubts about that, but they couldn't prove he wasn't.

In Fazlullah's presence they had slapped and kicked him around a bit, but it didn't amount to torture. The fact that Wilkins had come directly to them to offer his help and to betray the identity of a foreign spy in their midst counted for a lot. Wilkins felt sure that however unconvincing his story was about Stoner's real identity, and even as he was telling it to them, it sounded like a load of guff to his own ears, it was something they expected and wanted to hear.

He was sowing into a well-prepared field. Somehow they knew about Stoner's arrival in the Swat Valley and as soon as he had mentioned his name, Wilkins had their attention. In fact, Wilkins felt they seemed positively desperate to find a CIA man, so his unexpected arrival at their gate seemed a godsend. He actually heard one of them cry Allah Akbar after he told them about Stoner's presence.

Wilkins had never expected it to be so easy, so it had come as a shock when they had shoved him downstairs and tied him up in a cell. When they came for him, he was in a foul mood, but still not frightened. The men said nothing as they took the chains off his feet and took him back upstairs. He had kept quiet until he was in the courtyard and they took the hood off. The first thing he saw was the decapitated body and then the shock on Stoner's face. At that moment Wilkins thought he was going to die. His life was now in Stoner's hands, he thought, and he had betrayed Stoner to these murderous fanatics. If the roles were reverse, he would have let Stoner die.

Now, looking back at that moment in the relative safety of the jeep, he was pleased he had played and won a version of prisoner's dilemma, the fundamental problem in game theory he had learned a long time back in Cambridge.

Theory was one thing, reality was another. When he saw that Stoner did not react with any anger or hostility, Wilkins intuitively grasped that he had no idea that Wilkins had already betrayed him. On the contrary, that deep down, Stoner still thought of him as his friend. Wilkins winked and made a quick brave smile. To his surprise, Stoner spoke in a cracked voice. 'Stop it, please. I'll tell you whatever you want.' Then he added in a defeated, pleading way, 'Just don't kill him.' There was a pause. Wilkins swallowed hard and felt time stand still.

Fazlullah nodded and Wilkins felt the men holding him relax their grip. He got shakily to his feet. The interpreter standing behind Stoner then spoke urgently in his ear and, after a brief conversation, Stoner nodded and they went back inside. At once Wilkins knew he was going to live. The fierce energy that had sustained him drained away until he felt weak, almost trembling. He lowered himself to the ground and settled with his back against a wall. He stretched his legs out in the dust and lifted his face towards the sun. He had closed his eyes and savored the warm winter rays and the relief that flooded through his body.

The time passed him by in this blissful state, but it was not long before Fazlullah and his men re-emerged. They walked straight to him. Fazlullah embraced him and kissed him on both cheeks before he could recoil in shock, telling him something in Pashto. The translator explained that he should go back to Mingora and help them find some sort of laser device and then he would be free. He would be free and so would Aziza. At least he hoped so. Before leaving he had pleaded for her life. Fazlullah had warned him that if he played any tricks she would die just like her lover.

Wilkins looked out of the window at the poplar trees flying past along the road and wondered what Stoner could have told them. Enough to buy some time, but Wilkins thought he didn't have the imagination to invent a convincing story. On the other hand, he had that earnest ac- countant's demeanor and the flat pedantic way of speaking that suggested integrity and conviction.

Besides, thought Wilkins, Fazlullah's uneducated mind had a feeble grasp of the outside world and an even weaker understanding of modern technology. He would have been a credulous listener and all the more so because he was impatient. He and his team seemed to be in a big hurry. Stoner wondered briefly what they were up to and then put it out of his mind. It was nothing pleasant, that was for sure, but it didn't matter really. Impatience equaled desperation, so they wouldn't have time to check out whatever story Stoner had concocted. As long as they found something back in Mingora, Stoner would be able to fool the Taliban, at least for a while.

Unless, of course, he really was a CIA man. Wilkins almost smiled at the thought. The main thing was that Fazlullah and his thugs had believed it and that was what counted. He had gambled and won. Stoner had confessed rather than see him die in front of his eyes – the fool.

An almost idiotic sense of euphoria filled him. He had been reprieved at death's door and now he was going to start a second life, a life that would allow him to escape and become a different person.

Soon the driver slowed down behind a gaudily painted truck with a picture of Pakistani cricket hero Imran Khan painted on the back. He was dressed in whites and was wielding a mighty cricket bat. Wilkins felt a gush of nostalgia for his Cambridge days and an image of summer cricket played on green meadows came to mind. Yes, his life would be different now. Golden days of peace and calm were around the corner. In his second life he would be a better person, Wilkins thought, a wiser, more considerate man.

They were now in the outskirts of Mingora and a din of car horns and vendors' cries shook him out of his reverie. Ten hours had passed since he had fled Mingora and he was confident that this ordeal would soon be over. He could see skewers of lamb being grilled on the streets over charcoal fires and felt a sharp hunger. A quick meal and then he would be on his way.

The vehicle nudged its way through the now familiar streets and pulled into the court-yard of the foundation. Rasheed, the older of the guards was there. He got up and looked through the window and nodded grimly when he saw Wilkins at the back and the guns of the men accompanying him. He opened the gate and the jeep drove into the courtyard.

'Is Sally here?' Wilkins asked. Rasheed understood him, but shook his head and started to say something but the Taliban cut him short with a few threatening words. Rasheed looked cowed and fell silent, but he looked hard at Wilkins.

The three Taliban followed Wilkins upstairs to the bedroom where Stoner had left his bags and clothes. His trousers were folded neatly over the back of a chair. On a small wooden table lay a smart black leather attaché case. One of the Taliban went straight to it and picked it up. It was a lightweight traveling case shut by a small brass lock. The man picked it up, shook it and turned it around in his big hands. He tested the lock, then took out a large knife and sliced through the soft leather. Then he emptied the contents on to the desk and rifled through the papers, notebooks and tickets.

Wilkins could see Stoner's burgundy red passport. The man didn't see what he wanted, so Wilkins decided to help him. As he examined the inside pockets, Wilkins showed him the small round silver-colored device. He switched it on and a line of red light played on the whitewashed wall. The man grunted with satisfaction and hastily swept all the items scattered on the desk into the briefcase and turned to leave. In his hurry, he knocked some of Stoner's stuff on to the floor but he didn't care. The man looked Wilkins in the eye, shouted something and waved his hand in a dismissive gesture, and shot out of the door.

Wilkins didn't understand the words, but he understood the message well enough. He was being ordered to clear off. Then the Taliban thundered down the stairs and was gone. Wilkins stood there for a second listening as the men got into the Landcruiser, reversed out of the courtyard and disappeared. Then he bent down on to the floor and picked up Stoner's passport which had fallen under the bed. Inside was a plane ticket.

Wilkins slipped both into his pocket. Then he quickly packed Stoner's clothes into his suitcase. He checked around the room and before leaving tidied up the bed and re- arranged the furniture. He stopped to take a look. It looked neat and tidy, almost as if he Stoner had never been there. Then he took the suitcase back into his room and began packing.

Within a few minutes, he had bundled everything into Stoner's suitcase and had carried it downstairs. Rasheed, the night watchman, was at his post. Wilkins then checked in the kitchen and the living-room, but they were all empty. He noticed that Sally's jeep was absent and assumed she was away on a trip and would be back soon. He went out to ask Rasheed.

'Sahib Wilkie, sir, Sally today go Karram.'

Wilkinson guessed she must have left in the morning, well after he had made his getaway. He knew she was planning to deliver some computers and stuff to the village school. It was not surprising that she hadn't returned by now. Karram was good couple of hours' drive away but Rasheed seemed very agitated and worried and tried to tell him something, but Wilkins couldn't make it out from the torrent of Pashto mixed with odd words of English.

Wilkins went into the office and sat down to write Sally a note thanking her and explaining that he and Stoner had to left for Islamabad on urgent business. He was sure she would understand what that was. Then he thought better of it. Putting something in writing was probably a mistake. It was better to leave a cold trail for anyone who came looking for Stoner, as he felt they surely must. If they believed that he had died at the hands of Fazlullah, all the better.

Wilkins sat down in the office chair at Sally's desk and tipped it back so his head rested against the large map of Pakistan that hung on the wall. It was the first time he had actually articulated the thought in black and white. Fazlullah was never going to let Stoner go, especially now that they had found the evidence of this 'laser pointer'. It was certainly clever of him to re-member that he had such a lecture pointer in his briefcase. And typical of him to carry this vital executive tool on a trip to Pakistan.

Wilkins reflected for a moment and then came to the conclusion that even if he wanted to, there was nothing he could do about Stoner now. And he decided he didn't care anyway, but Sally was another matter. He felt he owed her something and so he picked up the phone and dialed her mobile number.

A recorded message from the Norwegian phone company informed him that the number could not be reached. Probably there was no cell phone reception out there. Well, he thought, he could try again later once he was on the road. Time to get some kebabs and naan bread inside him and then push off.

Then he noticed the red light on the answerphone was winking and on impulse he pressed the button. It was an old-fashioned model made of white plastic with a little tape recorder. There were twenty-three messages there. The tape started unwinding and he started as he recognized the voice of Sally's boss in London. She sounded panic stricken.

'Hello? Hello? Anyone there? Jennifer in London here. Please call me urgently. As soon as you get this message. Sally just called me. She is Karram and in trouble. She needs help. Immediately. '

Jennifer hung off. She called twice and in the final message added that she contacting the authorities in Islamabad. Wilkins stood still and started cursing. He felt caught in a violent tug of emotions. If he stayed in Mingora a moment longer he would certainly die so the impulse to run as fast and far as he could felt almost irresistible. But he couldn't leave Sally in trouble. The first thing as to get moving, he thought. Once he was safe, he could start helping her.

39

Wilkins peered anxiously through the front window, wondering why the taxi was slowing down. They were at least thirty miles out of Mingora, driving slowly and caught behind a convoy of over-laden trucks, but the taxi came to a halt. He cursed loudly.

It was another village check post and this time the militia men were carefully checking every vehicle going both in and out the valley. It was a more professional-looking affair, too, with proper sandbags behind which guards watched as the militia men forced everyone out of the vehicles. They had stretched a piece of cloth and rubber with nails sticking out of it across the road. Everybody was carefully searched before the vehicles could continue.

He wondered what they were looking, for, although he could guess what they were scared of – the Taliban's suicide bombers. He got out of the taxi and walked past the line of waiting trucks and a couple of minibuses. He could see everyone was nervous.

There were a lot more guns visible than was usual. He walked through the line carrying his backpack with him and waited in the line. He was hoping no one would notice him.

Two nervous youths came towards him. One held a worn-looking gun straight at him, while the other frisked him. Then he waited at the side of the road for the vehicles to pass the checkpoint, hoping no one would recognize him. Many of the men there were openly staring at him. The vehicles inched forward and he could see the taxi stuck behind two trucks, one carrying timber and the other all kinds of household goods. Then he saw Ali coming down a track between the fields heading towards the checkpoint and weaving from side to side with his big lolling gait. He was with two gunmen and was talking into a phone.

Wilkins turned his head away and lowered it down into his chest. He kept still, praying that Ali would not recognize him. He had been fighting with himself ever since he had left Mingora, knowing that he was making the wrong decision to flee. Deep down, he couldn't just abandon Sally but he had told himself that the best way of helping Sally was to get out of the Valley and get help. His inner coward had triumphed. He told himself he was out of his depth and the rational thing to do but he felt ashamed. He could see the taxi moving slowly towards him and, with a bit of luck, it would get to him before Ali did. For a second he hesitated, wondering if he should move to the other side of the road, but it was too late now. If he moved now he would only draw attention to himself.

Then the last truck was halted. The guards ordered the driver to get out of his cabin and he hopped down and started

laughing and joking. Wilkins could see the taxi just yards behind it yards and decided to walk to it and get in. As he did so,
he felt a large hand land on his shoulder.

'Inshallah!' Ali said 'You have come to look for me? And
now I find you.'

Wilkins found it impossible to shake him off. He was filled
with a new-found energy and he embraced Wilkins tightly. In
his enthusiasm, he did not notice the irritation which Wilkins
struggled to disguise. The taxi was only a few yards away now,
but it was too late to escape.

'Come! We are going to my house. I have important news.'

'Actually, I was on a trip. I have a taxi here,' he pleaded.
'No need to go anywhere else. We are ready,' Ali said and began
marching Wilkins back through the fields. As they started, Ali
turned round and gave some orders to the taxi driver, who had
half emerged from the car to demand payment. The sight of the
guns pointed at him quickly silenced him.

Wilkins felt a sudden relief. Fate had made the decision
was made for him and he felt oddly grateful. Soon after they
arrived at his house, in a village now familiar from his previous two visits, Ali led him directly to a stable. Inside he
saw armaments they had bought; stacks of old AK-47s with
worn folding-stocks, light machine guns, a collection of rifles from various eras, rocket launchers, small mines, hand
pistols, wooden crates filled with ammunition, holsters, web
gear and pouches and lots of second-hand camouflaged
clothing plus boots and helmets. Then he thrust an assault
rifle at Wilkins' chest, forcing him to take it and said triumphantly; 'Take it. This is for you!'

He walked around the pile and picked up a protective ceramic vest covered in dirty khaki webbing and held it out. 'You will need this, too!' Ali said. 'Special for you,' He smiled broadly and Wilkins just stared back uncomprehendingly.

'We are going tonight,' he explained. He looked proudly at Wilkins who just nodded.

'Where exactly are we going?' he said, unsure whether to give his assent or not. He was now pleased that he had not told Ali that he had been on his way to Islamabad.

'The villagers came here and said they are scared Fazlullah's men will kill them. All the girl students and Sally, too. They say we must attack now, tonight. In the morning it may be too late,' Ali said. 'That is why we are scared the Taliban may attack us first.'

So that is what had happened to Sally. He felt sick that he had even thought about deserting her. She was a brave girl he thought. So were these men. He was on the only coward here.

'Oh, I see, that's why you had the extra security on the road,' he said feebly.

'We don't know if they have spies among us. Or if this is a trap,' Ali said.

But Wilkins could sense how excited Ali was by the thought of action and itching to use the new weapons. His calculating rational side of mind was appalled by the thought of Ali and his amateurish friends trying to take on Fazullah. They wouldn't stand a chance. On the other hand, he felt a thrill at the thought of someone taking on these fanatics take on. He had bought their weapons and he would like to be there when it happened. He would be there when they rescued Sally. The anticipation grew as he watched the preparations and became infected by the nervous excitement of everyone around him. This was a buzz, he thought.

A few hours later, as it grew dark, he found himself sitting awkwardly on a donkey that trotted quickly along a trail that skirted the western side of the Swat valley. He had a pistol strapped to his right thigh and an AK-47 slung over his shoulder which bounced against the ceramic breast plate. Boxes of ammo were strapped on to another donkey which ran behind him. Just to be on the safe side, he had stuffed a couple of magazines into his pockets, even though he was still unsure how to clip them on.

The strike had been organized quickly and with an efficiency that had surprised him. At six o'clock, the leaders of the lashkar had met for a meal of greasy chicken and rice and decided on a plan of action. To avoid detection and ensure the vital element of surprise, the strike force had dispersed and been ordered to make their way in twos and threes to Karram and to assemble in darkness on a ridge overlooking the village. As a conspicuous foreigner, he had been ordered to leave first and accompany the baggage train carrying the weapons.

The donkeys followed a series of small paths that ran along the border of the last fields at the edge of the valley. In between the fields, they trekked through small woods and up and down small crags, occasionally fording a stream that ran down from the surrounding hills. There were about a dozen men with him, each leading five or six donkeys laden with their weapons and gear. Wilkins wasn't exactly sure how many were taking part or what the exact plan was. He was present at the council of war but understood nothing of what was said.

'You go with the donkeys, my friend. Then we will all meet before morning,' Ali declared, shook his hand and had hugged him. 'Don't worry. We will fight together. Sally will be safe.'

As he rode on the donkey, Wilkins had time to think. He wondered if there was still a chance to disappear. He could turn aside, perhaps in one of the woods. It was getting darker and darker and it would be a while before the other men noticed. Then he tried to imagine what would happen when they got there. He knew many of the Swati men were scared of Fazlullah's Uzbek and Chechen fighters. They were tough and well-trained professional fighters who would not run away at the first shot. If they had taken the children captive, they would be prepared for and even expecting an attack. It could turn out to be quite a bloodbath and everyone would get killed including Sally. Perhaps, it was not being brave but dangerously irresponsible. He began to think hard again about slip away and contacting the Pakistan military or British embassy. In a hostage crisis, they could send in the SAS. The only thing he would have to give himself up, and secondly it was now too late to stop Ali and his lashkar.

He pulled at the reins, some lengths of coarse hemp rope wrapped around the head of the donkey, so it turned right into the forest, and the other donkey behind followed obediently. After twenty paces, they could barely be seen in the gloom and he watched part of the caravanserai go past. For safety's sake, they were riding spaced out together, so it was easy to avoid notice.

The he began to think about Sally and what she must be going through. He thought about seeing her again and imagined the time they would have together. He thought about the way she would glance up at him from under that disheveled pile of hair, her head twisted a little sideways in a challenging, flirtatious sort of way. He knew he couldn't leave her there and he was going to get her out of there. There had to be a way. He felt a mixture of sexual excite- ment and danger stir him in an unfamiliar way. He jerked the rope bridle and kicked with both his legs until the beast cantered forward, following the line of donkeys ahead.

It took another six hours of steady travel until they reached the area of Karram village. They left the fields and took a steep pack trail winding up a precipitous valley and then traversed the shoulder of the mountain along a thin goat path until they reached another well-defined pack trail that descended in slow sweeping bends through the trees and into the valley floor.

When they passed through a clearing in the woods, there was enough light for Wilkins to recognize the village and its fields spread out below. The other men halted and stared at the sight and began talking in whispers amongst themselves. They dismounted and began carefully checking the horses and donkeys, tightening all the strap and bridles, to make sure they would travel the last stage in silence.

Several men unslung their weapons and held them at the ready and advanced down the path on foot. The rest followed them, holding on to the animals closely by the bridle. The final stretch of the path to the valley floor led through clumps of pine trees and the fallen needles softened the sound of the hooves.

The last evening light faded. Wilkins followed them at the rear, pulling at the donkey. It was turning cold, but he felt his hands were slippery with sweat.

40

When she had called Blashford ninety minutes earlier to abort the strike, the conversation had started better than she had hoped:

'You want to abort the strike?' he asked after listening to her explanation in silence. 'Now? With ninety minutes to go?'

'Yes, I do. This is a mistake,' Faiza had said levelly. She was now a professional with no room for emotion. 'We are targeting a school in Karram, not the shura. Those are school children inside the building.

'Half the bodies you can see there are girls. This is a new village school. The Taliban would never hold a shura there,' she said with a catch in her voice.

'A school?' he had said and she could picture him looking again at the image. 'It looks like a seminary next to a largish mosque.'

'Yes, recently built by the International Grassroots Literacy Foundation. It's especially popular with girls. The villagers wanted their daughters educated.'

'If it is a school and we blow it up, then the Taliban will have a field day,' he said slowly.

'And all those innocent children will lose their lives,' Faiza had added quickly. She couldn't control her sharp tongue, but Blashford didn't catch the acerbic tone.

'Yes, of course. Imagine the headlines,' he said. 'It would provoke a storm of public outrage. If what you are saying is correct.'

'If we make a mistake, it will cost us dearly,' Faiza agreed. 'Enough to doom the drone program in Pakistan.'

She hadn't expected him to accept so easily, and without question, that they had been targeting a school.

'But you seem to be saying that this is deliberate. That Fazlullah has set us up. Are you sure he is really that smart?' Blashford said. 'This guy never finished school. His biggest job was a ski-lift operator.'

'Remember the response to the attack at Damadola in 2006 and the attack on the semi-nary in Chinagai? The Taliban won a huge propaganda victory, stirring up public opinion against us. And remember that Fazlullah's brother died in the attack. I think he wants revenge,' she said.

Blashford had stayed silent for a moment.

'He is a Pashtun,' she said. 'A wolf cannot become a lamb.'

Saying nothing more, Faiza turned back to watching the seconds on the digital clock in the corner of her monitor. Then he had stunned her.

'Faiza, this mission is going ahead. We know Fazlullah is there. Two hours ago a Predator tracked him from Imam Dehri to this village. With him are other senior Taliban lead- ers – Faqir Mohammed from Bajour and Sadiq Noor from North Waziristan. Maybe Mahsud is there, too,' Blashford had said. 'Al-Zawahiri is there as well, I am certain of it. My hunch is he planned all this.'

'Your hunch? You are sure of that? So what do we do now?' Faiza had asked. She couldn't imagine how even the Predator's advanced telemetry could have identified these high value targets.

'We picked up a Telenor phone call. It was from Karram to a London number,' Blashford said. 'We are still trying to con- firm the identity of the recipient.'

'What was it about?' she had asked.

'It was a plea for help from a western woman speaking in English,' he had replied. 'That's why I think you are right. I have an idea of how we are going to turn this to our advan- tage.'

41

Wilkins had believed there was plenty of ammunition for everyone right up to the moment the shooting started. As soon as he and the rest had arrived on the outskirts of the village, the men had unloaded the crates of ammo from the donkeys and mules. They wanted to keep the animals out of sight in the woods, so there was no alternative but to open the wooden boxes and distribute whatever there was so they could carry what they needed to their fighting position. Wilkins watched the men grab the weapons and ammunition. Most of the unloading was done in silence with brisk efficiency. Then, one by one, the men, mostly wrapped from the cold in shawls and blankets, staggered off into the darkness to find their places. There they crouched, waiting for the signal to attack. Wilkins was impressed. They were more disciplined than he had expected and moved around quietly and stealthily. They were an odd assortment of ages and sizes. Some were in the twenties and looked fit and strong enough but many of them were middle aged and distinctly paunchy.

Not exactly an elite commando force, he thought, but they seemed determined. If they had surprise on their side, and with the advantage of greater numbers, the militants might just panic. It could all be over in ten minutes, may be just five minutes. He imagined a quick rush a bit of shooting and the militants surrendering. That was the plan. A simple plan.

Then again, these people were ready to die for their cause. If they were well prepared and stood their ground, then anything could happen. Some of these men might be dead or wounded in a few hours. There were no doctors or medics among them, he thought. Shit, everybody could die, including Sally. Who knew if they had booby-trapped the school and were ready to take everyone with them paradise? Stop it, he told himself. Think of something, anything else or you will get the heebie jeebies yourself. Don't want to get freaked out now. Think about how you are going to get out here if it all goes wrong. The best way was to run like hell and get lost in the woods above the village. As they say, you don't need to run faster than a tiger, just faster than the guy next to you.

Ali and his companions, who were traveling by road, arrived after midnight. The first men began to trickle in, arriving in ones and twos after circling the village on foot. Apart from a few whispered words of greeting, nothing was said. They each took the weapons issued to them and disappeared into the darkness.

Ali finally arrived and Wilkins thought he looked grimfaced. He shook Wilkins' hand solemnly but there was no smile and he said little. He gave his attention to the rest of the group, who were standing around waiting for orders. Then everyone settled down to wait for the night to pass.

Wilkins crouched on the ground, feeling cold and uncomfortable, and fidgeted. From time to time, he peered at his watch and then looked around at the men he could see squatting on their haunches and wrapped in their woolen shawls and blankets. They seemed to find it easy to sit motionless for long periods.

There was some starlight and a faint moon shadow across the roofs. He could hear dogs barking in the village, a ripple of barks and howls that spread, then died down, then started up again. Sometimes a light would flicker on in one of the windows and then be doused. Wilkins had only a vague notion of where the school and the mosque might be. Nobody was allowed to get up and take a good look around, but he guessed it was in the middle of the village where the houses were built closely together. Somewhere there Sally was spending the night in terror. He wondered if she was thinking of him too and what she imagined he was doing.

The plan was that before dawn Ali would fire a burst of gunfire, then everyone would else would open up and run towards the mosque from all sides, taking the sleeping guards by surprise. 'The dogs will die in their sleep,' Ali had promised.

At first Wilkins felt encouraged by his confidence. If it was going to be chaotic and no one could tell friend from foe in the darkness, the best option would be to stick like a limpet to Ali. The longer the wait, the more nervous Wilkins felt. His hands moved from the AK-47, touching the top of the barrel checking to make sure it was on single shot fire. Then to the two hand grenades fastened on both sides of the webbing vest pulled over a Kevlar plate. Finally, they would pass over the bulge in his trouser pockets, the spare bullet clips. After a few minutes' pause, they would compulsively start the ritual again.

In the same sort of compulsive neurotic way, his thoughts would plod around the same weary path again and again. They returned to the same old scenes: Stoner's sudden arrival in Swat. The executions at Fazlullah's headquarters. His terror. His escape. The last pleading look in Stoner's eyes. The absurd misfortune of being stopped just as he was getting out of the valley. Then the confident briefing about the attack before they left. Then his thoughts always re- turned to Sally and his feelings for her. He wondered why she had drawn away from him again and what she now thought of him. He badly wanted her to feel proud of him.

Yet he felt weary. Very tired, he realized, drained by his emotions and exhausted from a lack of sleep. Yet several thoughts came returning and he struggled to control them. There were things he knew he should understand but didn't: what was it that the Taliban wanted from them? They were obsessed about getting a laser pointer, but why? What use were they to Fazlullah? In science fiction stories, the aliens always fired laser guns. In the laboratory, scientists used lasers to split up light into its component parts. It was called spectronomy and shed light on things that were hidden to the human eye.

Then he wondered why Fazlullah had been in such hurry to get this weapon before launching the assault against this village school. When Ali told him about the attack he had automatically assumed it was part of the Taliban's campaign to shut down all the girls' schools and to punish anyone who defied their edicts. Perhaps, though, the two were somehow connected?

He felt small shoots of fear sprouting inside him which he suppressed. He feared they could grow out of control. For the first time in his life, he felt himself on the edge of a full-blown panic. The laser was some kind of weapon, like laser sights on a gun, he guessed. It must be something like that. He felt sure that the Taliban were expecting them. It must be a trap. A plan. For all he knew, they had been watched all the time. Then he was gripped by a simple conviction: as soon as the shooting started, the attack would go horribly wrong. Sally could get caught in the middle of the cross fire.

Fazlullah might have far more men than Ali expected and they were standing by ready to kill the attackers. These men were as ready to kill others as kill themselves. In the darkness his hands moved again from the gun to the grenades and then to the spare ammunition. He fought to control the panicky feeling inside him.

He decided to get up and talk some sense into Ali. He eased himself on to his feet in the darkness, trying carefully not to make a sound, and moved towards Ali. He could see a bulky figure dimly outlined against the door. The man was crouching down, peering at something. Then he stood up abruptly before Wilkins could reach him.

'Ali,' he whispered and reached his hand out to touch his shoulder.

Ali ignored him and stepped out of the hut and, unshouldering his gun, pointed it at the sky. He paused for a second and looked around him for an instant to make sure his men were watching him.

Wilkins gave him a horrified look, but he smiled briefly, then opened up with a brief burst of gunfire. It must have lasted just a few seconds. Wilkins hesitated and Ali turned, jerked his arm to pull him with him and then turned away.

He began to run forward, starting a lumbering sprint towards the mosque.

Wilkins felt he had no choice and began to follow in his footsteps. He moved slowly and clumsily at first, then with more confidence as the attack got under way. All around him, he sensed the other men leaving their hiding places and start to converge on the center of the village. Wilkins felt wild surge of excitement. He felt brave, so tough that he no longer considered the risk that he too might die here or kill anyone. At first it felt unreal, almost make believe but now he felt exultation and rage flood through him.

The men began firing at once so there was a sudden storm of noise. The firing came in intense bursts that started and eased off as if someone kept throwing handfuls of gravel at a window pane. Wilkins kept close behind Ali as he ran from one house to another, taking cover and shouting at the men, urging them forward. They needed a leader and they needed more discipline, he thought. Wilkins saw the fighters getting up, holding their guns above their heads and fire wildly. Then they would run twenty yards and stop behind a wall. Then they would put a gun round the corner and spray a bunch of rounds, again without aiming. He could see red tracer bullets flying. The fusillade of fire was intense but it soon began to taper off.

Wilkins wondered why. He stopped to look round and saw that some of the fighters had already run out of ammunition. He went past two men sitting on the ground surrounded by five or six empty cartridge clips. Ali was shouting at them and they were arguing back and gesticu- lating with their weapons. Wilkins guessed that a minute- long burst of automatic firing could empty a whole clip of twenty-five bullets. Now they had nothing left to fire.

Ali abandoned them, muttering to himself in frustration, and pushed on, striding between a row of solidly built stone and wood houses until they reached a junction with the wide mud road that ran through the heart of the village. Wilkins felt his resolve harden. They had to push on. It was too late to give up.

There was a ditch at the side of the road, partly covered by slabs of stone and Ali was about to step over it when he stopped and retreated, panting heavily. Then he fell back behind the corner of the house and crouched down. He turned and waved at Wilkins to do likewise. Then they both looked towards the minaret silhouetted against the night sky. Wilkins now felt a stab of fear. The enemy was right in front of him. He thought they would be waiting calmly with plenty of ammunition at hand. This is where it would start getting real.

42

Most the girls had fallen asleep and Sally felt alone waiting in the dark classroom listening and worrying. She sat near the door, leaning against the wall, straining her ears to catch the smallest sounds. She was waiting for sound of a vehicle approaching. Instead, long after midnight that she began to hear a distant sporadic tat- tat-tat that she struggled to identify.

Her thoughts and emotions twisted first one way and then the other. At first she had been calm, certain that Jennifer would have contacted someone in Mingora and that help was on the way. Then she became anxious as she pondered how she would react if anyone attempted to rescue her and the school girls. Hostage crises often turned bad, she recalled, with many hostages dying in rescue attempts. Then she thought about Wilkie and next about what Stoner had told her. What was he doing now? She tried to put the thought out of her mind but she couldn't help imagining what she would tell him when they met. If they ever did.

She was certain they were being held hostage for a purpose and she ran through the different scenarios in her mind. Then for a while, she held on to the thought that perhaps nothing would happen. She figured that anyone would first try to negotiate with the militants and there might be a long wait, perhaps even days before anyone would risk an all-out attack. After all, everyone is the Swat Valley knew that the militants were ready to die for their cause. They had used suicide vests before.

Then, she stopped. It was no good thinking like that way. She had no idea who was going to mount a rescue mission or even what the militants wanted. Did they have any demands? She shook her head in frustration.

In the early hours, her mind gradually slowed down as she felt more and more weary. Instead, she tried to think of better things like what she would do after they got out. She knew it had been foolish to stay in the Swat Valley. It was simply too big and dangerous a challenge. She recalled the meeting in London when Jennifer had warned her. 'De Nile is not just a river in Egypt she had said,' Sally smiled at the memory.

Then she thought about Wilkins and her feelings about him. She liked the way he had begun to change when he had seen what she was doing. She felt he had begun to see things her way. He had stopped making jokes about the Spanish donkeys. If he was in trouble in London, she was going to help him. The thought made her feel better and more positive. The thought of his presence, his large reassuring physical presence and warmth was good. She wanted to be with him again.

Around two in the morning, she was felt more alert and decided to stand up. She put her hands behind her in the darkness and groped along the wall. It was made from thin plaster and paint which came off easily. Underneath she could feel bricks and the mortar between them. She knew something about the building methods used in Karram because she had been involved in the construction of a number of new schools.

Sally began to wonder if it was not possible to dig loose a few of the bricks and take the door of the hinges or one of the windows? Or could they even dig a hole in the floor and escape out the back? All she needed was a few sharp metal objects and they could try.

Sally gently roused Shaleema and three of the other girls and whispered to them. 'Get up. Find something sharp or pointy,' she said. They began to move around quietly hunt around for anything metal to use. The classroom contained little except the wooden furniture and blackboard and some books. Sally didn't even have any keys with her. There seemed to be any utensil sharp and hard enough to scrape away the mortar.

Sally sat down again and tried to think. She had to get some nails or screws or a knife from somewhere. She looked through her bag hoping to find something. There only a few plas-tic pens and some loose coins. She tried using the end of the one pen to scratch the mortar but it broke after the third attempt.

By this time, they had disturbed some of the other girls who began making a noise, talking amongst themselves. She tried to shush them, fearing they would alert one of the guards. Yet no one came. Instead she began hearing in the distance the sound of the crack of a gun going off. First it was on shot and then another and then a steady pop pop. The whispering and movement in the classroom stopped as more and more of the girls began to listen. The sounds began to move closer.

Sally was startled. Then she began thinking again. 'Shaleema, Maleela, Get Up! We need to do something. Push these desks against the door,' she ordered them and started setting an example. She thought that barricading the door might help if the fanatics came for them. It would make it harder for anyone to get in. There were thirty desks and benches and they began working together to pile them up. She was quite pleased to see everyone getting involved. The pile of furniture created a kind of shelter too.

'Keep low and away from the windows,' she said. Then there was nothing more she could think of doing. When the girls stopped moving, they would hear the clear sounds of fighting and shouting outside. The girls started talking and a few began whimpering and crying. 'Stop that,' Sally shouted.

It was still dark in the room and Sally was struck by two things at once. The guards were no longer outside and secondly there was no need to keep quiet. She took one of the chairs and broke it against the wall on the other side of the room against the iron bars of the window. It broke easily into pieces. She took one of the legs and broken it by levering it between two of the bars so it cracked and splintered. The chairs had been crafted from local pine wood and some of the splintered pieces were sharp enough to attack the mortar with.

She began using one of them to start digging at the mortar underneath and above the window frame. The dry cheap lime mortar came away easily. She was joined three of the girls and they began frantically hacking at all four sides of the window hoping they could get loosen the frame enough to push it open. The closer the sounds of the gunfire and the fighting came, the more they tried.

They could hear people shouting and screaming. Some of the bullets could be heard hitting the metal of the outside gate. 'Shit, that's so close,' Sally said. Some of the girls were now shrieking and wailing. They were close to hysteria. Sally was soon panting and cursing with the effort. The rest of the girls crouched in the floor and had started whimpering with fear. Then they could hear the return fire coming from near the door. Sally stopped her helpers and began to pull at the bars hoping to pull the whole window frame loose from the wall. It moved but not enough to dislodge it. Any minute now and the fighting would be all around them. If they didn't get out they would be trapped inside a gun battle. She became frantic and tried to fight the waves of fear that rose up from the pit of her stomach.

43

'Possible new target approaching target building one,' one of the sensor operators said, speaking clearly in a calm Midwestern voice.

'Pilot copies,' Captain Miller said.

'Sensor copies,' repeated the second sensor operator.

She was not alone, but Faiza felt she was. Miller sat in front of her controlling four Predators which hovered 10,000 feet over Karram. He was being helped by two sensor opera- tors in the ground control station, each leaning back on large padded chairs.

Over in Langley, she knew that a dozen other intelligence of- ficers were watching the same data stream that was being bounced from a geo-stationary satellite suspended thousands of miles above the earth. All the data collected and processed by the counter-terrorism team from incoming signal and humintel traffic was being streamed on to a monitor screen in front of her. Everyone in the ground control center spoke in the detached neutral voices of officials going through a familiar routine, but an acute excitement gripped Faiza and she could feel her breathing tighten. Her enemies were going to die and she was going to watch it.

'If possible, keep eyes on the vehicle but the building has priority,' Blashford ordered from Virginia. He was in charge now.

'Pilot copies,' Miller said. 'Designate targets in minaret.' 'Pilot copies.'

'Designate targets vehicle one, two and three.' 'Targets found,' Miller said.

'Designate targets in guard post one and two.'

'Targets designated,' Miller said.

Faiza could see the laser range designator lock on to the shadowy white figures on the monitor. Two of the Predators were banking in a roll, but the targets remained locked in the cross hairs. She watched the truck approaching the outskirts of the village, seeing the heat of the engine in red and the people as white images, but clearly sitting inside the cabin or perched on the roof outside.

'Pilot, I need MQ102 to come off target and get in position and for 107 to come south. Get permission for 107 to come south,' Blashford said.

'Sensor copies.'

'Leave MQ101 to stay on target until we get permission,' Miller ordered.

'Roger wilco,' the first sensor said. 'Changing target,' Miller said.

'You can break lock on target six, change and turn sixty degrees,' Blashford commanded.

'Copy,' Miller answered.

'I've got eight missiles and two bombs on four Predators in the vicinity,' Blashford said.

'Request weapons load down,' Miller said.

'High value target entering vehicle,' the first sensor said. 'New vehicle approaching village,' the second said. 'Pilot copies,' Miller said.

'Pilot spin up a weapon on tail 101,' Blashford said. 'Copy,' Miller said.

'Prelaunch check list,' Miller said. 'Pr f-code.'

'88 power.' 'On.'

'A bit.'

'Passed.' 'Weapon power.' 'Passed.'

'Code weapons.' 'Coded.' 'Weapons status?'

'Ready.'

'Pre-launch check complete,' Miller said.

The next few minutes would tell if Blashford was right. Faiza felt her breathing tighten and time slow down. She started to chew her finger nails. Was she was wrong about this? She thought. Was Al-Zawahiri really there? These men in the vehicles were definitely militants and deserved to die but she thought Blashford was overconfident. If things went wrong and the children died, they might never get a chance like this again. She wished she had tried harder to get some voice recognition, perhaps she should have made a phone call, done something. If it went wrong now and the school kids died in the attack, it would be a triumph for the Egyptian. She hated that thought more than anything.

44

Wilkins hid behind Ali and looked over his shoulder at the mosque. He couldn't see anything moving. Then he looked towards the ground and saw bodies lying just in front of them. He could see a group of men lying twisted on the road with their weapons flung behind around them. They had been running towards the entrance of the mosque and another building next to it.

Before he could make sense of it, he could see and hear shots coming from above, hitting the rough stone walls of the house and smashing into the paving stones of the ditch. Ali suddenly turned, knocking him off his feet and falling on to his chest and the Kevlar plate. The heavy man knocked the wind out of him. They lay there for a second and then Ali got off and helped Wilkins back on his feet.

'Sorry, sorry,' he said, then he laughed. Wilkins slipped on the muddy ground and then he laughed, too, as he struggled to his feet.

'Good, good,' Ali said and patted his shoulder. They stood there for a moment listening to the sounds around them to assess how the attack was faring. The sky seemed to getting lighter. In a few minutes, it would be five in the morning. The firing was petering out.

'Is that the school where the girls are being held? And where Sally is?' Wilkins said.

Ali nodded 'There are Taliban fighters inside and in the tower. I think all the others are dead. Maybe five or six are left.'

He held up his hands and showed six fingers. Wilkins nodded.

'We will send them to hell. Come,' Ali said abruptly. He set off down the alleyway and Wilkins followed again after glancing nervously behind him. No one was following, but Wilkins thought he could hear someone moving in the darkness.

Ali rounded up a dozen men with heavy arms. They carried heavy machine guns, mortars and missile or grenade launchers. Ali led the way impatiently as they re- traced their steps in the alleyway and approached the mosque. Suddenly, he stopped and held up his hand. Wilkins, who was hard on his heels, glimpsed a band of men turning into the main street from the corner of the mosque about thirty yards away. They moved with a disciplined determination and purpose. As they saw Ali, they began firing carefully and deliberately at him.

Ali pulled both of them out of sight of the attackers and they sheltered behind a house. 'Uzbeks,' he said. The other men heard this and were afraid. Wilkins noticed the men looking at each other and whispering. He knew they held the Taliban's fighters in awe. Several began to edge backwards. Then one man, a broad thickset man, moved forward, holding his weapon at arm's length, and pointed it round the corner of the house. He opened fire.

45

'New target at outside school. He is pointing at something,' the second sensor operator said.

'Pilot copies,' Miller said.

On the screen Faiza could see a man standing about thirty yards from the school holding something in an outstretched hand that directed a thin red line at the school door.

'It looks like a lecture laser pointer. It's very low wattage,' the console operator said. 'What shall we do?'

'Take him out,' Blashford ordered. 'Designate new target.'

'Wilco,' the second sensor operator said 'Target found,' Miller said.

The green crosshair lines on one of the screens moved until they centerd on the man.

'Target locked,' Miller said.

Faiza smiled to herself. The Taliban evidently believed that a laser pointer used for lectures could confuse the Hellfire missile's homing device so it would hit the school. And it proved her theory was right.

'Launch check list,' Blashford said. 'Code weapons,' Miller said.

'Coded,' the other sensor operator said. 'Weapons status?' Miller asked.

'Ready.'

'Pre-launch check complete,' Miller reported. 'Laser selected,' the first sensor said.

'Laser selected,' Miller repeated.

'Go ahead and arm your laser,' Blashford commanded. 'Lasers armed,' Miller confirmed.

Faiza could see that there were now six Hellfire missiles primed to fire. One would hit the mosque, the second would take out the guard post, the third was locked on the man with the laser pointer and three others were locked on Fazlullah's jeep and the other vehicles parked nearby. With four Predators in the vicinity, that meant there were another two missiles to spare.

'Unidentified vehicle approaching guard post,' warned the first sensor operator.

'A group of men is approaching the village from the north,' said the second.

The video screen from MQ104 showed a party of about twenty figures moving slowly and cautiously out of the woods and then heading towards the village from the north side.

'What the hell! Who are these guys?' Blashford asked incredulously. Two minutes passed while they watched the group cautiously move towards the first house on the outskirts of the village where they took up defensive positions.

'My God, they look like they are getting ready to attack,' he said.

On another screen, they saw a truck stop on a bend of the road, just out of sight of the guard post. Faiza could see the guards moving around. They must have heard the truck approaching. A minute later she saw the guns in the hands of the guards turning white with heat as they opened fire.

'Pilot, you are free to engage the guard post,' Blashford said.

'Master arm is hot. Go ahead and fire laser,' Miller said. 'Lasing,' a sensor operator said.

'Within range,' Miller said.

'3 – 2 – 1 rifle,' the sensor operator said. '3 – 2 – 1 impact,' Miller said.

There was silence in the Ground Control Station as the Hellfire missile streamed away from the Predator. Its camera focused on to the guard post and then exploded. Within sixty seconds a cloud of grey and white dust billowed up and obscured the scene.

'Pilot, you are free to target the mosque and the man with the laser,' Blashford said.

'Pilot copies,' Miller said calmly.

'Sensor copies,' the second operator said. 'Go ahead and fire lasers,' Miller ordered.

46

Seconds later, a powerful blast exploded into the house, smashing against the corner and destroying it. Wilkins flew backwards in a cloud of dust and stone fragments. Half the house and the roof collapsed in a pile of rubble. The remaining eight or so men with him panicked and turned to flee. Some of them dropped their weapons and fought each other to run back along the alleyway to safety.

Wilkins, dazed and deafened by the blast, was left lying on the ground. He could feel some blood running down his face from small cuts and scratches. His torso had been protected from the blast by the Kevlar plate and underneath his back he could dimly feel his AK-47 sticking into him. He touched the hand grenades pinned to his webbing jacket. They were still there. Then he pressed his hands against his trouser pocket. The curved magazines were still there, too.

Next to him he could hear another man moving and groaning in pain. Then, he could hear men moving in the darkness and he lifted his head and saw several men coming cautiously towards him. He lifted his head and saw two men walking slowly towards him, holding out their weapons, the barrels pointed downwards. He let his head fall back and closed his eyes. He felt powerless. If they were going to shoot him, there was nothing he could do now. Except take some of them with him.

He let his hands move back up to his jacket and the hand grenades. Then he felt himself lifted off the ground by a tremendous blast as if a giant hand had picked him up and dropped him. A rain of small brick fragments and stones fell on him.

When Wilkins came to his senses, he felt he could barely see or move. Stunned and deafened, he lifted his head with difficulty and looked around him. His face was caked by thick dust and he gingerly brushed it away. When he could see better, he looked around. There were other bodies crumpled on the ground, but it was hard to tell if they were dead or, like him, in deep shock.

From his prone position, he could see that the mosque and its minaret had disappeared. A cloud of dust still hung over the cratered site. In the semi-darkness, he struggled to see what else had been destroyed. The first dawn light was filtering through the dust and he could see that the school next door looked as if it had escaped the blast undamaged. He could no signs of movement. The troop of Taliban fighters had disappeared.

Then he began to hear the sound of crying from the school and a thin high-pitched keening. He could hear men moving around, shouting at each other and a car engine kick into life. He began to crawl along the ground so he could reach the wall on the other side of the alley where he could poke his head round and get a clearer view of the school. Then the earth shook again underneath with other massive explosions that slammed into the ground like two huge punches, each lifting his body off the ground like a rag doll.

For minutes, he lay there, staring up into the night sky, gathering his strength. He could see the sky brightening, but could hear nothing except a ringing in his ears. They felt wet and sticky and he wondered if his eardrums had been burst.

Then he thought about Sally and the school children. He held on to the wall and pulled himself to his feet and looked round the corner. He had been lucky. The wall had shielded him from the blast. In front was a crater around which were scattered the fragments of a vehicle and half a dozen bodies. The gate to the school was torn open and inside he could glimpse several fighters holding their guns in front of them, ready to spray the street. It looked like they were preparing to make a run for it, but were waiting for a signal.

They hadn't seen him yet. Wilkins realized that he still had his gun with him, hanging from his back. He pulled it round so it was pointing at the gate, wondering what to do.

Sally was probably inside. He could see the fighters looking at the sky.

Without thinking, he squeezed the trigger at them. The gun was in single shot and he kept firing until the magazine was empty. He still couldn't hear much or think straight. Then he ducked back behind the corner wall and slumped down.

A few minutes later, he felt a hand on his shoulder shaking him roughly. It was Ali, with three other men. He smiled at them weakly. 'We go now,' Ali shouted grimly. He pulled

Wilkins to his feet and then looked at his weapon. Ali pulled out the magazine and snapped in a fresh clip. 'Go!' he shouted.

Wilkins couldn't really hear him, but nodded. Then all four of them peered round the corner. One of the men fired an RPG at the gate, and then they started a rush towards it, firing and spraying the gate with gunfire.

47

Sally felt a giant hand smash into the ground. It shook the walls and roof of the classroom. It was like a pile of steel girders had come crashing down at once. The blast tremor traveled underground and the force exploded into the room lifting her and everyone else off the ground. It dropped them onto the ground like rag dolls. A wave of hot air generated by the shockwave blasted the air out of the room smashing the glass windows. The blast had destroyed the mosque and the massive explosion had blasted a shower of masonry that hit the school buildings and smashed against the walls and the door. The classroom door splintered and was ripped from its hinges but was held up by the pile of desks and shares that had been piled against it. The roof held firm too.

Sally could just see what was happening but could barely hear anything. The room quickly filled with thick dust. She felt her lungs had been crushed and twisted inside by some horrible force. She struggled to inhale and when she did, she chocked feebly on the clinging filthy dust. It was her ears that hurt the most. She wondered if they had been ruptured and she put up her hand she touched one of them, checking for blood. There was nothing there but she couldn't hear anything but inside there was a dull pain. Sally could barely think but she tried to concentrate on identifying on other pain on her body. Had been hurt anywhere else? She patted her legs and arms. Everything seemed intact.

She kept her eyes closed to keep out the dust and visualize where her body was. She was lying on her back, she thought. Her feet were pointing to the door and her head towards the window. She could feel colder air drifting in. Then she started trying to think about the others around her. She couldn't hear anything but she could sense the children and their movements. She wondered if anyone was dead or wounded. Perhaps they were just stunned like her.

After a while, - she couldn't tell how long – the air began to clear and she struggled to feel her lungs with her bruised chest. What she needed to, she thought, was to get up and put her face outside the window. She summed all her will power and forced herself onto her knees put her hand on a wall and raised herself onto her feet.

At that moment there was a second blast. The giant hand slammed onto the ground and the force waves slammed her against the wall. She cracked her head against something and fell to the ground. This time she senses the explosion was a little further away. The hot air blew over her, blasting out of the door and through the two windows at the back. There was another rain of debris but she couldn't hear anything. This time, she herself blacking out for several minutes.

She came too with a ringing sound in her ears. Perhaps her eardrums had been perforated. She might never hear anything again. She again felt around her ears and this time there were small cuts on her face and neck. Her face was covered by a thick coating of dust and dirt. She groaned softly. She wanted to get up and see to the others but she felt weak as if someone had shaken her all over.

After a long while, she began to breathe easier. She scrambled to her knees, got up and put her head to the window. The bars had gone. She started breathing the clean fresh air. Everything felt sore inside. It was getting lighter outside and she could see the outline of a few houses and some figures lying on the road.

She gazed at the scene blankly and began wondering what had happened. What had caused the explosions? What happened to the guards? she asked herself. The main thing was she was still alive. They hadn't killed her. She had a vague feeling that the guards must have be dead but she couldn't quite articulate any kind of reasoning of why that should be so. Her brain felt completely fogged over. She looked at the sky lightening up and the hint of pinkness on the horizon and entertained briefly the thought that the worst was over. Sally concentrated on getting the air inside her.

After what seemed a long while, she felt strong enough to look into the classroom. All twenty girls were still lying haphazardly on the floor. The door was wide open. I still can't hear anything she thought to herself. Is anyone screaming or shouting for help? She walked around trying to help one girl and then other to their feet. She couldn't hear what they were saying although she could see they were talking to her. She shook her head and pointed her ears. She found Shaleema and was glad that she seemed alright and even managed a smile.

Then Sally began to think it was best if they got out there. She started pushing aside the desks and chairs and clearing the way to the door. The girls started to follow her. Then she went outside. The mosque had gone. It had simply vanished. Then she could do no more and collapsed. She leaned against the brick wall and slowly slid down it.

48

Faiza watched as the missiles struck the minaret, which exploded in a cloud of debris. At the same time another cloud obliterated the Taliban figure who was standing outside. Blashford
had left the school untouched and there were five more missiles
to fire. On the other side of the village, she could see that the
unidentified group of fighters had opened fire and were now
running into the village. Their guns showed up brightly on the
screen as their barrels became hot. At the other end of the village, there was now a small crater where the guard post had
been. The other group of gunmen had become visible. They
were lying on the ground now and opening fire, but she could
not see what they were firing at. She counted eleven men. Some
of them seemed to be looking up at the sky and searching for
the source of the explosions.

She switched her attention back to the school, but there
was no movement in any of the buildings. There was silence

in the ground control station as the team waited for fresh or- ders from Blashford. He and the rest of the team were watching the mosque, waiting for the clouds to settle down so they could see what was happening. A minute passed. Then she could see Miller twisting the joysticks around so that two of the Predators completed turns and offered different angles of the mosque. The minaret had collapsed and the missile had torn away the dome, leaving a crater and heaps of beams and bricks.

'Keep eyes on the mosque and wait for any targets leaving,' Blashford said. 'Mosque has top priority, but monitor vehicles.'

They waited and watched the courtyard of the mosque for the first sign of fresh movement. Faiza knew that the next few seconds would be the defining moment of the mission.

'High value targets visible,' the second sensor operator said in a neutral voice. Faiza suddenly felt a surge of hope. She could see a handful of shadowy figures moving slowly and cautiously out of the rubble. They emerged from a corner of the courtyard behind the mosque

'Pilot copies,' Miller said.

'They are coming out of the bunker. We've got them now,' Blashford said with relish.

'High value targets are leaving the mosque,' the second sensor operator said.

'Engine starting on vehicle one,' the first operator reported.

'Engines starting on vehicle two and three,' the second operator said.

'Designate new targets,' Blashford ordered. 'Vehicles now have top priority.'

'Wilco,' the first sensor operator said. 'Copy, targeting vehicles,' the other said.

'Pilot, you have permission to engage at will,' Blashford said.

'Lasers selected,' the first sensor said. 'Lasers selected,' Miller repeated.

From a rat hole in a corner of the mosque's back yard, a dozen men emerged one by one. Then they scrambled to their feet and sprinted across the smoking rubble towards the waiting vehicles. This was what the team called 'squirters'. Faiza guessed the squirters had been hiding in a store room or possibly even a bunker hidden beneath the mosque. They must have assumed that the Predator attack was over, or they had simply been panicked by the attack. She saw them running to the vehicles in the hope of fleeing.

She struggled to identify any individuals. As they passed by the rubble, their heat signatures blurred against the heat given out by the smoldering debris. Miller was waiting until they entered the vehicles before destroying them.

On another screen, she could see that the forces attacking the village from both ends were getting closer and steadily firing their guns as they moved forward. She puzzled about the identity of the attackers. If they were the Pakistan army or police, she wondered how they had timed the attack to coincide with the Predator attack. It seemed impossible that Blashford had coordinated this without her becoming aware of it. But she knew he wanted to capture al-Zawahiri and the others rather than see them killed. Before she could reach any conclusions, she saw them reach the waiting vehicles. As they did so, the rest of the village sprang into life. People began to emerge from their houses to look around.

'Targets entering vehicles,' the first sensor operator said. 'Sensor confirms,' said the other.

'Designate new targets, vehicles one, two and three,' Miller said.

'Targets designated,' the first sensor operator said. 'Pilot copies,' Miller said.

She could see now that there were four bodies inside the four-wheel drive and the green cross hairs were locked on to Fazlullah's vehicle. Its engine was hot enough to register red on the screen.

'Master arm is hot. Go ahead and fire laser,' Miller said coolly.

'Lasing,' the first sensor operator confirmed.

'3 − 2 − 1 rifle,' the second sensor operator said. '3 − 2 − 1 impact,' Miller said.

There was a delay of just five seconds between the command and the explosion. The vehicle had already begun to pull away before it was hit by the 100 pound explosive and disintegrated in a blossoming black and white cloud. Then she watched as Miller fired the next two Hellfire missiles at the two vehicles with the same effect. A Hellfire was designed to smash through the toughest tank armor and she knew that anyone in a civilian vehicle would be killed instantly.

'Excellent,' Blashford said. For a moment there was silence in the GCS as everyone watched the screen to see what was happening. Faiza could see that the vehicles were now blazing away.

The village was a confused scene, with people running in all directions. She couldn't see if any of the Taliban had escaped or how many had been killed. Some figures were running away from the vehicles and the mosque, while others were moving towards it. No one moved out of the school buildings, but she could see that some individuals, including the attackers, were moving towards the school and opening the gates. Some of the remaining Taliban were directing their fire at the attackers, who were now less than a hundred yards away. She could see streaks from regular gunfire. In the chaos she was no longer sure who was who. Then she saw a number of armed men running into the school, smashing down the gate and entering the classrooms. Other figures ran out from the houses into the orchards and fields around the village, chased by ribbons of gunfire. If it had been daylight, they could have seen and identified the men.

'Some squirters are escaping,' the first sensor operator said.

'MQ101, 102, 103, and 104 laser target and lock on suspects,' Blashford said.

'Sensor copies,' the operator said.

Faiza watched on different screens as the Predators circled over the area target locking each of the fleeing men. Each Predator could track more than one target simultaneously, but the images were confusing as they moved through the trees and among the sheep, goats and other animals. The survivors had spread out. She knew that with only two Hellfire missiles left Blashford would soon have make decision which, if any, of the survivors to target. She reckoned that at least ten men had been killed in the vehicles and at least six others killed in the first attacks. How many had been there in the first place? How many had been hidden under the mosque?

Faiza gave herself no time for celebration. She switched her attention back to the other Taliban fleeing through the orchards, hoping to identify them for Blashford. She could see that some of them were being pursued by the attackers. One of them could be al-Zawahiri. A man in his fifties who was overweight and unfit from staying underground for weeks on end would surely be the slowest on foot. The Egyptian was also shorter than the average Pashtun. She as- sumed, too, that he wouldn't be carrying a heavy weapon and would probably be shadowed by a bodyguard.

'Target 3 on MQ101. Can we get a close up?' she said. Faiza could see more clearly now a man moving more slowly than the others and struggling to follow another large man who stood still and waited for him.

'That one might be al-Zawahiri. I can't be sure,' she said. 'He looks like he is wounded. If it is him, he is going to be captured,' Blashford said. 'He can't get away.'

'Yes, he can. We must destroy him,' Faiza shouted angrily. 'Kill him now!'

'Target designated,' the first sensor operator said. 'Laser primed,' Miller said.

'Copy that,' the operator said.

'Wait, he's more valuable alive,' Blashford. Miller hesitated and Blashford saw her start to move. 'Faiza!' he shouted.

At the same moment, Faiza reached over Miller's shoulder, and pressed on Miller's hand as it hovered over the control panel, activating the missile. Miller tried to fend her off, but he was taken by surprise. Although he was stronger, it was too late to stop the machine. Within five seconds, the two figures were obliterated in cloud of debris. Faiza saw the explosion and smiled with triumph. It was over and she felt free.

49

Under a silver warmer, a plate of scrambled eggs, toast and real butter waited for her attention. Between her hands she nursed a fine white bone-china cup from which she took a sip of hot coffee. Sally was wrapped in a fluffy white bath robe and contemplated Wilkins across the gilded breakfast table. He was reading a newspaper and ignoring her.

Sally slipped down in her seat to get a better angle for her foot and touched his leg under the table.

'Aren't we just the old married couple?' she said fondly. 'Ah hem,' Wilkins said.

She looked at the thick blond hair and pink cheeks and decided she liked him better without his beard.

'You could do with a haircut, too, you know,' she said. 'Ah hem,' he repeated and did not look up. Sally wondered why he sounded distracted and briefly criticized herself for going too far. Then she decided that she didn't care. She felt no desire to go anywhere or do anything. The best thing would be to go back to bed.

The windows in the air-conditioned room blocked out the usual din from the traffic on the streets below. She felt Pakistan was far away. The thought came to her that a new era was about to begin and she might never go back to her old life in the Swat Valley.

'Reports of my death seem to be premature,' Wilkins said and raised his head to look at her with a smile. 'It says here in the Dawn newspaper that several westerners are reported missing after fighting broke out in the Swat Valley.'

He reached across and thrust over some smudged pages. She put down the coffee cup and read through the article. It was a small news story on the front page, followed by a longer report in the inside news section.

Swat Valley: Maulana Fazlullah, the leader of the Tehrik-i-Taliban, is reported to have been killed in a battle between Taliban militants and local lashgar forces which erupted early on Saturday morning.

Dozens more are reported dead or wounded in fighting which began after lashgar forces attacked a Taliban stronghold in Karram, a village forty miles north of Mingora. "Fazlullah is dead. His reign of terror is over," local sources said.

The 33 year-old Swat Chieftain, known as the DJ Mullah, had led a small army of militants who had imposed a strict form of Sharia law over the district.

"He is still alive. These are baseless rumours spread by his enemies and the CIA," Taliban spokesman Muslim Khan told AFP.

Army sources could not confirm the report, but noted that previous reports of his death had proved inaccurate. An army spokesman said they were investigating the reports of large explosions at the village in which a mosque was destroyed.

"We heard three or four explosions early in the morning. We think the insurgents' ammunition dump exploded," said a local resident. Another resident blamed the explosions on Taliban suicide bombers attacking a girls' school.

A number of western aid workers working in the Swat Valley are also reported to be missing during the fighting. Western diplomats in Islamabad said they had so far received no reports of any missing citizens, but warned foreign nationals it was unsafe to travel to the region.

'It seems pretty vague, doesn't it? None of us is mentioned by name,' she said. 'The British High Commission knows about us, though. Jennifer must have told them.'

'Yes, they know about you and that you are all safe and sound,' Wilkins said.

'And how Prince Valiant rescued me?' she smiled happily and kicked his calf again. 'Shouldn't you be rewarded for showing uncommon valor and chivalry?'

'Oh, I don't know, haven't I been well rewarded already?' he said.

'That's not what I meant,' she giggled.

Then she leafed through the pages to read the stories on the inside pages. There was a longer interview with the Taliban spokesman in which he charged the Americans with attacking the mosque in Karram with missiles fired by a drone and killing dozens of innocent students. An American spokesman was quoted, saying that they never commented on drone attacks in Pakistan. Despite the outraged tone of the Taliban spokesman, the reporter noted that there had never been any previous UAV attacks in the Swat Valley. The majority of attacks took place in North and South Waziristan and other regions along the border with Afghanistan. The report also noted that, unlike other occasions, no video footage or photographs had emerged to support the Taliban's claims.

Sally thought she could well understand why. Neither the villagers nor the lashkgar would have allowed Fazlullah's men to do that or even to go back to the village.

'So do you think Fazlullah is really dead?' she asked.

'Of course he is. I saw him go down,' Wilkins said. 'He can't have survived.'

'I know he was shot, but they took him away before I really got a chance to look at him,' she said. 'There are no pictures of a bullet-ridden body, either.'

'Well, it's a bit early yet,' Wilkins said. 'I think the locals might have returned the body to the Imam Dehri as quickly as possible. They wouldn't want to give his men another excuse to come back to the village.'

'In this longer story about the Swat Valley, it quotes one resident, Ishmail Khan, as saying that the war with the Taliban is not yet over. They don't believe peace will come back to the Valley until they see for themselves that Fazlullah is truly dead,' she said.

Then she thought that if he wasn't dead, she was never going back to the Valley. In fact, she wondered if she really ever wanted to go back anyway. She didn't want to be alone again. Ever.

'But what were those explosions?' she said. 'I still don't understand what they were and how it happened just as you were attacking the village.'

'Well, fortune favours the brave,' he said and put the paper down. 'Any more coffee?'

She poured him some more. Then he got up and went to the mini-bar and found a bottle of brandy, unscrewed the top and emptied the contents into the coffee. 'Here's to luck,' Wilkins said and raised his cup. 'Our luck.'

'You are right, it was very odd. I can't really explain it, but it was jolly lucky for us,' he went on. 'It was a sort of deus ex machina, an intervention from the gods, wasn't it? The missiles hit the village just as we were attacking it. If it wasn't for that, we might have been done for. The lashkar were a pretty hopeless sort of Dad's Army outfit. They had these new weapons, but they didn't know how to use them.'

Sally eyed him curiously. 'And do you?'

'You know me better than that,' he said. Then he turned serious and for the first time gave her a detailed account of what happened.

'Do you think these missiles were planned? I mean, did Ali know about it beforehand?' she asked.

'Well, that's a mystery, isn't it? He seemed just as shocked by it as anyone else. Actually, he was screaming with fear,' Wilkins said slowly. 'Only when he realized that the missiles had killed his enemies, did he get up and bravely lead the attack.'

Sally tried to capture his gaze. 'You are not telling me the truth about everything, are you, darling?' He smiled modestly.

'But I suppose it doesn't matter.' And she touched him again with her foot.

'Look at this in the paper,' Wilkins said, changing the subject. He held a page of the paper in his hand to show her. 'The International Herald Tribune here says that intelligence sources in Washington are saying that al- Zawahiri is also dead. He's the one who planned 9/11, isn't he? That's almost as good as getting Osama bin Laden. It says he probably died in a drone attack in North-West Pakistan. My best guess is that this explains the mystery. Those missiles were destined for al-Zawahiri.'

'You mean he was there?'' she asked.

'The Taliban are denying he is dead, but they would, wouldn't they?' Wilkins said. 'And so is the Pakistan Army. Who knows? But is Fazlullah really dead? What did you see?'

'We kept hoping something would happen after I spoke to Jenny. I knew something was going to happen. The guards had prepared to die. They had shaved off their beards and cleansed themselves as if they were expecting martyrdom,' she said. 'I was praying myself.

'After the explosions, I got out of the door completely shell-shocked and deaf. I could see there was some shooting going on and thought I saw Fazlullah lying on the ground.'

'Yes, I thought so too,' he said.

'Then some of the men, I don't know who they were, came over and lifted him up. There was a lot of shouting and they took him away,' she said. 'He wasn't moving, but groan- ing a lot.'

'Well, whatever happened, I don't think that he will be troubling anyone for a while yet,' Wilkins said.

'Do you think so? I wonder if there is a chance now that peace will return to the Swat Valley and I can go back there and rebuild the schools,' she said.

Wilkins didn't reply at first, weighing his words with care. He wasn't sure whether he should encourage her stay, or to go with him. In a way, it would be neater if they both disappeared at once. It would leave fewer traces, making it harder for anyone to trace him afterwards. The Grosvenor Bank was still looking for him. The markets would re-open the next day and he had yet to decide how to handle that.

'It certainly a major setback for the Taliban in the Swat Valley, whether Fazlulluh survives or not,' Wilkins said slowly. 'My guess is that they will lie low for a while. They know they are not safe anymore. Remember how Ali and his men celebrated afterwards – all that chanting and dancing around and firing into the sky? They won't be cowed again so easily now they have tasted victory.'

She remembered with pleasure how the villagers had feted her as the savior of their children. They had even sung a special song in her honor and given her a gift of a soft pashmina shawl embroidered with red roses. The children still needed her in the Swat, she thought. The terrorists must be defeated and she would help re-open the hundreds of schools that had been fire-bombed or forced to close.

'But remember you are now a prominent target for them.' He put his hand on top of hers 'You know, Fazlullah came close to executing Aziza.'

'Yes, she says you saved her life. Is that true?' she said looking at him again with that admiring look.

'Well, not exactly,' he said with a deep breath, feeling uncomfortable. 'But I tried.'

'Fazlullah caught her and her lover. I think I saw them the first time I met him. Fazlullah wanted to execute them then and there. Then I tried to bargain for her life in exchange for a laser thing they wanted. But after that I don't know what happened,' he said modestly. The last thing he wanted to do was talk about what had happened.

'Well, she spoke highly of you,' she said. 'How is she doing?' he asked.

'She is very low. You wouldn't recognize her. You know they executed her lover right in front of her. She thought was going to be next. She can't stop crying and stays in her house now and never goes out,' she said slowly.

'She wants me to stay and take over her work,' she said. 'But I can't.'

Sally began to cry softly. The emotions of the past twenty-four hours broke through her guard and for a long time she could not stop. Wilkins came over to her, stood behind her and put his arms around her.

'I am going to make sure that you have enough money so that you can carry on and change things here,' he said.

She nodded slowly, still choked. 'I don't think I could manage to go back, not now, not alone,' she said weakly. Wilkins froze for a moment and then chose his words carefully.

'She believed in what she was doing. She knew the risks and accepted them,' he said in her ear. 'When people need you, you can't just run away.'

Sally gripped his arms and took a deep breath.

50

Wilkins paid off the taxi and waited patiently in line at the airport entrance. It was still early in the morning and the air felt fresh and cool. The airport was all shiny steel and glass. In front of him was a large and overweight family heading back to Britain, and further down the line gangs of sad-looking young men going off to work in the Gulf, plus a handful of westerners in suits. Wilkins was the only tourist. He carrying just a small backpack and his thick anorak made him look like one of the climbers returning from an expedition to the Himalayan peaks bordering India.

All he had to worry about now was getting through passport control with Stoner's pass-port and he would be able to disappear without a trace. Stoner was a few years older, but he reckoned the officials would not look too hard at a Brit leaving the country. To help matters, Wilkins had put on some dark sunglasses and had covered up his hair with a woolly hat. He opened up Stoner's passport for another look, memorizing his date and place of birth – Lon- don, August 27, 1965 – in case he was questioned.

Stoner had only been gone a week and Wilkins was sure that over the weekend no one at the bank would have become concerned enough to alert the authorities. Wilkins had thought it best to make an early start just in case. There were still four hours before anyone at the Grosvenor Bank would be in the office. Mervyn, he knew, wouldn't be in before ten. He would be chauffeured into the City from his house in the Cotswolds where he spent the weekends and would occupy his time read- ing the Financial Times and calling up Tokyo and Hong Kong.

When he got into the first-class lounge, he thought he might send off an e-mail just to reassure them. He knew that Stoner's phone had been taken away and he couldn't have been in contact with London for two days. The line inched forward and at last Wilkins stood before the X-ray machine. He showed his ticket and passport, took off his shoes and his belt, and then slung his bag into a plastic tray. The guard motioned at him to take off his anorak and he obeyed reluctantly. He knew the money would show up, so he had left what remained as a part- ing gift to Sally.

She didn't know it. He had sneaked out, leaving her still sleeping in the big emperor-sized bed, quickly closing the door behind him and feeling a little like a thief. A thief who had left behind a small fortune. He smiled happily at the guard as he was frisked and then walked into the departure lounge and headed towards the ticket counter. He had left behind a brief but affectionate note and was gone without checking out.

As he waited to check in, he wondered whether Stoner was still alive. He probably was, but not for much longer. Wilkins thought that the Taliban would still be in shock and confusion after the attack on Karram had gone so disastrously wrong. Fazlullah was either dead or very close to it and his followers at his headquarters would still be confused and leaderless. While they were licking their wounds, he thought they wouldn't have taken the decision to kill Stoner. Or would they? Maybe they would have already taken out their revenge and frustration on him. He thought about it dispassionately.

At the first-class check in, the pretty dark girl with too much make-up under her scarf for Pakistan gave him a brilliant smile along with his boarding pass. 'Going home, sir? A pleasant flight, sahib,' she said. He smiled pleasantly and moved on towards passport control, beginning to feel a mixture of nervousness and high excitement.

Was Stoner still alive? He might by now be in a shallow grave, but Wilkins imagined him still chained to a pipe in that basement room with a hood over his head. In the darkness, listening and trying to interpret the sounds of movement in the floors above. Waiting with time crawling by like a blind worm, fearing the sound of a door opening: or perhaps hoping that freedom might be at hand. Perhaps he still believed that Wilkins might save him or perhaps he was cursing his decision to save Wilkins from execution.

Altruism was always a mistake. In the classic version of prisoner's dilemma, defect is the dominant strategy. You shouldn't really trust anyone, not even your mates. Hanging in and believing the best of people always got you into trouble.

That was why, after all, Wilkins had decided to come to Pakistan in the first place. He hadn't trusted Stoner when they were under investigation not to sacrifice him up and to save himself. When Stoner came after him in the Swat Valley, he knew he had made the right decision. Stoner could now go to hell, for all he cared. Stoner had been out to trick him into returning to face the music after Stoner had set him up back in London. He didn't doubt that Stoner had revealed their secrets to Mervyn and hidden his own involvement.

Shit, if the exchange rate pairing had gone the wrong way, he would have caused the bank losses running into the billions. The bank would take him to the cleaners. It would be at least three years in the slammer for abuse of trust, proprietary trading. He'd have to pay back all the money locked in that secret account, he forgot how much exactly, maybe 100 million pounds – and he would become such a celebrity, the notoriety would follow him throughout his life. The man who destroyed a 300 year-old bank, the most famous name in Lombard Street, and brought down the Grosvenor.

Wilkins was now standing in the passport control line holding his boarding pass, passport and exit form. He checked to see if they had any cameras, but there was no tell- tale black eye above the counter. So there would be no video record of his presence here. He took off his jacket and stooped a little to make himself shorter and to resemble Stoner more. He figured the officer would check his passport, scan it, glance at the photo to be sure that it resembled the person before him and then wave him on. There were still six people in front of him but the line was moving quickly.

Wilkins put himself in Stoner's shoes for a moment. He might believe that it was Wilkins who should now be feeling guilty. After all, Wilkins had run before there was any proof that Stoner had betrayed him and was doubly guilty for having saved him from Fazlullah. Even if he did – which he didn't – there was nothing he could possibly do. It was too late for any heroic rescues. That one night had been more than enough. But it was natural for people to hope, to hang on to hope for too long.

Stoner was a dumb fuck, though, to think that he had ever been one of his mates; that was his mistake, but he knew all about games and the trouble with these games is that they took no account of human feelings like loyalty and hatred, or of chance. They could never account for chances such as the 'jailer' being a religious maniac like Fazlullah, who delighted in killing people.

Wilkins slid the burgundy-red passport through the tray under the window and then stood there, waiting. The officer, young and clean-shaven, took it briskly, looked at Wilkins, opened a page to look for the visa and placed it face-down on the scanner. Then he took another look at Wilkins. 'Sir, please take off your sunglasses,' he said.

'Oh sorry,' Wilkins mumbled.

He tried not to look the officer directly in eye so that he would not see his blue eyes. He took the glasses off and then slowly folded them and put them in his shirt pocket. He was pretty sure that Stoner didn't have blue eyes, but he couldn't remember what color they were.

'I hope you enjoyed your stay,' the man said politely. 'Well, it's been eventful,' Wilkins replied.

'Mr Stoner, do you know your passport is about to expire?' the officer said helpfully and handed back the passport. Wilkins nodded and smiled and then took the passport and walked past him with relief.

He walked straight into the first-class lounge and helped himself to a celebratory cup of coffee. He took in for a moment the wood paneling, the blue plastic armchairs and the plastic flowers in cheap vases under the spotlights. It was quiet, calm, sterile and safe.

There were forty-five minutes to go before boarding and only a handful of people sat quietly reading newspapers. On the other side of the room, he spotted a row of computer terminals and went over to log on. He first scanned through the news briefs on Google. He noticed an AP story that Congress had approved a deal for the Pentagon to buy more Predators, citing the proven effectiveness of the new weapon which was going to revolutionize warfare. There was a separate article on fresh drone strikes against al-Qaeda groups in the North-West frontier. A training camp in North Waziristan had been hit, but there was nothing further about the Swat Valley.

He looked at Bloomberg to see what had happened to the yen and his heart leaped. Two days earlier, the Japanese prime minister from the ruling Liberal Democratic Party had unexpectedly resigned. 'Third Japanese Prime Minister in 18 months steps down,' said the headline. The article compared Japan to Italy and said the decision opened the way for fresh elections, which the opposition was expected to win.

The announcement had caught the markets by surprise and prompted a sudden sell-off against the yen. Analysts were predicting that the Japanese Central Bank was expected to lower interest rates to a post-war low in a bid to revive the flagging growth. At the other end of the scale, the Icelandic krone was doing better after the stricken government had announced that it was applying to join the European Union.

The two events meant that instead of a loss, he was looking at a huge profit on the interest rate swop. He turned to the news from New Zealand. It was good as well. The central bank had followed Australia in raising interest rates. He opened up the calculator on the screen, to check the figures but he didn't need to. He already knew that the positions he had taken were going to show a very handsome profit.

He sat back for a moment in surprise. For the last five days, he had completely forgotten about the markets for almost the first time in ten years. He realized with an even greater shock that he didn't really care anymore. The addiction was gone. There was no adrenalin rush, but he didn't need it. It was out of his system, as if he was a heroin addict who had gone through a period of enforced cold turkey. All he had to do now was to close the positions in the next twenty four-hours before the end of the month.

Then he thought for a moment. He could do that now, from here, if he could get into the system using Stoner's passwords. He knew his own access would be blocked.

Wilkins looked up at the clock, he had just forty minutes to do it before boarding started. Or he could just do nothing. It didn't really matter. Not to him, anyway. He sat there and stared into space for a while. It was just money, not even real money, just figures on a screen, digits on an accounting ledger.

In fact it was even more insignificant – just a series of binary codes that changed almost at random every day. Nobody had forced Taro Aso, the Japanese prime minister, to resign on that day. Whether he lost or won, it was just up to chance, not quantum calculations, just the random actions of people moved by emotion.

It was nothing compared to the taste of physical excitement he had felt during the raid at Karram village and the joy and happiness he had seen in Sally's face when she had seen him with a gun in his hand. That was real. He could taste the smoke and dust again. It was real life that he craved now.

'Would you like more coffee, sir?' the hostess interrupted his thoughts with a tentative smile. 'Or some breakfast?'

'Yes, you know I think I would,' he said smiling. 'I am feeling pretty hungry for more.'

He couldn't stop smiling. He wasn't going to spend any more of his life sitting in windowless rooms staring at computer screens looking at numbers. He would just do nothing. The bank could liquidate the positions without him. The deal with the Landesbank would go through now without a hitch. With good profits, the bank wouldn't care much about creating a scandal by going after him now.

Besides, he was dead, wasn't he? Destroyed by a missile which no one had expected and which no one was even now acknowledging had been launched. What were the odds on that happening? What could be more random?

There was just one more thing to do. He opened up a g-mail account in Stoner's name and addressed an email to Janet, Mervyn's secretary. 'Dear Chairman, I regret to inform you the sad news that Mr Samuel Wilkins is reported to have lost his life in the Swat Valley. He was last seen after being seized in Mingora by militants loyal to the local Taliban leader Fazlullah on Saturday and is reported to have been killed when fighting erupted between the militants and local militia. The situation here is still extremely tense and dangerous and until I can ascertain for certain his fate, I will stay on here and continue the investigations. In the meantime, I have found his belongings which were left at his lodgings and discovered his notebook. It contains the details of a number of a bank accounts and passwords which might merit further investigation,'

Wilkins paused there and asked himself again whether he really wanted to hand back all the money. It was true that they had used the bank's money but he and Stoner had made it themselves by proprietary trading. If he gave it back, then it would more or less close the case. Everyone would lose interest in Wilkins, but what about Stoner? If Stoner didn't return, the bank would be suspicious and try to find him.

Damn it, it didn't matter, he thought. Sooner or later, the authorities would find out that it was Stoner who was dead and by then he would be long gone. Once Mervyn had the money, there would be no criminal case, nothing that he would want to make public. He continued the typing, listing a series of bank account numbers and passwords from memory and then added. 'I shall be back in touch within a few days as soon as I have confirmation of Wilkins' death. At present I fear that I remain under surveillance by the militants who still pose a lethal threat here in this lawless region. Please do not attempt to contact me by telephone or to alert the authorities in Islamabad. Yours sincerely, P. Stoner.'

Wilkins stopped to read what he had written and then pressed the send button. It was done and Wilkins felt a sense of liberation. He was free, could go wherever he pleased and be whatever he wanted. Without the money, he was free. He pictured himself alone on a beach in Thailand watching the sunset.

There were just fifteen minutes to go before boarding started. Wilkins signed off the computer, got up and gathered up his anorak and bag and walked out of the departure lounge. He walked down the long corridor back to passport control and joined a group of arriving passengers. Within minutes, he arrived at the border control with an entry card. 'Is this your first visit to Pakistan for the first time, sir?' the man asked him.

'No, not the first time.'

'Will you be staying for tourism?'

'Yes, this time it's for pleasure. I rather like the people here,' Wilkins replied.

'Enjoy your stay,' the man said and stamped his passport automatically.

Wilkins walked on, whistling the tune from 'Dil Dil Pakistan'. He could be back in the hotel before Sally woke up, he realized. It was still just 7.30 in the morning. They would have breakfast together and discuss her plans to rebuild the schools. He saw her jolly smile dimpling her cheeks and the sunny idiotic enthusiasm for doing good. They could buy some more computers for the girls in Islamabad. He saw himself in the villages working up a sweat by laying bricks and hefting sacks of cement while Sally looked on with approval.

THE END